# Iruses to Ashes

Charlie Hudson

*Enjoy!*
*Charlie Hudson*

**Outskirts Press, Inc.**
**Denver, Colorado**

Irises to Ashes
All Rights Reserved.
Copyright © 2011 Charlie Hudson
v2.0

Cover Photo © 2011 JupiterImages Corporation. All rights reserved - used with permission.

Outskirts Press, Inc.
http://www.outskirtspress.com

ISBN: 978-1-4327-7389-2

Outskirts Press and the "OP" logo are trademarks belonging to Outskirts Press, Inc.

PRINTED IN THE UNITED STATES OF AMERICA

# Acknowledgements

My loving husband, Hugh, has once again given me the support I need to bring *Irises to Ashes* to life. I also want to thank Cathy Milton and Lisa Jones, my author's representatives at Outskirts Press, the professional staff that handles the production side, and Reality Premedia Services for the beautiful cover design.

# Part One

## Maggie's Beginning

**Summer 1976 – Summer 1978**

# Chapter One

I was thinking about whether I should relinquish my virginity to Billy Ray and forgot about the pothole that Monday's downpour had enlarged. I hit the edge of it so hard the canvas bag of quilting squares that Mrs. Watkins gave me for Mamma tumbled onto the floorboard. Good thing the bag was zipped. I wasn't in the mood to pick up dozens of pieces of fabric.

"Oh hell," I muttered and jerked the truck to the side of the gravel road. I didn't feel the telltale list of a flat tire, but still I jumped out to check. It was sticky hot with the June humidity at August levels, and I didn't feel like having to wrestle a tire jack with a nearly full bed of produce. Even more than that, I didn't want to waste time listening to my brother cuss about me not taking care of his raggedy-ass truck. Crazy Miz Hatcher's was my last stop, and I was supposed to meet Billy Ray at The Drunken Gull after dinner.

The tire looked okay. I ran my hand around it, glad to see that the jolt didn't seem to have done any harm. I climbed back in, cranked it, and started to tap my fingers against the steering wheel to "You Can't Hurry Love." I liked the song even though I wasn't looking for love to start with and that was part of what was bothering me about Billy Ray. Him telling me he loved me was just plain nonsense, and he should have known better than to say it. He and I had been going out more or less steady since

February, and he was cute enough, plus a good kisser. And it wasn't as if I was particularly saving myself for some future husband, despite last Sunday's stern warning from the preacher about my generation's lack of respect for family values.

No, my hesitation was pretty much rooted in stubbornness rather than moral concern. Billy Ray was already more possessive than I liked, and I figured taking the big step with him would hardly improve his attitude. On the other hand, he seemed to be getting impatient, and if I didn't give in soon, he would probably take up with Rita Simpson, who everybody knew was no stranger to sharing a blanket on a beach come sundown. Did I care? That was the question I'd been asking myself all afternoon. Well, unless Billy Ray demanded an answer tonight, I guess I could take awhile longer to make up my mind.

The dune line and stone cottage came into view. The road dead-ended at the back of the single-story house with dark green shutters on wide windows. It was an oddity compared to the white frame or gray-shingled exteriors common to the Outer Banks. Even more out of character was the fence. Instead of hurricane fencing like everyone else had, this was split logs for rails interspersed with four-foot-high square stone columns instead of posts. The inside yard was devoted almost entirely to a vegetable garden, although different varieties of flowers bordered three sides of the large rectangle. There was a separate oval bed of purple and white irises between the garden and the black wrought iron gate and another bed with roses between the garden and the stone garage. The driveway that led through the gate and the rest of the yard was covered in gravel. Two paths of crushed oyster shells curved around either side of the house. I'd never seen the front, although I assumed it would be partially visible from the beach.

Crazy Miz Hatcher was kind of a hermit, if a female could be a hermit. She was one of three people who couldn't deliver to Watkins Farmers Market where my older brother, Bobby, worked. Bobby and Mr. Watkins said her tomatoes, carrots, cucumbers, and strawberries were the best in the region, if not the whole state. Today, I was picking up strawberries.

I never saw her, of course. My instructions were to stop at the gate, load the crates into the truck, and leave. Mr. Watkins handled payment privately. Ronny Fuller, more commonly called Ronny Retard, always carefully laid the containers out in tidy rows for me, and when he was near the gate, he would wave or call my name. He was a hard worker no matter that he was slow in thinking, and at his size, he was good help with any heavy tasks. As far as anyone knew, he was the only one Crazy Miz Hatcher allowed around the place. I was thinking about how to dress for the evening and reaching for the last of the strawberries when I noticed a movement of fur to my left. I jumped back, not sure of what it was, and tripped over a pail sitting between the gate and the containers. Two rabbits bounded from under the irises as the bucket spun in one direction and I landed on my butt.

"Ah hell!" I sat still for a moment, my heart pounding foolishly. Rabbits! Nothing but stupid rabbits!

Ronny stood at the gate, cradling a black rabbit in his arms, grinning at me. "Did they scare you, Maggie? Did they make you fall?"

I shook my head and got to my knees, groping for spilled cartons of strawberries. "Just a little bit, Ronny. I didn't know you had rabbits."

"Miss Melly's rabbits," he said. "They feel soft. You aren't afraid of them, are you?"

"No, Ronny, they just surprised me, that's all."

He opened the gate and came through, easily holding the rabbit in one beefy hand and pulling me the rest of the way up with his other. He was taller than most of the boys in school and had shoulders that made the football coach growl in frustration because Ronny wasn't capable of following a playbook. He'd more or less been passed along through grades because he tried hard, could read at about a fifth-grade level, did basic math, and didn't cause trouble.

"Your bottom is dirty now. Do you want to pet Blacky?"

I brushed the dirt from the seat of my jeans and watched him stroke the animal. It was big, with long ears, a breed I wasn't familiar with. The other two, brown versions of this one, hopped within ten feet and stopped.

Ronny put his finger to his lips. "Shhh," he whispered loudly and handed me Blacky. "I have to catch them for Miss Melly."

I started to protest, but Ronny seemed so intent I decided a few more minutes couldn't hurt. He stepped noiselessly, calmly, some of the spilled strawberries in his hand, extending them to the pair. He stopped within less than an arm's length, far more patient than I would have been. The larger of the two took a single hop forward, nose twitching at the scent. Ronny laid the berries by the fence, poised for the next move.

The second rabbit joined the first, and in the snap of a finger, Ronny grabbed them both as they emitted tiny squeaking sounds. He began to laugh with delight in his accomplishment.

"I did it good, didn't I? Got the bunnies for Miss Melly."

"Yes, you did, Ronny. You did a good job." I laughed with him, the bunnies squirming in his grasp.

"You! You girl, stop laughing at him!"

The sharp voice startled me, and I turned to see a woman

striding toward us. Her white hair was pulled into a bun, large strands escaping to lie loosely around her face. She wore an ankle-length print cotton dress and carried a straw hat in one gloved hand, a pair of pruning shears in the other.

"You have no business staying here," she said harshly as she approached. "Get the containers and leave! And what are you doing with that rabbit?" She reached out, glaring at me.

"But Miss Melly, Maggie is my friend. The bunnies got out," Ronny said, his voice earnest.

"Ma'am, I'm not hurting anyone," I said, trying not to snap. "I didn't let the rabbits go, and I'm certainly not laughing at Ronny." I thrust the black one into her arms, anxious to be away from this strange woman.

"Maggie is nice. She's my friend. She helped me catch the bunnies," Ronny repeated. "Don't be mad at me."

The woman's face relaxed at his tone. She spoke softly to Ronny while ignoring me. I picked up the last of the produce and loaded it in the truck, gritting my teeth as I listened to her.

"No, no, Ronny, I'm not angry with you. You did a good job catching the rabbits."

"Maggie helped me. She's nice to me at school."

"Then perhaps I spoke inappropriately," she said and looked at me closely. "You're one of the Stewart girls, aren't you?" Her green eyes searched my face as though trying to decide if she'd seen me before. With my oval face, hazel eyes, and chestnut hair, I resembled my mother more than my sister did.

"I'm the youngest," I replied. "Look, I'm sorry if you thought I was making fun of Ronny, but I wasn't. I've got what I need, and I'll be going now."

"Wait just a moment, please." She glanced at Ronny. His face was puckered in the way of a child still expecting a scolding.

"You did a wonderful job, Ronny. Please put those two rascals back in the pen and then you can take Blacky. After you finish, we'll have our lemonade."

He nodded, obviously happy to know that the woman wasn't angry with him, and walked toward the cottage, the rabbits tucked close to his body.

"I may have reacted too strongly, but Ronny is treated so badly most of the time," she said once he was out of hearing.

I slammed the tailgate shut. "Yes, ma'am, I guess you're right about that, but a lot of the kids don't mean any harm; they just don't think he cares."

My desire to leave was mixed with curiosity. I didn't personally know anyone who had ever talked with Amelia Hatcher. People sometimes saw her on the beach, but never any closer. If this was her, of course. After all, Ronny did call her "Miss Melly," but that was sort of like "Amelia."

"So why are you different?"

"What?" I stared at her, puzzled at the odd question. "What do you mean?"

"You don't take the opportunity to engage in easy, thoughtless cruelty? And at your age? That makes you different."

I couldn't tell if she was laughing at me, but there was no smile on her face. Even though her hair was completely white, her face wasn't deeply wrinkled and I wondered how old she was.

I shrugged. "I don't know, I guess it's that Ronny is like some big kid. He may not be as smart as he's supposed to be, but he's a nice guy and it doesn't seem right to poke fun at him."

Ronny turned the corner, ready for the last rabbit.

"Look, I'd better be going," I said. "Bye, Ronny."

He grinned and gently took Blacky. "Do you have to leave,

Maggie? Miss Melly said we would have lemonade. I like lemonade." He looked at Amelia anxiously. "Can Maggie have some, too?"

"Thanks, Ronny, but I have to finish working," I said quickly and climbed into the truck. "You take care of those bunnies, and I'll see you next time."

I drove away and watched the old woman and boy through the rearview mirror. She was only an inch or two taller than I was so she barely reached Ronny's shoulder. She put the straw hat on her head and patted his arm as I cleared the driveway.

Bobby, my older brother by eight years, wasn't curious about what I'd seen. I told him what happened while we unloaded the truck, and he said no one had seen that crazy old lady for ten years or better. He accused me of making shit up just to explain why I took so damn long making the run today. I flipped him the bird and ducked when he threw a chunk of dirt at me.

Jed, the only other one of us kids still living at home, wasn't around for dinner much now that he was almost eighteen. He'd been working the summer at the Hortons' farm and often as not, Mrs. Horton would feed him, then he'd swing by the Bursely house and hang out with his pal, Greg. 'Course Jed was planning on joining the Army soon as he was done with high school, so we might as well get used to not having him around. As we finished one of my favorite meals of fried pork chops with cream-style corn, I told my parents about the encounter.

"Do you think it really was her?" I asked.

They exchanged one of the parental looks that immediately make you want to ask more questions.

"Don't much matter," my father finally said and wiped a biscuit around his plate. "She's nuttier than a fruitcake, and you don't need to be talking to her anyway."

"Well, doesn't it sound like her?"

"I told you, it don't matter. If she was acting crazy, it probably was. You just do your chores like you're supposed to and leave it be." He stood up, the conversation over, ready to head for his chair in the den. "You help your mamma with the dishes and bring me a beer."

"So what made her crazy?" I asked when Mamma and I were alone.

She sighed, squirted soap into the sink, and filled it, adding almost no cold to the sudsy water. "Oh, I don't guess anyone really knows. She isn't from here originally. Her family was over Manteo way."

"Do you know her, then?" I picked up a towel and began drying the dishes.

Mamma shook her head. "No; it's been a long time since she set foot off her property, and she wasn't much for socializing even before that. I used to see her in town, but then she stopped coming in at all, made arrangements for everything to be delivered. She may not be crazy—she may just be an old lady who doesn't like to be around people."

My curiosity was on full alert. "Well, is she rich? And how did she come to be in that cottage? Wasn't it a part of the old Thornhill property? Why is it built funny?"

Mamma slid the knives and forks into the hot water. "Now, Maggie, there's no sense in getting all excited. No one really cares about her anymore. She was Mrs. Thornhill's maid, or companion, or something like that a very long time ago when the big house was open. Mrs. Thornhill went off to Europe, got sick, died over there, and her son and daughter used the house in the summers until they were killed in that plane crash better than twenty years ago. Then there was some kind of legal confusion, and the house caught fire while the lawyers were trying to figure it all out."

"Doreen, Maggie, one of you bring me a beer!"

"I got it, Mamma," I said, hoping she would be willing to keep talking. This was exciting, no matter what anyone said. Why hadn't I heard any of this before?

Mamma was rubbing down the frying pan when I returned. I grabbed a dry towel, scooped up a handful of silverware, and began wiping each utensil carefully.

"Well? What happened then? And is she rich?"

Mamma sighed again. "You're not going to let this go, are you? It's not nearly as mysterious as you think."

"But Mamma, that old lady alone on a place that used to belong to some rich folks, she hides from people, nobody knows how she came to be there, and you don't think that's mysterious?"

"Maggie, if I tell you what I know, will you be quiet about it?"

I nodded vigorously.

Mamma put the frying pan on the stove and rinsed a rag in the sink. She began to scrub the counter and talked quietly.

"Like I said, Mr. and Mrs. Thornhill lived in Raleigh, and for some reason, their two children didn't usually come to the big beach house. It was quite a house, I must say, the biggest one around here. One of those Victorian things with scrolled woodwork and a porch that could hold half the village. I don't know how Amelia came to be with her exactly; I've heard stories of her being left an orphan or something. However it happened, she was just a teenager I guess, maybe about your age. Mrs. Thornhill went on a trip to Europe, sometime in 1933 I think it was; got sick; and died in Paris, or maybe it was London. For whatever reason, Amelia stayed overseas. Anyway, Mrs. Thornhill's son and daughter were the sole heirs and took over all the property, but they were both killed in a plane crash. Lot of sadness in that family, even if they were fancy folks. Then, not long after the crash, Amelia Hatcher suddenly shows up after being gone all those years. The way I understand it, Mr. Harvey Trotter, the lawyer on Main Street, took care of getting her here. The big house had burned, but Amelia had a trailer brought in for a while. She up and moves into it, hardly ever speaks to a soul, brings in some Yankee builder, and has the stone cottage built, then she puts in the big garden and that fence. Nobody around here had ever seen anything like it."

"So she is rich."

"I suppose so, but it's hard to tell. Like I said, she used to come to town some but drove an old Ford, and you sure couldn't tell anything by her clothes. I do know Lilly and George Campbell kept French wine in the store for her. Not much call for that around here. Or not at that time anyway."

"Real French wine?"

Mamma nodded and wiped the counter for the third time. "Oh, people talked a lot as you can imagine, but no one was welcome at her place. The preacher went out, and she told him she didn't believe in the church or God and to get off her land."

I stared but could believe it after what I'd seen today.

"A couple of the ladies tried and were treated about the same. Like I told you, wasn't but a few years until Miss Amelia Hatcher made arrangements for things to be delivered to her, paid everyone by check, and stayed put right where she is today. I suppose Mr. Grayling at the bank, Doc Rundle, and the lawyer were the only ones ever talked to her."

"So how did the business with Mr. Watkins get started?"

"Same way as with Lilly and George, I guess. Like I told you, she had the big garden put in, and after a while she got hold of Herb Watkins and offered to sell her produce. That's why I'm not so sure she's got money. Why would she bother if she was rich?"

That was a good point, and the clothes she was wearing today looked like she'd gotten them at some secondhand store.

"She just stays at that place all by herself? And why does Ronny work for her?"

"Oh, she's always had someone around helping with the heavy work, but not anybody who would talk to folks. I imagine she picked Ronny for the same reason. Good boy he is, but not able to be telling many stories, at least not any that could make sense to regular people."

That was true. "So that was her today?"

"The way you described her sounds right, but like your daddy said, it's best you leave her alone. Even if she isn't crazy, she surely is strange."

"Maybe she's got gold or boxes full of money hidden around the cottage, and that's why she never leaves and doesn't want people coming around."

Mamma hung the rag across the faucet, wiped her hands on her apron, and rolled her eyes. "Maggie child, you do have an imagination on you. That's downright silly, and I've talked enough about Amelia Hatcher. You go on over to Ruth Ann's house and get me a spool of black thread. I'm about out, and the store's closed."

I glanced at my wristwatch.

Mamma looked at me sternly. "I know all about you meeting up with Billy Ray tonight, and you've got time for this first. And speaking of Billy Ray, you have yourself home before eleven unless you want a belt across your backside. Don't think your daddy can't hear when you come across the porch."

"Yes, ma'am," I said with a straight face and scooted through the back screen door, my curiosity about Crazy Miz Hatcher taking a lower priority to my plans for the evening. If Ruth Ann wasn't exhausted after a day with her kids, she might be willing to let me borrow the pink eyelet sundress I liked. I'd decided not to give in to Billy Ray yet, but it wouldn't hurt to remind him that I was way better looking than Rita Simpson would ever be.

# Chapter Two

My parents meant well, but ignoring their warning about Crazy Miz Hatcher wasn't an unreasonable act of rebellion considering that I was already resisting premarital sex, drugs, cigarettes, and limiting my underage drinking to special occasions.

I adjusted my schedule to make sure that the cottage was my last pick-up, and Ronny was always eager to show me his handiwork in the garden or let me help feed the bunnies. I didn't actually see Miss Amelia, as I'd begun to think of her, even though I caught glimpses of her around the corner of the cottage or passing by one of the windows. She didn't come to chase me off again, so I figured that she didn't really mind. I got to where it was kind of fun talking with Ronny, too, and it wasn't as if he had a lot of people who would carry on conversations with him. Well, limited conversations. After nearly a month of this routine, Miss Amelia approached me with a look like my English teacher had when I handed in a sloppy report because I hadn't bothered to do it right.

"Ronny, please go in and wash your hands," she called gently to him while holding my eyes with hers. I thought of the color of clover, darker than most green eyes.

"I suppose you might as well join us for lemonade and satisfy your curiosity," she said.

"Uh, I…" That wasn't what I meant to say. Ronny had disappeared around the side path.

Her mouth curved a little even though you couldn't call it a real smile. "I would be far more concerned, if you were accomplished at duplicity at your age, but do me the courtesy of not denying that's the reason for your continuing interest in Ronny."

"Yes, ma'am, I mean, no ma'am, I don't mean any offense," I managed, absurdly pleased that I knew what *duplicity* meant.

She slapped her wide-brimmed gardener's hat against one leg and motioned for me to walk beside her on the crushed oyster shell path. She was dressed as she had been the first time I saw her, in an ankle-length, short-sleeved, lightweight floral print dress that looked like something I'd seen in photographs of my grandmothers. She wore scuffed brown leather clogs, and her white hair was wrapped in a bun at the base of her head.

"I have everything set on the terrace," she said. "I prefer it when it's not too windy. We'll walk around front so you can see the entrance."

We reached the edge of the house, and I slowed my pace to take in the view of the Atlantic. The Outer Banks had more than twenty miles of beaches that stretched from Corolla to the north and southward to Hatteras, with towns like ours of Duck, sprinkled along Highway 12, the beach road. The massive dunes of Wright Brothers' fame were inland on the opposite side of the highway. Ocean-side dunes weren't as tall, and people who wanted to keep a house intact from hurricanes and winter storms knew to build just behind the dune rather than on the beach below. Since this was a single-story house, you wouldn't be able to see the entire dwelling from the beach. As with most of them, it was positioned so the dune itself provided a wind break, and this house had close to forty feet between it and the crest of the dune. Low growing native sea grass covered all but the path that led from the back.

A single wide stone step led up to a small, covered entry-way with a closed dark solid wood front door. Two casement windows to the left of the door were cranked open, giving me a glimpse into what I assumed to be a den. Miss Amelia by-passed the door and walked on the path to an opening in the low stone wall of what I would have called a patio. *Terrace* was the word she used, and it was an expanse of flagstone that stretched the width of the house and extended out twenty feet, if not more. The dune was lower here to provide an unobstructed view of the water, and a flight of wooden steps with handrails provided access to the beach. Huge reddish brown urns filled with flowers anchored the two far corners. A wooden chaise lounge and matching round table were angled to one side. A big table that seemed to be made of heavy planks and six equally heavy weathered chairs took up most of the space to the right. Ronny stood by one of the chairs, watching the waves. Two sets of green painted French doors were open to the house, but my attention was drawn to the table. My God, it looked like silver!

Ronny grinned when he saw us. "Miss Melly has pretty things, doesn't she?"

A silver pitcher with all sorts of curlicue designs on the handle sat on a fancy silver tray and three crystal glasses filled with ice and a lemon slice wedged on the rim, were in front of three chairs. A tiered china plate like I'd seen in a bakery once was also on the table, layered with cookies, tiny frosted squares, and little triangle sandwiches with the crusts cut off. A pair of silver tongs rested on top of three matching china plates.

"Holy sh…, cow!" I blurted and felt my face turn red.

Miss Amelia acted as if I hadn't said a word. "This is a little ritual Ronny and I enjoy, don't we?"

Ronny nodded vigorously. "I'm very careful with pretty stuff," he said proudly and held the chair while Miss Amelia sat down at the head of the table. "I don't break things."

"No, you don't," she agreed. "You are quite the gentleman when it comes to our afternoon repast."

Ronny took his seat to her right, and I slid in next to him so I could face the ocean. My only regret was it also meant that I couldn't see inside the house. If this was how Miss Amelia did lemonade, what did the rest of the place look like? I rubbed my hands rapidly against the side of my shorts, wishing I'd washed them. I nervously lifted the crystal goblet, glad the stem was thick.

"A little of everything?" She held the silver tongs in one hand and a plate in the other. Ronny passed me a dark blue honest-to-God cloth napkin.

I sipped quietly, nodding, and remembered I'd seen the frosted squares at my cousin Ellen's wedding. Patty-somethings.

"These are *petit fours;* the cookies are gingersnaps, one of Ronny's favorites; and chicken salad finger sandwiches," Miss Amelia explained and handed the plate to Ronny, who focused hard to set it in front of me without spilling anything.

"I wasn't expecting anything like this when you said lemonade," I said, not sure how she would take my comment. "I mean, everything is really lovely." I held my hands together in my lap, knowing that I shouldn't start until Miss Amelia did. My home ec teacher thought I paid no mind to her boring class on etiquette, but as with most of my teachers, I took in more than I let them know.

"I learned a long time ago that it doesn't hurt a bit to use elegant things every day," she said with a tiny shrug and finished serving Ronny and herself. "The other day you said you were Doreen's youngest. There are four of you if I recall correctly."

"Yes, ma'am. Only two of us are still at home, and Jed, next to me, is going into the Army as soon as high school's over."

"Pa said I couldn't be in the Army. I'm too stupid," Ronnie said and smiled when the cookie made a *snap* as he broke it in half.

"But you're a big help to me, and you're going to make a fine shrimper," Miss Amelia replied immediately, patting his arm as I'd seen her do that first day.

Ronny nodded vigorously. "Uncle Cecil is gittin' his own boat, and he said a big boy like me should help him." He crunched his face and turned toward Miss Amelia. "I'm sorry I'm going off, Miss Melly. Uncle Cecil says I got to start leaning early so's I won't make mistakes on the boat come the season."

Another pat. "That won't be for a couple of months, Ronny. Don't you worry about me. I'll get some more help, and you can visit when you have time."

"And see the bunnies and have lemonade with you."

I pressed my lips together hard to keep from giggling because I was sure Miss Amelia would think I was laughing at Ronny and get mad again. But holy shit, how were you not supposed to laugh? Here was Ronny who could probably lift this table over his head without breaking a sweat, being so careful with the crystal and china, talking about bunny rabbits. I was dressed in my usual scruffy shorts, a faded cotton shirt, and worn down sneakers, and Miss Amelia was taking no mind as if I was in my Sunday best.

I thought quickly to keep from laughing. "I heard about your uncle Cecil's boat deal. He asked Daddy to check the engines and stuff. He's getting the boat from Mr. Pooley, and it's kind of old, but in really good shape."

"That's right. Your father is a mechanic of some kind, isn't he?"

"Yes, ma'am, he's been with Wheeler's Marina all his working life."

Ronny half-closed his eyes, seemingly lost in the taste of cookies. Miss Amelia brushed a loosened strand of hair behind her ear. "Do your parents know you're here?"

I squirmed too much before I answered, and she held her hand up.

"Never mind. I will assume you are capable of making such decisions for yourself. Do you read by any chance?"

"Ma'am? You mean books?"

She pursed her lips instead of smiling. "I assume you read books in school. I meant do you read for pleasure, for enjoyment?"

I wasn't sure what to say. My teachers would have said *No, she barely manages required reading.* I was the only one in the family who had a library card, and our little library didn't have much I hadn't read. We didn't have books around the house, not because anyone was against it, but with four kids to feed and clothe, costly books were more like a luxury. I bobbed my head. "I'm not much on schoolwork. My teachers say I don't concentrate."

She flicked one finger as though thumping a fly. "Not concentrating is one of those convenient labels teachers use when someone doesn't fit into their precise mold. In your case, I assume that means you don't cause much trouble but also don't do as well as you could. You haven't answered my question though—do you like to read?"

I nodded, confused as to how she could know this about me and my teachers. It had never been that schoolwork was hard—it was just so boring that it didn't seem worth the bother. And it wasn't as if anyone was figuring I would be going off to college.

"Have another cookie, Ronny, I have to show Maggie

something inside," Miss Amelia said, standing and pointing her finger toward the open double French doors. "Come along, little country girl."

I followed her inside, into my first glimpse of what lay within those out-of-place stone walls and felt the involuntary *"Gosh!"* escape my mouth, which was no doubt hanging open.

It was sort of like walking into an antique store, but not crammed together to where you were sure you'd bump into something. Even though the furniture was big and a large black iron chandelier spread across the ceiling, the room had an airiness that I wasn't expecting. Sunlight came in through the doors and the open windows, where gauzy curtains stirred in the mild breeze. When my eyes adjusted to the interior light, I could more clearly distinguish the array of objects that caused my reaction. Against the wall to my left, crystal, china, and silver filled a cabinet that nearly reached the ceiling. The wall to my right was taken up almost completely by massive book cases that did reach the ceiling. The shelves were heavy with books, candles in fancy holders, and knickknacks that probably had some fancy name. There was a rolling library ladder slanted from the ceiling like I'd seen in old movies. A smaller version of the wooden table and chairs on the terrace sat beneath one of the large windows. An old record player in a cabinet with legs and a lid that opened on hinges stood at the back wall. Alongside it were three sets of wooden bins like they had in the record stores, lined up next to each other. Another tall bookcase ended at the edge of an arched entry that probably led to the kitchen.

I looked down at the planked wooden floor and suspected that the old rugs were more likely antiques than the kind you ordered from Sears.

"Come over here," Miss Amelia said, once again ignoring my astonishment at what I could only think of as treasures.

She waved her hand across the first set of books. "I think you should start at this end."

I closed my mouth, determined to stop being embarrassed, and stepped to her side. "Start with what, ma'am?"

"Reading for the fun of it—reading about the world outside this place." She turned her face to the books and surveyed them as if she hadn't looked at them for a while. "I suppose it can be a bit overwhelming," she said with not quite a smile.

"Where did all these come from?" My intent to stop acting the complete doofus lost out to the idea that anyone would own this many books.

"I live alone," she said in the softer tone she seemed to save for Ronny. "I have no use for the obnoxious intrusion of television—reading, my music, my garden, and the beach serve me nicely." She reverted to the crisp, nearly sharp voice in her next breath.

"I have an arrangement with a book dealer in Raleigh," she continued. "Contemporary literature is at the other end, but I suggest you begin with some of the older works—I imagine you'll enjoy them more than you think. And no, I don't mean you need to focus on Shakespeare, although his complete collection is on the top shelves."

She tapped the gold lettered spine of leather volumes at my eye level. "There's nothing wrong with starting with Agatha Christie, but take your time and look while I check on Ronny. The upper shelves in the second case have mostly French and German works."

With that, she left me to wander slowly, now deliciously, her purpose in this abrupt offer no longer important. So many books! Books she was obviously going to let me borrow. Why should I care what her motive was? I tentatively stroked the spines as I edged from section to section. It was as orderly as if the town library had somehow gotten a gift of quality classics—alphabetized and no catch-as-catch-can, random offerings. At least two dozen Agatha Christies, more Hemingways than I knew had been written, Fitzgeralds, an interesting absence of Faulkner, and on down through every letter of the alphabet. I lifted my eyes to see strange sounding names I did not know and script that I recognized as French and what must have been German. Did she actually read in those languages? If not, why have them? If so, where would she have learned?

"Ah, you want to begin with Sir Arthur Conan Doyle? Not a bad choice," she said, slipping so quietly beside me that I had hardly heard her footsteps. "If you don't mind, please take just one and we'll see how this goes."

"I'll be careful with it," I promised, afraid she was about to change her mind.

She gazed at me with that intense teacher-like stare. "I'm sure you will be, but now you'll have a logical reason to return. It's not as though the produce season will go on much longer and that has been your primary excuse for coming here, hasn't it? Shall we rejoin Ronny?"

I held the copy of *The Lost World* to my chest, following her silently, and felt an oddness that I couldn't define. It was more than the comical quality of having lemonade from crystal glasses when I would have expected plastic cups, and it wasn't the dozens of questions I ached to ask. Where had Miss Amelia gotten so many lovely things, or even why she would be willing to lend me books? It was, perhaps, a flickering understanding that by answering the invitation to come around the corner of the house, I had been drawn into a set of secrets as surely as the kind you have with a makeshift clubhouse and whispered passwords. Not that I'd ever had such things, but everyone knew of them. I already recognized that I would not speak of this afternoon at the dinner table, nor during the shared time with my mother as we washed the dishes. The book would be easy enough to explain if it was noticed at all, I thought.

As we came out of the house, I suddenly realized that it was almost closing time at Watkins Market. Bobby usually locked up, and sometimes he needed help with last-minute tasks.

"Miss Amelia, I have to go," I said quickly and clutched the book more tightly. "I mean, thank you for everything, but…"

"No matter," she said with her shrug of dismissal. "Ronny and I have more work to do, and it's almost time for my afternoon walk. Don't forget to latch the gate."

"No, ma'am, and thanks again for everything," I said and left them clearing the table, Ronny's face tight with concentration as he held crystal glasses in both hands.

I navigated my way to Watkins Market unconsciously, puzzling as to what had happened that afternoon. Had I unknowingly said something to reveal the love of reading that I kept as a quiet part of myself? When I was ten, my grandmother lost her sight, and for reasons I never quite understood, it became my chore to read to her until she passed away.

"Does a body good to get a picture in words," she would say, having me linger over descriptions in passages of Victoria Holt. Even though I wasn't really impressed with the heroines who always seemed in need of rescue, I agreed it would be wonderful to see a castle someday. It was through her that I came to know the librarians who suggested books like *Pippi Longstocking* and *Little Women*, until I happily found Jack London and other adventures.

"You get lost today or what?" Bobby opened the truck door nearly before I stopped in the graveled yard behind the market stand. "We got to go to Sheila's mamma's tonight, and I still got to lock up. Let's get this shit unloaded."

Bobby, like Jed, had Daddy's lean hardness and muscled forearms built from working with his hands. His light brown hair, which didn't have my coppery hues, was from Mamma's side, and I was always glad I hadn't gotten his thick eyebrows or patches of freckles that were like splotches. Bobby was okay as far as big brothers went, but he got bossy awfully quick at times. Every so often he'd treat me like I was ten years old instead of practically seventeen.

"It took me longer than usual at Miz Hatcher's," I said, climbing into the truck bed and sliding crates of fruit and vegetables onto the open tailgate.

Bobby lifted them out and aligned the crates inside the fenced storage area. "That crazy lady? You see her, you mean? She give you any trouble?"

"I told you I've been seeing her and you hadn't believe me. Besides, she's really not so bad if she's not yelling at you. She needed a little extra help with getting things picked today," I lied for no reason I could figure.

"Yeah, well, way I heard it, she took a shotgun to a couple of guys fishing last week when she caught 'em sitting on the steps going up to her place. Blasted a hole in the sand at their feet and told 'em to get on down the beach out of her sight."

"Could be," I said and smothered a smile. Bobby straightened and shooed me with his arm.

"That's it. Don't forget we gotta clear out the back shed tomorrow. I promised Mrs. Watkins we'd load that shit up and haul it out."

I waved my agreement as I backed from the lot, grinning at the thought of Miss Amelia threatening fishermen with a shotgun. It was the kind of story that if it wasn't true, it should be.

# Chapter Three

March must be a dreary month in some parts of the country, but not on the Outer Banks. It is not the glorious flowering season of April and May, although daffodils and star magnolias make appearance and the bird population thrives. I loved the emptiness of the beaches; the winds across the Atlantic, which were not the sharp ones of winter; the less frequent rains; and the sun that was willing to warm you with no more than a light sweater needed. It's not so much that I minded the tourists that come and bring dollars to fuel the towns; it's more that I cherished the quiet days before the first cars filled with groups of men, who were escaping whatever their lives were outside, who arrived to rent the wooden fishing cabins. Spring break will be followed by Memorial Day, the traditional start of tourist season when families come, loaded with beach toys, suitcases, and stair-stepped children whom they will alternately indulge with mounds of saltwater taffy and restrict with screams to not go so far into the waves.

Rumors were bouncing around town that franchise hotels were being considered for the Outer Banks to fill empty spots on the beaches—name-brand hotels that would draw more people. More suspicious was the idea of large structures being built with some strange sounding thing called timeshare and bigger houses that would be owned by people who lived elsewhere. Not the modest fishing cabins we had now, but three- and four-bedroom structures to be filled with weekly renters who would either bring new prosperity or doom the region to escalating prices and overcrowding, depending on who was doing the telling.

"Sally Watkins said Myrna Billings said they're going to put a Holiday Inn up in Nags Head," my sister, Ruth Ann, announced as we finished Sunday dinner, a weekly event my mother took pride in. "She said it was only the beginning because all those beach towns in Maryland and New Jersey had gotten so crowded in the summer that you couldn't hardly walk on the beach for stepping on somebody and people were looking for some place new. She said maybe this year, and if not, then for sure before the end of 1978." Ruth Ann's face was more narrow than mine with a sharper chin. She got her looks from Daddy's side of the family and when she was trying to be serious, she'd squint her eyes up just like his mamma used to.

"Yeah, and I heard some big developer was looking to put up some fancy resort over the sound side," her husband, Kenny, added.

"Fishing and camping been what folks wanted here for as long as I can remember," Daddy grunted. "Places like the Dolphin Inn plenty good enough for somebody wants a motel, 'stead of a cabin or tent. No reason for changing it."

"We been hearing the same thing in Elizabeth City," Uncle Merl said and popped the last bite of pecan pie into his mouth. "Word is land's going to jump up here, and in ten, fifteen years, you won't know the place. Lots of talk about putting in a bypass on 58, and putting up shopping and stuff. "

"Got nothing to do with us," Daddy replied stubbornly, his forehead creased. He had more forehead now that he was losing his hair. He was beginning to look more like the pictures of his daddy, who'd died when I was just a baby.

"That's enough of that," Mamma said firmly, knowing that Daddy and Uncle Merl could squabble over the time of day if they wanted to. "Maggie, if you're done, you can clear the table and go on. Ruth Ann and I will do the dishes."

I jumped up and started stacking plates in case she changed her mind, or Ruth Ann thought I was shirking. The last thing I wanted to do on a Sunday was hang around the house, and that would have been true even if Uncle Merl hadn't brought a new camera for me. Well, not new, but a really nice Leica he wasn't using any longer. He owned a small camera shop and studio, the kind of place where brides got their pictures made. I can't remember how old I was when I first watched him develop a roll of film, although I do remember the strange smells of the darkroom. He let me start helping him not long after my thirteenth birthday and said I had a natural eye for taking pictures. I hadn't told anyone yet, but I knew the business was doing well and I was thinking that maybe after I graduated from high school, he might take me on in a real job.

This was part of my planning as I dashed from the house, camera strapped around my neck. I hurried from our neighborhood of gray-shingled houses down the short street and across the Beach Road through a cut in low dunes, where sea grass bent in the breeze. I stopped at the base of a dune to slip my sneakers off and leave them. If I stepped through the surf, I didn't want to slog home in sodden shoes. I'd already changed into a pair of denim shorts and a green cotton sweater with three-quarter sleeves, the color more like sage now from repeated washings. It was a hand-me-down from Ruth Ann, like most of the clothes I wore that once belonged to my sister or cousins.

I stood for a moment, watching the wave pattern. The hard

blue sky and wispy clouds that didn't blunt the sun gave the water the aquamarine tone that meant as waves crested, you could see shimmering blue-green before the waves crashed into shallows, white foam rolling onto sand. If I had color film, I would have tried to set the exposure and time the shot to capture the curl, but with only one roll of black and white, I would concentrate on my task.

Miss Amelia's birthday was in April, and even if I had more money to spend, what could I possibly buy her that she would want? I'd decided on a photograph of the beach she loved—well, not the exact beach beneath her steps, but the few miles between her place and this part of town had the same flocks of brown pelicans, assorted gulls, and pipers that were bound by region, not property lines. I carefully scanned the stretches of sand left and right as I thought of Miss Amelia's offer to have me replace Ronny. It meant no more making up silly excuses to have access to books, paintings, and descriptions of parts of Europe that Miss Amelia occasionally shared with me. She suggested that I present the practical matter of money to Daddy, recognizing that cash was never in plentiful supply for us and knowing that was one of the few things likely to influence my father.

"Don't know this is a good idea. You got enough to do with school, Watkins on the weekends, and helping your mamma," Daddy had said, when I braved the subject of working for Miss Amelia.

"It won't interfere," I promised, alone with my parents at the dinner table. "It's just a few hours a week really, helping her around."

"Thought that retarded kid, that Fuller boy, helped her," he continued, his frown not the dangerous glower that meant the discussion was over.

"He does Daddy, but his Uncle Cecil got his boat, so Ronny'll be shrimping. And Miss Amelia pays good, I mean pays well," I corrected immediately. "Three dollars an hour."

Mamma drew her breath in and shot a glance at Daddy as he drained his beer and plunked the can onto the table. "Huh," he grunted. "What's she got you doing?"

"She's kind of old," I said quickly. "I help with moving some of the heavy stuff, stacking firewood for her, that kind of thing."

Mamma reached for Daddy's plate and shrugged. "Clarence, I'm not saying Amelia Hatcher isn't strange, but she's always had somebody giving her a hand at that place, and I've never heard bad about that part. If Maggie keeps up with everything she's supposed to, we can always use the money. You know the roof needs to be tended to before long."

"Don't be letting your chores go around here," he warned as way of permission. "And half of what you earn goes to your mamma. Groceries ain't getting any cheaper."

"Yes, sir," I said and held my smile inside. I fleetingly thought about giving them a hug in thanks and knew the gesture would be brushed aside. Ours was not a family that carried on with emotion. I was sure Mamma wanted to ask more questions, but she kept quiet, no doubt worrying about Ruth Ann who was pregnant again. I knew part of my wages would be slipped to her, and if she wasn't married to somebody who got fired from damn near every job he ever got, I wouldn't mind so much.

A sand crab the size of a quarter refocused my thoughts as it darted from my path and gulls wheeled and squawked. I wasn't in a hurry and didn't have the luxury of shooting roll upon roll of film and then deciding what picture I liked. Uncle Merl told me that was the way real photographers did it, and as

I searched for the right subject, I relished in my fantasy about how it would be to go all over the world taking pictures.

It wasn't that I didn't appreciate the Outer Banks, but to travel to places like the Grand Canyon or across the ocean, maybe to Egypt or Africa, or see the Alps in the winter—what a life that would be. I'd given up trying to get Miss Amelia to give me more than glimpses of what France and Germany had been like, and I wasn't sure how many countries she'd been to.

"It was all a long time ago, and no one cares anymore. The past can stay where it is," she'd said in a way that I recognized meant she didn't want to talk about it.

After I became familiar with her book collection, I asked about her records; old ones made before I was born. Once when I mentioned rock and roll, she narrowed her eyes and said it was yowling racket; that jazz, blues, and classical should be good enough for anyone. And cook—she could spend all day tending a pot to do nothing more than make plain soup, or stock, she called it. It's not that Mamma wasn't a good cook, but I'd never seen anything like the ingredients Miss Amelia cooked with.

"It's an herb garden," she'd explained, when I asked her why one section of the garden seemed filled with odd-looking weeds. "Rosemary, basil, oregano, and so forth—there's more to life than salt, pepper, and bacon grease, you know."

Time spent with Miss Amelia meant I became accustomed to the sight of her floured hands kneading dough, to fragrances I couldn't identify, to the idea of wine being used in a dish.

"There are more ways to cook fish than to roll them in cornmeal and drop them into a pot of hot oil," she said the first time she suggested I stay for lunch.

"Watch carefully while I create the sauce," she instructed. "Fresh ingredients and patience are key to all French cooking and don't turn your nose up because it's something you've never tried."

How was I not supposed to be suspicious of poached fish smothered in a sauce whose name I couldn't pronounce? On the other hand, she dismissed my weak protest of not being allowed to drink with a contemptuous, "Don't be barbaric. A glass of wine won't kill you, and you can't possibly ask me to believe you've never had a drink. I'll start you with an easy white and teach you more later."

"Don't pretend you don't like it," she said tartly, when I tentatively nibbled the portion of fish balanced on my fork.

"It's okay," I replied, determined not to gush. I was already regretting that she'd made only two servings.

"Nonsense—it's delicious," she said and almost smiled. "Don't worry, we'll do this slowly. Now, pay attention while I tell you why the table is set differently from the way you do it at home."

Perhaps I should have felt some sort of conflict as I moved in and out of Miss Amelia's isolated life and my everyday routines. I still couldn't understand why she never ventured from the two acres she called her own, except to walk the beach at times when she was unlikely to meet anyone else. Since I saw no signs of recent wealth, I came to the conclusion that her possessions were maybe all she had left of what had been a prosperous time. But how and from where? Had she been married to some rich man in Europe? Had he been killed in the war? Was she divorced? Had there been some terrible scandal she ran away from?

"I have no use for people in general," she said calmly, when I asked if she didn't get bored. "My traveling days are over, and I have everything I need here. Once you get to be my age, you'll understand."

It didn't take long for me to stop asking questions and simply accept lessons she meted out as the mood took her. I equally accepted her silence on the days when she had no desire to discuss what book I'd read or talk to me about food.

My own response to the few questions put to me about Miss Amelia was a mumbled, "She doesn't say much about anything, but she's okay," and my family ceased to inquire as to what I did for her.

The truth be told, my routine world wasn't anything to be excited about, not like what Miss Amelia could talk about. My relationship with Billy Ray had drowned in a wave of disgust with his escalating badgering for sex, and the other boys in town weren't a bit different. Why would I want to go out with any of them? I couldn't really say that I had girlfriends either. The smart ones had visions of college that held no interest for me, and the rest were younger versions of my sister. Constant assessing of potential husbands at age seventeen was not my idea of a future. I didn't think of myself as a loner, although I suspected that's how my teachers described me. I didn't dislike people, but I saw no reason to pretend to enjoy silly conversations just so I wasn't sitting alone at a lunch table. If I didn't keep my nose stuck in a book to win a scholarship, that was because I knew there had to be other ways to leave our narrow barrier island. The time I spent with Miss Amelia strengthened my intent to someday board an airplane or take a train cross country.

I hadn't told Jed that I was hoping he would be stationed far away when he finished his Army training so I would have a ready-made excuse to travel. I wasn't sure where all he might go, but I sure didn't want him to be at Fort Bragg like Mamma was hoping.

Thoughts of exotic places disappeared when I saw a large

piece of driftwood that had been left when high tide receded, jagged branches angled to make perfect perches. I slowed, not wanting to disturb the kind of scene I had been looking for. Water was pooled where the chunk of wood indented the sand, and most of the piece was still dark from being wet. The longest branch in full sun had the gray of dried wood; a brown pelican was poised on the end of it. Two willets ignored a black-bellied plover as they probed wet sand on the far side of the chunk of wood.

I readied the camera and eased into position, noiselessly drawing as close as I could. The afternoon light was good, and I quietly watched until the birds clustered closer. The pelican swiveled his head and prepared for flight, and I rapidly snapped four shots. My movement sent the other birds hopping away until they determined I was no danger. The pelican launched, and I resisted the urge to capture his wing motion—I didn't have the shutter speed set for that.

I wandered for more than two hours, never rushing the shots; I paused at another small tidal pool carved into the sand with a couple of crabs, and then I saw an old man surf fishing. He had his poles jammed in at an angle, tips bent forward as lines and hooks floated out, waiting for a strike. His short-legged lawn chair was settled into the sand, a small white cooler beside it. He had ambled to his truck, parked at the edge of the beach, and nodded permission when I waved the camera. I waited for him to stroll back and politely inquired as to his catch. We exchanged opinions about it being too early in the season for red drums to be running, but sea mullets and croaker were doing okay and it was a pleasant way to spend a Sunday afternoon. I left him easing onto his chair and headed home, knowing I would choose between the pelican and the fishing poles.

I wanted to make arrangements with Uncle Merl to develop the film as soon as I could, and I already knew what I would do about framing. Despite smirks, I'd signed up for shop class, and I was earning A's as well as the grudging, "not bad for a girl" comments. There was always scrap wood, stain, and paint around the classroom that I could use to build a frame. I recovered my shoes and slipped them on, thinking that while I was at Uncle Merl's store, I could talk to him about getting another lens. I didn't know how many different ones real photographers used, but it was sure as hell more than one.

# Chapter Four

"This is nice composition for someone your age," Miss Amelia said, when she peeled the newspaper wrapping from her gift. "I like the way you presented these together. Did your uncle develop them?"

"Plain old developing? I've been doing that for ages," I said. I'd struggled with which photograph I liked best and then thought to make the frame large enough to fit two side-by-side. I'd caught foamy waves around the base of the fishing poles with the small cooler wedged against the chair in the sand; the contrast in elements noticeable in black and white. The more I looked at the other photograph, I decide that the birds weren't clustered as tightly as I wanted. The pelican beginning his launch, webbed feet barely in contact with the driftwood branch was a better shot.

"We'll hang this above the phonograph later. Don't wrinkle your nose at the cheese. It's served in practically every house-hold in France. There really is more in life than cheddar, you know."

We were on the terrace, Miss Amelia's favored spot, a red wine she called Beaujolais in our glasses. She gently corrected me when I pronounced the *s*. "Remember, in French, you don't pronounce the consonant unless there is a vowel at the end. You did soften the *j*, so that's an improvement."

Her decision one day that I should learn French was delivered in the same way as most of her ideas for me. "It's good for you, and don't pretend you haven't thought about it."

Her technique was the simple approach—the first hour I was with her we spoke only French. Or rather she spoke and I tried to follow, tried to understand what she wanted me to do. She switched to English precisely sixty minutes after we started, and when we took our afternoon refreshment, she explained pronunciation and basic grammar rules. I stumbled through the first two weeks then began to hear the cadence of her words, locking nouns and adjectives into memory before I grasped verbs. It was more enjoyable than I cared to admit, although it wasn't as if we had hordes of French tourists wandering about. I wasn't sure what practical good it was doing me.

"Do they really have three hundred kinds of cheese?" Popular or not, the creamy goo I spread on a thin slice of toasted bread was too sharp for my nose and mouth. I liked the firmer ones better.

"More than four hundred actually, and it would be unfair of me to discount some lovely Swiss and Italian ones, plus the Brits do well with a few, and I suppose one should grant the Dutch their gouda. Try one of those black olives—I prefer Spanish over Italian."

"How do you get all these things? No one here sells them." I nibbled reluctantly and gave in again at being proved wrong. The only kind of olives I'd ever seen were the green ones people sometimes brought to church dinners. We certainly didn't have any in our house.

"We're not the end of the earth, you know, and arranging to have items shipped to you isn't terribly difficult." A persistent fly hovered around the cheese plate, and she batted it away with the back of her hand.

Her answer was as clear as many she gave when she answered at all about how she lived in the cottage with such little outside contact.

"I want to replant begonias this week. Can you go to Pinkham's one afternoon and pick up some flats for me?"

I nodded. "I can do it tomorrow if he has them. Do you want me to call?"

"I've already done that," she said sharply, as if I should have known better. "I'll let him know to expect you after school. He'll put it on the bill. Now, I want you to pay attention while I explain the difference in this wine and something full-bodied like a burgundy."

It was too bad you couldn't get wine and food lessons at school—my grades would improve for sure. I'd started keeping a roll of mints handy to chew on when I left Miss Amelia's. My parents might overlook a sneaked beer on a Saturday night, but smelling booze on my breath on a school day was a recipe for trouble. In spite of what some people would no doubt think, Miss Amelia's lessons were for real and not just an excuse to get drunk before five o'clock. We rarely had more than two glasses each, if that. She was taking her time with reds, having brought me from whites through rose. She said champagne would have to wait until I could appreciate it properly.

"Did you know the Army has bases in California? If Jed gets stationed out there, I could go visit. I heard California has good wine, too."

"Fledgling but promising," Miss Amelia said and tapped the bottle. "The French have been making wine for centuries, not decades. No doubt California wines have a future, but I'll leave that to you youngsters. In the meantime, learn the basic rules so when you venture more than fifty miles from home someday, you'll at least have a rudimentary idea of how to order in a restaurant."

I listened to Miss Amelia as I envisioned traveling to California, or Colorado, or whatever exotic place the Army might send Jed. I'd checked the map, and even if he went some place like Fort Polk, Louisiana, which he said everyone said sucked, it wasn't far from New Orleans. Mamma and Daddy didn't know that the last time I'd been to Uncle Merl's shop, I'd gone right into the bank down the block and opened a savings account. I'd given Miss Amelia's address without asking, and it took me more than two weeks to attempt a sheepish explanation since I figured the bank would start mailing things before too long.

She'd snapped at me a bit for being presumptuous rather than asking permission but then shrugged—secrets were something she was used to. When time came to visit Jed, I wouldn't have to ask anybody for help. I don't know why I wanted to keep it to myself, but from the minute I had money building up in the bank, it felt good. It was mine—not meant to be spent on anything except what I wanted to. I didn't know what that was yet other than planning to take a trip, but it didn't really matter. I would figure it out later.

# Chapter Five

Pinkham's graveled parking lot was empty. The wood frame, L-shaped building could use a new coat of red paint, unless the owners were trying to emphasize the rustic look. It was the only nursery open year-round although its inventory would be basic until later in the spring. The long side of the L was kept stocked with indoor plants, gardening supplies, and decorative pots. The large section out back defined by steel hurricane fencing contained drought tolerate shrubs, grasses, and plants as well as pallets of landscaping stones and bags of river rock. Split firewood, measured by the pickup truck load, was set against the back of the fence and covered by heavy tarps. Within a month, the loads would be divided into smaller bundles for summer people who wanted the smell and sound of a crackling fire for a romantic evening. The smaller section of the yard would soon be filled with flowering plants, from bedding plant size that you could hold in the palm of your hand to small trees in black plastic containers.

Pinkham's was a second-generation business that started small and expanded when cash was available, as had Watkins Market. Like anyone on the Outer Banks who didn't want to see their life's work repossessed, businessmen knew better than to take out loans based on expectation of money coming in. One bad hurricane season with damages and lost revenue could wipe a family out when the money men came looking for mortgage payments. You could hear tourists chat during summer months about how quaint the set-up was, never realizing that rambling add-ons were economically driven rather than architectural design. Bobby said Mr. Watkins was thinking about putting in a Bar-B-Q stand next year if business stayed good. He had the space, and everybody knew his sauce was always in the top three winners in the regional competitions.

I stepped inside, a little surprised to see Old Mrs. Pinkham sitting on a stool at the register. She set aside some kind of paper she was working on and looked up when she heard the door open.

"Why, Maggie, I haven't seen you in a coon's age. How's your mamma and daddy?" Her round face was less wrinkled than you would expect of a woman her age, but my sister, Ruth Ann, swore she'd read in a magazine that the only good thing about being fat was your face didn't wrinkle as fast as it did if you were skinny. Not that I'd call Mrs. Pinkham fat exactly. At a full head shorter than me, plump was probably the right word. Her gray hair had that bluey tint and wavy look all the ladies at church seemed to like. I wondered if it was some kind of rule for old ladies that they whispered to you later in life.

"They're fine, ma'am. Is Mr. Junior around?"

"No, Junior and Rhonda are down to Nags Head for a while, and I'm minding the store. It's been pretty quiet this afternoon. Did you need something special?" Her brown eyes were squinting a bit like she should have been wearing glasses.

"Yes, ma'am. I think Mrs. Hatcher talked to Mr. Junior about a couple of flats of begonias, and she thought they might be ready for pick-up. I can come back tomorrow though."

She pursed her lips to where her entire face looked puffed up like a balloon before you let the air out of it. "Amelia Hatcher.

That's right, you've been doing chores for her, haven't you?"

"Yes, ma'am," I replied, not overly concerned about getting the flowers. One day more or less in planting wasn't going to matter.

Mrs. Pinkham edged her way off the stool and ran her index finger across several notes taped to the side of the old metal cash register. "Amelia Hatcher, now there's a woman I never expected to see again. She ever mention folks in town?"

"Uh, not really, ma'am, she's kind of a private person." I guess Mrs. Pinkham would be about Miss Amelia's age, but hadn't Mamma said Miss Amelia was from Manteo?

"That she surely is. I grew up in Manteo, you know," she continued, "lived in the house next door to them. Oh, here it is." She moved her face close to the note. "Two flats of begonias; A. Hatcher, pick up. Oh, they won't be here until Wednesday." She shook her head. "I never did understand what happened to her after that night, and I really liked her mamma, never mind how ugly her daddy was."

"Ma'am?" I craned to try and see the note.

She poked at the note and looked at me, still squinty-eyed. "Amelia Hatcher, a strange story if ever there was one. You know she spent most all her life off in France or some such place, don't you? Might have been England, I guess. Went to live with Mrs. Thornhill when she was no more than fourteen. I was seventeen that year, the summer I married Mr. Pinkham, God rest his soul." She hauled herself back onto the stool and wagged a finger slowly. "She hasn't told you about Mrs. Thornhill and the fire?"

I knew I should say, *No, ma'am,* thank her for her time, and leave. If Miss Amelia hadn't told me this story, then it wouldn't be right of me to ask questions of Mrs. Pinkham. "She doesn't say much about those days," I said with a tiny little sigh that wasn't really like asking a question.

"Well, let me tell you, it was about the strangest thing I'd ever seen happen in my life. You want a Coke? I was just thinking about one when you came in. Junior has some in the refrigerator in the office there. Why don't you get two and bring another stool over? I could use a break from these sums I've been messing with."

I could hear Mamma telling me I should mind my own business as I slipped into the small office at the far end of the counter. But how was I supposed to pass up a chance like this? I mean, Mrs. Pinkham was a nice lady; she wasn't the kind to be spreading stories, and if she really had lived near Miss Amelia, it wasn't really like she was gossiping. I grabbed two cans of Coke in one hand and hooked a stool with my other.

"That's a girl; you just sit down for a spell and let me think for a minute about that family." She accepted the cold can, pulled the pop top, and set it on the counter. "Mr. Pinkham, God rest his soul, was like your daddy, born right here in Duck, but my family was over in Manteo, where my daddy was a carpenter. I met Mr. Pinkham at an ice cream social when I was sixteen years old. A fine looking young man he was." She took two sips of her Coke, and I wondered if she forgot what she was supposed to be talking about. *That would serve you right*, I could hear Mamma say.

"But that's another story. Let's see, I must have been about fourteen when the Hatchers moved in next door, and I must have known where they came from at the time, but can't for the life of me recall. Anyway, there was the oldest boy who was my age and had a terrible scar on his arm, but it's not like we thought anything about it at first. Then another boy a year younger, then Amelia, and then the little one, another girl. No one in the neighborhood had any money to speak of so when they moved in without much of anything, it wasn't unusual. It was a small house, like everyone else's, but the only one that was rented." She paused for another sip, and her mouth tightened like she tasted something bad.

"Naturally, Mamma sent me over with a pot of peas and a pan of cornbread to welcome them, and Mrs. Hatcher, Miriam was her name, thanked me all proper like and said she didn't want to be unneighborly, but her husband didn't care much for socializing. Well, let me tell you, it took no time at all to understand that Mr. Hatcher, Roscoe is what he was called, was as mean a man as you'd want to meet. He was always hollering and beating on the kids and her for no reason. Not a one of them hardly ever walked around without bruises."

"Didn't anyone call the sheriff on him?" If this was true, that would explain why Miss Amelia never talked about her family.

Mrs. Pinkham shrugged. "It's not like today. Most folks didn't think to interfere with another man's family. Thing is, the oldest boy wasn't there long. He ran off maybe four or five months later after he and his daddy had a fight. Then that first winter the little girl died of pneumonia. Mamma got Mrs. Hatcher alone and tried to talk to her about maybe complaining to the sheriff, but all she said was it might help if she could bring in some money. Mrs. Hatcher had a gift for sewing, and she could stitch up clothes out of almost nothing. Amelia was sort of pretty in a skinny kind of way, and even though I think she only had three dresses to her name, her mamma kept them darned up to where they looked nice. Anyway, that was how Mrs. Hatcher got to know Mrs. Thornhill."

"The rich lady from Raleigh?" Mrs. Pinkham didn't seem to be in a hurry.

"That's right, from Raleigh. She and her husband had this

grand house in Duck that was damaged during a hurricane, and my daddy was one of the carpenters working on it. Mrs. Thornhill had taken a house in town while the beach house was being repaired, and it so happened she was looking to have a bunch of new draperies and stuff sewn up. Mamma took her a sample of Mrs. Hatcher's work, and she gave Mrs. Hatcher the job right away. Mrs. Thornhill was a nice lady, fancy though she was. She didn't carry on about their money, gave to the church, and that kind of thing. Mamma thought Mrs. Thornhill felt sorry for Mrs. Hatcher because even after the draperies were finished, she would send her driver, her driver mind you, in to pick Mrs. Hatcher up, two, sometimes three days a week, to come out to Duck to do tailoring and such."

I nodded politely, the picture of Miss Amelia as a skinny girl—had she been blonde or dark haired? With green eyes, it could have been either—well, she could have been a redhead, too. "Did the extra money help them out like Mrs. Hatcher hoped?"

Mrs. Pinkham shifted on her stool and scrunched her face in a way that mixed pity and disgust. "That mean old man. Things were getting hard those days, and he was a mechanic like your daddy—worked on big stuff like boats and farming equipment. With his drinking, it got hard for him to find work so turns out they weren't much better off. Mind you, I don't think the money really had a thing to do with it. I think he'd of found excuses for beating on her and the kids no matter what. Not that we knew exactly. See, they stayed to themselves, hardly anybody really saw them. The other boy didn't bother with going to school most days, and that second winter, he ran off, too. Amelia, now she was just flat quiet, didn't take up with any of the girls at school." Mrs. Pinkham blew a stream of air out of her pursed mouth. "The truth be told, I'd have to say that nobody really tried to be friends with her."

I didn't know what kids were like in Mrs. Pinkham's days, but I suspect they weren't all that different. There were always a few loners that nobody seemed to notice. "So Mrs. Hatcher used to take Miss Amelia with her to Mrs. Thornhill's?" I wasn't in a terrible hurry, but I figured Mr. Junior would be coming back before too long and I might not get to hear the whole story.

"Yes, that was pretty much it. Amelia would go with her mamma sometimes, although she didn't have her knack with a needle. Anyway, Mrs. Thornhill promised that the next summer when she came up, she'd hire Mrs. Hatcher again for work. That winter was when the boy ran off, like I told you. Seems he shipped out on a freighter, and once in awhile, he would send a postcard from way off somewhere like Japan. Don't really know what happened to either boy, because after the fire, they had no reason to come back even if they'd meant to."

*Finally, the fire. What was the deal with the fire?* I was about ready to scream the question but held my words not wanting to seem too eager to hear about Miss Amelia's past.

"Anyway, things went along pretty much the way they had been. I admit I wasn't paying a whole lot of attention to the neighbors since I'd met Mr. Pinkham and we were keeping company. By the time spring came around, he'd proposed, and we were planning a June wedding. Good to her word, Mrs. Thornhill sent for Mrs. Hatcher soon as she opened up the house in Duck, and it was like before with her going out there. Now let's see, Mr. Pinkham and I got married on the twenty-fifth of June so it must have been maybe the tenth or right around there. It was dark, must have been close to nine o'clock at night. Mrs. Hatcher came knocking on our door with Amelia; she had an old suitcase with her. Lord, they were both a mess. Amelia's lip was bleeding, her cheek was starting to swell, and her hair looked like someone had dragged her around by it—and that's probably what happened. Mrs. Hatcher didn't seem to be hurt, but you could tell she'd been crying; her face was all smudged with dirt and sweat. Mamma offered to send me for Doc Wilson, but Mrs. Hatcher said she didn't have money for the doctor. Said that Mr. Hatcher had passed out and if we could just help clean Amelia up and let her call Mrs. Thornhill, then she'd send Amelia over there to spend the night. Said Mr. Hatcher was in a fierce mood, but he'd be fine if he could sleep off the whiskey. She kept apologizing and saying it wasn't going to happen again, and she sure was sorry they hadn't been better neighbors."

Mrs. Pinkham shook her head slowly. "It was strange the way she was talking, and, of course, Amelia wasn't saying a thing—just gritting her teeth like she wanted to bust loose with something. Daddy called Mrs. Thornhill, and you could tell he felt like going over to have it out with Mr. Hatcher, but Mrs. Hatcher asked him please not to do anything, that she would take care of everything. We got Amelia as fixed up as we could, gave Mrs. Hatcher a cup of tea, and sure enough, Mrs. Thornhill's driver came for Amelia. Mrs. Hatcher walked her out to the car, hugged her, came back to apologize to us again, and then went home, even though Mamma told her we'd be glad to put her up."

Mrs. Pinkham drained her Coke and set the empty can down on the counter. She tapped her finger against the top and stared past me for a moment. "It was early in the morning that we heard a racket. It was confusing, being not light yet, and then we smelled smoke before we rushed outside and saw the flames. The Hatcher house was burning, and I'm not talking about any little woodstove fire. Daddy and the other men tried to get inside, but flames were coming out of almost every window. It didn't seem right that the fire could have spread so fast, and there was nothing anybody could do. It was a good thing the houses were set apart and there was no wind, because I think it would have spread as hot as it was burning."

"What happened? How did the fire start?" I couldn't stop the question tumbling out.

Mrs. Pinkham sighed. "No one ever knew, but it seemed so strange. The timing of it, I mean. I'd never seen Mrs. Hatcher like that. I remember that I kept thinking she looked like some cornered animal. And when they were finally able to get into the remains of the house after the fire died down, they said it was as if neither one of them tried to get out. Said his body was in the bedroom and hers was in a chair, like she'd been sitting next to him. Of course, if Mr. Hatcher was drunk like she said, that would make sense for him. And who knows, maybe she fell asleep in the chair and the smoke got to her before she woke up. Anyway, there was nothing left in the house, and talk was that Mrs. Thornhill paid for the funerals. Not that they'd been church folks so they just had a graveside service. Amelia didn't say hardly one word to anybody, but then it must have been a shock to her. No one saw her after that. Talk was that Mrs. Thornhill took her in as a companion, and she went back to Raleigh with her. Then Mr. Thornhill took sick so they didn't come to the house for the next summer. After he died, Mrs. Thornhill went off to Europe. The way I heard it, she got sick unexpected like and died over there. Her son had to go bring her body home. There was no mention of Amelia, and I guess we all thought maybe she met some man and got married. You could have knocked me over with a feather when I heard tell she was back, all set to rebuild after the Thornhill house burned down."

"And she had the stone house put up?"

"And what a shock that was. I'm not sure anybody but maybe Harvey Trotter, the lawyer, knows how she came to have the place. Guess it had something to do with the Thornhill boy and girl being killed in that plane crash. Anyway, I was right here in this store, working with Mr. Pinkham and in came some Yankee landscaper telling me what kind of plants he needed for the Hatcher place. I tried to do the neighborly thing and drove out myself to say hello, see how she was doing and so forth. Let me tell you, she was as standoffish as you could ask for. Told me flat out that she'd be glad to do business with me, but preferred doing everything by telephone and delivery and had no need to talk about people that were dead and gone. She wasn't nasty like I've heard she is with some folks, but no question that she wanted to be left alone."

Her look pulled me from what was almost a trance as I listened to the story. Uh-oh, was she expecting me to reveal something about Miss Amelia in return for what I had to admit was a lot more information than I'd expected?

"Uh, yes, ma'am, like you said, she's real quiet, and I've never seen anybody visiting her. She pretty much gives me a list of chores and then goes off walking on the beach while I'm there," I said in a convincing voice. It wasn't altogether a lie because there were times Miss Amelia did just that.

Mrs. Pinkham nodded her head like she understood. "Well, her holing up in that house she had built isn't as crazy as what some folks do, and she has been a good customer all these years." She shifted her bottom again and gave a tiny laugh. "Well, haven't I been running off at the mouth today? Funny how you get to remembering things. Anyways, you tell your mamma I said hello and those begonias should be in tomorrow. I'll take that can if you're done with it, if you'll carry that stool back into the office for me."

"Yes, ma'am, and thanks for the Coke. The story was real interesting, too."

She waved her hand as if she'd already forgotten, her mind now perhaps on how nice-looking a man Mr. Pinkham had been when he proposed to her.

I drove home slowly, wondering if I could possibly ask Miss Amelia about what I'd heard. It did go together pretty well with what Mamma told me. I thought about the truly loner kids at school, the ones who had bruises from claims of falling down stairs, the ones who just sort of disappear into the walls, that you never give a thought to. It was hard to imagine Miss Amelia being like that, but it had been a long time ago, and if her little sister died and her two brothers ran off, there must have been something bad wrong with the family. Even if brothers and sisters were pains in the asses at times, it's not like you'd want everybody *gone*.

And if her daddy and mamma did burn up in a fire, that sort of explained why she was taken in by Mrs. Thornhill, which would have been a whole lot better than being sent off to some orphanage.

"Jesus Christ, Maggie, you shouldn't be driving if you've gone blind. I've been flapping my arms like a damn scarecrow." Bobby slapped his open palm against the hood of the truck as he came from the back door of the house.

"Sorry," I said through the open window. "I was…"

"Who cares? Mamma's been on me to get Mamaw's trunk to Sheila, and I can't carry it by myself. Get your scrawny butt out of the truck and give me a hand," he grumbled in a way that meant Sheila had probably been busting his ass a whole lot more than Mamma had been.

I stuck my tongue out at him for general principle and

dodged the half-hearted swat he aimed toward my butt. I decided that asking Miss Amelia about Mrs. Pinkham's story would be a waste of time, and she was liable to get mad at the very idea of me listening to someone talk about her. I'd just have to decide what to believe for myself.

# Chapter Six

"Fort Sill, Oklahoma for training and then assigned to Fort Riley, Kansas. Kansas, can you believe it? Why would I want to visit Kansas?"

I was seriously pissed at the United States Army. Jed was supposed to have gone somewhere exotic. I mean he'd already told me other boys were going to places like Germany and Hawaii. Why was he off to some Army fort out in the middle of Kansas? How could that be fair?

"I haven't the faintest idea," Amelia said and tossed a weed into one of her shallow rectangular gathering baskets. "I never went to the Midwest, although I met people from there who didn't have two heads if I recall correctly."

She had told me to stop referring to her as *Miss* Amelia, not liking the school teacher sound of it. I was still having trouble thinking of her in that way, but I had more important matters on my mind today. I sighed. "I just meant I was really hoping for something…"

"I'm aware of that," Amelia interrupted flatly. "Instead of planning your own way out, you've been depending on Jed to do it for you." She stuck her trowel deep into the soil and extracted another weed.

"Uh, I, uh," I wasn't sure what to say. That wasn't fair either. Not that Amelia tended to sympathize about much of anything, but me wanting to get away was something I assumed she would understand.

She turned her head, her wide-brimmed straw hat held by the strap under her chin. It was her *fine, I'll explain this* look. "Listen little country girl, if you want to leave here after high school, then do so. You don't need to trail after Jed. Surely someone in that school of yours is going off to college. Or for heaven's sake, join the Army yourself. I hear that young women are doing that these days. Or maybe it's the Air Force."

"It's all the services," I said defensively in a tone I knew better than to use with her. "We had recruiters come in, but they didn't really want to talk to the girls." Actually, I had thought of it and quickly concluded that volunteering for something with more rules than school and my parents was not for me.

"So go to college. Your grades are respectable." She straightened from her kneeling position and gazed across the bed of iris for weeds that may have escaped her.

I took my cap off and ran my fingers through short hair that I wasn't used to yet. I'd grown tired of ponytails and treated myself to a Christmas present of a short bob. I was glad I had enough natural curl to avoid the stinky permanents that Ruth Ann subjected herself to.

"We can't afford college and I haven't done enough to earn a scholarship. It isn't that I couldn't work part time and I guess we'd qualify for loans, but I don't really like school all that much."

"My, my, it does sound like you're stuck, doesn't it?" Amelia tapped the edge of her trowel against the stone bed border. "Well, if you're not overwhelmed feeling sorry for yourself, let's dump this batch of trash and have a glass of wine. A lovely little Vouvary and some quiche will help your outlook."

I twisted my body slightly away from her and nodded,

drawing in a breath to avoid a smartass remark. It was too bad the French lesson was over for the day – I could have asked what the phrase was for, "Up yours, you old hag."

"In case you're wondering, the French word for shit is *merde*," Amelia said and pushed the basket toward me. "Take this and I'll lay the table."

"That wasn't quite what I was thinking," I said with a grimace. "But it was close."

"No doubt," she threw the barb over her shoulder and entered the kitchen through the back door.

I deposited the jumble of weeds in the compost bin near the stone garage that had been turned into a repository for Amelia's gardening needs. It was only a one-car garage and she'd stopped driving years before, although I wasn't any more sure of when that happened than I was about other things in Amelia's past. It was another topic that she dismissed as unimportant and nobody's business.

"I saw a poster the other day for the Peace Corps," I said when I joined her on the terrace. "South America or wherever they send people isn't exactly what I was thinking of, but it's a way to go somewhere and I could practice taking photographs of monkeys and giant snakes and naked natives." I lifted the bottle from the chilled white ceramic holder and filled the glasses.

Four slender slices of quiche were nestled among a cluster of red grapes on a plate. A tin of chocolate coated butter cookies was to the left of the place where I usually sat. Oh, cookies instead of sympathy.

"Why don't you go to Paris?" Amelia asked the question as I concentrated on pouring the wine without dribbling any down the outside of the glass.

"To Paris? The Peace Corps has teams in Paris?"

She swiped a clinging tendril of hair off her forehead. "I hardly think so. I mean go and live for a while. Take a job as a photographer's apprentice."

I served us each a piece of quiche accompanied by a stem of grapes instead of doing the eyes roll thing that she deserved. "Well, I didn't exactly see a poster for that."

"Despite having a good ear for language, I'm not sure I can teach you the proper inflection to carry off sarcasm in French," she said dryly. "What I am proposing is quite practical."

I set my glass down and stared at her. "I don't understand." I kept one hand on the base of the glass and the other clutched the edge of the table. I didn't want her to see trembles of anticipation, but I could feel that something important was coming.

Her eyes were as neutral as if she was giving me a shopping list. "I maintain contacts there of course and it so happens one is a well-established photographer who would be willing to take you as an apprentice. A small apartment in a decent, yet reasonable part of Paris would not be terribly expensive and if you're not extravagant, you could manage for probably a year between what you have saved, what I will give you, and the pittance you will make in wages. If you spend foolishly, you will have perhaps five or six months."

"You would do that for me?" I could hear my voice cross between a squeak and a whisper.

She turned her lips vaguely toward a smile and poised a fork over her plate. "Well, it would be silly to waste the lessons I've given you, wouldn't it?"

I moved as if in slow motion, my brain and stomach seeming to whirl in opposite directions. Was this a joke? No. Amelia was stubborn, terse, stinging in her opinion of others, admittedly strange in many ways, but not cruel.

"Dear God, I didn't expect you to be struck with silence when a simple, *Yes, thank you,* would be an adequate response," she said with the same impatience as when I stumbled over verb conjugation. "And please don't bother me with questions as to why. The *why* I'm doing this is not of any particular importance."

A giggle burst through my paralysis. "Yes, yes, God, yes, I want to go. Of course I want to go," I managed through laughter.

She picked up her glass and raised it toward me. "Oh good, we're going to swing back and forth along the pendulum of teenage emotions. I don't need hysteria from you either."

I didn't care if Amelia wanted to pretend she wasn't doing something wonderful – even she shouldn't deny it was something a fairy godmother would do. I stopped laughing and didn't try to get rid of a grin that I'm sure looked stupid. "How would you like me to act? This is just super terrific fantastic."

She nodded. "Well, I suppose we shall see if your parents agree. In fact, there is really no need to get into any details this afternoon, so the subject is closed for the day."

"Of course they'll agree," I said, completely convinced I was right. Why would they object?"

# Chapter Seven

I bounced up the steps onto the porch, aware that I'd stayed so long at Amelia's that I barely had time to set the table before supper. I yanked the screen door open and caught it before it slammed shut.

"I've got the most terrific news," I said to Daddy as he sat in his chair, the television tuned to the weather report. "I can't wait to tell you and Mamma."

"What you've got is fifteen minutes to help your mamma," he said without looking at me.

I scooted into the kitchen, undaunted by his lack of curiosity, and opened the dish cabinet as Mamma glanced over from the stove. The smell of hot grease meant we were having fried pork chops or fried steak—couldn't be chicken since it wasn't Sunday.

"You wash those hands first, child," she said, stirring what was probably a pot of field peas. "What are you in such a dither about?"

I could feel the grin that had been fixed to my face since leaving Amelia's. "It's something wonderful, about after I graduate." I soaped and rinsed my hands at the sink and dried them on a flour sack towel hanging from a drawer pull.

"You mean Billy Ray has come to his senses and proposed?" She turned the burner off under the pot and reached for a platter with a folded paper sack on top of it.

For the second time that day, I was nearly startled out of words. I stood with my hand touching the stacked plates and stared at her. "Billy Ray proposing? Mamma, we haven't had a date for months."

"I know you two haven't been keeping company regularly, but he's a nice enough boy. I thought maybe you'd gotten back together," she said, transferring golden pork chops from pan to platter. "Pour the tea while I dish up the rice and tomatoes."

Wondering how on earth she could have come up with such an idea, I said, "No, ma'am, this has nothing to do with Billy Ray. I . . ."

"Maggie, you can tell us after we eat. If you don't get that table set before the news is over, your daddy will think we're late."

I sucked in a breath to keep from snorting. How being five minutes off schedule was going to bring the world to a screeching halt was beyond me, but Daddy was dead set on supper being on the table by the time he turned the television off. I pressed my lips together and tried to calm down. I guess it wouldn't kill me to wait twenty minutes.

Once we were set down, Daddy said as short a grace as he could get away with and launched into a list of reasons why Mr. Wheeler shouldn't depend on his new son-in-law learning how to run the marina, mainly because the boy was an idiot. That could either mean he was an idiot or it could mean Daddy just didn't like him what with the boy having worked in a bank instead of with his hands.

I thought I'd have my chance when he ran down, but then Mamma remembered that Ruth Ann said their window screens weren't going to make it much longer. Somehow I got volunteered to find some spare rolls of screening as well as cut and install the new ones.

Daddy said he'd have dessert later and pushed his plate to one side. He reached for a toothpick from the little glass holder that was kept next to the salt and pepper shakers and looked at me. "Now, what was that you were carrying on about when you came home?"

I wiggled and then sat up straight, not wanting to act like some ten-year-old. I was careful to refer to Amelia with the proper *Miss*, not wanting Mamma and Daddy to think I was forgetting how to respect grownups, and I sure didn't want Mamma distracted with my manners when I had such great news.

"I was over at Miss Amelia's this afternoon, and she has this most wonderful idea. You know how I've been using Uncle Merl's old cameras and taking pictures and he says I'm a natural at it?"

"Uh-huh," he said suspiciously. "He mentioned he might have a job for you come summer."

"I know and that's kind of what I'd been thinking, but Miss Amelia knows this photographer in Paris who she says is willing to give me a job, too, and she's going to give me money until I get my feet on the ground, and I've got some saved up so it's not like I can't pay part of my way. Isn't that wonderful? Me, going to Paris to learn how to be a photographer?"

I faltered as I saw their faces—Mamma's forehead crinkling in bewilderment and Daddy's jaw clenching.

"What in the name of God are you talking about, girl? What's that crazy woman been telling you?"

I plunged on, words gushing out. "It's not crazy, Daddy. She's been teaching me French and everything, and she used to live there so it's not like she doesn't know the place. She says she knows someone who will find me an apartment there . . ."

His fist crashed onto the table, his face reddened with the stormy look we'd dreaded as children.

"You stop that nonsense right now, girl. Doreen, this is what comes from lettin' her have her own way too much. Damn fool notions like going off to Paris." His finger stabbed the air. "I don't want to hear anymore of this, and you tell Amelia Hatcher she has no cause interfering in this family. In fact, you tell her you're done working for her. She can get somebody else to do her fetching. I knew no good would come of you being around her."

"That's not fair," I shot back, my shock at his reaction mounting to anger. "You just said working for Uncle Merl would be okay, and this is tons better than that. I couldn't even get a chance like this if I was to go to college."

Both of his fists were planted on the table as he raised his voice above mine. "You hush that mouth of yours, Missy. For starters, I don't know why you think you need a job at all. You ought to be finding a decent husband and getting ready for a family, not thinking about going off to a place full of Frenchy frogs. Bad enough you think you need some job instead of a good man, but you're not about to take charity off Amelia Hatcher."

"Not every girl in this town plans to get married and start having babies as soon as high school is over," I flared, pushing my chair back. I swung to Mamma, who was holding her hands up in a plea.

"Maggie, don't sass your daddy. Clarence, don't shout at the girl so much." Her voice lacked the firmness she usually settled arguments with. "Maggie honey, you need to slow down. Now, what brought all this on, and what do you mean Miss Amelia has been teaching you French?"

She laid a restraining hand on Daddy's forearm although

his glower didn't soften.

I breathed hard, trying to control my voice. "It's just something we started awhile back, and Miss Amelia said I picked the sounds up real well. Maybe that's what got her to thinking about it, and she knows I like taking photographs. I told you already that I was planning to go work with Uncle Merl if his business stayed good. I never dreamed of anything like this, and it isn't charity, not really. I mean, some of the kids at school are getting scholarships for college, and you wouldn't call that charity. Plus, if the Army wasn't sending Jed to Kansas, they could send him off like to Korea and that's way further than Paris."

"Jed's a boy, a man, doing a man's work for his country," Daddy snapped and threw his toothpick onto the table. "You want to think being a wife and mother is old-fashioned, that's fine, but I don't want to hear one more word about this Paris business. You work out some kind of deal with your Uncle Merl if you're dead set on this camera stuff, then you tell Amelia Hatcher tomorrow that you're done."

I clenched my fists on the edge of the table in an unconscious imitation of him. "I'm almost eighteen years old. That's full grown, and you've got no right to be this way about Miss Amelia."

"I set the rules when you live under this roof and don't think you're too old for a whipping, Missy."

"Clarence, that's enough of that," Mamma said, a tremor in her voice. "Maggie, I'll do the dishes. I think you should go take a walk and cool off that temper of yours."

I jumped from the table and whirled toward the door as Daddy barked more instructions. "You better get your head put on straight and come back in here with an apology ready."

I couldn't make out his next words to Mamma. I bolted

across the porch and down the steps, barely mindful of Mamma telling me I'd need a sweater. Not tonight I wouldn't, not with the heat raging through me. How could they? How could they not be happy for me, much less take this attitude? Never, never, never had I sat around mooning about getting married, acting as if the only thing in the world was keeping house for a husband.

What shit was this? Okay, maybe I'd never talked about college either, but I hadn't made any secret about going to work for Uncle Merl. Until this afternoon, that's what I had intended to do. Work with him, learn more about photography, and save money to go visit Jed and who knew what after that. It was kind of fuzzy. I was on the beach before I knew it, a three-quarters moon giving the only light other than what filtered from the houses behind the dune line. Most of the beach cabins were still shuttered. I didn't need light, though—the sand was pale, and it was easy to tell the water line by the white cap of waves as they broke on the shore. I'd spent my life running up and down this stretch in all seasons, in daylight and dark.

I slowed my pace, soft sand resisting speed, my anger focused ahead of me like a beacon. I might not be a perfect daughter, but I'd done more than my share of helping, and I sure hadn't been a burden to anyone. How dare they think my rightful place was to marry Billy Ray or anyone else for that matter? Husbands and babies be damned—I was not my mother or sister.

Even if Duck wasn't more than a fishing village, that didn't mean we were stuck in the last century. A couple of the teachers at school weren't married and so what that people called them old maids or spinsters? I'd never done that, and I didn't make jokes about them either. The fact that I didn't know any women photographers didn't mean there weren't any, and there was nothing wrong with the idea. I was going to learn from Uncle Merl, but I didn't want to be stuck taking baby pictures and trying to make some bride look pretty no matter if she was or not.

Wait a minute. Uncle Merl did more than regular pictures. I remembered a lady came in for passport pictures not long ago. She and her husband were going on one of those bus tours—the kind that went to a bunch of countries in two weeks. I was going to be eighteen in July. Was that old enough to get a passport? If it was, it couldn't be that hard to find out how. I was using Amelia's address for my bank account, so I could use it for the passport, too.

Orange from a bonfire in the distance pierced the darkness, small showers of sparks spiking into the night when someone tossed a piece of driftwood on it. I paused, not in the mood to move forward to see how many people there were or if I knew them. I shivered from the combination of cool night air and renewed anticipation as the seed of a plan took hold. I turned toward home, refocusing my indignation into how I could pull this off.

Daddy wanted an apology? No problem. A little sulky to make it believable. A made-up school project to get Uncle Merl to do the passport photos. An initial hedging with Amelia about how my parents were thinking about letting me go to Paris. That wasn't a complete lie. If I had to finally tell her the truth, I was sure I could find a way to convince her it was all right. After all, I would be eighteen, and that was older than when Amelia herself had left the Outer Banks if what I'd heard was true. My rebellion-fueled scheming faltered as I neared our house and saw the outline of someone sitting on the porch.

"Maggie, come put this sweater on, and we'll talk," my mother's voice floated across to me.

Shit. I wasn't prepared yet. I stopped, one hand on the short wooden rail, one foot on the bottom step. "Where's Daddy?"

She held the sweater out. "Gone to bed. Don't pretend you're not cold. That shirt is nothing but cotton."

I took refuge in silence, having calculated that they'd both be in bed and I'd have until morning to perfect my story.

She was sitting sideways on the porch, her bent knees covered by her house dress, one of her heavy shawls draped across her shoulders, the crisscrossed ends touching the porch. "I told your daddy you meant no disrespect, that you just got caught up in too much excitement. He'll likely be okay in the morning."

I wrapped the sweater close around, sat on the second step, my back against the rail, and nodded. I tucked one leg up like hers and let the other dangle.

She tilted her head back, not looking at me. "Maggie child, you can't come up with something like this out of the blue and expect us to act as if it was normal."

"Does that mean you'll change your mind after you think about it for a while?"

She turned her head toward me. "No, but I would like you to tell me why Amelia Hatcher would be making promises like this. I can't say your remarks about Billy Ray took me too much by surprise, but I thought you were pleased about the idea of working for your Uncle Merl. "

I inhaled deeply, wondering how much truth I could say. "I was Mamma, and don't be thinking it's Miss Amelia's fault that I want to do more than that. Working for Uncle Merl is what was going to get me started, not all that I ever planned to do. I've been wanting to travel since I can't remember when. I was figuring that if Jed went somewhere far off like California, I was going to visit him. I could take a bus or a train and go all the way across the country for a while. I don't know exactly what it is that I might be doing in a few years, but why can't I spend time seeing other places?"

"I guess I never gave it much thought. My folks and your daddy's go way back. Some stuck to farming, some preferred fishing, and your daddy took up as a mechanic. Boys went off for military duty, 'specially in the wars, but nobody wanted to stay gone. You've always been more independent than your sister, trotting around with your brothers more than caring about what boy might make eyes at you. But child, think about people who pay to come here as tourists. Seems that means it must be a pretty good place. Awfully nice to be able to stroll down and watch the sun rise out of the ocean even if we don't have a fancy house."

I shifted my butt, found a pebble by my foot, and tossed it into the yard, trying again to put my emotions into words. "Me going to other places has nothing to do with the good things about here. I look at pictures of the Alps mountains and pyramids in that Egyptian desert, and it makes me just want to get on an airplane or boat and head out myself. I'd rather spend my money taking trips than have pretty clothes or a new car. I don't know why; I just know it's the way I feel."

Mamma nodded her head slowly once. "Well, we've had a few wandering folks in our family somewhere. Your Uncle Merl's coming to dinner Sunday. Make your arrangements with him so's you can start having a regular job after you finish school, and you might can find a room to rent in Elizabeth City if you want that."

*Elizabeth City. Oh yeah, Amelia offers me Paris, and Mamma thinks I'll be satisfied going up the road.* "Yes, ma'am, I'll do that," I said quietly. *You bet I would. I was going to make those plans at the same time I was working out the details for my real adventure.*

Mamma unfolded her legs as a prelude to rising. "Tomorrow you tell your daddy you're sorry if you were sounding sassy, and I'll make it right for you to keep working with Miss Amelia 'til after graduation. I think she meant well by her offer, but once you're working full time for your Uncle Merl, she'll need to be finding someone else. You won't be able to do both, 'specially if you decide to take a room up there so you can be more independent. I reckon that might be part of what you're looking for."

I scrambled to standing, suddenly realizing that I was a full head taller than Mamma. "Yes, ma'am," I repeated, edging in what should have been the right measure of good daughter tone. "I'll be in shortly."

She entered the house with no further word, and I leaned against the porch railing. We had few street lights in this part of town, and most house windows had darkened with working people gone to bed. Frogs, insects, and the occasional cat yowl or dog howl were our night noises—the surf wasn't heavy enough for the sound to carry this far.

I waited until only silence came from inside, and then I slipped into my room. I wondered if I would dream about the Eiffel Tower as I planned my escape.

# Chapter Eight

If I couldn't get to Paris by being honest about it, then it wasn't really my fault that I had to be sneaky. Daddy grouchily accepted my apology and truly believed I'd given Amelia notice that I was moving to Elizabeth City. Uncle Merl officially offered me a job starting in July and assured Mamma and Daddy that Mrs. Blakely, a widow lady, had a real nice room with a bath to rent cheap that was just what a girl like me needed. I waited until I was working with him one Saturday to explain about the school project I had invented to justify passport photographs. By the next weekend, I added them to the passport application form hidden in my room.

I participated in the pregraduation crap I was expected to, and in a moment of nostalgia or more likely because of a couple of extra beers, I gave in to Billy Ray's insistence that even if I didn't want to go out with him anymore, I shouldn't graduate from high school as a virgin and who better to trust than him? He had the courtesy to bring a blanket and sheet to soften the bed of his pickup, and I suppose being on the beach under an almost full moon was sort of romantic. At least he was a pretty good kisser, and if his sweating and hollering meant anything, he must have had a good time. The mess was more bothersome than the pain, and I didn't feel the earth move even if such a thing could happen. It didn't change my mind one bit. As far as I was concerned, other girls were welcome to get goofy over boys.

Amelia seemed to accept my explanation that Mamma and Daddy had been really surprised at her offer. She didn't ask for details of their reaction, nor did she question my explanation of waiting to apply for a passport until after my birthday. She said no one in their right mind went to Paris in August anyway, and as soon as I got my passport, she'd book me on a flight for either September or early October. She now only allowed me thirty minutes of English; the rest of the time it was French, although she refused to teach me slang or profanity. She said slang would have changed too much since she'd been there and that I would no doubt pick up obscenities on my own.

The only problem was the gap between July and when I left because everyone in my family thought I was going to work for Uncle Merl. The easy solution would be to lie to Amelia and make up a story about how Uncle Merl really needed my help, but then I'd be cut off from her, French lessons, and the excitement I felt each time she described a section of Paris to me.

I was puzzling over possibilities when Bobby came by the house a week before graduation. He said that Mrs. Watkins's oldest daughter, who was pregnant with twins, was having complications. Mrs. Watkins wanted to go over to Manteo to be with her daughter for the summer, and if it wasn't too much of a burden to me, could I delay my plans with Uncle Merl for a few months? Mamma said if I didn't mind, it would be the Christian thing to do, and she was sure Uncle Merl could manage okay.

If God was upset with me for lying to everyone, would he have sent such a perfect solution my way? It had to be a sign that he understood my deception was for a worthy cause. In fact, it was probably another positive sign that Mr. Wheeler's son-in-law went back to work at the bank and Daddy was in better spirits. He didn't ask point-blank about Amelia, and I didn't bring the subject up around him. Mamma said that as long as I wasn't shirking the Watkins or sassing Daddy, then I might as well finish out the summer working for Miss Amelia.

I was feeling pretty pleased with the way everything was falling right into place until Amelia mentioned the shots.

"I'll need what?" I'd been half listening to her explain the difference in a work visa and a tourist passport.

"Proof of immunization, little country girl, and maybe some updated shots. It's a small yellow book where the doctor writes in things like smallpox vaccination. Doctor Rundle, or that horse of a woman who runs his office, can look up what shots you need for France, give them to you, and put everything into the book. You'll need to keep all your documents together, you know."

"Yes, ma'am, you've told me that, but I didn't know about shots." I hadn't been to Doc Rundle since I'd broken my arm when I was twelve.

"Don't tell me you're afraid of a silly shot," she mocked. "It won't be more than one or two at the most."

"I'm healthy," I protested. "I don't see it should matter."

She shook her head and waved her hand in the way that meant she didn't want to discuss it. "It's one of those things that are required for travel. What you need is called an International Shot Record; Doctor Rundle will know exactly what it is."

Just when I thought I had no more obstacles! As I drove home that afternoon, I came up with a plausible enough story. I could make the appointment without Mamma knowing, and I had money where I could pay cash. Doc Rundle was a busy man, and he wasn't likely to know that Jed was in Kansas. I could say the Army was considering sending Jed to France, and

I might be going to visit him. I'd tell him I want to be prepared. Nobody in the family had been sick for ages, and Doc Rundle was a Methodist so there wasn't much chance Mamma would run into him at church or anything.

Even though the story was bullshit, I practiced it until the words came easily and reminded myself not to volunteer information. Talking too much was what almost always got you into trouble. I whispered one more thanks to God when I arrived at Doc Rundle's and discovered his regular nurse was on vacation. The substitute, Mrs. McGinty, didn't seem especially interested in me, and I got away with no more than a few medical questions, two boosters, a tetanus shot, and the precious shot record validated with Doc Rundle's scrawl.

Mamma thought I should have a family dinner for my eighteenth birthday. She made all my favorites plus a devil's food birthday cake with chocolate icing. Somewhere in the middle of seeing all of them crowded around the table, everyone reaching and talking, the kids pestering to go down to the beach, I realized that it would be my last big family dinner for who knew how long. Mamma's birthday wasn't until late October, and there'd be no reason to have another one until then. Oh, not that my brother or sister didn't bring their broods some Sundays, but it wasn't like when we had them all at the same time. I'd have to be sure and send postcards for the celebrations that I was going to miss. I could imagine them passing the cards around—the first one would be of the Eiffel Tower, of course, and I could send Mamma a little bottle of real French perfume.

I had a real nice letter that I'd been composing in my head to explain everything—that there was no sense in blaming Miss Amelia and that at eighteen I was old enough to be on my own. I was going to carefully put the letter where they would find it right away. It wouldn't do for them to think I had just run off. I mean, I was running off, but only in a way so it didn't cause another big fight. Once I was in Paris and sent them a few letters, they'd come around to see that it was the right thing for me, and they'd get over being mad

Miss Amelia's celebration for my eighteenth birthday included my first champagne, which I had to admit didn't taste like I thought it would. She drank most if it and told me I would acquire the taste. I mailed my passport application the very next day and hoped whoever did these things didn't screw it up.

The single piece I hadn't quite figured out was how to get to the airport up in Norfolk. Amelia didn't drive, and even if she did, she would naturally assume that someone in my family would take me. We might not gush all over each other for no reason, but me leaving for France for a year would surely be worth a farewell gesture. I couldn't very well take the truck and leave it at the airport with instructions for someone to come get it. I couldn't risk asking Billy Ray—he couldn't keep a secret for shit. The only reason he hadn't mouthed off about us being together is because he knew Bobby would beat the hell out of him. This was one of the infrequent times I regretted not having a girlfriend who'd be willing to take chances for me. It would probably have to be the bus, and I bet it didn't go straight to the airport. I'd maybe even have to spend the night depending on how that worked and then take a bus or a taxi. I didn't know how much any of that would cost, but I was being careful of my money and should have plenty to cover it.

I was puzzling over this latest detail when I turned down the road to Miss Amelia's and saw one of the town's few taxis waiting to enter the main road. I waved at the driver I didn't recognize and wondered if Amelia had made one of her rare trips off the property.

A partly cloudy sky held no threat of rain in the heaviness of summer heat so I wasn't surprised to see the yard empty. Miss Amelia would have spent the early morning hours in the garden followed by perhaps a short nap after a light lunch or the afternoon passed in reading. I'd come to know her rhythm of movements by season.

I clambered out of the truck and retrieved a roll of chicken wire from the back. A section was coming loose by the rabbit hutch, and I wanted to tend to it before the rabbits nosed their way through. I carried the wire around the side of the house and was startled to hear voices coming from the terrace—a woman's voice, too low to distinguish the words. While that would explain the taxi, a female visitor was a greater rarity than an outing into town.

Amelia knew I was coming, so I didn't hesitate to join them and stopped in mid-stride as I reached the low stone wall. Oh my God, how had this happened?

"*Bonjour, ma petite. Nous avons le plasir d'un visiteur.*"

I don't know if I opened my mouth to speak or not. Mamma, in her lavender Sunday dress, held a glass of lemonade in her hand and sat at the table, watching me with a quiet expression.

"*Ce n'est pas polit de dire rein,*" Amelia admonished as if I wasn't supposed to be dumbstruck.

*Hello, little one, we have a visitor, and it's not polite to say nothing!*

"*Pardon y je m'excuse, madame,*" I stammered, still unable to swing my leg over the wall. "Mamma, I . . ."

She set the glass on the table, half-rose, and gestured me forward. "Come sit, child. I would say it's time for all of us to talk."

"Yes, ma'am," was all I could mange as both women kept their faces maddeningly calm—not a hint of how angry they might be or the sense of disappointment I knew Mamma could project without a word.

I swallowed hard, determined not to let my trembling show, and approached the table. My stomach clutched with fear—not of the whipping I expected would come later when Daddy got hold of me, but of seeing the dream I'd built for weeks now crumbling before their gazes.

I sat down, my spine erect and my hands clasped together on the table to keep them still.

"Why Maggie? Why did you lie about this?"

Mamma's voice was oddly soft, and the defiance I meant to muster melted from me. I swallowed again to hold back un-wanted tears. "I-I-, all I can say is that I wanted this more than I ever wanted anything in my life. When y'all said I couldn't go, I didn't want it to be that way."

Mamma turned her head for a moment to Amelia, who was watching us carefully, and then nodded once.

"Maggie, I think you should take a stroll on the beach while your mother and I discuss this. Not quite an hour should do it," Amelia said, as if they had already made an agreement.

I stared at them. *What?*

"Miss Amelia is right, child. Go on now. We have some things to get straight between us."

I knew that tone too well. I stood stiffly, then whirled and hurried down the steps, wanting to be out of hearing, wanting a chance to think of what to do. What could I do? How had I given myself away? A bank of clouds mercifully blocked the sun from my unprotected head— I'd left my cap in the truck— and I suddenly checked my watch. An hour—that would be about down to the finger of beach that diminished with each passing storm.

I stumbled, my heart seeming too large for my chest. I forced myself to stop and breathe deeply. I refused to look behind to see if I was being watched. The pounding in my ears lessened as I struggled to focus. Walk, walk slowly, walk and think. Think what? Why did Mamma want to talk to Amelia anyway? What was there to say? That I would be forbidden to come again? That Amelia had interfered too much in our family? Resentment rippled through me, refusing to stay submerged in humility. Damn it, I was eighteen—the same age as Mamma when she married Daddy, only one year younger than when Ruth Ann married Kenny, the same age as when Jed joined the Army. Nobody was worried about him. He could be sent off to God knew where and that was just fine because he was a boy—a man listening to Daddy. Ruth Ann was a respectably married woman, never mind that she probably couldn't find Paris on a map. It wasn't fair—not at all—and okay, maybe I shouldn't have been lying, but what choice had they given me? They hadn't listened when I told them the truth.

Jed. Wait a minute, didn't women join the Army? Sure they did, those recruiters had come to school, and I'd seen Army women in movies if not in real life. Well, I was eighteen, and by God, they might think they could shame me into not going to Paris and refuse Amelia's money, but they couldn't keep me from going in the Army or Air Force or even Navy, I guess. That was a way to get to travel, and no one could stop me. I mean, the Army had turned one of Billy Ray's brothers down, but that was because he'd broke his leg real bad in a car wreck, and it hadn't healed right. I was healthy without so much as a cavity. That would be my way to travel, although with the way my luck had turned, I might wind up in Kansas with Jed. My pace quickened as this new avenue opened in my mind.

I wasn't going to duck whatever penalty Daddy and Mamma meted out. Maybe it wasn't really their fault they couldn't understand and I *had* lied to them—well, to just about everyone. And I *was* letting Uncle Merl down when he was trying to do right by me.

Pipers and gulls pecked at tiny scuttling crabs and other creatures on the elongated patch of beach that thrust outward for twenty feet or so. Ropes of seaweed were strewn among mostly broken shells that stirred as lazy waves barely lapped over them. The water was a murky shade because the clouds broke up the intense blue of the summer sky. I could see people in the distance and hear faint shouts; a cluster of cabins was further ahead, and they were no doubt filled with tourists this time of year.

I pivoted, my new plan emerging from the destruction of my old one. A month, I could wait for a month, be penitent to pay for my lying, and then I'd go see the recruiter. I'd get all the information, tell them I'd be happy to go to another country, and find out if I could go to France right away. For sure, I knew there were Army units in Germany, and I didn't even care if they wanted to send me to Korea. Mamma and Daddy would be upset about this, too, but it sure as hell wasn't charity, and I bet the recruiter would have some photographs of women soldiers and tell them how patriotic it was of me. And wasn't there some kind of deal where the Army would pay for college later? Even if I didn't want to do that right now, I might want to later. How many years had Jed signed up for? Four, I think, maybe more. Four years was a long time. If it got me away, though, I could do that. Hell, it was the same amount of time as high school if you thought about it.

Okay, this was just a setback then, not the kind of disaster it had felt like when I saw Mamma on the terrace. I almost wanted to shout out loud, "So there! I'm not giving up, and nobody can make me!"

Slow down. I had to slow down. I was supposed to be upset, and I still was—my new idea was going to be a lot harder on me what with having to go through basic training and that kind of crap. I wasn't so good with following a lot of stupid rules, but Jed seemed to be doing all right with it and we were a lot alike.

I might have to stop seeing Miss Amelia for a while. Even if I could sneak over, she might be pissed off about the lying, too. I shoved aside the thought of her refusing to see me. She, of all people, would understand why I lied. She'd give me a tongue lashing no doubt and then let it be. A wave raced toward me, and I dodged to my left to keep from getting my feet soaked. The steps were in sight again. It was time for me to grit my teeth and take the punishment I had coming to me.

# Chapter Nine

I looked up, startled to hear voices that sounded anything other than upset. What was going on? I mounted the steps cautiously, and Mamma curved her lips into a half-smile when she saw me.

"Ah, a few minutes early, but no matter. You must be thirsty." Amelia had a third glass of lemonade on the tray, ice cubes not yet melting, moisture just beginning to collect on the outside of the glass.

"Yes, ma'am," I responded automatically, suddenly feeling sweat trickling beneath my shirt. I swiped the back of my arm across my forehead then rubbed it against my shorts.

"Drink your lemonade, child, then we'll be going. There's time for us to talk while we're cooking supper." I'd never seen Mamma like this, and another surge of worry nearly over-shadowed my new resolve. Why wasn't she getting on to me? I guessed she wanted to wait until we were alone.

I silently accepted the glass, thirst overcoming my anxiety, and drank greedily. The tang of the lemonade stung my throat as I tried not to gulp noisily.

"Thank you for your hospitality; you have a lovely place," my mother said astonishingly, as if this was a visit with some-one like the preacher's wife.

"I'm glad we had a chance to talk," Amelia replied in a

pleasant tone that I certainly wasn't used to hearing from her. "I apologize for any confusion, and I'm sure that Maggie feels badly about it."

I nearly choked on a sliver of ice. "Yes, ma'am, I do and I . . ."

Mamma held her hand up in my direction as she stood. "Later, child. You might want a moment with Miss Amelia. I'll be in the truck." She gathered her purse from by her feet and disappeared around the side path.

"We don't have time to get into this," Amelia said, when I opened my mouth to speak. "I know you must be burning through with curiosity, but it is not my place to explain. I hope to see you soon, *ma petite*. Now go, and don't keep your mother waiting."

"*Oui, madame,*" I said automatically, wishing I could have five minutes with her. At her wordless command, I handed Amelia my empty glass.

Mamma was sitting in the truck with the window rolled down. I shot her a questioning glance as I slid into the driver's seat and cranked the truck, the rumble causing a vibration as it always did. I quickly twisted the radio knob when sound blasted out.

"You pay attention to your driving, child. Talk can wait until we're home." Mamma then turned to look out the window, her profile impossible to read, her posture straight without being rigid.

Making me sweat was obviously part of the punishment. Mamma knew, of course, that I was about ready to explode wanting to ask what had happened. Where had I messed up? How had Mamma found out?

We were halfway to the house when she swiveled her head. "Those books at Miss Amelia's—the ones she showed me. You read all those? Even the ones in French?"

"Yes, ma'am, but Miss Amelia had to help me with the ones in French."

"I know I've seen you with books from the library, but your teachers claim you don't care for reading."

I hesitated. "I guess maybe what I don't like is being told what to read," I said with a flash of self-awareness.

"Could be that," she said and averted her gaze again.

I slowed way down when I got to the driveway so as not to bounce Mamma. She shifted sideways, one hand still curled in her lap and one hand resting lightly on the dashboard.

"Maggie, I'm not going to ask you how you came to think up all of this. Amelia Hatcher is a strange woman, and she hasn't seen the inside of a church in a long time, but I believe she means you well."

"Miss Amelia didn't have part in this," I said, trying to keep my voice steady.

"What you did was wrong, but you're not the first young one to get up a head of steam and leave the truth behind. You come inside now and get started peeling potatoes while I change my clothes. Then I think it best to tell you what we talked about while you were on your walk. I want this all said before your daddy comes home."

*Finally.* "Yes, ma'am," I repeated, beginning to tire of the words.

I thought to pour us both a glass of tea. When Mamma came in, having changed her dress, I was at the table, the first potato in the battered colander, five more lined up on the table, the scrap bucket on the floor to toss the peels into.

Mamma took cucumbers from the refrigerator, the small paring knife she preferred, and her wooden cutting board and sat across from me. She acknowledged the tea by taking a sip and nodded for me to scoot the scrap bucket in between us.

She picked up a cucumber, sliced one end off, then began to carefully work the knife, the strip of peel curling over the back of her hand.

"You don't know that you had a great-aunt who flew airplanes during World War II, do you?"

I was so startled I wasn't sure what to say and shook my head.

"Great Aunt Daisy, on my mamma's side—she was the second oldest girl, not quite two years before Mamma. Headstrong, stubborn, mind of her own, and a tomboy, like you. She didn't care what people said about her. She was funny, though, and could make you laugh. That's mostly what I remember about her. Anyway, you know about the way women went into the service during the war?"

I briefly wondered if my mind had become completely transparent. Was Mamma onto my new scheme about the Army already? "Like nurses?"

"All sorts of things, more than just nurses. Once all the able-bodied men were gone, Aunt Daisy said she was going to do her part, too. See, when she was in high school, she started hanging around Mr. Sikes with his crop-dusting business and took to learning about airplanes. Nobody would let her fly, but she knew everything there was to know about how that thing was put together, and she'd heard they were training women to be pilots. They were using women to fly airplanes to Europe so the men pilots could go into combat."

Unlike Mamma who was peeling the cucumbers, talking, and catching my eye every few seconds, I was having problems concentrating. I put down the potato to stare at her.

"She did that? Got trained and flew airplanes during the war?"

Mamma nodded. "She did, and it caused a ruckus in the

family. But that died down because it was part of the war effort. It was afterward that caused the problems."

I almost momentarily forgot that I wanted Mamma to get to the point about what this had to do with my problem.

"See, most of those women that went into the factories and such understood that when the men came home, it would be time for them to give the jobs back. Not that we had any factories in these parts, but for your aunt Daisy, it was kind of the same thing. They just didn't need the women flying anymore, not with plenty of men available. It wasn't only the flying—it was like she'd been too many places, done too many things, to be satisfied being here."

There was that half-smile again.

"Like how I've been feeling, you mean?" Why hadn't I ever heard of Aunt Daisy? Wait, wait, a sister that died—— I remember seeing a photograph at my grandmother's.

"It would seem so," Mamma said quietly. "Aunt Daisy came back for just a little while and said she wasn't about to settle down with some farmer or fisherman. She and two other women who had been pilots were taking an apartment in Washington, D.C.—said there was plenty of work to be had, and it was an exciting place. That got the family all stirred up again, and my mamma tried her best to talk Aunt Daisy out of it."

"So what happened?"

"Aunt Daisy went on about her way, kept in touch, but hardly ever came to visit. She went to work in the government doing something that I don't recall, and she'd go off on these adventures for vacation. Just couldn't stay still, the way Mamma said it. Anyway, she took off one summer, oh, I guess it was right after your daddy and I got married—sent us a generous check as a present but didn't come to the wedding. It was out to the Rocky Mountains, I think— somewhere out west—and there was an accident. A car wreck. The car went over the side of a mountain, so it took better than a day to get to it and get the bodies out—or what was left of them."

Mamma finished the last cucumber and looked me in the eye, her face sympathetic. "They couldn't have the casket open for the funeral. Years later, when Mamma was reflecting one time, she said that Aunt Daisy had asked her five or six times to come up to Washington to see the city, to see how she lived, to see why she thought it was a wonderful place. Mamma hadn't gone, of course, and she told me she regretted that—that maybe if she'd gone, she would have understood a little better."

"Is this part of what you and Miss Amelia talked about?"

"Not exactly, and to be honest, I'd put Aunt Daisy out of my mind, but the story popped right up when Amelia told me how hard you'd been working, how much you had learned."

I realized that I was holding my breath. I didn't trust myself to ask another question.

Mamma positioned a cucumber on the board and began cutting it into thick slices, slowly so she could look across at me as well.

"I suppose blood will tell out, and I can't say as I like the idea of you going off to some place like Paris, especially not alone, but Miss Amelia promised me that she had people that would take care of you."

"I can go? You mean that?" I was shocked into an almost whisper, afraid that I'd heard wrong.

She laid the knife down and held up a hand in caution. "Don't go rushing headlong, child, and running your mouth about me visiting with Miss Amelia. Your daddy is a good man who works hard; none of us have had to do without food on the table or shoes on our feet. If he's set in his mind on something, you don't change it easy. I'll not be tearing this family apart over this, so you be patient and let me make it right with him. It'll be about a week, probably two until things will be settled. Do you hear me?"

I nodded, mouth clamped shut to keep from yelping with joy. My eyes felt wide with curiosity.

Mamma turned her hand and shooed me. "I imagine you're about to bust open, and those potatoes aren't going to peel themselves. I'll take care of them. You run on to the store and get us milk and a loaf of bread—it's too hot to be baking biscuits. I'm cooking up ham and red-eye gravy tonight. And don't be dawdling, either."

I jumped up, caught the chair as it tilted backward, and then swept to Mamma's side, wanting to hug her. I pecked her on top of her hair instead, the smell of hairspray tickling my nose. "Thank you so much, Mamma, thank you more than I can say."

She patted my forearm briefly. "You just be patient, like I told you, and you better be planning to be in church come Sunday asking forgiveness of the Lord, too."

"Yes, ma'am," I grinned, backing up. When I reached the screen door, I stopped and swallowed. "I truly am sorry about the lying, Mamma."

She reached for the potatoes. "Catherine McGinty was standing in line behind me at the post office this morning. Guess you didn't know she joined our church about a month ago. She was wondering if you'd had any kind of reaction to your shots and went on about how I must be proud of Jed and how nice that you might go pay him a visit. All I could figure was this had something to do with Amelia Hatcher. I gave her a call, and she reckoned it would be better if I came to see her. Things get around in a small town, Maggie, no matter how smart you think you're being. Best you remember that from now on."

I nodded solemnly, choking back a laugh, because I knew she would think I was being disrespectful and scrambled to get outside to the truck. My God, I was going to Paris. I didn't know what Mamma and Amelia had planned, and for now, I didn't care. Since everything was going to work out, I was almost glad to be caught—sneaking a beer and letting Billy Ray into my pants were one thing, but carrying on the kind of lying I'd been doing was more of a strain than I thought it would be. The problem was trying to keep straight what I'd told everyone—it had been getting downright confusing. Mamma hadn't said anything about me staying away from Amelia, so I figured it was okay for me to keep doing the way I had been.

I would ask her about what she and Mamma talked about even though I expected she would ignore my question like she usually did when it came to private things. Amelia and Mamma were about as different as night and day, but I was willing to bet that they had both agreed that not telling me their plan was the dollop of punishment I deserved. If it took the whole two weeks, or even three, I'd be okay because Paris was going to be worth it.

# Chapter Ten

Daddy was home when I returned from the store, and the way Mamma was acting, you wouldn't know it had been anything except a normal day. As soon as we finished supper, she sent me off to Ruth Ann's to help shuck and clean a bushel of corn. With the way my sister yakked and the distractions from the kids, Mamma knew I'd be gone until bedtime. It was her way of emphasizing the message that the subject of Paris was closed for the time being.

Amelia didn't wait long to speak her mind the next afternoon. She'd barely said hello before she directed me up on a wooden step stool to take down the collection of crystal bowls in the large cabinet, which had open shelves in the lower part and glass-fronted doors on the upper part.

"They accumulate dust with the way I keep the terrace doors open," she said. "It's not wise for me to be climbing up and handling fragile things at my age. And no French today, little country girl, I think we need to make certain that we both understand each other."

"*Oui, madame,*" I said without thinking. I gently handed each bowl to her, and she carried them to the dining table where she had towels laid down. Once the shelves were emptied, I sat at one end of the table, reached into a dishpan filled with a solution of warm water and vinegar by the smell of it, squeezed one of the two dishrags until there was no excess water, and then picked up a small, heavy, emerald-colored bowl. I began a carefully rehearsed apology that she interrupted with a "Don't bother."

"Providing you moral guidance has never been a part of our arrangement," she said in that schoolteacher tone. "And for your information, I never did buy your story about your parents' unquestioning acceptance of my offer, but it wasn't particularly important, either."

"Not important? And you knew I was lying?"

Amelia sighed. "Most people lie to some degree or another to get what they want— it is merely a matter of how often. What I meant was that it wasn't important that you might not go to Paris at this particular point in time. You would have managed to go under my patronage, or you would have bowed to your parents' wishes for at least a while. We would have continued in your training until you came up with your own scheme, and don't bother to tell me you hadn't developed an alternative plan. As far as the money goes, I would not have made the offer to you if I could not afford to do so. The money I set aside for your adventure would have simply continued to do whatever it is that my money does when it is not being spent. Therefore, neither the timing of your departure nor the expenditure of funds was of importance in the larger scheme of the world."

She paused while I puzzled over her comments. "However, since you chose to lie to me as well as to your parents, when your mother telephoned with her question, I saw no reason to keep the truth from her. Despite our obvious differences, I was most impressed with how she responded to my explanation. We had quite an interesting discussion about you."

Ah, that was something I understood. "Yes, ma'am, I was wondering . . ."

"Absolutely not. It is your mother's choice of when she wishes to enlighten you, not my place to do so. After all, a bit of unfulfilled curiosity is a small price to pay, *ne c'est pas?*"

"*Oui, madame.*" A small price, is it not? I was expecting her to say that, and I knew it wouldn't do me any good to ask what the real plan was. "Will you at least tell me if I'm going in September?"

"I would think the third week of September would be appropriate for planning, although your mother is not completely certain that she can win your father over." Amelia's smiles were so infrequent, that when one played across her mouth, it disappeared almost before you realized what you were seeing. "I have great confidence in her, however, based on what I observed during our visit. So it might be a good idea for you to arrange all your farewells."

"There won't be many of those," I said with a shake of my head. "Other than family, the Watkinses, and you, I don't really have anyone to say good-bye to."

"Ah, that's right, you aren't exactly a big joiner, are you? More the loner type."

I tried to read the meaning in her eyes, unsure of how I was supposed to react to that. "I haven't found much of interest to join. Girls are always carrying on about what boys they like, and the boys my age are mostly silly."

She shrugged. "I didn't mean the remark disparagingly—as something bad," she said when I mentally stumbled over the word. "I wouldn't have been able to tolerate you if you'd been some flighty girl who thinks a moment of silence should be filled with nonsensical chatter. You're too young to understand the value of not needing external validation to run your life. You'll be able to make your own way once you've seen a bit of the world."

"Is that what you did when you left? Made your own decisions? But you came back here."

"I was gone a long time. All this talk, however, will not prepare you for your trip. When we finish this task, I have a new map of Paris as well as information for you about the Metro. That and walking are likely to be how you get around, and the more you understand about it before you arrive, the less you will look like some dumbstruck tourist who has never set foot in a city."

"I haven't been to a city—not even a place as big as Raleigh. And what is the Metro?"

"One of the first subway systems ever put into operation. Now while I never personally had much dealings with it, I have kept up with the city through magazines and newspapers and understand that it has grown considerably during the past few decades. I have another new guide book for you—the off-the-path type that gets beyond the Eiffel Tower. Now that we have that settled, we can switch languages after all, *ma petite, seulement francaise pour une heure.*"

The hour of conversing only in French went quickly as it always did in my excitement, and our lack of English spilled into the second hour, when we moved outside to the terrace for a glass of wine, cheese, and my introduction to paté. Amelia sighed in exasperation when I incorrectly identified it as potted meat and nodded approvingly when I nibbled a bite and smiled.

"If you don't like all the different types of paté, at least you'll know what it is," she remarked and said my next food lesson would be how to eat an apple with a knife and fork. "Peaches are easy enough, but if you haven't practiced, you'll spin an apple off the plate onto the floor." Although I had no idea why anyone would bother to eat fruit that way, I didn't see any reason that I couldn't master the skill.

As it came time for me to leave, I reluctantly agreed that it was best to leave the map and guidebook at her place for the time being. I arrived home to help get supper ready, and Mamma gave me what I took as a secret smile. I mentally swore again to myself that I would be patient. I would pretend it was a test of strength, like seeing how long you could swim underwater with your lungs burning, aching to surface, but knowing that if you could wait just another two seconds, you'd have everyone else beat. Even my brothers had to admit that I was the best in the family at holding my breath underwater—well, really the best in the neighborhood.

Nine days after I thought all my plans were gone to hell, I came into the house just as it was time to wash up. The aroma of chicken and dumplings drifted from the kitchen, and I was surprised to see Daddy sitting in his chair, a glass of ice tea on the table next to him and the television turned too low to hear. Mamma was in her rocking chair, leaning forward; it was obvious they had been talking.

"I'm sorry I'm late. Mrs. Rundle came in right about closing, and she's a real good customer so I stayed to take care of her. She said to give her regards."

"Guess we're not having supper on time no ways," Daddy said and pointed a thick finger at the coffee table, then at the couch. "You better open that and let's see what it's about."

I slid onto the couch, my eyes fixed on the bulging envelope that lay waiting to be touched. It was a creamy color with a New York postmark addressed to Miss Margaret E. Stewart. I forced my hand to be steady as I loosened the flap, trying not to tear it. I pulled out a sheaf of papers, heavy stock with embossed black lettering on the top.

"Sinclair College in New York." I scanned the cover sheet

rapidly, reading aloud, stunned at the words.

*Dear Miss Stewart:*
*Congratulations on your initial acceptance into our Fine Arts*
*Program . . .*

Mamma bounced a finger off her lips. "My goodness, that must be from that competition you entered awhile back."

Daddy's expression wasn't a glower yet. "What competition, girl? And what's this New York business?"

I couldn't seem to speak. Mamma reached over and patted Daddy's arm, smiling as sweetly as I'd ever seen her. "Now, Clarence, it was sort of an impulse thing for Maggie. A teacher at school told her about it if I remember right. She sent in some real pretty photographs, and they must have liked them. Go ahead, child, and read. Let us see what it is they have to say, Clarence."

I tried not to stumble, beginning to understand the idea. I cleared my throat and conveyed the offer of a one-year scholarship to the small, but well-established Fine Arts School of Sinclair College with its New York City campus and opportunities to study abroad in Florence, Italy; Barcelona, Spain; and Paris, France. Details were enclosed in the packet, and more would be forthcoming once Sinclair received my completed application, which was also enclosed.

"Well, isn't that something?" Mamma shifted in her rocking chair studying Daddy's face.

His voice was firm. "What kind of nonsense is this? Never heard anything like it. Why would these people be offering such a thing to Maggie?"

I didn't know if I was supposed to say anything so I let Mamma go ahead.

"Now, Clarence, you heard yourself that Merl said Maggie had a lot of talent for someone her age. No reason other people wouldn't recognize that. Does the letter say what all they're offering?"

"Uh, a one-year scholarship, all paid up, except their New York campus is full so I can go to one of the overseas places or go on a waiting list for New York. I have to let them know when I send in the application." I hoped my voice wasn't quavering because my insides were as wiggly as Jello.

Daddy was shaking his head. "Off across the ocean or to New York? Doesn't set right by me, and I can't believe you'd want to let her go off like that, Doreen. Merl can teach her everything she needs to know, if she's all het up to be one of these career women they're always blathering about." He turned and looked at me with more confusion than anger. "I guess if you got something against picking a good man to settle with and you got itchy feet girl, you don't have to go off halfway around the world."

Mamma shot me a warning look. "Well, I tell you what. Let's have supper, then we'll call Merl and ask his opinion about this. Maggie, bring those papers, and you come on with me. You check on the weather report, Clarence. We'll get food on the table in about ten minutes."

I grabbed the envelope and scooted through the kitchen door as Daddy turned the volume up. Mamma followed almost on my heels.

"Don't be asking questions yet," she said maddeningly. "Amelia Hatcher has some kind of connections with that college in New York. You get the plate of sliced tomatoes out while I dish up the chicken and dumplings. Soon as supper is done, you remember you need to go out for a while, but be back here right at eight-thirty. You can take those papers and read them while you're gone. I imagine your daddy will come around, and there's no reason to keep him up past his bedtime."

As anxious as I was to ask just what in the hell was going on, I couldn't very well argue. I saw she'd cooked butter beans, and there was an icebox lemon pie in the refrigerator when I opened it. That was bound to put Daddy in a good mood. With the way she was behaving, I didn't think the menu was an accident.

I somehow made it through the meal with small talk, having suddenly recalled that I had a library book due today that I should take to the book drop. Mamma said that since I was going to be out anyway, that I ought to run over to Bobby's and pick up a new pattern that Sheila had for her.

I said I'd have a piece of pie later, asked if I could be excused, and scurried out of the house clutching the envelope and a library book I hadn't had a chance to read yet. I drove straight to the library and parked underneath a light. I deposited the book lest I forget and carry it back home. Then I yanked the letter, application form, and information brochure out of the envelope. Sinclair College? I had never heard of it, much less sent any photographs in, but the letter and the brochure sure looked official. There was a cluster of red brick buildings behind a black iron fence with a decorative scrolled gate and *Sinclair College* in big gold letters arched at the top.

If I thought it would have done any good, I would have rushed to Amelia's and demanded an explanation. The letter was deceptively simple, and if I didn't know better, I would think that I actually had entered a competition. How did Amelia get them to agree? Or was this maybe a thing where she just knew someone who was willing to write a letter on fancy paper? I forced myself to read slowly through the brochure, and then I went by Bobby's. I got in and out with the pattern as quick as I could without raising too many questions. When I re-entered the house, Daddy was sitting with a can of beer, and Mamma was crocheting one of the baby jackets she planned to contribute to the annual church bazaar. A baseball game was on the television, but the sound was down low like they'd been talking again.

Mamma smiled as I felt suddenly leaden and stood with the pattern in one hand and the envelope in the other.

Daddy swung his gaze across her and then to me. "Your Uncle Merl says he'd be glad to have you like he offered, but figures this is better than he can do for you. Thinks we ought to let you give it a try. You sure that paper ain't asking for money?"

I breathed in deeply and didn't flinch from his scrutiny. "Uh, no, sir, they're not. I read it over real close. It sure says it's an all-expenses-paid scholarship. Travel and a place to stay and everything. Something called a stipend to pay for food and incidental stuff."

"I guess it can't do no harm to send in the form, if this is what you want to do. Your mamma heard tell about some lady at the church got a niece doing something like this, too. I'll not be having you get a swelled head about it, though."

"Maggie will be fine, Clarence," Mamma said firmly and lowered her eyes to the yarn in her lap. "Turn the sound up so your daddy can hear the game."

I walked to the television, turned the knob until Daddy held up his hand, and then disappeared into the kitchen before he could think of a reason to change his mind. I waited a few minutes to see if Mamma would come in. When she didn't, I found a pen in a drawer and began to fill out the application. I'd take it to Amelia in the morning and find out just what in the hell this was all about. I'd waited long enough for answers as far as I was concerned.

# Chapter Eleven

Jumbled dreams disturbed my sleep. I rode waves of snatched conversations, flashing colors, and shapes that would not take solid form. It was full daylight when I finally kicked the sheet to the foot of the bed. I was shocked to see that it was a little after eight o'clock. I, who often saw the sun rise, had slept late. Daddy would have been on his way early, and judging by the silence of the house, Mamma was gone, too.

The white speckled blue coffee pot was still warm on the stove and a plate with biscuits and two slices of ham sat on the table. *Got the quilting ladies at church today. Best you go see about having that paper filled out. Mamma*

I made sandwiches of the biscuits and drank a cup of coffee, knowing that Amelia would not be ready for a visitor for another hour yet. Her morning routine was unvaried—a walk along the beach unless it was ferocious weather when she would substitute an hour of reading, a light breakfast, and then her toilette as she called it. Thank God, I wasn't needed at work until noon. If I didn't get a few real answers soon, I was going to have to pick a fight with someone just to un-bottle all the emotion swirling around my insides. I did think to telephone Amelia as soon as I got dressed rather than risk showing up unannounced and having her get stubborn on me. Sounding all casual-like as if she didn't know what I wanted, she said it was fine for me to drop by.

When I slammed the truck door, she called out that she was at the potting table. I left the envelope on the passenger seat and had my gloves in hand just in case she intended this to be one of those work-while-we-talked conversations.

The large wooden table, silvered as was every other piece of lumber left outside, was attached to the wall of the converted garage by a series of bolts. The surface was gouged, and dirt was embedded into the joints of the planks. Three of the indoor plants and three empty containers were on one end of the table. Amelia had a trowel in hand, and she waved it towards the garage door.

"The bag of potting soil is inside—there's no sense in me wrestling with it now that you're here."

Of course, that's where the bag was; I'd delivered it not a week ago.

"Considering your early arrival, shall I assume you received the letter from Sinclair College? And shall I further assume your mother did not explain it and that your father was reluctant? He wasn't actually angry, was he?"

"Yes, ma'am; yes, ma'am; and not exactly," I said, lifting the bag onto the table and slicing it open. "Is it for real? I mean, what am I supposed to do with the application?"

She pushed a circular copper pot over to me. "Fill this new container while I remove the plant from the current one." She inserted the trowel into the soil around the ivy and began to gently loosen the plant. "By your question of *is it for real,* I assume you mean Sinclair College. I can assure you it is precisely what the letter says it is. As for your scholarship, that is a minor modification of the truth."

She was concentrating on the plant instead of looking at me, even though I knew she could repot these blindfolded. "I guess I don't understand," I said, tired of the games she and Mamma had been playing with me. "I'm real sorry that I lied about everything, but could I please be told what's going on?"

The side of her face twitched a bit, and it might have meant she smiled and her voice wasn't as sharp as she could be. "What is going on is a tiny bit of a ruse that I suggested and your mother agreed to. While I have chosen to live as much without the presence of people as I possibly can, that doesn't mean I don't know people." She wiggled the plant free, and I slid the old pot out of the way and placed the new one within reach. She nodded and began to pluck the tangled roots away from the knot they had formed.

"An acquaintance of a friend accommodated me with the packet to you. As soon as you send the application to the individual, and do be certain to address it to him personally, he will return a packet to you with all sorts of useful information about your contact in Paris. It will include the address of the apartment where you will stay."

She finished with the first plant, and we progressed to the next one. "But I'm not really going to the college?"

"No, although there is no reason for your father to know that. This is merely a slight diversion of the original plan. The apartment that you will have, the bank account established, and your apprenticeship with Jean-Claude Reillard, a photographer of some international note, is the same as we discussed. I think we can safely assume that none of your family will be popping into Sinclair College for an unexpected visit. Considering your dislike for formal academics, it should come as no surprise to anyone that you decide college is not for you after the year is over."

"And at the end of the year?"

She stilled her hands, resting her fingertips on the table,

and turned to me, one eyebrow raised. "If you survive a year of tutelage under Jean-Claude Reillard, you will be as skilled a photographer as if you had attended Sinclair, and you should not be lacking job offers. He will pay you very little, which is why you will be provided a place to live and have an allowance that will be neither extravagant nor miserly. You will be far better equipped for a year in Paris than many students are, while not as catered to as some spoiled rich brat who can't appreciate the opportunity. What happens to you at the end of the year will be entirely up to you, little country girl. Who knows, the big foreign city might frighten you after all, and you might choose to flee back here and become the housewife and mother that your father thinks you should be."

I felt heat flush my neck and face. "I won't do that."

She began to work again. "I don't expect you to," she said with a shrug. "I don't honestly know what will happen, Maggie, and perhaps we will both be wrong. What I have done, what you have done, what your mother has done, for that matter, is prepare you as best we can, and not until you are in Paris on your own, will you know how it is."

"It's going to be the most wonderful thing that has ever happened to me," I said quickly. "And I'll work harder than I ever have. I don't care if this Jean-Claude guy is awful or not. I'll learn from him."

Amelia actually laughed, a sound that startled me. "Jean-Claude awful? No, my dear, he is incredibly talented, demanding, and temperamental, not some grizzled ogre. In fact, when you come tomorrow, remind me and I'll give you a book of his photography. You might as well study it until you leave. Anyway, let's get done with this, and you can fill out the application. I'll sign your mother's name, and you can mail it when you go into town."

With that, my frustration disappeared like what happens when you have a headache and the throbbing pain stops; gone as if it had never hurt. It was like with the plants we were repotting. I was root bound, too hearty for the container that was home—I was about to be transplanted, and I would thrive. I knew it as surely as I had ever known anything.

# Part Two

## Maggie's Time

### Fall 1978 – Spring 1992

# Chapter Twelve

My last weeks at home were surprisingly uneventful. My decision was accepted by my puzzled family with more warnings than congratulations. I refused to allow their gloomy predictions about what I would find in a foreign place filled with smelly French people dull my excitement.

The promised packet of instructions came with a one-way airplane ticket, the address of where I would be living, assurance that someone would meet me at the airport, and a telephone number to call if anything went wrong during my travels.

My parting from Amelia was as routine as if I were just going to the store to run an errand for her. She simply handed me an envelope. In it were the name and account of the bank where my allowance would be promptly deposited each month and from which my rent would be paid directly; and a stack of French francs to take care of expenses until I made it to an exchange, which came with a reminder from Amelia that it only looked like an enormous sum because I was forgetting the exchange rate. Amelia had already replaced me. She hired Gus Pickens, a sturdy man who was a deaf mute but fully capable of communicating through notes. He was an acknowledged hard worker; no worries about him gossiping. I did not believe that Amelia had no feelings about my going, nor did I know how to express what I felt; so I followed the same path as with my family and didn't prepare good-bye speeches.

Bobby said he would drive me up to Norfolk so no one else had to take off work, and Mamma made me a lunch to carry just in case. With little more than a "I guess you know what you're doing. Be sure and write Mamma soon as you get there or she'll worry," Bobby deposited me at the airport with a pat on my shoulder instead of a hug.

And so, my grand adventure began with me standing in the terminal, repeating what I was supposed to do inside my head as I waited in the short line to be checked in. A small airplane to the JFK airport in New York City and an evening flight to Charles de Gaulle airport. I was supposed to have plenty of time to get from one place to another, according to Amelia, and I wasn't to be afraid to ask questions as to how to make connections. I didn't know if it was on purpose, but I had a window seat, and after fumbling with the seatbelt, the older gentleman sitting on the aisle asked if it was my first time flying and what my final destination was. I supplied the information being sure to say, *sir.*

"It sounds like a wonderful opportunity," he said and explained how the take-off would be. He offered me a stick of gum for when my ears would pop.

Awareness that I was actually on my way banished nervousness at the unfamiliar engine sounds, the speed of the plane, the vibration, and the sensation when we began to climb. The gentleman retreated into a newspaper, and I spent the entire flight staring at extraordinary cloud formations. When we entered the clamor of the New York airport, he touched my elbow and guided me toward a pretty woman in the same uniform as those who'd been on the airplane.

"This young lady is going to Paris. Please make sure she knows how to get to the correct terminal. Good luck to you,

Maggie," he said with a smile as the lady studied my ticket.

I silently thanked God that I had nearly four hours between connections. I'd never seen a place so crowded, with little carts whizzing about and announcements going off every few minutes. Careful to follow the airline lady's scribbled directions, I poked along, taking it all in. I was astonished at the prices of the food stands I passed. I decided to spring for a Coke and find an empty chair where I could eat the sandwiches and cookies stuffed in my backpack. I tried not to gape at the assortment of people I saw, the snatches of foreign languages I didn't recognize. When I wasn't dawdling in shops, I gazed out the large windows, watching airplanes being prepared, taking off, and landing. Perhaps it was seeing the lumbering crafts by the dozens lifting safely into the air, but once I followed the other passengers onto my next airplane, I settled calmly into my seat. I was surprised to discover I had a row to myself and accepted a small pillow and blanket, wondering if I would be able to sleep. Nine hours to fly—it seemed to be both a long time and a blink of an eye that in only nine hours I would be carried across the Atlantic Ocean, away from all I knew.

I paid attention to instructions from the stewardesses and observed other passengers, some who appeared to be as novice as I was, and why shouldn't that be so? It wasn't as if every human being on the planet except me was used to flights across the ocean. I reluctantly made my way to the bathroom and discovered it wasn't that hard to manage. After an edible meal of chicken and a glass of white wine, the lights were dimmed, and despite what I expected, I began to feel drowsy. I drifted in and out of light sleep, shifting positions as best I could.

The interior of the airplane came to life again when we were two hours out. Stewardesses served a breakfast of juice, croissants, and coffee; then afterwards they came by with a tray of little rolled towels that had been steamed. It was a refreshing treat, and I retrieved my backpack from underneath the seat. I ran a brush through my hair and found a pack of breath mints. I was still rumpled and would have liked a shower, but that would have to wait. I inhaled deeply when the pilot said we were beginning our descent, pressed my forehead to the window, and could hardly believe the vastness of the city that stretched beneath us. I managed to get through customs and passport control by following and observing two couples who looked comfortable with the ritual of arriving in a foreign place. I saw a young, black-haired woman holding a sign with my name when I exited customs, still clinging my stamped passport. I was absurdly relieved and suspect it showed on my face.

"You are Maggie, the American, no? I am Felice Gaigneau, Jean-Claude's assistant." Her English was distinguishable with a pronounced accent, and her dark brown eyes were welcoming. Although she was not much taller than I, she was thin like a model and dressed like one, too: slim black jeans, a black scoop neck stretchy top, and black leather low-cut boots.

"*Oui*," I mustered, feeling more disheveled than ever. "*Preferez-vouz que je parle en francaise?*"

She laughed instantly. "What a charming accent you have. No, you do not need to speak French with me. I wish to use you to practice my English if you do not mind." She looked at my feet where I'd set the backpack and the Army duffle bag Jed had sent me. "This is all for you? No other cases?"

"I, no, this is it," I said, slipping my passport into an inside zip pocket of my brown fake-leather shoulder bag.

"Then we are to go. I will explain to you the city as we drive." It was difficult for me to concentrate on her rapid chatter as she dodged more traffic than I imagined could exist, squeezing into gaps between cars, trucks, and buses; allowing mere glimpses of landmarks I had dreamed of. The blur of tall, modern buildings gave way to older structures with carved stone, spires of churches, and streams of people on the sidewalks.

"You know the *Rive Gauche*, the Left Bank of the River Seine, yes?" Felice had careened through a set of lights, passing Notre Dame as I twisted to gape at the massive shape of soaring stone. "*Voila*," she continued before I could answer. She had turned down a side street, bumping onto the sidewalk and whipping into a spot vacated by a gray paneled truck with some sort of advertisement on the back and sides. "It is the building two from here. Floor two, one from the top, and no elevator I am sorry to tell you."

She flashed a grin and took my backpack, either not noticing my desire to linger on the street, or not realizing how strange all this was to me. What a dizzying assault of sounds, scents, and colors were crowding in on me. Most of the buildings were narrow and stone with wrought iron balconies; many had window boxes filled with flowers. We walked through a tall, ancient-looking door into a tiled entryway, where there were a bank of nine mailboxes on the right-hand wall, one door next to them, a door to the left, and a wide stairway directly ahead. I saw no one about and heard no sounds. Felice climbed slowly with regard to the extra burden that I carried. We stopped at the second floor, well, it was really the third if you didn't count the ground floor as the first floor — I suddenly recalled Amelia explaining they counted floors differently in France.

Felice moved to the left and stopped before a door with a bronzed number 6 mounted on it. Producing what looked to be a skeleton key from the pocket of her jacket, she unlocked the door, swung it open wide, and gestured me inside. My first impression was of light, its source a set of glass French doors. The room was about the size of our living room at home, and I sensed the age of it, like when we used to visit my great-grand-mother. The walls were devoid of decoration, nail holes pocked in the off-white plaster, and the plank floor was worn to a light brown. A short sofa in a faded red and gold floral print was centered in the room underneath a hanging light with little gold lampshades over the four bulbs. A chair with arms and a dark red upholstered seat was angled to the sofa, and a trunk was evidently intended as a coffee table. A square table was set against the left wall with three mismatched chairs, each painted a different color. The right wall was actually an alcove no more than three feet deep. Felice waved her hand toward it. I could see a counter with a two-burner hot plate and a small sink with a single wall cabinet to the right of it. There was what looked to be a refrigerator under the counter, a little one like they had in older motels. "We will find you a coffee press, a skillet, a pot, and a kettle. Other than that, you should not need." Felice was as quick to announce that as she had been everything else.

"The bedroom now, and the W.C., a water closet, but with the little shower also. No walking down the hall for you, even though Madame Blanchard gives only six hours of hot water each day—from five until eight in the mornings and then hours twenty until twenty-three in the nights, but she is a good landlady all the same and she has the pleasant disposition."

I followed her through the single door that stood open to the right of the French doors. A double window almost over-powered the rectangular room that had a bed in a black iron frame, one nightstand with a lamp, and a chest of drawers with four drawers that was made of a lighter wood than the tall wardrobe on the left wall. A door to the right of the bed was no doubt the bathroom; I peeked in and it was indeed quite small.

Felice deposited my backpack on the bed and tilted her

head. "It is not grand, no, but a very sturdy apartment."

"It's fine, better than I had hoped," I said truthfully. What did I need with anything more?

Felice looked at her watch. "Maggie, I must go. It will be good I think for you to have time to walk about. You will see that much of what you need is close by. No one should spend their first night in Paris alone so I will come for you at seven o'clock to take you to a restaurant. I will go later to meet with some friends, but I think tonight you will be much sleepy. It is said that you should not have a nap because that makes the body harder to adjust. *Adjust,* is that the correct word?"

"Uh, yes, you mean because of the time difference." I had changed my watch before we landed. I overheard one of the stewardesses tell the couple across the aisle from me that the secret to recovering from jet lag was to stay awake until nine or ten o'clock at night. Felice needn't worry about a nap. I didn't intend to spend my first afternoon in Paris sleeping for God's sake.

"The difference of the hours, that is it exactly. Oh, I have a map of the *environs*, the close streets, for you in the car. It will be of good use because I do not think you should try to go very far today, not on the Metro yet. We will do that tomorrow. Jean-Claude's studio is near a Metro, and I will show you how to get from here to there. This is good, yes?"

She handed me the key and started for the door. I scrambled after her, not bothering to lock the door. At her car she rummaged through items on the floor of the backseat until she emerged with a thin folded map. "It is not all of Paris, only here because that is enough for now, yes? And I have put my telephone number on the front, but I will not be home until perhaps the five o'clock. Madame Blanchard will return soon, and it will be good for you to perhaps make your introduction and give her a small flowers. You can buy them from the streets. You have francs, yes?"

I nodded, fighting the urge to cling to the only person I knew. Good Lord, within seconds I was going to be alone.

"Then I say, *à bientôt*, Maggie. You know the French custom of kissing the cheeks?" She stretched forward and lightly kissed my left cheek, then my right.

I tried not to stiffen and smiled instead. "Thank you for everything, Felice. I will be ready at seven o'clock. And Madame Blanchard, does she speak English?"

Felice was in the driver's seat, the door still open. She laughed, "*Mais non*, with her you will speak French." She flipped her hand in a cheerful farewell, slammed the door, and lurched into the street, inches from an oncoming car.

I drew in a deep breath, momentary indecision freezing me into position. I was alone in Paris, a city I knew only from descriptions and books, where I thought I could speak the language, but could I really? I slowly retraced my steps to the apartment and discovered that I was trembling when I pushed down on the curved handle of the door. Was it anxiety, fatigue, or the thrill of adventure? Why couldn't it be all three? Stop. I was in my apartment. My a-p-a-r-t-m-e-n-t. In Paris. Me, Maggie Stewart. I had a map and money. Felice would return later. This was it; this was what I had dreamed of, planned for, lied for, and now I was going to quiver and be afraid? Bullshit.

I shook my head fiercely and marched to the French doors to fling them open. The dramatic gesture was ruined when I found I had to wiggle them loose, but no matter. Even though the balcony would hold no more than a tiny table and two chairs, there were four window boxes hanging from it; two spaced along the front with red geraniums and one on each side with purple and white pansies. I didn't know if the last tenant had left only a short time ago or if Madame Blanchard was watering them. My apartment was on the back side of the building, and the street I overlooked was narrow with apartment buildings rather than shops, none of the buildings taller than the four stories of the one that I was in. It was quiet, as could be expected in the middle of a workday. A few windows were open, music from radios softly drifting out. A black and white cat that looked well-fed sat on the stoop of one building, its tail curled around its paws.

I inhaled a mix of scents, realizing I was thirsty and feeling the first tug of hunger. It would take me no more than fifteen minutes to unpack, and despite what Felice said about no hot water during the day—a puzzle I would have to ask about—I thought a cold shower would perk me up. I was sticky from having slept in my clothes, and my mouth had the fuzziness of not having brushed my teeth. That was it, then, the positive action that would propel me into this world I had chosen. Damn, what would I use as a towel? I opened the wardrobe. Yes, there were linens for the bed and bath—nothing luxurious, merely utilitarian white sheets, two towels, and a washcloth. It would do for now, and I could buy more. I would buy what I needed to make this place a home for me, a place where no one else except Amelia believed I belonged. I was here, and by God, I would use the year to prove that we were right.

# Chapter Thirteen

Thirty minutes later it was done. My belongings stowed, my skin tingling from chilly cleanliness, my eyes wide taking in the sights, I stood for a moment on the sidewalk in contemplation, not tired confusion. The key to my apartment was tucked securely in my jeans where I could feel it, while one of the small guidebooks and map protruded a bit from the outside pocket of my purse, which I held firmly by the strap. I took careful note of the street sign at the corner; Rue Danton was my street—*my street*—in Paris. The name bounced like a chorus inside my head. I set off in the direction we'd come in Felice's car, remembering that I had seen shops as we turned and passed Notre Dame. There was no reason to be too ambitious my first afternoon, four or five blocks might easily overwhelm my senses. None of the buildings on this street were taller than four stories either; all were made of a similar stone with gray or black tile roofs of what looked to be slate. Some had dormers arrayed along the front, and I could see pigeons clustered on peaks as well as gliding to and from one old building to the next. The modern architecture that I had noticed on the way from the airport was not evident here.

I straightened my posture and turned left at the corner to see a store with fruits and vegetables in cases propped at just the right angle to make them easy to pluck, but not roll out.

Bouquets of fresh flowers sat in a white plastic bucket by the door, which was wide open. An old lady dressed in an ankle-length, dark blue dress stepped outside with a straw basket on one arm and a purse clutched in her other hand. I could see a bunch of carrots lying across the top of her purchases. A younger woman politely waited for the woman to clear the narrow doorway before she moved inside. Two doors down was a shop with a *Pharmacie* sign; it was filled with people and aisles of bottles and boxes. On my side of the street was a *Boulangerie/Patisserie,* where a woman behind the counter chatted with a customer. I stared in amazement. The window to the left of the door held breads and rolls in cloth-lined baskets; incredible cakes and pastries were arranged on glass plates in the window on the right. There were beautifully decorated chocolate cakes, others in white with fresh fruits atop, little apple tarts, and sandwich-type cookies covered in confectioners' sugar. I felt a surge of hunger, but thought it better to not go for sugar immediately. I smelled something enticing and looked to the far end of the street. Two people stood in line at an open window. As I moved closer, I saw the girl in front, who looked to be my age, extend her hand and take something that appeared to be a paper-wrapped triangle. She said something, walked away, and the man behind her stepped up.

As I neared the window, I saw the word *Creperie* painted in an arc over the window; the window reminded me of the one at the Dairy Queen back home. Crepes. Amelia didn't make them often, but at least I knew for sure what they were and she'd told me they were the French equivalent of fast food. The menu was written in chalk on a blackboard on a stand to the left of the window. I could translate most of it without looking at the dictionary in the guidebook, and the prices were cheap. I watched the man's transaction, withdrew two ten-franc notes from my wallet so I wouldn't be fumbling for money, and approached the window with more confidence than I felt. Cans and bottles of beverages were displayed on a shelf immediately behind the lanky man in a white T-shirt and a less than sparkling white apron. "*Un jambon y fromage y un Coca-cola,*" I said with a smile and held my breath.

"*Oui,*" he said and, without another glance, dipped a ladle into a container of batter and poured it onto the large round griddle. He took a can of Coke from the cooler behind him and set it on the counter inside the window. He added a thin slice of ham and sprinkled shredded cheese on the crepe, folding it into a large triangle with a flourish and flipping it for about one minute. He slid the crepe into the paper wrap and handed it to me. "*Sept francs,*" he said as he took a straw from a box, tore the tab off the can, and inserted the straw before passing me the can. I gave him a ten, took three one-franc coins as change, and stuck the other ten in my jeans pocket, leaving my hands free to manage the crepe and the can of Coke.

I moved beyond the window and bit off a corner of the crepe. My God, it was delicious. The ham and cheese that I thought was Gruyère were melted into what my family would have called "some funny looking pancake." The combined slightly tangy taste was vaguely like a really thin toasted ham and cheese sandwich. I had to slow down to keep from devouring the crepe and going back for a second one. I didn't know what other delights I would find and wanted to pace myself. After all, I would pass the patisserie again. I savored the buttery balance of ham and cheese and did not think of this simple street food as my first French meal since Felice intended to take me to a real restaurant. I unabashedly licked my fingers before I used the napkin and deposited the waste into a small black metal trash can mounted to a light post, then I continued to where I saw more people passing, standing in clusters and knots, and a bus stopping to disgorge passengers.

Within paces of that, I doglegged onto another short street and stopped again in surprise. Before me was a huge bronze fountain that rose above my head. The curved basin was filled with water, and a handful of young people sat on the edge of the fountain, smoking and talking, their backpacks propped at their feet. Others passed without so much as a glance at the fountain, hurrying toward the Metro sign, *Saint-Michel*, with stairs leading to the subway. Another sign showed *RER St-Michel*, and there was a busy street to my left, flowing with every type of vehicle, a stone bridge within sight. Two restaurants, a large bookstore, and other shops opened onto the square. This appeared to be some sort of a hub. I sipped my Coke, moving out of the way as I needed to in the swirl of people. Horns honked, air brakes hissed, bits of conversation flowed around me, and I heard the sound of a guitar. I shifted my stance and saw a long-haired man standing near the entry to the Metro, a black guitar case on the sidewalk at his feet. He was playing a song I didn't recognize, singing in French, and a small group of people had gathered to listen. A woman made brief eye contact with the musician and dropped coins into the open case before she moved on.

My temptation to explore was greater than my desire to stay and listen, and judging by the reaction of most people, this was a regular occurrence. The Seine and Notre Dame called me. No matter that the famous cathedral held no religious meaning for me, I simply had to see it. I crossed with the crowd and headed to the bridge closest to Notre Dame, where I leaned against the wide stone railing and inhaled deeply, quietly taking in the sight. This was the front view, a picture of the soaring steeple and fantastic carvings of the ancient building. It sat on its own island in the Seine. Tall trees were spaced within the park-like setting, and dozens of people strolled about, some obviously with tour groups, others in pairs, and a few solitary figures. They all looked a bit less than life-size from my vantage point. Barges and tour boats moved ponderously up and down the river; I could hear the faint sounds of a speaker, a tour guide describing points of interest. A wide path ran along the river, and it was occupied by people, too. Sets of stairs leading to the street level were shaded by trees from above and to my right. Rows of kiosks were side-by-side in the space between the sidewalk and the drop off of the bank. I vaguely recognized the scene from Amelia's books, although those had been black and white photographs. I had admired the images but not been able to imagine the colors, smells, and sounds.

I could see another bridge in the distance and thought that rather than try to see too much at once, I would meander to the second bridge, cross to the other side of the river, and make my way around in a giant loop. That would take me past the kiosks, allow me to see the cathedral from every angle, yet keep clear of the crowds. I had managed to order lunch, and I thought I could keep my bearings using the two bridges as boundaries. As far as I was concerned, I was accomplishing a great deal and had no reason to be embarrassed over my desire to take things slowly.

I tossed my empty can into another trash receptacle and realized that the first kiosk appeared to be a used bookseller, as was the next one and the next, then someone selling prints and postcards and more used books. There was at least one person browsing or engaging in discussion with each vendor, and my presence aroused nothing more than a brief nod as I picked up rapid phrases wreathed in strong cigarette smoke. I would have to ask Felice, but if the prices weren't too expensive and haggling was a common practice, I was already thinking as to how a few books would fit nicely into my apartment. When I cleared the line of kiosks, I looked toward Notre Dame again, glassed-in tour boats dotting the waterway. Of course, I had seen photographs, so it wasn't as if I had no idea what the cathedral would look like. The age of it was incredible though, the carvings like nothing I'd ever seen before, and yes, there really were gargoyles with contorted faces, poised as if ready to leap. I was glad it was daylight—I was betting that they were spooky in the dark. Now I understood what was meant by flying buttresses—I'd read about them. To think that the massive arched supports—well, the entire huge structure—had been created by hand; stone carvers, masons, horses, I supposed, and pulleys all working together to hoist and join the pieces into something so magnificent. And the stained glass. My God, how long had it taken to make windows that large?

I absorbed the sheer wonder of it, knowing I would wait for another day to venture inside. I didn't want to rush anything; I wasn't on some quick tour where I was being hustled along to the next monument. By now I'd crossed the Seine and saw a series of small stores, cafés, souvenir shops, and restaurants to my right. Round tables and chairs, complete with umbrellas of different hues, edged the sidewalk. The umbrellas sported logos such as *Cinzano,* and many of the tables were full, waiters in black trousers, white shirts, and black vests carrying trays or scribbling on pads. By tomorrow, after having dinner with Felice, I should be ready to give it a try. What was it Amelia had told me? That it was nothing for a meal in France to require two hours or more? I had to admit that no one seemed to be in a hurry, but how on earth did you spend that long eating?

Another store with buckets of flowers on display reminded me of Felice's suggestion that I buy a bouquet for my landlady.

I checked my watch, surprised that I had been walking around for almost three hours. My stomach began to protest the single crepe I had allowed it, and I remembered the store closest to my apartment also had flowers and an assortment of other items. Since I had no idea what the plan for tomorrow was, it might not be a bad idea to gather a few snacks and some beverages. There were plenty of places to eat, but what if I woke up hungry in the middle of the night? I completed my elongated loop, still in no hurry, watching the flow of people, the maneuver of vessels up and down the river, and listening to city sounds that were so different than what I was accustomed to.

I was mildly disappointed to see that the patisserie had closed by the time I got there. So I headed straight for the shop by my apartment. The L-shaped counter with the cash register was a few steps inside to the right, and a stout woman in a faded print dress was ringing up a sale for an elderly woman, who looked a great deal like the other older woman I'd seen coming out of the shop earlier. A refrigerator section ran across part of the back next to a door marked, *Interdit*, do not enter, I thought. Merchandise was crammed closely together; it was basically a convenience store, even though I suspected that wasn't the word that was used. I found the snack section and suddenly realized there were no brands that I recognized. It wasn't something I was prepared for, but the packages were colorful and potato chips were potato chips no matter who made them. Ah, chocolate bars—and a tube of Smarties that looked a lot like M&Ms. Cookies, too, plain and chocolate covered. I gathered essentials, then found cans of Coke—so much for no American brands.

I inhaled a deep breath, let it out slowly, took my purchases to the counter, and carefully pronounced a full sentence of what I hoped was, "I would also like some flowers."

The woman looked at me quizzically for a moment as I pointed outside to the bucket. *"Oui, les fleurs,"* she said and motioned for me to choose.

I selected a bouquet of mixed carnations and handed the woman a twenty-franc note. She gave me change and made no movement to bag my purchases.

"Uh, madame, *un sac?*" I was pretty sure that was the word. How was I supposed to carry everything?

She wrinkled her brow. *"Ah, vous ete Americaine,"* she said instead, then waved her hand to a stand with a sign, *Sac, 3 franc.* Multicolored string bags with canvas-like handles were on display, and I flashed back to what I'd seen on the street— people with baskets and these bags, not paper sacks.

*"Ah, oui,"* I said, plucked off a dark blue one, and returned most of the change. *"Je comprends."*

I did understand, and she rewarded me with a smile of crooked teeth. *"Vous ete un etudiente?*

I filled the bag and picked up the flowers, no tissue paper offered as a trickle of water ran down my arm. *"Oui, merci."* Well, I was more or less a student.

*"Merci y au revoir,"* she said, turning her head as a new customer entered.

I smiled in parting, figuring I'd be using this store a lot and should try to be on friendly terms. Okay, my second successful transaction and my first cultural mistake.

When I went by the door with the discreet engraved brass plaque of Apartment Number 1, I saw a light on and heard faint music. Okay, I would take things up, run a brush through my hair, bring the flowers down, and say hello. I ought to be able to manage that. I rehearsed my opening statement as I climbed the stairs.

I tried not to be nervous when I later rapped on the door,

the bouquet clutched in my left hand, my guidebook dictionary tucked under my arm just in case. The woman who answered my knock was strong featured—black hair streaked with gray done in what we would call a French twist—did they? Her dark brown eyes were set wide apart under thin, arched eyebrows. Her nose was substantial. She was taller than I, the size of a center in basketball.

"*Bonjour, Madame Blanchard. Je suis Maggie Stewart,*" I said carefully.

Her eyes noted the flowers. "*Ah, l'Americaine. Entrez-vouz, s'il vous plait.*"

"*C'est pour vouz,*" I continued and stepped inside as she accepted the bouquet with a slight nod. Her hands were large, with faint scratches on her knuckles and no polish on the short nails. I wondered how much of the upkeep of the building she did herself. "*Parlez-vouz anglais?*"

"*Non, mais vous parlez francais, ne c'est pas?*" She gestured toward the interior, a living room substantially larger than mine, but with the same set of doors that were opened onto a terrace rather than balcony.

"*Uh, pas tres bon,*" I countered. Lord, the woman didn't speak English. Not at all, unless she was putting me on. How was this going to work? My response to her remark that I didn't speak French all that well was met with a shrug, another smile, and a gesture toward a couch.

Immediately after her assurance of "*Nous parlons lentement,*" she did speak slowly, posing a question that had "tea" in it and pantomiming drinking from a cup.

"Don't be silly, little country girl," I could hear Amelia mock. "We've done this many times."

"*Oui, merci,*" I said somewhat weakly and sat gingerly on the couch.

Madame Blanchard carried the flowers into the direction of what was probably the kitchen and gave me a minute to collect my thoughts. I could do this, if we took things slowly as she promised. Surely my landlady wouldn't expect me to discuss anything complicated. I had no idea what Felice had told her about me when she collected the key to the apartment, but she would have at least some background. She would perhaps inquire as to my journey and health— safe subjects. I could compliment her on the room and allowed my eyes to roam, picking out objects that I knew the words for.

It was a lovely room with lots of sunshine pouring in and furniture that was well worn, but well cared for. It wasn't as if the furniture was from a matching set, but everything fit together, a lot like in Amelia's house. From the size of this room and the piece of hallway I could see, it was probably two bedrooms, which would make sense if she managed the building. Now that I was relaxing, I breathed in floral smells, traces of vanilla, and maybe hints of lemon. Without sound, a gray, shorthaired cat padded into the room, paused for several seconds, and leapt onto the other end of the couch. I held my hand palm down below its nose. It sniffed delicately, jumped down, and proceeded toward the open terrace door. I didn't know if I'd passed inspection or not.

When Madame Blanchard reappeared carrying a tray filled with two cups, a teapot, a small plate, a cream pitcher, and a little bowl of something, I automatically scrambled to my feet to take it from her, but in seeing my intent, she smilingly shook her head.

She set the tray onto the coffee table. The plate held some of the chocolate-covered rectangular cookies I'd seen in the store, and the bowl was filled with little sugar cubes, a tiny set of silver tongs resting next to it.

Madame Blanchard motioned for me to help myself. "*Nous parlons lentement*," she repeated, and with that, we did speak our words clearly in short sentences that must have reminded her of carrying on a conversation with a child.

But converse we did with few awkward pauses. After inquiring as to my trip, she got across to me that she had been in this position for nearly twenty years and had seen many people come and go, most quite nice. She didn't permit some sort of something that I wasn't clear on, but I'm sure meant boisterous. Otherwise, she didn't have too many rules. If I understood her sly smile, I would be permitted to entertain gentlemen callers without interference. That wasn't exactly on the top of my priority list, but maybe it was of concern to other residents. With my arrival, all seven apartments were rented; four tenants were French, one Chinese, and one Lebanese. The Lebanese girl, perhaps spoke English, but she didn't know about the others.

When Madame offered me a second cup of tea, I declined, not sure of what the proper response was and feeling the strain of too many unfamiliar things catching up to me. She walked me to the door, thanked me for the flowers, and welcomed me to the building.

My footsteps seemed heavier than before, and I exhaled a deep breath. Thank God, Felice wanted to practice her English on me and did I ever have questions to ask. Hell, I'd better make a list so as not to forget. Most important, though, was the postcard I bought in New York that I would write a few lines on to let Mamma know I was okay. I'd get Felice to help me mail it in the morning.

I finished my tasks and turned to the problem of what to wear. I didn't know where we would be going, but if it was one thing Paris seemed to have, it was lots of restaurants. Mamma had insisted that I bring my three good church dresses, but even if I didn't know shit about fashion, I was willing to bet that what passed for Sunday best in Duck, North Carolina, wasn't about to compare to Parisian clothes.

I decided on a pair of black jeans and a long-sleeved purple knit top underneath a black crocheted hip-length tunic that Mamma had made for me from a pattern she found in some woman's magazine. I stood back from the framed mirror mounted on the bedroom wall and could see myself well enough to be satisfied with my choice.

I could feel my shoulders sagging from fatigue and gave myself a shot of caffeine with a Coke that I took out onto the balcony, watching lights begin to flicker on in other apartments. Although open shutters gave me views into several rooms, I didn't let my gaze linger on any particular window—I wasn't prepared for more than quick glimpses into other people's living habits.

I crossed into the living room literally as I heard the knock at the door. When I opened it, Felice cocked her head to give me the once-over.

"You have a little tired in your face, but it is nice your appearance. Is that the right word, appearance?"

"Or you could say, 'You look nice, just a little tired', and you look gorgeous," I said, not feeling too underdressed. Felice was wearing a forest green pencil skirt that brushed the top of her knees and a navy blue and forest green striped long-sleeved sweater with a scooped neckline. Three tiny jade-colored buttons, all unbuttoned, revealed just a glimpse of cleavage. Her jewelry was simple gold, a pair of small hoop earrings and a pendant of a half moon that rested below the hollow of her throat.

"The night is cool, and I thought for us to walk," she said, patting a black wrap draped over one arm. "A restaurant I like is close by. You are ready, yes?"

I nodded, grabbed my blue windbreaker from the couch, and locked the door, slipping the key into the inside pocket of my purse.

"It is a walk not far, and I will tell you of the streets. Okay? You were today where?"

"I went to the river and around Notre Dame," I said, still trying to get used to the way Felice mixed the sequence of her words. Of course, I probably sounded like that when I spoke French. We exited the building, the block now unfamiliar as darkness settled.

"Ah, she is beautiful the cathedral. We go this way." Felice gestured in the opposite direction from what I had taken earlier. "The restaurants on the square and around the cathedral are not bad, but we go to a place for not as many tourists. It is belong to a friend of my mother. You saw the fountain, yes? It is a famous place where to meet. Everyone knows the fountain at Saint-Michel."

"The fountain, yes, it is beautiful." I could see how it would be a convenient landmark to give someone. I kept pace with her as we turned a corner, and I was assaulted with lights, noise, and intermingled smells. There must have been five or six restaurants and small bars on the street, another creperie, *Chez* something and *Chez* something, large menu boards at the entrance, rooms not very crowded.

Felice took off on an oddly angled short street, past a *bar-tabac* on the corner, the door open and smoke drifting from the dimmed interior. A man behind the bar dangled a cigarette from the corner of his mouth as he surveyed the three old men sitting with glasses of red wine in front of them. Several shops were closed and too dark for me to see what they were.

"*Coq du Pays*." Felice pointed at a lighted sign down the

street. The wooden sign was framed in black wrought iron as I had seen in other places. On the sign, a rooster sat on a stone wall with a slight hill in the background, two cows grazing; an accurate depiction for Country Rooster. A closed *boucherie* was across the street and a *boulangerie* just beyond it. I liked the idea of having a restaurant within steps of a butcher and bakery.

"The coq du vin is a specialty, if you know of it," Felice said, leading the way in. "It is an early hour for dinner in Paris, but for tonight, you are tired. I will invite you in two nights when you have sleep, and you will meet some friends."

Ah, that explained the empty tables I'd seen, and I was grateful for Felice's idea. I couldn't possibly manage trying to talk in a group.

"*Bonsoir*, Felice," a man greeted her with the traditional double-cheeked kiss. He was not much taller than she, and the fringe of brown hair on his balding head was sprinkled with gray. His deep-set brown eyes were pleasant, though, and I wondered at the faded scar that ran along his left jaw.

"Yves, *c'est mon ami*, Maggie," Felice introduced us. His handshake was firm, his palm lightly callused.

"You are American?" His voice was surprisingly deep for his size, his accent not terribly heavy. How could he tell when I hadn't even opened my mouth?

"*Oui*," I said anyway.

"Welcome, Maggie. Felice, Chantal, and Jean-Paul are not here tonight, but the second chef, he is good." He smiled a row of yellowed teeth, led us to a table against the stone wall, and handed us leather-bound menus when we were seated. "You wish what to begin?"

"Campari for me."

"Me also," I said quickly, determined to pass on some

of what Amelia had taught me about the preferred French aperitifs. "Please show a little sophistication and don't order a beer unless it's for a mid-afternoon drink," she'd instructed. Although I had gagged when I tried the licorice-tasting Pernod, and the hint of bitter in Campari took some getting used to, I was okay with it.

Felice smiled her approval, and Yves raised an eyebrow that looked vaguely like a squashed caterpillar.

"We look at the menu and then talk of tomorrow, okay? I think four courses tonight for you to sample the good cooking. Okay?"

I nodded, my eyes already studying the meals offered. My first, honest-to-God sit-down French restaurant, and it was all three-, four-, and five-course meals, nothing listed separately. There was no English translation, and I was relieved to recognize enough dishes so that I wouldn't have to ask for help. Amelia had made coq au vin, the country-style dish of chicken simmered in red wine, on several occasions. If that was a house specialty, why not have it?

I would pass on the snails, mussels, and frog legs as appetizers, choosing country-style paté instead, then a cheese course after the entrée, and end with a peach melba. If I stalled, maybe Felice would order the wine.

She did after a rapid discussion with Yves that I caught only part of. I didn't mind and looked around the rectangular room. It was not a large restaurant, maybe twenty or so tables. Two that could seat six were in the back of the room near the short bar that had only four stools. Tables to seat four filled the rest of the room's center, and two-person tables lined the wall on either side. It was a room of exposed stone and heavy wood, a beamed ceiling, and a stone floor with noticeably worn spots. The door to what must have been the kitchen was to the right of the bar, and an opening to the left would be the bathrooms, I supposed. The restaurant had a certain warmth, giving the sense of a country kitchen with dark red tablecloths and an oil and vinegar cruet in a straw holder on each table. Oil paintings, mostly landscape scenes, decorated the walls.

"The restaurant is two generations with Jean-Paul and his mother is from a farm near Chartres," Felice said after we ordered. "That comes the name Coq du Pays. And now, *a votre santé.*" She offered the traditional toast of "to your health" and touched her glass to mine.

"You have questions, yes, or do you wish me to talk first? We do not have hurry here. Not in France for the meals."

I sipped the ruby-colored liquid, a wave of energy buoying me, knowing the odds were that I would sink later. Not at the moment, though, not when I had so much to ask. "You talk, please, and I will ask questions. Oh, thank you for the suggestion about flowers for Madame Blanchard. We had tea."

"That is a good beginning." Felice brushed her bangs with her fingertips. "I will come for you in the morning at eight hours, and we will go for the breakfast, then take the Metro to the studio. Jean-Claude does not have the too busy schedule tomorrow, and he will leave for other things. It is better for me to show you without him. Jean-Claude is brilliant, much the artist, but he is of a temperament."

"Do you mean he has a temper? Becomes angry easily?" Oh great.

Felice frowned slightly. "He is quick for to shout, but it is not for a long time. Like a shower, not thunderstorm, yes?"

"I understand," I assured her. "Where is the studio?"

Felice laughed. "The Avenue Montaigne, of course, near to the great houses of fashion. It is models that Jean-Claude became famous with, and he stays close to use them often in his work. No matter the subject, Jean-Claude will have a reason to have a beautiful woman to shoot. Your aunt, she did not tell you this?"

I felt my mouth tug downward. "My aunt?"

"Your aunt, she is the one to know Jean-Claude, I think. That is what he say to me. That she is friend to his family and why he agrees to have you. It is very difficult to be to work for him, you know."

"Oh, yes, I understand that and I am quite honored," I said to smooth the confusion on Felice's face. I suppose you could think of Amelia as my aunt, and claiming me as family probably was easier than trying to explain our real relationship.

"Ah, our first course," Felice said with the delivery of my paté and her escargot. The red wine she and Yves agreed upon came in a blue ceramic pitcher emblazoned with a rooster.

I had to give credit to Amelia for all the times she'd badgered me with terse remarks about how to behave when dining in France. I was more comfortable than I'd thought possible, falling into the rhythm of the meal with Felice, listening to her hints about apartment living in the city, inserting questions about things I'd seen. She laughed delightedly at my mistake in the little store and promised we would go to the bank as part of our errands. Dishes appeared and disappeared, smoothly and without folksy chatter like we would have back home. Each customer that entered was greeted by name, until two-thirds of the tables were filled; groups, couples, several single diners. I noted that, thinking it could be a good place for me when I was alone.

I couldn't believe that more than two hours had passed when we ordered coffee, Felice gently suggesting that I might wish to not have an after-dinner drink. It hadn't actually occurred to me, and I felt my shoulders droop once more, fatigue beginning to eclipse excitement. She did not insult me by insisting on paying. We split the bill as is the custom, no trying to work out who had what, leaving only the coins on the table since the tip was automatically included.

I made a mental map of the route as we returned to the apartment building and thanked Felice for all of her help, especially coming back to guide me through dinner. She smiled in farewell, explaining that she was on her way to meet up with friends at a trendier spot.

I held the rail as I climbed the stairs, hearing bits of music and voices coming from closed doors. I'd forgotten to leave a light on, but the dark did not seem eerie to me, despite being utterly alone in a strange place in a city thousands of miles from home. I stumbled toward the bedroom, a heaviness in my body; hardly a surprise considering the day. I peeled my clothes off, exchanging them for the rose-striped cotton nightgown I'd left on the foot of the bed. I slid underneath the sheets, pulled the thin coverlet on top of me, and used my last bit of strength to switch off the lamp on the bedside table. My final thought as sleep drew me into blackness was that I didn't know what time it was in North Carolina.

# Chapter Fourteen

The sound of church bells pulled me awake—an overlapping musical peal that confused me, uncertain of what I was hearing. Paris. I was in my apartment in Paris, and I was hearing church bells.

My eyes opened fully, light fragmenting into the small room through bright blue shutters that I'd latched closed, leaving the window open. I kicked off the bedclothes and turned my head to the travel clock that had been the going-away present from my family. Six-thirty. Why were bells ringing at six-thirty in the morning and it wasn't Sunday?

I swung off the bed still groggy, almost as if I was hung over, but that wasn't it. This was the jet lag I had been warned about. Felice, what time was she coming for me? The bells faded to quiet, and other sounds drifted in. Not for an hour yet. My stomach gurgled, not entirely sure if it wanted breakfast or dinner.

As my head cleared, I made my way into the tiny bathroom, trying to recall how long it was until the hot water would be turned off. Felice explained that her instructions from the man at the bank that had my account was for her to find me an apartment that was "adequate, inexpensive, and within easy walk to a Metro." Felice knew of Madame Blanchard's residence because a cousin of hers had lived on the top floor during her studies at the university. Allowing hot water for only a set numbers of hours was commonplace as was no elevator. Not that I cared about that—it wasn't as if I were planning to haul furniture upstairs.

I padded to the window, pulled back the shutters, and let in the morning sounds of delivery trucks and calls of *bonjour* between early risers. The smell of coffee drifted in from probably more than one apartment, and I made a note that one of my errands today would be to purchase the limited kitchen supplies that I would need. Previous tenants had left a mixed assortment of dishes and flatware that would serve my purpose. There was the expected corkscrew mixed in with a few standard utensils.

I downed a Coke and ate two cookies to quiet my stomach and considered what to wear. I was going to meet Jean-Claude Reillard, a famous photographer who would be my boss and quite probably change my life one way or the other. Mamma would insist I wear one of my Sunday dresses, and if I were being given a job as his secretary, that might be a good idea. Why would a photographer's apprentice show up in something like that, especially to meet a man whose studio was populated by models wearing fashions from some of the world's leading designers? Jeans and a simple cotton knit top was the sensible attire.

I emptied my backpack of all except my camera and the two precious lenses—used equipment that might bring more of a scoff than would my clothes, but I could take better pictures with it than could most people with the newest cameras on the shelf. Even though I was here to learn, and learn from one of the best, that didn't mean I was completely ignorant.

Felice knocked on the door and was smiling when I opened it. "Hallo, Maggie, I am some minutes early. You are ready, yes?"

"All set," I said, having decided that I might as well use idioms around Felice and extract a promise that no matter what language mistakes we made, we would tell each other straight up and learn.

"Breakfast, the Metro, and a stop at the Post near to the studio. It is too early for the bank," she said as we descended the stairs. "I did not bring the car today. I too live near a Metro and do not drive except when it is for to carry something special or when I go to visit my parents."

We were on the street and took off in the only direction that I hadn't explored yet. Felice waved one hand toward the vicinity of the fountain. "The cafés and restaurants at the main corner, they are always more cost than the ones to the side. I will show you."

She led me to the Café Michael with half a dozen round tables for two and metal chairs in front. Four old men sipped cups of coffee, their faces hidden behind newspapers. Two of them had pipes sitting in small white ashtrays, smoke tendrils rising, and one held a smoldering cigarette so close to the newspaper that I didn't know why it wasn't catching on fire.

We stepped inside, where there were not many more tables and a bar that ran three-fourths the length of the narrow room. There were no stools at the bar, merely a brass foot rail. Younger people had cigarettes clasped between fingers that punctuated the air as they talked. A thin man behind the bar was taking orders and calling them out to a girl who looked to be my age. She was standing at the end behind the bar, two large baskets nearby. One held a mountain of croissants, the other a pile of what looked to be bread cut diagonally into four-inch lengths.

"*Deux petit dejuener; café au lait*," Felice said to the man and looked at me. "Do you want juice of the orange?"

I shook my head, and the girl nodded acknowledgment of

the order for two breakfasts. Felice took the closest open table. It was already set with a plain white plate that held three white containers. One had some sort of dark red jelly—currant, I thought—one had orange marmalade, and one had a chunk of butter that was paler in color than the margarine I was used to. A separate white dish held paper-wrapped sugar cubes.

Felice smiled when the girl brought a tray with a basket of two croissants, four chunks of bread, and two cups of coffee already whitened with steamed milk. "For us, we do not have the big breakfast. I forgot to ask if you wanted tea instead of coffee."

"No, I like coffee. So, I just ask for breakfast and don't tell them what?"

Felice shrugged. "Oh, the large hotels might have a choice, but for most, it is simply croissants or bread, or like here, a bit of both. What to drink is the choice."

I filed away the information, suspecting that I would usually eat breakfast in my own apartment. Why pay extra money for something as simple as bread, butter, jelly, and coffee?

Felice, as I expected, launched into more advice. I didn't mind though because I wanted to learn as much as I could. I didn't quite understand why it was important to me to avoid looking like a tentative tourist—probably a reaction to Amelia's constant badgering for me to adapt as quickly as possible. Or perhaps it was a stirring sense that this could be a place for me to become whatever I wanted—to reach far beyond the small-town girl that took school and wedding photographs and definitely beyond being a duplicate of my sister.

My lessons continued as we navigated to the post office and the Metro—a means of transportation I could see as being useful after watching Paris traffic. I saw the logic behind the routes, and changing stations didn't look that difficult. I hid my surprise at the blatant sexuality and partial nudity of some of the ads that adorned the station walls and breathed shallowly at the smell of what seemed to be unwashed bodies where up-raised arms grasped the overhead rail in the crowded cars.

We emerged from the underground tunnel into busy streets, no hint of rain in the cloud-streaked blue sky. I could not linger as I wished—this was a day for business, not sightseeing, and I tried to adopt Felice's confident stride to Jean-Claude's studio. I almost wished I did understand fashion so I could better ap-preciate passing names that even I recognized—Chanel, Dior, Vuitton.

Our destination was an ordinary stone building, a glass dou-ble door with the street name and number and Jean-Claude's name the only adornment. The reception area was a decent size and manned by a stunningly beautiful raven-haired woman be-hind an uncluttered desk, telephone to her ear. An armless up-holstered burgundy sofa sat against the right-hand wall; opposite, against the left-hand wall, were two coordinated chairs in blue and burgundy swirled fabric. Fresh flowers in cobalt glass vases topped the black modernistic coffee table and small round table between the chairs. The floor was pale gray, marbled with darker gray, black, and cream. The white walls displayed Jean-Claude's work—a small gallery showcasing the talent that made him fa-mous. I could have easily spent an hour studying the enlarged photographs had Felice not steered me past the receptionist and through the black lacquered double doors.

"You will meet Madelaine later," Felice said and swept her hand grandly. "The heart of Jean-Claude's studio."

I puzzled at the interior size until Felice explained. "Jean-Claude made the purchase of the buildings on the right and left for more bigness. The shooting is for the center. Come, I show you."

Photography equipment and light sets dominated the room with a triple screen device in the center. It seemed to be hinged from behind since the two outer sections were slightly angled and no hinge apparatus was visible. It was obviously a back-drop setup; there were stools of different heights, other types of seats, and risers pushed to one side. Two metal tables held more supplies and three black canvas bags.

"The right side is for the dressing, a W.C., and a room for the storage." Felice went left across the concrete floor. Two doors were closed. "Jean-Claude's office," she said with a wink. "Large and very nice. The darkroom, also large." The third and fourth doors were open.

"Our office is not so large, and we have the small kitchen." I followed her into the room and thought it was just fine. It wasn't great; I would have liked a window, but it was func-tional. There were two desks, three glass-fronted bookshelves, and two four-drawer wooden filing cabinets. The white plaster walls were surprisingly devoid of photographs.

"That is for you," Felice said, pointing to the empty desk and dropping her handbag onto the larger desk cluttered with magazines, manila envelopes, and other correspondence. "You understand that much of what you work for Jean-Claude will be not at a desk."

"I wasn't expecting it to be," I said, and placed my purse and camera bag on the floor next to my chair. The telephone on her desk rang with that odd sound, more a *brrrng* noise than a regular ring.

She spoke rapidly, nodding and gesturing with her free hand before she made an annotation in the calendar sitting close to the telephone.

"An excellent shoot for Jean-Claude," she said with satisfac-tion. "For Rome in three weeks. Perhaps you will be ready to travel with him. I think it will be some too early, but it is hard to say."

I drew in a breath and tried not to look startled. Rome? Go with Jean-Claude to Rome? It wasn't important that I might not be considered ready yet. It was the casual assumption that at some point it would be expected for me to travel to somewhere like Rome. My God.

"*Eh bien*, Felice. You have the American girl?"

We both turned to the doorway. He was taller than I thought he would be, nearly six feet. Lanky, with oversized hands that hung loosely at his sides. Dark hair that curled over his ears and a longish face with penetrating brown eyes. Not quite handsome; a face that would hold your interest though. Late thirties would have been my guess even if I hadn't read everything I could about him. He studied me, although I didn't have the feeling of being undressed like they were always talking about in books and movies.

I stepped forward, my hand outstretched, as Felice came from behind the desk. "Pleased to meet you, sir. It's an honor."

He took my hand and held it without shaking it, his eyes moving from me to Felice and back to me. Then he dropped my hand and shrugged. "At least you are not ugly. Come with me to the table." He turned abruptly, and Felice shooed me out the door. I wasn't sure what kind of reception I had expected, and I didn't know what I was supposed to say. He was at one of the tables, four photographs spread in front of him. He crooked his finger and then passed his hand across them.

He had less of an accent than Felice, and his tone was hard to read. "Tell me what is wrong with these." He stood to one side, his palms pressed against the table.

Shit, it was like a pop quiz. Well, hell, so what? I looked at the photographs carefully, all seemingly perfect at first glance. The women were breathtaking, the poses all appearing to be from the same shoot. It was an outdoor setting, apparently the back of a mansion. A cobblestone terrace was bordered by a low stone wall, and huge urns of flowers flanked the wall of French doors that led inside. Wide expanses of green grass sloped gently toward a sculpted garden, but I focused on the women. Two of the shots showed all four women, and two featured only one of the four. Exquisite gowns and lavish jewelry, sultry looks and pouty lips.

Jean-Claude did not press me to speak. "The sun is reflecting too much from the doors in this one. There is a shadow across this one. The balance of the four women is not correct in this one." I hesitated, waited another minute or two, and looked at him. "And, I'm sorry, I don't see what is wrong with this one." I tapped the second photograph, a close-up of a gorgeous woman, her glistening lips pursed, her hand poised as if to blow a kiss, a collar of diamonds sparkling around her neck.

He straightened and moved his mouth upward, but not what I would call a smile. "It is Maggie, yes? A small name for Marguerite?"

Close enough. I nodded, wondering when he was going to tell me if I passed his test.

"Do you know why I agreed to have you come here? A man I respect asked for this. Have you studied at a school?"

"No, just with my uncle."

His mouth twitched. "Better no school than to study with idiots. I love women but have trouble with women who wish to be photographers. They too often whine when the weather is bad or the bags are heavy or they do not have the glamour." A shrug. "Maybe they become jealous of the beautiful women.

How is that with you, Maggie?"

I stared into his eyes without flinching. "I know you have your choice of apprentices, and I realize it is a privilege for me to be here. I work hard, and I don't whine. I am not pretty, but I do not mind that other women are. I will do whatever you need and not complain. I want to learn."

His gaze shifted to the photographs. "You are correct on the three." He touched the corner of the one that I could not find fault with. "This one was perfect—a spectacular moment. It is good that you did not make some silly remark to try and impress me." He put his hand on my shoulder and almost smiled again. "The photographs I saw from you have promise. You will not begin immediately to take pictures, but we will see if you are willing to learn. I must go. Tomorrow we shoot at the Opera. Felice will tell you what you are to do."

He withdrew his hand, gathered up the photographs, and left me standing alone. Felice clapped her hands enthusiastically; I didn't know what she had heard. "Bravo, Maggie. He is pleased with you, I can tell. Come to meet Madelaine and to learn about the habits of Jean-Claude. It will be a much busy day tomorrow, and it will be good for you not to make too many mistakes."

I was tempted to say that I wouldn't make any mistakes and realized that the odds were not in my favor. I knew nothing about how Jean-Claude worked other than to figure it was a hell of a lot different than Uncle Merl. I better listen to Felice and pay damn close attention to Jean-Claude. I was sure he was the type who would rather have you learn by watching than asking lots of questions.

I missed whatever Felice was chattering about and hoped it wasn't too important. I scooted behind her to meet the gorgeous Madelaine and thought that she must surely have been a model or maybe still was. All I really knew about this non-sense of skinny women being dressed up like dolls was that it involved a lot of rich people and lots of photographs. If being around this silly business was what it took to teach me what I wanted to learn, then I didn't mind, and it sure as hell wasn't going to bother me to be an ugly duckling among swans. Oh, yeah, that's right—Jean-Claude had said that at least I wasn't ugly—guess plain Jane would be more like it.

# Chapter Fifteen

I was not, in fact, ready to travel with Jean-Claude to Rome, although he was kind about it in his own way.

"Maggie, you have promise, but Rome is too soon. I must have someone who requires no instruction to my needs. You understand this and will not run back to America in a temper while I am gone?"

It was early evening, the last of the nearly naked models clothed and departed. Madelaine was gone, Felice was on the telephone as usual, and we were selecting equipment for Monday's shoot.

"It's okay, Jean-Claude. I don't mind. It's only a week." Felice had already probed my feelings, assuring me that even though he wouldn't tell me, Jean-Claude thought I was clever and quick and he was glad he had gotten to me before I developed too many bad habits.

"Good. I think perhaps Nice in March. You know the French Riviera?"

I shook my head, nestling the Nikon into a foam cutout in a black case that I could easily handle.

Jean-Claude checked his leather-banded Cartier Roadster watch and actually winked; an uncharacteristic gesture for him. "You will like Nice. The colors are not in Paris in March, but in the South, there will be many flowers. And now, little Maggie,

I must go. You finish here and tell Felice that she is to send two dozen red roses to Arianne—the Portuguese beauty today. She was excellent, don't you agree?"

"Yes, quite lovely, and, yes, I will finish here." So that was why the supple Arianne had required such close personal attention from Jean-Claude. Felice had mentioned that she thought his affair with the Russian ballerina was in the final stage. Was tonight his farewell to her or his beginning with Arianne? I didn't particularly care, and Felice would fill me in anyway. I had learned that one of her duties was to keep romantic conflicts from Jean-Claude's packed social schedule. She swore that once, before her time, he appeared at a gallery with a new Egyptian lover only to realize that one of the featured artists was a woman whom he had broken up with only two nights before. I was glad that all I had to worry about was Jean-Claude's lens preference.

Rather than being disappointed about Rome, I was glad for the break from the famous photographer. It had nothing to do with his demands—despite his quick, impatient bursts, he was nowhere near as bad as Amelia when she had a bug up her ass. I had been right about the fact that he wasn't the kind of man who would give me lessons exactly. I watched him carefully; listened when we prepared equipment; made mental notes of the lenses, film speed, lighting, and composition that he used. I marveled one day when he moved a model's foot back a fraction of an inch to capture the pose he wanted. I now understood what the word *perfectionist* meant, and I could open a magazine and recognize Jean-Claude's work with a glance.

Even with my admiration for him, though, I found the drama surrounding the models to be tiresome—like being around whiny, plastic mannequins. They fawned over Jean-Claude, of course, and treated everyone else with disdain. My

French had improved to the point that I recognized most of the snooty remarks directed toward me. Felice held her own with them, reminding me that their career expectations could reasonably be less than ten years before they became "old" in the eyes of a world where always younger women waited to take their place.

We had been relaxing over a bottle of red wine in the studio, a common way for us to review what Jean-Claude would need done for the next day or two.

"Too much, these bitches, they think it will not happen to them," she said, as she tapped a page in the desk calendar. "The fame disappears like the candle burning, and what do you think they have done with their money?"

"Invested wisely," I replied with a grin.

Felice snorted in an unsophisticated way—was my Americanism rubbing off? "Ah, yes, Maggie, this is, what word—*payback?*—that makes me to laugh. Age thirty and off they go. Oh, yes, a few it is not so, but for most—the work it is no more. The money it is gone because they have no brains in their pretty little heads." She momentarily held her glass to the light and watched the burgundy hues, then looked at me. "You do not seem to get the anger with them. You have the great patience."

I shrugged. "Not really. Or maybe. To me, they're no different from the clothes they wear. They're living sculptures. I have no interest in them."

"Ah, yes, Jean-Claude thinks you care more for the animals, the flowers, the buildings, and not so much the people. Is this true?"

"People are too complicated," I said and refilled both our glasses.

I thought about that conversation later while I planned my

days with the boss gone. I didn't mind photographing people as background or coincidental to a scene, but I much preferred taking early morning shots of Parisian streets, gargoyle gutter spouts, or the fabulous bridges spanning the Seine any day of the week over photographing all the Ariannas in the world.

I divided my personal photography into two categories. I went around and took pictures of the famous sites and sent two or three in my short letters to Mamma and Jed. My real photography, the stuff I let Jean-Claude critique, was of the animals, flowers, and buildings that Felice teased me about. I was not the least bit ashamed to admit that I was in love with Paris. Not the crowds, the ridiculous trappings of the celebrity world that Jean-Claude moved in, and certainly not the noise of politics. The magnificence of the city itself though was something else. I had yet to see the brilliant colors of Paris in the spring, but even when autumn faded into cold winter and I hurried, bundled in coat, scarf, hat, and gloves, there was the beauty of hundreds of years of architecture that I was only beginning to be able to identify. There were the bare branches of trees playing against dove gray skies in the thinly populated Jardin des Tuileries, the barges and other vessels that plowed the brownish waters of the Seine.

I equally embraced my small apartment in all its sparseness, cherishing early mornings when I sat with my coffee and croissants, watching the street stir for the day, listening to bells peal. There were countless neighborhoods similar to the one where I lived, each with its church or churches, small cafés, bakeries, butcher shops, pastry shops, little grocery stores, and apartment buildings lining streets often barely wide enough to park vehicles on one side and squeeze traffic by. I spent my first month exploring every foot of the four streets around me, learning the names of the proprietors in these family businesses, which were much like what we had at home. They laughingly corrected my French, praised me as I got better, and accepted that I was a student of photography. If they hated Americans, I neither heard nor saw it. That display seemed to be reserved for those who found voice in newspapers and on television.

These people of the neighborhood allowed me to snap away at anything I found of interest, and I obligingly took photos as they wished of their family, taking little time to do more than make sure the shot was in focus. My attention was drawn to images such as a big woven basket with long thin baguettes of bread protruding like sticks, or the trio of cats that claimed the front steps and lobby of Madame Blanchard's building. One sunny afternoon I waited patiently until they were arrayed as I hoped; the black and white one lapped delicately from the bowl of milk Madame set out twice a day on the top step. The solid black one sat, tail curled around one front paw, the other paw lifted as he licked it, and the gray one on the bottom step extended her paws as she arched her back in a languid stretch. I clicked rapidly, knowing the fleeting moment was exactly what I wanted. I almost held my breath when I developed it and saw the depth of black and grays, the curve of the cats' tongues, the contrast of their fur against the stone, their fluid movement projecting from the photograph.

"Bravo, little Maggie," Jean-Claude later said. "It is the eye that you must have. Technique can be taught and how to frame the models, but not the instinct of the eye to see the precise shot."

This was how I passed my first three months in Paris — working, learning, exploring. I was comfortable in my routine and taken utterly by surprise during one of our late afternoons when Felice nonchalantly asked if I had been to bed with Jean-Claude yet. I couldn't stop the look of surprise that caused her to laugh as it always did when my naiveté spilled out.

"But, Maggie, Jean-Claude always seduces his assistants. You have not had the invitation to his apartment for a special lesson in darkroom procedures?"

"No, and I don't think I'm his type. He's been seeing the Greek model he used in the layout for the Louvre piece."

"Jean-Claude is quite for the world in the definition of his type, although he does like more the models. The story is that he only became a photographer because all photographers can ask women to take off the clothes. And voila, he discovered he had the true talent with the camera. It was a good coincidence, do you not think?"

I was curious now but didn't feel particularly disappointed that Jean-Claude had not turned his attention to me.

"So, you mean you and he were, well, an item?"

Felice laughed. "Item? What a funny word for *l'affaire*. It was for, oh, I do not remember exactly, two months, perhaps three, until a beautiful blonde from Denmark caught his eye. For all of his skills, which are considerable, he is not to give your heart to. He tried to marry three times, but always the new one makes his eye to wander. Oh, I did not think to ask, you are not still as the virgin, are you?"

"Well, no," I said, still unaccustomed to the casual French approach to such personal questions. "But I mean, there was just the one guy back home."

"Only one and you have almost nineteen years? Hmmm, we shall have to make for you the introduction to some older men; they are really much better than an inexperienced boy. Oh, unless, of course, would you perhaps prefer the women? I do not think that of you, but it could be so."

I nearly choked before I could answer. "Uh, no thanks. And it's okay, Felice; I'm doing fine just the way I am."

She laughed, amused once again at my lack of sophistication, and I was grateful when she changed the subject.

Despite her warning, the night Jean-Claude asked me to bring some rolls of film by his apartment I was unprepared for his relaxed, debonair manner. By the time I'd had two glasses of wine and felt his body pressed against mine in his private darkroom, I didn't care that he was only fulfilling what he viewed as his obligation as a true Frenchman.

I didn't mind admitting that until the night with Jean-Claude, I didn't know how incredible sex could be. His hands and mouth were so certain, so much like when I'd watched his artistry in photographs, that I had no hint of embarrassment. It was more like I recognized that, for the moment, I was his work of art. It was my body that he was attuned to, me that he kissed and stroked in his passion for the female form. And even as he held me afterwards and I was gripped in the lingering sensation from multiple orgasms, I kept Felice's words close to the conscious part of my brain. Jean-Claude was as skilled as she claimed and under no circumstances the kind of man to fall in love with.

It was easy to adopt Felice's advice, to enjoy Jean-Claude for a brief few weeks before a Eurasian dancer drew his affection away. We amicably reverted from lovers to mentor and protégé, an arrangement that we both knew was more practical. Felice uncharacteristically never asked me the direct question about him. She probably figured it out on her own and decided we had already discussed what we needed to.

My reward for both my good work and my easy acceptance of his inevitable attraction to a new woman was to accompany him to Nice. March had not yet brought full spring to Paris, but Felice assured me the south of France would be alive with color.

"Jean-Claude will be at the Negresco, of course, as to be near the beautiful women, but I think you will want to be not so close at the end of the day, no? I have for you a so precious room at the Fleur Rose, only fifteen minutes to walk. Madame Duvall you will like much." Felice had given me a thick folder with schedules and other instructions surrounding the logistics of taking the train, ensuring Jean-Claude's equipment arrived safely, and being prepared to deal with whatever crisis popped up.

As it turned out, Felice's skill at making arrangements and what turned out to be the Negresco's flawless attention to its guests meant that I really had nothing out of the ordinary to deal with. Even though I had read a little bit about the famous hotel, I was unprepared for its pink, white, and gold opulence. It did, indeed, look for all the world like an incredibly decorated wedding cake with its landmark domes. The massive lobby with marble floors, rotunda of gold leaf, stained glass, paintings, statues, and ornate furniture might as well have been part of the Louvre or the Palace of Versailles. I forced myself not to gape, knowing that was the reaction that Jean-Claude expected. I instantly understood Felice's real motive in not booking me into the sumptuous hotel—I wanted to enjoy my first visit to the Riviera, not be intimidated by a liveried staff.

I turned the boss over to people who wouldn't let him run out of champagne and strolled along the Promenade Anglais. The wide, palm-lined avenue stretched as far as I could see with other hotels, restaurants, and shops catering to most needs. Across the avenue was the Mediterranean Sea, or actually the bay, sparkling vivid blue-green in the late afternoon sun. I'd glimpsed startling colors of sky and sea from the train windows as we moved south, but I wanted to wait until the next morning to explore the water's edge.

I found the cross street for the Fleur Rose, and Madame Duvall welcomed me with a smile of crooked teeth and a pronounced overbite. The lobby and breakfast room were airy with a large vase of fresh flowers in each room. The wooden floor was a light color; framed prints of what could be the city and surrounding countryside decorated the white-washed walls. I accepted her traditional offer to show me the room she'd selected on the second floor with a balcony overlooking the street. I assured her it was perfect and nodded to her instructions about when breakfast was served. The room was similar to my apartment, but with a sun-washed feel. My duffel bag, which had been among the luggage whisked away by the car service that met us at the train station, was propped against a white painted armoire. The iron frame of the bed was also painted white, and the rose-patterned comforter and plump crisply white pillows looked new. Two armchairs, one with a faded floral pattern and one in pink, green, and yellow striped fabric, were angled toward each other with a round wooden table between them. Ah, another vase of mixed flowers. A short table with a straight-backed chair near the armoire held the telephone and a floral motif porcelain lamp with a rose-pink shade. I quickly unloaded the contents of the duffle bag, retreated into the small bathroom, and took a fast shower. I slipped into a clean pair of jeans and a dark green long-sleeved cotton top with a scooped neck. I wore no jewelry. I hurried, not wanting to miss the nightly transformation of the marketplace, which Felice had told me about.

The *vielle ville*, the old village center, was nearby, a wide expanse of cobblestone bound on three sides by buildings, many that were restaurants. Stalls of various sizes filled the space. Huge arrays of fresh flowers were on display in the open-air setting along with fresh produce, cheeses, and other products.

Serious shoppers had finished for the day, and the stall owners were beginning the process of packing up. I purchased a can of chilled Coke and walked slowly, savoring scents of herbs, spices, and roasting meats. I moved toward one end, staying out of the way, watching the orchestrated movements that occurred here nearly every evening as the merchants withdrew and the restaurants took over. Waiters and restaurant proprietors flowed outside, carrying umbrellas, tables, chairs, linens, and large grills. They efficiently converted the market into al fresco dining. Strings of tiny electric lights were strung, and I salivated at the serving trolleys that were rolled to the entrance of the restaurants. Whole fish, mounds of mussels, clams, oysters, shrimp, and lobsters were attractively arranged on beds of cracked ice.

Felice had explained the almost daily practice. "Oh, yes, even in the winter when it is not too much cold, they bring the small heaters and you eat out of the doors. You will see for yourself, this."

I no longer wanted to eat at six in the evening, just as I no longer thought of dinner as supper. I planned to seek out my habitual smaller, less expensive bistros for other evenings, but tonight I would splurge in this special setting, starting with the thick fish soup that was supposed to be a regional specialty. I was adept with dining alone now, comfortably familiar with making my way through a multi-course dinner.

The next morning, the memory of succulent grilled shrimp lingered when I awoke early enough to grab my camera and head to the beach, which had not yet begun to fill with bikini-clad beauties and overly clothed English tourists. It was the post-dawn stillness that I loved when few other sounds competed with gulls shrieking through pink-tinged clouds in the blue sky, and waves washed quietly onto the beach, which was oddly made of rounded stones instead of sand. I snapped a roll of film as the noises of the city coming to life increased. Then I returned to the hotel for warm brioche and café au lait before I set off to attend to Jean-Claude.

The schedule was as fast-paced as all of Jean-Claude's shoots. The three days in Nice blurred into continuous motion around the Negresco, at the beach, and up to the ruins of the old chateau with its breathtaking view. I kept up, though, having learned Jean-Claude's needs so well that I could have his array of cameras set up quickly, anticipating when he would want a different camera or another lens. I knew to have Perrier handy and the extra pack of cigarettes. The models and their wardrobe were someone else's responsibility, thank God. Once Jean-Claude was returned to the care of the Negresco staff, I enjoyed my private snatches of Nice, filled with a desire to return on my own someday. When the three days ended, I relaxed on the train ride to Paris, fixed by the window, watching the scenes change. The car had emptied at the last stop. Jean-Claude was, of course, in first class.

I still couldn't put my feelings into the right words for Mamma to understand or, Lord knows, anyone else in the family. Even Jed talked about returning to Duck as soon his Army time was up. 'Course, I guessed that Fort Riley, Kansas, wasn't much more exciting than what we'd grown up in, and there wasn't a guarantee that he'd get something better while in the Army. Not like Paris and now Nice. I could see why the painters were drawn to this part of France, with its rich colors and scented air that would inspire anyone to want to pick up a brush or a camera.

But it wasn't just here that drew me. There were so many places that I knew Jean-Claude and others routinely traveled to. I didn't care that people spoke strange languages or that I might accidentally order a plate of cow's intestines. If I could learn French, I could pack a dictionary and get by on not too many sentences in other languages as well. I wasn't sure yet if I meant to travel the whole world, but why not? Pyramids, herds of animals in Africa, the Amazon; hell, the Grand Canyon and the Black Hills of my own country, for that matter. Why would I trade that to marry Billy Ray, or anyone like him? Sure, some people in Duck went on vacations, but a yearly vacation wasn't enough for me, not after this.

Would Amelia understand? I mean, she's the one who sent me here—no, it was a lot more than that. She had done everything to make it happen. But why had she turned away from this? I didn't know how much money she had, but I thought it was plenty to still travel, even though she was old. Maybe that was it, maybe she needed a companion to go with her. That would make sense, that she wanted someone who could help her out, and I could do that now. I could talk more with Felice and learn how she made all the arrangements that she did—hell, it couldn't be that difficult. Was it possible for me to combine photography with accompanying Amelia? I wouldn't want to depend on her for money, even if that was what she had planned. I bet I could do both, though. Jean-Claude didn't work for only one magazine; he was in such demand that he could pick and choose his projects. Not that I expected to be famous like him, but there were bound to be plenty of travel magazines and stuff that would buy photographs. I smiled at nothing in particular. I was an apprentice to an amazing photographer, and unless I did something really stupid, he was going to teach me everything that I needed to know to make it on my own.

My stomach interrupted, preferring thoughts of *steak frites* rather than future plans. I had yet to tire of the thinly sliced sirloin pan-seared in butter with a warm red center, juices seeping into the fries that were called *pommes frites,* not French fries. And what was *steak frites* without drinking red wine? Hell, maybe I'd have two glasses—I had certainly worked hard enough on this trip to deserve it.

# Chapter Sixteen

It was hard to believe that a year had passed. Wasn't it really only a few weeks ago that I'd sat on the terrace with Amelia, enjoying a bottle of white Cotes du Rhone, a plate of cheeses and fancy crackers, a crock of paté, and Belgian chocolates? Except this time, I had provided the paté and crackers from the store around the corner of my apartment in Paris.

"What on earth gave you the idea that I wanted to travel again?" Amelia's hair, still the mass of white waves that hung below her shoulders, was clasped loosely at the nape of her neck. I saw no slowing in her motions, no hesitancy in tart responses.

"I've been there now," I said, unable to quell my excitement. "You saw the photos—Majorca last month and Venice before that. I understand, and I've learned how to take care of airplane tickets, trains, hotels. You won't have to do a thing, but tell me where you want to go next." I paused as she cocked her head. "Jean-Claude knows that I want to go off for special trips, and I can pay my own way. Well, maybe not as far away as Africa yet, but for sure all around Europe."

Amelia shook her head firmly, her eyes closing the subject as they so often had when I had asked about her past. "Maggie, I truly don't know where you got this notion. I'm not surprised that you have succeeded, nor that you are anxious to see more of the world—that was the point, after all. My time with that is done, however, and I never intended it as otherwise. Does your family know you aren't home to stay?"

My surge of enthusiasm fluttered from me as if it were a napkin blown from the table by the wind. So much for my theory of why Amelia sent me to Paris. "I only got home two days ago," I reminded her. "I haven't really talked to anyone yet."

Amelia refilled our glasses and didn't comment for a moment. It was unusually overcast, the sky a high ceiling of pale gray, the water pewter with intermittent whitecaps. The ever-present wind of the Outer Banks was moderate, and I was comfortable in jeans and an old high school sweatshirt. My hair, which Felice had insisted be cut into a fringed cap, stayed in place, and the truth is that the style did fit my face.

"So, France, Spain, Italy, all in one year. Quite the debut to Europe. Tell me more about Jean-Claude. Is he as brilliant as they say? There's no question that your photographs have improved. Has he acknowledged that?"

"He enjoys saying that he was glad he got to me in time, that I will owe my future to him." I hesitated. "He is remarkable. Before I left, he said that if I came back, he would have me ready to go out on my own within another year, that I had more to learn but would be good enough to earn a living."

Amelia gave me a look that I couldn't read. "And all of that at the bare age of twenty. Is it what you had hoped for?"

"It's so different from here," I said slowly. "I don't really know anyone, not any women anyway, who left here and went off other than to college or to follow their husbands. I mean, some of the guys go into the military and their wives go with them, but this is not the same thing." I stared out at a V-formation of brown pelicans, gliding across our field of vision. "Jed's coming back in January. Daddy's got him a job lined up at the marina repairing boat engines. Jed said he's had enough of being gone."

Amelia flicked her eyes to the pelicans and then I felt her stare, regaining my attention. It was a look I remembered from the times when she demanded that I speak French for an hour, when she insisted that I master eating a peach with a knife and a fork.

"Maggie, if you bothered to read newspapers and magazines rather than just looked at photographs, you would see that women are involved in many new things that have nothing to do with being a housewife. I don't mean that silly nonsense of burning brassieres. I'm talking about women joining the military like men always have, going into corporations, starting their own businesses. There are interesting as well as some ridiculous predictions for the 1980s. My point, however, is that you have already made the decision to do something different. Although your mother and I have not had a single conversation since you left, I think she alone in your family probably understands that you aren't likely to be satisfied being the star photographer for the local newspaper or working for your uncle, much less suddenly marrying a man like that Billy person. I'm not saying that you need to map out the rest of your life, but you do need to recognize that you *are* different."

I couldn't hold her gaze and shifted in my chair. "More like you? Is that why you were in France so long?"

She shook her head sharply. "What happened in my life is not the point. My reasons for returning and choosing to stay alone are my own. You have to be honest about your own reasons, no matter what those are."

I set my wineglass down, reached for a cracker, snapped it into four pieces, and tossed them to the edge of the terrace where a sparrow eagerly pecked them. I drew in a breath and felt a half-smile forming. "It's not enough here. Maybe someday, but not now."

"Then that should settle it,' Amelia said with a shrug. "Practically speaking, how are you for money?"

Maybe having this conversation would make it easier to explain to Mamma—I hadn't bought a round-trip ticket because I wasn't quite sure of the date to return, but I had paid Madame Blanchard a month's rent in advance. The next important shoot wasn't for nearly six weeks. Did I want to stay away for over a month? "I'm okay," I said quickly. "Jean-Claude is paying me for real, and he gives me all the film I want. It's not like I need fancy clothes or a car; I've got one of those plain scooters. I like wandering the city, and that doesn't cost much."

She waved her hand toward the water; the ocean that I would cross again. "I'll take care of your return ticket as soon as you tell me when you want to go. Now that we have that subject settled, tell me about Venice. I don't remember why I never visited there."

I could only stay another half-hour since Mamma had asked me to go by Ruth Ann's and pick up some fabric, but I promised Amelia I would bring other photos tomorrow and come for lunch.

Ruth Ann was alone in the front yard when I arrived. She wore jeans, an oversized blue shirt with the sleeves rolled up to her elbows, and tennis shoes. Her hair was pulled into a ponytail, and she wore a frown that didn't disappear when she saw me. A scraggly yellow cat darted behind three old tires piled together at the end of the empty driveway, which was splotched with oil stains. The place was months past when it should have been painted, the first step of the front stoop had a corner cracked off, and one of the posts of the hurricane fence was listing badly.

Ruth Ann put her hands on her hips as I swung out of Mamma's old Dodge. "Nothing's really changed. Bet it's not like the castles you've been seeing, is it?"

What was that about?

"Mamma tell you she wanted me to pick up that cloth?" I asked instead. "She said it was real pretty, and she's going to make up a dress for Katy."

Ruth Ann dropped her hands and jerked her head. "Bag's in the kitchen. Kids keep growing out of everything. I got no time for keeping up with them and sewing, too."

We went through the side door where the walk-thru space was cramped with an old washing machine, a basket of wet clothes on top, a jumble of dirty ones on the floor, and the water heater in one corner. Fishing gear and stacked plastic buckets were jammed into the remaining space.

Keeping up with the kids apparently didn't include spending too much time cleaning house. Mamma's insistent scrubbing wasn't a trait that Ruth Ann had inherited, but it looked more chaotic than I remembered.

"Got tea if you want some. Guess they don't drink tea in France, do they?"

Sweet tea in a tall glass of ice was something that I missed. "Hot tea," I said, "They don't use ice a whole lot either. I need to get on back though."

Ruth Ann narrowed her eyes and reached for a brown grocery bag with folds of a pink print fabric sticking from the top. "Got this on a good sale because it was the end of a bolt, but, of course, it's not some kind of high Paris fashion."

I looked hard at my sister, her face pinched in disapproval, and stuck my fingers into my pockets. I felt a knot of anger in my chest. "Look, you got some kind of bug up your butt? If you do, I'd just as soon get it done with."

She tossed her head. "That mouth of yours sure hasn't got any better, but wouldn't expect it to what with you traipsing around with a bunch of foreigners. You know Mamma thinks you're going to church and all, but I bet you haven't set foot near one since the day you left. Carrying on with Frenchmen like you are."

I shoved my fingers in deeper. "I'm not carrying on with anybody, Ruth Ann. I work damn hard, and I'm studying. It's not like I'm living some life of luxury, sitting around eating chocolates all day."

"Who knows what kind of life you're living these days? It's bare gone on four o'clock, and you think I don't smell booze on your breath? You been with Crazy Miz Hatcher all afternoon, haven't you?"

"There's no cause to call her that." My face was as flushed as Ruth Ann's was drained.

She thrust the bag at me. "That old lady might not be crazy like some folks, but everybody knows she's the one put these ideas into your head. Just because you think you're too good for the rest of us now, don't mean we can't see things plain as the nose on your face."

I snatched the bag to keep from slapping her, my breath ragged. "You're full of shit."

"That mouth again." Her voice was tight. "Let me tell you something else, Missy. You think bringing little bottles of perfume makes you all high and mighty, then you're the one don't know crap. In case you hadn't heard, Billy Ray's got married and has a kid on the way. He didn't waste time waiting on you. So you want to come back and settle down like a Christian woman ought to, you better plan on another husband."

"Whoever got Billy Ray is welcome to him," I snapped and

backed out of the house, glaring, wanting to say something hurtful without saying the string of curses that came to mind. I yanked the car door open, threw the bag inside, and gunned the engine, resenting a quiver in my hands. What in the hell was wrong with Ruth Ann? I thought to the dinner we'd had last night when I gave out presents. Everybody but Jed was there, and it'd been hard for me to think of what to get what with so many to buy for. Little colored tins of fruit candy for all the kids, a different flavor for each one; small bottles of cologne for the women plus a porcelain thimble for Mamma with the Eiffel Tower painted on it; an Italian leather wallet for Daddy; and knit watch caps for the men. Come to think of it, Ruth Ann hadn't said much the whole while they were there, but everybody had thanked me, and it wasn't like I'd been carrying on about stuff—not too much anyway. Why wouldn't I show some of my photographs? It wasn't as if I'd laid out that many. The truth is that Ruth Ann had always criticized me. Didn't like me taking after my brothers with learning how to use my hands to fix things or surf fish, said I was too gawky. Oh, the hell with her.

I slipped into the house, not ready to let go of my anger, and Mamma called for me to join her in the kitchen. She was at the table, a folded dishtowel underneath the dented colander filled with wet-skinned potatoes. She poised with the old paring knife in her hand, glanced at the bag I clutched, and inclined her head. "You can put that by my chair in the living room and then get us both a glass of tea, if you don't mind. Did you have a nice talk with Miss Amelia? Is she well?"

"Yes, ma'am," I muttered, realizing that my shoulders were tight. I tried to shake them loose, got the ice tea, and sat when Mamma toed out one of the chairs.

She wasn't even looking at the knife as she peeled the

potatoes over a plastic bowl, the skins falling in curls. "You and Ruth Ann have words?"

I almost choked as I swallowed the icy, sweet tea. I bit my lip without answering.

"It's been a hard year on them," she said quietly. "Prices up a lot on everyday things. Kids been sick more than usual. Kenny got fired 'bout six months ago; took him awhile to find work. Pay isn't quite as much as before, but looks like it's going okay for him now."

"None of that's my fault," I said more sullenly than I intended.

Mamma picked up another potato, her rhythm uninterrupted. "Ruth Ann's got a sharp tongue and a mind of how things should be. Likes to tell people how to behave; always has."

I took another sip, stopping to take a good look at Mamma, seeing wrinkles etched into her face, her hands reddened. I should have brought her some nice skin lotion.

"Let me finish those," I said. "You take a break."

She curved her mouth and shook her head. "This isn't much of a chore. You sit and tell me what's on your mind. You didn't bring but one little suitcase and a duffle bag home. Not a lot of stuff if you plan on staying."

I held her steady gaze, softer than Amelia's, but no less probing as she continued. "It's not hard to see changes in you, child. Don't imagine you can tell, probably come to you a little at a time."

"I wasn't bragging and putting on airs, Mamma."

"Didn't say you were. It's all over your face, happy with what you're doing, almost wiggling like a puppy to get back to it. Hair's different—looks nice though. I thought maybe you'd get this out of your system, but that's not how it is, is it?"

I hesitated, feeling a mixture of relief at having her ask the question and still simmering from my sister's unfair attack. "Why can't everybody be glad for me? I'm making a living, I'm learning more than I ever would in some college, and I'm not doing anything wrong. Jed's been gone longer than me, and nobody's fussing about him." Well, maybe the fling with Jean-Claude might be considered a little bit shocking, but it hadn't lasted and he was the only one. Ruth Ann had no call making that nasty crack about Frenchmen, not when she knew that I knew she had no business wearing white at her wedding. I hadn't forgotten that she'd been with Neal Watkins before he dumped her and she married Kenny on the rebound.

Mamma shrugged. "It's the way things are, Maggie. Jed went into the Army—lots of men do and he'll be home for good right after Christmas. What you're doing is different— not saying that should matter, but it's not what folks are used to. 'Specially not with you going off to a place like France on your own." She gave me a silencing look, stopped her task, and drank some tea. "I know people with money send their children to Europe on trips and off to college. Some go clear across the country and don't come back. That's not us, child. We start working early in our lives and keep doing it with no time or money to spare. We mostly have work, family, and church. Far as I can recall, other than Aunt Daisy, there hasn't been anyone in the family, your daddy's or mine, has gone beyond Elizabeth City, except for the wars."

I ran fingers through my hair, the flush starting again. "I don't know why I want this. All I know is that I do—that I'm good at what I'm doing and that if I think about staying here and marrying Billy Ray or someone like him, I can't hardly breathe."

Mamma's hand extended, not in a touch, but as a signal for

me to stop. "Maggie, I'm not saying you're wrong. You take a deep breath and listen for a minute."

I was trembling again, even though I clasped my hands together on top of the table and gulped twice to try and keep it from showing. The unwavering look on Mamma's face was calming, and I inhaled slowly.

"I don't truly know why you feel this way, not more now than before, but I do see it in you, and I'm not making judgment like Ruth Ann. I don't see that this is doing you harm, and anybody willing to be honest likes your pictures. If you can make a living at that and you're dead set against getting married, there's no call to say being a photographer is any less respectable than being a schoolteacher. Are you hearing me?"

I nodded once, relaxing my fingers, idly noticing that she'd peeled all the potatoes.

"I think we've had enough carrying on, then. I just need you to promise me three things in all of this. First, let everyone keep thinking you're in school—not that I imagine anyone will ask. Second, you don't get so stubborn that you feel like you can't come home if you run into trouble of some kind. You hear that?"

"Yes, ma'am." I hoped the third promise wasn't about sex—I didn't want to have that conversation with my mother.

"I've seen in magazines about French soap, that it's something real special. Will you send me a couple of bars come Christmas time?"

I pushed up from the table, threw my arms around her shoulders, and pressed my lips to her hair. "Mamma, I'll send you a whole box of soap."

She patted my forearm once and gave it a light pinch. "That's all right, two or three bars will be plenty. For now, you run up to the store and get a bag of flour. Don't be dawdling, though, because I want to do a peach cobbler. That'll make sure your daddy stays in a good mood."

"Yes, ma'am," I said, lifting the colander of potatoes and moving it to the sink for her.

I covered my laughter until I was out of the house, then it spilled into the afternoon air. No more pretending and the hell with Ruth Ann's jealousy or narrow-mindedness or whatever was eating at her. I was returning to Paris and having peach cobbler.

# Chapter Seventeen

"A lot of people come to places famous for skiing to, you know, ski." His name was George from Minneapolis, and he professed only mild disappointment when he learned that the lithe models had departed earlier that day.

"I gave it an honest try," I said, glancing as a burning log tilted sideways in the massive stone fireplace, glowing embers falling from it. "My brain refuses to accept that I can make it safely down the side of a mountain on two thin sticks. Doesn't matter that little kids are doing it."

"You don't have a heavy drawl, but do I detect some South in your voice?" He moved his elbow comfortably onto the back of the long black leather couch. The après-ski crowd had not descended in force, and we had this side of the fireplace sitting area to ourselves. It was only yesterday afternoon that Jean-Claude had the quartet of beauties arrayed in the same spot, their sultry looks competing with the flames. Before that they'd been photographing absurdly expensive ski ensembles brightly colored against the snowy background of the slope. One French, one Italian, one Austrian, one German—a cross-section of Alpine loveliness.

I breathed in cinnamon from hot spiced red wine that I'd discovered our first day on location. Glühwein was too sweet to enjoy in quantity, but in that first half-hour when I came in from the frigid temperatures, it was perfect. "The Outer Banks in North Carolina. That's probably why my brain doesn't connect to skiing."

"I've seen pictures of the beaches in travel magazines—good fishing, I understand. You're here working? With the models? I mean, I was watching at the ski lift yesterday, and you were the one who seemed to be doing the real work. The guy, the one with all the cameras, it was like you knew exactly what he wanted. He kept taking photographs, and you were swapping out stuff for him without talking to one another."

George had approached me earlier when I stood at the bar, asked if he could buy me a drink, and suggested we grab the prime fireside spot.

"I'm Jean-Claude's assistant," I explained. I hadn't noticed George in the small crowds that inevitably collected around a shoot when it was in a public setting.

George had a large glass of beer and took a swallow as he looked at me curiously. "French, he sounded like. You a student? Like on some kind of exchange program?"

I shook my head. "I'm in my second year as an apprentice. Jean-Claude went home; I'm staying for another day or two on a small assignment. There's a lady in Paris who wants some photographs of the Matterhorn."

Did it sound casual? Was I masking the fact that this was my first actual independent assignment? December had been a moment of triumph for me when Jean-Claude did a special newspaper holiday shoot. His focus, as always, was on the models daringly draped in little more than furs, and he hadn't wanted to bother with an intricately carved crèche that was the centerpiece of a display window. I captured the manger scene beautifully, and he included two of my photographs in the spread. Smaller than his, of course, and on the second page of the article, but there with my name. Yvonne, one of Felice's friends, was a travel agent, and she was gathering photographs for a new brochure. She heard about the upcoming trip to Zermatt and asked if I would take the job that was well beneath the dignity of my famous boss. Jean-Claude had laughingly patted my shoulder when I tentatively mentioned it to him. "A beginning for you, little Maggie, a beginning. I will tell Felice to pay for the hotel for two days more so you can concentrate—it will be my present to you."

George's brown eyes registered approval. "That's cool, an international photographer. Now I understand why you're here and not skiing."

"You're with a group?" I countered, hiding my surprise at the label. International photographer? Me? Well, I was in Switzerland taking pictures for a client in Paris. Yvonne was a client, even if she was taking advantage of the fact that my travel expenses were covered by someone else. I guess that did make me an international photographer.

"My uncle and aunt were stationed in Aviano, Italy, back when he was in the Air Force. They did like a quick weekend here once and always wanted to come back when they could afford it. He's done pretty well in the furniture business in Minneapolis. We usually ski Wyoming or Idaho, but my aunt put this together and brought my youngest sister and me along. They don't have kids."

George launched into a discussion about Minneapolis, so very American in his expansiveness. I knew his nationality before he opened his mouth. The buzz cut of light brown hair was part of it, and he had the husky openness that slender European men lacked. He didn't have the ruddy Germanic face I would have also recognized or sheer Nordic blondness. His solid build would soften if he wasn't careful, but it sounded as if he enjoyed a lot of outdoor activity.

"Hey, listen," he said, after draining his beer, "we're leaving tomorrow. How about having dinner with me? My sister is going out with a group she met from Colorado, and I figure my aunt and uncle should have one romantic night together."

"Uh," I faltered. "I, uh . . ."

"Oh, sorry, I wasn't thinking. You probably have plans," he said quickly. "A pretty girl like you."

That comment was even more surprising. "No, it's just that, I, well, I have to get up early—I'll be doing a sunrise shot." Not that sunrise was all that early in February. The truth is that other than the fling with Jean-Claude and dinner with Felice and some of her friends occasionally, I hardly ever went out.

He swung his glass in a semi-arc. "Not to worry, we can call it quits whenever you're ready. I haven't had that melty cheese dish everyone talks about, and there's a place nearby that's supposed to be good."

I laughed at his description. "Do you mean fondue or raclette?" At his size, I guessed either would do as a first course, but then he probably would enjoy a hefty serving of steak and potatoes.

"Either, both," he grinned. "This is my first trip to Europe. You can show me the ropes."

"Okay," I said and agreed to meet him in an hour. I returned to my room and laid everything out for the morning. Then I changed into a fresh pair of black jeans and the beautiful black and teal sweater Felice had given me for Christmas. She had insisted I pack it, and I was feeling a little guilty about not having worn it yet. I wasn't completely ignorant about fashion; it was more that I didn't particularly care what I wore. My loose-fitting, nondescript wardrobe served me well. Or maybe seeing the price tags of high fashion had made me want to stay away from all that craziness. I mean, why any woman was willing to spend a thousand dollars on an evening bag was beyond me. On the other hand, if George from Minneapolis wanted to believe I was more sophisticated than I was, the least I could do was look the part.

I didn't regret my decision about dining with George. He was one of those talkative guys who enthusiastically explained the joys of snowmobiling and ice fishing as we worked our way through raclette, the bubbling cheese that dripped from the tabletop grill and was delicious with thin slices of toasted bread. I suggested an entrée of steak with herbed butter and rosti, the Swiss savory potato pancake-like dish. And, of course, we finished the meal with apple strudel. I let him drink most of the wine, which he insisted I select, and pretended not to understand his hint at a one-night stand. Despite Ruth Ann's accusations, I had no interest in short-term sex. It had nothing to do with moral judgment—I simply couldn't see why you would want to become intimate with someone you barely knew. I didn't share Felice's philosophy of "sex, why not let it be just for fun sometimes?" I did accept a kiss on the cheek, took his card, and wished him a good trip home.

I was properly bundled when I left the lodge the next morning, the groomed streets of Zermatt almost empty. The village was a postcard image of stone and timber-framed buildings, smoke curling from chimneys. The Matterhorn rose in magnificent quiet; I had maybe another two hours until crowds converged onto the ski lifts to either expertly swoosh or awkwardly careen down the slopes. I'd spoken at length with the head bartender about the layout of the area, and he told me which hiking path would give me the vantage point I desired. The pale gray predawn light was adequate as I made my way in air so crisp that I wondered if there was a spot on earth where it would be cleaner. Although I was not overly enamored of the cold, my boots were sturdy, and I was adequately protected. The weather was predicted to be clear again today, and the colors I hoped for wouldn't linger for long as the sun rose higher. I was in position, camera at the ready, when gradients of pinks tinged in gold transfused across the expanse of a sky becoming a soft blue. Stillness enveloped me, the sound of the shutter audible in the silence. I clicked frame after frame—I would select the exact photos later. I captured the famous peak centered in my viewfinder, shots of the adjoining mountains, the village for good measure, figures not distinguishable as individual people, a handful of electrical vehicles moving in the town that banned gas-powered cars and trucks. I was done in less than an hour, ready to return to hot coffee and the robust breakfast that the lodge provided.

I readjusted the wool cap to sit lower on my ears, slipped heavier gloves over the light wool ones that left my fingertips exposed, and began the mile trek to the lodge. I puffed air to see my breath, and as much as I appreciated the grandeur of the Alps, I was glad Jean-Claude's next shoot was scheduled for somewhere in the Greek islands.

# Chapter Eighteen

I was accustomed to train travel by now and passed the time on the return trip to Paris thinking of what it was like being on my own without needy models and an exasperatingly talented boss, the easy way in which George from Minneapolis accepted my explanation of my livelihood. An international photographer. No raised eyebrows, no "why would you want to do that?" Maybe I should have had sex with him out of pure gratitude. I silently laughed at the thought of ever becoming that French in my outlook.

This was, however, one of those times when Jean-Claude's sexual exploits provided me with some needed breathing room since he was taking a few extra days off to be with the Austrian model. I would have the darkroom to myself, and I arrived at the studio even earlier than usual the next morning, anxious to develop the photographs. I selected the ones that I thought would please Yvonne and tried to disguise my nervousness when I delivered them. She studied the spread, complimented me on capturing the exact look she wanted, handed me an envelope of francs with a small bonus in addition to my fee, and promised to recommend me to others provided I gave her first priority for future work. I kept my composure until I was far enough down the street where she wouldn't see the silly grin and my lips pressed to the envelope. My first assignment and probably more to follow. Okay, a travel brochure wasn't *Paris Match*, but hey, everyone started somewhere.

I hurried into the office to tell Felice that I was taking her to lunch to celebrate and stopped at the look on her face. She held a piece of paper.

"Maggie, it is bad news from your brother. The one, Jed. He is called to say that your *maman* is very ill, and you should come home."

"He called? While I was out? Mamma's sick?" I stared, hoping it was a mistake. There's no way Jed would call long-distance to Paris if he wasn't worried.

"There is room on an airplane tonight if you wish," she said quietly. "Your brother, you want me to make the call for you?"

I nodded, moving slowly to the chair by her desk as she lifted the receiver and spoke rapidly to an operator. It was what, a little after 6:00 a.m. at home?

"Hello." There was a faint buzzing on the line.

"Jed? It's Maggie."

"Mamma's real bad sick," he said with no introduction. "Got pneumonia. She's in the hospital in Nags Head. Doc Rundle says it's not good, not at all."

"Pneumonia? That's what happens to old people," I said faintly.

I heard the fear in his voice. "There some kind of complication. She got the flu, and you know Mamma. Didn't stop her none—she kept doing for everyone. Ruth Ann came over yesterday and found her out cold in the backyard. Guess she was hanging laundry and must have passed out. Nobody knows how long she was like that, but it's not good. Doc says she's real weak, and he thinks it'd be best if everyone is around."

"I'm taking a flight tonight," I said hurriedly. "Can you come get me? I'll call as soon as I know when I'll be landing."

"Yeah. Yeah, I can do that. Best you call the hospital and give them the information. We're kind of taking turns, and you might not get anyone at home."

I copied the number, read it back to him to make sure I had it, and replaced the receiver as if it were fragile. Felice's tone was gentle. "I will make the ticket. You go to do the suitcase, and I come to take you to the airport. This is okay, yes? It is more easy for me to do this."

I nodded, squeezing my eyes shut for a moment. "Yes, yes, thank you. I'll go to the bank and get money."

Felice snapped her fingers. "There is no worry of money. Jean-Claude, he does not pay you enough. This is for him to do. He is gone for five days more anyway. I will make the ticket for one week, and maybe it will be better than your brother thinks, yes? Maybe in a few days, it will be okay."

I swallowed hard, nodding rather than speaking, touched at her generosity, latching onto her optimism. Did pneumonia kill people? I mean, old people, sure, but someone Mamma's age? It just couldn't be right.

I repeated that thought for fifteen hours, giving it greater strength as I snatched catnaps on the long flight to New York. I stumbled through customs and caught the shorter flight to Norfolk with little time to spare.

I smiled in reflex when I saw Jed waiting at the gate. Although taller than Daddy by a head, he shared Daddy's build and hair color and texture. He briefly clasped my upper arm in greeting, never mind that others around us were welcoming passengers with hugs and excited shrills.

"Got the truck close by," he said and reached for my backpack. "Thought we'd go straight to the hospital, unless you need to go to the house first."

A shower would have been nice, but I didn't like Jed's low-pitched tone. "Is Daddy there?"

He shrugged. "He's at work. Nothing he can do, and he don't like sitting around. You know that about him."

It didn't take long to be on our way, and I saw that Jed had a pillow on my seat. "Thought you might want to sleep a little. You want to stop to eat?"

"I'm not hungry," I said, my eyes stinging from fatigue. It was obvious that Jed didn't want to talk so I bunched the pillow into as comfortable a position as I could find and drifted into a light sleep. I didn't have time for jet lag.

I understood Jed's somber mood as soon as we entered the waiting room. Sheila, my sister-in-law, rose from conversation with Mrs. McGinty and Mrs. Watkins. My God, the church ladies. I imagined there was a ham at home, casseroles, pies, and maybe a cake or two. They might as well have told me when the funeral was going to be. The church ladies did not turn out in force unless it was serious.

"You came," Mrs. Watkins said with half a smile. "The pastor is in with her. You want Jed to take you down?"

I nodded dumbly, silently acknowledging the ladies who squeezed my hands quickly before they drew Sheila back into their hushed conversation.

It was early afternoon, but only weak light came into the room through the gray-clouded sky. Mamma's bed was close to the doorway, the bed by the window empty. Her eyes were closed, her face unsettling in its lack of color, a tube fixed to her arm. Brother Gibson stood, a Bible in his left hand.

"I was reading her favorite Psalms," he said, a practiced handshake ready. "She's mostly sleeping, but rouses sometimes. She'll be pleased to see you. Jed, why don't we go get Maggie a Coke?"

I stood at the side of the bed, not wanting to sit yet. Where was the doctor? Why wasn't she in a different part of the hospital, more being done for her?

Her free hand was palm up on top of the blanket, rough skin pale, veins showing blue, her chest barely rising. I laid my fingers on her cheek, and she stirred. Her eyes fluttered open, and her mouth moved, but no words came out.

I leaned in slightly as she focused, not wanting to startle her by getting my face too close. Her smile was faint and her voice raspy. "Maggie?"

"Yes, Mamma, I'm here."

"Water."

I looked at the glass on the stand, crushed ice floating in water, a paper straw bent. I brought it to her lips, telling her not to strain to sit higher. She took only two sips and pulled back into the pillows.

"Tired."

"I know, Mamma, it's okay. I'll sit right here, and you can sleep for a bit. Later, I can get you something to eat. Something to get your strength back."

"Tired." Her eyes closed as if they were too heavy to stay open.

I sank onto the chair, pulling a tissue from the box on the stand, and stabbed at the welling tears. Blubbering wasn't going to help anything.

I straightened when I heard footsteps in the hallway and Jed returned with two cans of Coke.

"Pastor went on to see some other folks," he said quietly, leaning against the foot of the bed. "Mrs. McGinty is going to come in when we're ready, read some more scripture to her."

Scripture? How about a damn doctor instead? I set my jaw, the can of Coke chilling my hand, and motioned him to the other side of the room even though there was no sign that

Mamma could hear us. "Isn't there a better hospital, one with other treatment?"

Jed's voice was barely above a whisper. "Maggie, that's got nothing to do with it. The intensive care is full here, and she and Daddy don't want to be going off up somewhere else after Doc Rundle said he doubted it would matter. Like I told you, Mamma got the flu first and wouldn't hardly slow down. She kept saying she'd be all right, didn't need to waste time on the doctor. A little chicken soup and hot tea and she'd be fine. Turns out she's got low blood pressure that nobody knew about and now advanced pneumonia that isn't responding to antibiotics. It's a mess of stuff, and Doc said it happens more than folks realize. All we can do is make her comfortable. He's letting us keep round-the-clock watch, so you know, so she's not alone. That's why I called you."

I sucked in a shuddering breath to keep from lashing out at him. It wasn't his fault. I was able to envision Mamma doing exactly as he said. It was her way; it always had been. But this? This wasn't right. Anger mixed with the jet lag I wanted to ignore, and I suddenly felt as if I couldn't stand. I gripped the edge of the windowsill with my free hand.

Jed's eyes widened. "Maggie, you okay?"

I let go of the sill and rubbed my forehead. "Look, I'm the one who doesn't have a job, no kids to look after. It'd be best if I take the night time. Let's go to the house, so I can get cleaned up and catch a few hours sleep, then I'll come back."

"Sure, there's a ton of food there, too. Bet you haven't eaten for a while. I'll go get Mrs. McGinty, and we'll head out."

I studied Mamma's prone body, a woman who cared for a husband, four children, her church, her neighbors. A woman who darned socks to make them last longer, hemmed and re-hemmed clothes to pass from child to child, always took bones from the grocery store to make a richer broth when meals could be no more than soup and cornbread. A woman who scrubbed floors on her hands and knees, swearing that not having much money didn't keep you from having a clean house. And this was her reward? Her end?

"We sure do thank you for this," Jed said politely, entering with the plump woman. "Ruth Ann will be here shortly."

"Y'all go on now," she replied, her face grave. "Maggie, you look like you're about to topple over. I guess it was a real long plane ride for you."

"Yes, ma'am," I said automatically and stepped aside so she could take the chair. We left, stopping briefly in the waiting room to explain the plan to Sheila and Mrs. Watkins.

"I'm going to go to the marina, do a little work, and bring Daddy to the hospital after quitting time," Jed said, as we crossed from Nags Head into Kill Devil Hills. "Shouldn't be nobody else at the house, so you can rest awhile. No reason for you not to use Mamma's car. Keys are on the peg by the door."

I nodded and shifted in the seat to really look at him. "How are you doing in all this? Before Mamma got sick I mean. The job and all? You didn't like staying in the Army?"

He didn't turn his head. "Too many rules, couldn't say I liked Fort Riley either. Wasn't sure where I might wind up next, and there's not many Army posts on the ocean. Saved up some money though. Got the truck, was able to put a down payment on the old Fuller house. You remember it?"

I was surprised. "Sure, but why a house?"

"Got to live somewhere. I stayed with Mamma and Daddy for awhile. 'Sides, Susie Grayling and I been seeing each other since I got back. Mamma told me she was a good match and no reason to be dragging my feet about it."

"I didn't know about you and Susie. Mamma didn't say anything in her letters."

"Well, I hadn't asked her yet and she might say no—it wouldn't be like Mamma to spread word of something that's not sure."

"No, it wouldn't. So the job, it's good for you?"

"It's honest work, and the truth is that Daddy's slowing down even though he won't admit it. I think he's got a touch of arthritis—makes it harder for him to handle the tools. Can't get in the tight spots like he used to could. Plus, old Mr. Morton's been the head guy for a long time, and I keep going like I am there's nothing's to say I can't work my way up." He swiveled his head and briefly caught my gaze. "You had enough of being gone? You coming home to stay?"

Well, it didn't take long for that question to come up. "I like what I'm doing, Jed. I had a lady just paid me for some of my photographs. Do you know I was in Switzerland a few days ago? The Alps, Jed, I was in the Alps."

"We got mountains in North Carolina, but I guess those are bigger," he said with an indifference that stung me.

He hauled my bag into the house and put it into my room, which still looked like it had since the day I left. He asked if I wanted him to call later to wake me up. I told him I'd be fine, and as he drove away, I realized how empty the house was. I stood in the living room, no sounds from the kitchen, no ra-dio, the television dark. Not that Mamma ever watched TV by herself, but she did like music from the clock radio that we all pitched in to buy her one Christmas. I crossed the room and turned it on, catching a quick weather spot promising a high tomorrow of forty-seven and partly cloudy.

My stomach urged me toward the kitchen, and as I had expected, two pies covered in plastic wrap, a chocolate cake with a glass cover over it, a foil-covered plate that probably had cookies, and a platter of fried chicken were on the table along with several notes. Those would explain what had been put into the refrigerator—probably a tuna noodle casserole, macaroni and cheese, maybe some potato salad, a ham.

I didn't want to take time to cook anything so I picked the potato salad. I devoured some of that, a piece of chicken, and a slice of pecan pie, my hunger kicking in with the first bite. I washed up the dishes, wondering if Ruth Ann or the church ladies had been tidying things—I knew that Daddy wasn't likely to have been looking after himself. I took an almost full beer in with me to the bathroom and finished it while I waited for the shower to get hot. Things became a little fuzzy after that, and I barely managed to crawl under the covers before my body shut everything out.

I had left the light on in the bathroom, knowing I would be disoriented if I awoke in the dark. As it was, I drowsily opened my eyes to the silent house and hoped I hadn't slept too long. No, it was a little after seven o'clock. I dressed quickly and drove to the hospital unimpeded by traffic. The Outer Banks was not a winter destination, and people were mostly at home on a weeknight.

Jed and Daddy were standing outside Mamma's room when I walked down the hallway, visitors trickling out from other rooms. Daddy's shoulders were slumped, and his clothes looked like he'd been rolling around on the floor. The look of resignation on his face held not so much as a trace of joy in seeing me. I had the fleeting, disturbing sense that my presence held no special meaning for him. "Jed said you were figuring on staying here at night."

"Yes, sir, I thought it would be easier for me to."

"Mind you don't tire her out if she wakes up. Hard for her

to talk about much."

"I won't," I said, wondering if I should just give him a hug.

He coughed, rubbing a hand across his mouth, a hand with scarred knuckles and embedded grease, which no amount of scrubbing could completely wash away. "Then we'll be going. You be sure and get the nurse, anything goes wrong. Don't press that damn buzzer waitin' for her to come check."

"I'll be careful about that," I said, as Jed patted my shoulder in parting. My father hadn't touched me.

"We'll come by in the morning before work," Jed said, Daddy steps ahead of him. "Sheila comes early sometimes, though, so if she does and you want to go, that's okay, too." He glanced at Daddy's back, then at me. "He's taking it hard, Maggie. He's not talking to anyone, not really."

"Yeah, okay," I said, trying not to let my disappointment show. "I'll probably be here when you come by."

"Call if something happens. Oh, Susie brought some magazines and a couple of books. They're in the stand." He hurried after Daddy, and I slipped into the room, a pole lamp behind the chair providing light for reading. Mamma's breathing was as ragged as before, and she didn't move. I sighed and opened the drawer to see what Susie had brought.

My vigil was only two nights. Any hopes I had for a miracle disappeared in the early afternoon while Ruth Ann was by Mamma's side and Brother Gibson was making his visitation rounds. It was Sheila who took charge, making the calls outside the family, starting the ritual of more food flowing in, alerting the funeral home.

Jed called me, though, his voice bleak, and I held the telephone too tightly to my ear, wishing I'd had a real conversation with Mamma. "You'll be okay, Maggie. You're a strong girl," she'd whispered in the middle of the night when she woke for not much longer than five minutes. She had tried to squeeze my hand, and I had gently pressed her fingers, wanting to keep her with me. If I had known those would be our last words, I would have told her that I loved her. I knew the house would fill with visitors soon so I called Amelia while I had some privacy.

"I truly am saddened," she said, her voice as gentle as I had ever heard it. "Your mother was very special. You will have a great deal to do the next few days. Come see me when you're ready, and we'll talk."

It wasn't that I had a lot to do as much as it was that a lot happened around me. There was no question that Daddy didn't want to make decisions and that Ruth Ann was speaking for the immediate family. Cousins whom I barely recalled showed up in groups. Between them, neighbors, and Mamma's church friends, condolences washed over us the day of the viewing and the funeral. I tired of it within hours, aware of awkward pauses in conversation with people whom I no longer had anything in common with. I smiled sadly, constantly, and handed people off to Ruth Ann or one of my brothers. I lost count of the times when I was asked if I was home now, done with traveling. I murmured a polite lie: "I have to see how things are," when in my head, I was wondering how soon could I leave? What was it that I was supposed to do to help? There couldn't be that many tasks to see to.

It wasn't as if Daddy was giving me the time of day anyway. Keeping close to Uncle Merlin, who seemed to know what to say to people, he acted as if I were some vaguely remembered distant relative.

It was the day after the funeral when I got up early as always. I had my coffee and surveyed the stack of dishes that would need to be returned to friends and neighbors. Would they come by, or was I supposed to deliver them? There was food enough to last through the week, including extra eggs, bacon, and cans of biscuits. I had a pan of biscuits baking in the oven, thankful for someone's thoughtfulness. I'd never picked up on how to make Mamma's from scratch. Ruth Ann could, but I didn't have the right touch, they both told me. Probably the same reason I couldn't make a decent pie crust.

I heard Daddy in the bathroom and pulled out the cast iron frying pan, seasoned from years of use. I knew the rhythm—fry up the bacon, drain the grease into the aluminum container next to the stove, cook the scrambled eggs in the residual fat, not too much salt, no pepper. I set the tub of margarine and a jar of homemade grape jelly on the table while the bacon sizzled. The biscuits were a minute or two from the right golden brown color. I turned the oven off to make sure they stayed warm.

I heard a chair scrape and poured Daddy a cup of coffee before I turned to see him at the table. "I'm getting ready to do the eggs," I said, as he looked around the kitchen.

His face was expressionless as though he wasn't sure of where he was. He blinked when I put the plate of biscuits and the coffee in front of him. "You girls go through your mamma's things. Get what you want and don't be fighting over anything. Sheila is a good woman, too. I reckon she ought to have the sewing stuff."

I stepped back toward the stove. Ruth Ann had said she'd be over after she got the kids to school.

"Okay, Daddy. Is there something special you want to keep?"

He split a biscuit. "Plenty about her around the house. You pay attention to those eggs— can't stand 'em cooked hard."

"I remember," I said and checked the flame under the pan.

He dropped back into silence until I set the plate of bacon and eggs down in front of him. I sat in my regular chair, leaving Mamma's empty, and took a biscuit and two slices of bacon.

It was not a comfortable silence. "Jed said he was doing well at the job," I ventured.

Daddy grunted. "He's got a lot to learn yet. Least he's working." He ran a piece of biscuit around the plate, wiping it almost clean. He pushed it to one side, drained his cup, and shoved the chair back. "Ruth Ann be here soon. Maybe she can teach you to make real biscuits, she got time."

I stared at him without responding, and he strode from the room. What in the hell kind of comment was that? I tossed the rest of my food into the trash, thinking balefully that Mamma would chide me for waste. I managed to get most of my third cup of coffee down before Ruth Ann stomped into the room, shedding an outer coat.

"You got coffee? I need another cup. Good, you got Daddy's breakfast for him. You do his eggs the way he likes them?"

"Yeah, but seems he doesn't like canned biscuits."

She dumped two spoons of sugar into her cup, her gaze raking the table. "Well, he may have to get used to that. You never had the touch for doing them right. Don't figure you'll do better even if I try to teach you again. Speaking of food, I imagine there's enough leftovers for a few days. You shouldn't need to go shopping until later."

I inhaled deeply. "Shopping for what?"

She blew across the coffee cup. "Groceries, of course."

My stomach clutched, knowing what she was hinting at, and I spoke as calmly as I could. "You want me to stock up the refrigerator before I go?"

Her eyes narrowed briefly. "Go where?"

"To my apartment, to my job. The one in Paris."

She set her cup down and ran a hand across her forehead. "Maggie, Mamma is hardly cold yet, and you want to start that nonsense? You're not married; you got no kids. Who do you think ought to do for Daddy? Nobody's saying you can't have a job, but I was talking with Mrs. McGinty at the viewing and she knows of two openings. I'm sure you can fit one of them, or there'll be something else come up. I heard that the girl in the front office at the marina was leaving next month to have her baby. What with Jed working there now, they might be willing to have you, too."

What she was saying was bad enough. The matter-of-fact way she was saying it was worse.

"Ruth Ann, I don't know where this crap is coming from. I am more than willing to do whatever needs to be done around here to help out, but if you or Daddy or anyone else thinks I'm moving back in here to cook his meals and wash his clothes, you've got another thing coming."

"It so happens that everybody expects you to do exactly that," she snapped. "How can you stand there and not know that? You think Daddy's not expecting you to do your family duty?"

I set the cup down so hard that I might have cracked it. "Family duty, my butt. Daddy's not a cripple. He can damn well learn to scramble eggs and run a washing machine."

"I can't say that I'm surprised at you disrespecting Mamma and Daddy like this…"

"Stop it, Ruth Ann," I interrupted. "This is ridiculous. I'll stay as long as until next week, but then I've got to get back. I was planning to talk to Daddy about this tonight anyway. So you let me know what it is that we need to do about Mamma's things and let's get started."

Her hands went to her hips. "Well, Missy, if your time is

so precious, don't let me stand in your way. I can handle everything here just fine without you. You tell me what you want of Mamma's, and I'll leave it out. 'Course maybe nothing she had is good enough for you."

God, I wanted to slap her! "You want to talk about disrespect? You think Mamma would be proud of how you're behaving? She wouldn't expect me to give everything up."

Ruth Ann narrowed her eyes, and her nostrils flared. "What would you know about what she really thought? You only paid attention to what you wanted to hear. She kept thinking that just a little bit longer, and you'd come to your senses, find a good man, and settle down. That's what she wanted from you, not more postcards."

I couldn't listen to this, couldn't take another second of her mean-heartedness. "You make sure I get the locket that I gave her, and I don't care what you do with the rest. You take it all."

I swept past her to get my purse and coat, clenching my hands to keep from striking her, and missed whatever other hateful thing she said as I slammed out the front door. Dear God, what was happening to us? I drove, my hands clinging to the steering wheel to keep them from shaking. I headed to Amelia's, the only person I could think to turn to. I would call the travel agent from there and see if she could change my ticket. If I was lucky, maybe I could be on my way to Paris tomorrow.

# Chapter Nineteen

I was wondering how ten years could have possibly melted away and almost missed Felice's affectionate chiding.

"Only a lunch for a birthday is not much celebration," Felice said, her English now charmingly accented instead of mangled with the mixed phrasing of our early years together. "And for you, Jean-Claude sends a kiss."

"I got the bouquet," I laughed. "I thought two dozen roses were reserved for his lovers."

Felice moved her glass so the waiter could refill it. "You are special to him in a way that they are not. You look well, by the way, but I could take you shopping after we are done here."

I smiled appreciatively as the waiter brought the first course of mussels steamed in cracked pepper and white wine for me, escargot for Felice. "I give you credit for trying, but you look terrific enough for both of us. Come on, I dressed up in khakis and a nice blouse for you, and I'm wearing real shoes instead of boots. What more can you ask for?"

"American Hush Puppies?" She raised her eyebrows and held a snail above the shell until the garlic butter stopped dripping, then delicately popped it into her mouth.

She was the quintessential Frenchwoman who showed up in every crowd scene of Paris: perfectly coiffed with impeccable makeup and flawless nails manicured in rosy-beige; attired in a cap-sleeved dress of sapphire linen with deceptively simple lines that fit her precisely; accessorized with a print silk scarf of the same shade of blue draped exactly as it should be with a silver clasp that matched her earrings.

"Comfortable, Felice, Hush Puppies are truly comfortable. So, you're finally going to leave Jean-Claude. How is he going to manage without you?"

"My replacement is well trained, and she had her affair with him almost a year ago. My Philippe is much regarded by the senior partners as an architect, and it is time for us to begin a family." She smiled with a trace of her old teasing way. "Who knows exactly when that is to be, but now we try. Very often."

"Well, congratulations in advance, in case I'm not around when you succeed." I tipped my glass against hers.

"Thank you, and speaking of success, where is it, your next assignment?"

"South again. Saint Paul de Vence."

The waiter delivered our entrées of herb roasted chicken for Felice and pork medallions with apple brandy glaze for me. He exchanged my wineglass and brought a half pitcher of the restaurant's superb table red, one of those that came from a vineyard that had no desire to distribute its wares beyond the borders of France. He emptied the half pitcher of white wine into Felice's glass and acknowledged her signal for another one.

"Ah, yes," she said, "The fortifications of Saint Paul de Vence are wonderful, I hear. The village is a bother to get to, although many tourists find their way."

"I'll go early while most of them are still in bed. Lots of shots of the medieval stonework, the art embedded in the walls, scenic views of the Alps to one side, the Mediterranean to the other. I don't need to include people."

"I cannot argue the quality of your photographs, Maggie, even without human subjects."

"I don't need the drama of people," I said with a shrug. "Never have cared for that."

We ate in silence for a few minutes, appreciating the perfection of the food, the leisure of a lunch that would take us almost two hours, a dining room filled with the choreography of a staff that would seem inefficient to tourists looking for a quick meal. The Café Rive was one of my favorite restaurants, not of the popular Parisian brasserie type and not on the tour guide circuit. It was third generation with a wise great-grandparent who had snagged a location with a view of the Seine but far enough from the major attractions so that most of the patrons were either regular customers or brought in as friends of a regular. One of my clients had brought me, and I had introduced Felice.

"You said you had some news, though," she reminded me. "I do not suppose it could be of a romance?"

I swallowed the last bite of pork and laughed. "Not hardly. No, after I finish this shoot, I am returning to America for a while. I have a wonderful assignment to photograph some of the national parks. The daughter of one of my clients is working on her master's degree in literature, and she has an apartment in New York. We're going to do a sublet swap for six months. I'll actually be on the road for weeks at a time so it doesn't really matter where I live."

Felice lifted her glass in a toast. "*Ah bon.* You have been here for almost ten years, Maggie. Is this six months to be a test for you? To see what it will be like to live again in America?"

Her insight was keen as always. "I never could fool you. Just think, I left when I was eighteen, learned more than I ever expected to, and instead of running home frightened, I found a career, have traveled throughout Europe, and have a nice nest egg built up." I paused and felt my face soften. "And while I would have had none of it without Amelia and my mother, and Jean-Claude does get credit professionally, you are the one who made the difference here, the one who showed me the ropes."

She inclined her head in acknowledgment. "Maggie, my friend, it has been a pleasure. You were so young, so eager, and wanted so much not to fail. Never did you complain. I have no younger sister, and for me, you have been that."

We were both nearing that poignant moment when women burst into tears of affection, and I didn't want to see her make-up damaged or have us dip into a maudlin mess. "Well, here's to birthdays and new beginnings," I said cheerfully to break the mood. "The future of motherhood for you, a tentative and perhaps triumphant return to the United States for me. And on that, I think it's time for dessert and coffee."

Three days later, my arrangements were completed, and I was in the dinged, yet highly serviceable Peugeot that I had acquired my fourth year in France. The little black sedan was all I needed to crisscross my way from country to country on this side of the Iron Curtain. While I was cautious to remain in the slow movers' lane when faced with prowling Porches and BMWs on the German autobahns or sleek Ferraris on the Italian autostradas, I was fully able to get from point to point and easily navigate narrow village streets and country roads. My duffle bag, backpack, camera bag, and photographer's vest continued to be the mainstays of my travel. My client list was respectable, and the offer from the magazine for the national parks piece had come about through word of mouth as work so often did in the freelance world.

I had been offered a staff position with a publication and had considered it for several hours. An adequate, reliable paycheck;

some decent benefits; an agreement that I could accept other assignments if there were no conflicts—it was an opportunity that, if nothing else, validated my talent. Then I spun the scene further out. A steady job first, then why not a nicer apartment, furniture to fill it, maybe a better car—before I knew it, I was likely to find myself encumbered, unable to say, "Of course," when a call came in apologizing for short notice but asking if I could pop over to the Isle of Skye to provide photography support for a new birding guide.

It was Amelia, as always, who'd shrugged away the need for a conventional job. "Go right ahead if you think you need that, but having an unpredictable flow of income as a freelance person is easy enough to handle. Go sit with your bank and tell them what you are doing. They have trustworthy investment advice for people who have that up-and-down sort of revenue business."

That had been the time I was briefly home for Daddy's funeral. The stroke that felled him was virtually instantaneous, and I felt like a distant relation who had shown up. My family and I were quietly polite, quickly running out of anything to talk about. Few people attended the service. There were new nieces and nephews, vague questions as to how I was doing. I relieved Jed of chauffeuring duty by renting a car, and Ruth Ann's resentment didn't erupt this time, perhaps because I signed a piece of paper relinquishing claim to any part of Daddy's estate. There were rumors that the house would bring a good price because of the location. I didn't care about the money, and I sure as hell didn't want to hang around waiting for the outcome or be tracked down to go through the hassles of long-distance documentation. They could have it all.

It was Amelia's friendship that I truly valued. She was the one who wanted descriptions of the Pyrenees at dawn and of a regatta in Greece. "I spent most of my time in cities," she said in explanation, when I showed her selected additions to my portfolio.

After that, my visits diminished, none of my siblings urging me to come for the holidays or for any other event for that matter. I routinely sent Amelia postcards with scribbled notes, especially when some of the postcards featured my photographs—I wasn't a snob about clients. Calendars and travel brochures paid, too.

So here I was in the south of France again, less than a week before my flight to New York. I planned to finish the shoot early, spend the night in Nice, return to Paris to develop and deliver the photographs, meet the girl who was to take the apartment, introduce her around, receive instructions from her as to whom I was supposed to meet in New York, have a farewell lunch with Felice, and entrust the car to Madame Blanchard's favorite nephew.

The weather was fragrantly warm rather than sticky, and I cranked open both windows of the Peugeot, relishing the scent of the countryside. The road was comfortably wide with gentle curves. I was no more than a mile or so from Cagnes-sur-Mer when I spotted a new, silver Peugeot pulled as far off the road as the hill allowed. I slowed and looked at a slender woman sitting in the front seat, her head resting on the steering wheel, her face scrunched. A Hertz sticker identified the car as a rental. I wasn't in a hurry, and since there were no other vehicles approaching, I pulled in front of her. She opened the door and swung long, lean legs out of the car.

"Model" might as well have been stamped on her forehead. She unfolded her remaining height. With her wavy, glossy dark hair and liquid brown eyes, she could have been European, but she had that familiar American look.

"Uh, pardon. Je . . ."

"It's okay," I said quickly. "What seems to be the problem?"

"Oh thank God! You're American? I have no idea. I was driving and it was fine and then it started to slow and, pfft, just like that, it quits. Pfft. It's making starty noises, but that's it."

I groaned inwardly. *Starty noises.*

"This is a good car, but that sounds as if you have a fuel problem. May I try?"

"Oh God, yes, have at it. I mean, I was thinking I'm close to town so someone ought to be coming by, but then, how was I going to explain? I left my phrase book back at the hotel."

At least she had a pleasant voice, not the squeaky or breathy type. She stepped aside as I slid in, pumped the pedal a couple of times in case she'd flooded the engine, and turned the key. It was cranking but not firing. I slid back out and popped the hood, looking for an obvious leak along the fuel line. But the engine compartment was as clean as one would expect from a new car. It was one of those quirky failures that just occur.

"I really appreciate you stopping," she was saying. "I was not looking forward to walking to the village in these shoes."

Her ensemble was designed for lunching, not strolling; a crimson mid-calf wraparound skirt in a fluid fabric that revealed the long legs with certain movements, a not-quite-off-the-shoulder crimson top with yellow flecks, matching enamel jewelry, and a pair of crimson and muted yellow-striped espadrilles.

I closed the hood. "I'm pretty sure it's the fuel pump, and I'm afraid that's not something we can take care of here. Are you in a hurry?"

The shake of her head sent her dangling earrings into motion. "Not really. I mean I have a party to attend this evening.

If you could possibly give me a ride back into town and help me manage a telephone, I'll call the hotel or, I guess, the rental place. I've got friends staying near Saint Paul de Vence. If there's going to be a long delay, they can come get me."

Well, at least she wasn't going all hysterical. "You're staying in Nice? At the Negresco?"

She brushed her hair behind her right ear and laughed unexpectedly. "Oh God, am I that stereotypical?" She flipped a hand at my expression. "It doesn't matter. Yes to both questions."

"Okay, look. We'll run back into town and make the call. I assume you booked the car through the concierge at the hotel. He'll make the necessary connections, and I'll give you a ride back—I'm staying not far from there. Take the keys with you, though; they'll bring another set."

She eyed the car for a moment. "It's okay to just leave it here?"

"Sure, it's far enough off the road."

She gathered the inevitable straw purse that matched her outfit and settled into the passenger seat of my Peugeot without disdain. She glanced into the backseat.

"That looks like a photographer's bag. Is that what you're doing here? Oh, by the way, I'm Christina Donnetti."

"Maggie Stewart," I said and started the car. "Yes, I'm a photographer. As a matter of fact, I was up in Saint Paul de Vence this morning."

"Isn't it a lovely village with the walls and everything? A girlfriend of mine and her husband are renting a villa near there, and I was with them last night."

I did a U-turn, a little surprised that no other vehicles had appeared as yet. It only took twenty minutes or so to explain the situation to the owner of the closest *Bar-Tabac* and explain again to the concierge at the Negresco, who assured me that

Mademoiselle Donnetti need not worry about a thing.

"You're all set," I said and took the chilled Coke Christina had bought while I was on the telephone. She was drinking mineral water, of course.

I offered to roll up the windows, but she was unexpectedly not concerned about her hair becoming windblown. "Listen, would you like to come to the party tonight? The yacht company is throwing it, and so far, they've done everything with a lot of style."

Ah, that was it. "You're here on product promotion?"

"You do know your stuff, don't you? Yes, me and three others—I'm the brunette. Two blondes and a redhead. All tall, looking lovely in bikinis and filmy evening wear, standing at the railing, martini in hand—the perfect complement to a ninety-foot yacht—not the largest one they make, but it will do in a pinch." She was grinning this time.

"They brought you in from the States?" There were usually plenty of regional aspiring, or aging, models/actresses who did these gigs. Those starting out to become noticed or those in the beauty world who were looking at careers ending at age thirty were prime for this type of work. I guessed Christina had a couple of years to go yet.

"Yes and no," she said lightly. "I have a cousin who works for the company, and he thought it would make a nice swan song for me. I only agreed because Sophie, the friend with the villa, was here, and she'd been raving about the place. It was one of those fortuitous things, sort of like you coming along."

*Fortuitous*—now there was a word most women who looked like her didn't use.

"Swan song?" I prompted instead.

"My mother's term. I'm making a leap and assuming you know that in my line of work, I'll soon be past the juicy assignments. Not to mention that I was never a ramp star anyway."

"Model, you mean?" I said and waved to a Citroen that passed us coming from the opposite direction; it was one of a short line of other vehicles strung behind a lumbering delivery truck.

"Right. Anyway, I was never overly serious about it—well, not after the first three months of having every tiny flaw pointed out to me and realizing that I began to hate every new woman who walked into the agency. That's a hell of a way to live. Better to enjoy it for a while and then make other plans."

I turned to actually look at her briefly then refocused on the road. "I—yes, I'd have to agree with you."

There was a giggle this time. "Yeah, I know—hard to believe that some of us do figure it out early on. Anyway, you haven't answered me about the party."

"Thanks, but it's not really my scene," I said simply.

"I got that," she said, taking no offense. "Hey, have you had lunch? The party doesn't get going until nine o'clock or so. We can have a late lunch, and I get to eat real food now. Do say yes."

I'd eaten breakfast and grabbed an apple after I finished my work.

"Come on, you can even pick the place, since you seem to know your way around. Oh, and how is it that you speak such great French? It doesn't sound like something you've learned in a classroom."

She suddenly reminded me of Felice. "There is a place not far from Le Chateau. It's nothing fancy."

She waved a lovely hand that had probably been featured in lotion advertisements. "Listen, I'm getting fancy from the yacht crowd. I trust your judgment. Besides, I haven't had that scallop dish yet—the one . . ., which one is it?"

"*Coquilles Saint Jacques?*" I supplied. "They do have that at the Silver Fish."

Traffic was picking up as we neared the city limits, and I navigated through to the Poisson d'Argent. The main room held a short bar with only six stools and fewer than twenty tables, while the terrace overlooking the bay accommodated two dozen more, about half of them still occupied with other late diners. Madame Cartin spotted me as we entered. After the kiss to both cheeks and a warm welcome to Christina, she guided us to a waterside table and said she would send paté and crudités for us to begin with. A pitcher of white wine appeared along with a basket of sliced bread and a small white ceramic pot of butter.

Christina studied the harbor, which contained more working boats on this end than pleasure craft. "They treat everyone like this?"

"It's mostly regulars. Even though I don't come down that often, I qualify." The waiter brought the chalkboard with the handwritten menu. "Their *coquilles Saint Jacques* is excellent."

"Sold," Christina said happily. "And now, Maggie, I intend to extract your life's story. I'm from a big, boisterous Italian family—we can't help but be nosy, and don't be grumpy about it. I really am interested."

I laughed in spite of myself and managed to get away with an abbreviated version that elicited a pause of genuine sympathy about the death of my parents. I skirted my relationship with Amelia, allowing Christina, like Felice, to think she must be a childless aunt. I brushed over the strain with my siblings with a vague statement about not being close. And I discussed my upcoming visit to the States.

"No, no, not New York—you do not want to do that,"

she said, as we moved into coffee, both of us declining dessert. "Come to Philadelphia."

"Philadelphia?"

"Absolutely. It's a quick train ride to get into New York when you need to. If the girl you're swapping apartments with has a decent place, she can sublet it to someone else in a heartbeat. You come to Philly and meet my family; you'll have a ready-built network. Pop has the clothing boutiques, Uncle G has the restaurant end, Uncle Frank is in the car business, and that's just my family. Richard, my fiancée, he's an only child, but his father is in real estate. What a deal we'll be able to get you on an apartment, or a house, well, rowhouse, if you're ready to buy. Or maybe a loft."

I stared at her, nearly speechless at the rapidity with which she was ready to draw me in. "Look, I am enjoying the lunch, but that really is enough payment for making a telephone call and giving you a lift."

"Don't be silly," she said laughter still in her voice. "Don't you believe in fate? I mean honestly, if my car had broken down ten minutes later, you'd have already passed by. Trust me, this was meant to be. Besides, you said yourself that you're going to be traveling a lot on this assignment. Come to Philly and try it. If I'm not right, I'll even help you find a place in New York if you decide to stay around. It's not as if I'm giving up all my contacts there."

"How about if I think about it?" There was a certain logic to her proposal. The truth was that I didn't really know anyone in New York other than at the three publications I routinely dealt with, and that was strictly business. I had no particular desire to live there, except that it seemed to be convenient to be in the same area as so many of the major magazine publishing houses.

Christina radiated a smile at the waiter, signaling for the bill. "If you insist. I leave the day after tomorrow; I'll give you all my contact information. I'll be expecting a telephone call soon, or for that matter, you can just show up at the house if you'd like. I'll tell my mother not to be surprised if you do."

"I won't do that," I said firmly. "I will call, though, one way or the other."

Christina handed the waiter more francs than required and waggled her fingers in a way that meant, "Keep it,"—a gesture that could make her a favored patron. "Okay, I won't push anymore. You're smart—you'll figure it out for yourself. I suppose I should get back to the hotel and decide what I'm going to wear. Sure you won't change your mind about tonight?"

I shook my head, and we left with one more round of kisses from Madame Cartin and a promise to not wait so long for the next visit. I wheeled into the Negresco, grinning inwardly at the discipline of the staff that would not permit them to visibly show their disapproval of my lowly car.

"Thanks again, Maggie, and I'll see you in less than a month, I bet."

"We'll see," I said in parting. After all, I might like New York.

# Chapter Twenty

"So New York wasn't for you?" The unopened present lay in Amelia's lap.

We were in our familiar places on the terrace—how many times had we been like this since that long ago that day Amelia allowed me to step within the fence?

"I can't say exactly why. It might have had something to do with the fact that during the three days I was there trying to make up my mind, I saw a lady's purse snatched in broad daylight, a drunk threw up on my boots at seven o'clock in the morning when I was coming off the subway, and the bill for lunch was practically as much as the rent for my apartment in Paris."

"You weren't paying for it," she pointed out.

"That did help," I agreed. "Seriously, I don't know if there was one exact problem, and I wasn't even sure if it would be different in Philadelphia. It was though. I mean, it's a big city, and while I'd just as soon not have the traffic and shit like that, I do need easy access to a major international airport, and it is easy to get to New York when I need to. I've got a great place a block from South Street. Can you believe it? I finally own a house, well, sort of a house."

"I have no idea what you're talking about from a location perspective," she said tartly. "You converted an old grocery store?"

"It's terrific," I said, momentarily forgetting the present. "Christina's father-in-law found it at a bargain price—one of those transitioning neighborhoods. It was a shop three or four different times during its history ending as a corner grocery store. There was a two-bedroom apartment over it and a small enclosed parking/delivery area. Believe me, dedicated, enclosed parking in that part of Philly is a nice perk. Anyway, I gutted the place and built an absolutely perfect studio downstairs, and I have plenty of room upstairs. It's a one-bedroom now instead of two, and while that isn't as good for resale, I don't really care."

"Well, it does sound practical, and quite frankly, real estate is usually a good investment."

"I travel so much that it didn't seem worthwhile, but there's not a lot of maintenance. I don't have a yard to keep up, and I have an arrangement with a guy who keeps an eye on the place while I'm gone." I gestured to the package she was holding. "And speaking of gone, I got that for you as a memento of my first trip to the Caribbean. I had this great shoot of an annual sailing event in St Croix. What a beautiful little island, even though it is very different from the Mediterranean." How nonchalantly I made the comparison, now that I lived in a world I had once barely dreamed of. Not that it was a dream world without hard work.

"I have little need for gewgaws," she said, her hand on top of the flat, square box.

"Which is why I don't bring you such things. Now don't spoil my fun."

She slit the tape with her fingernail, pulled away the tissue paper, lifted out the scarf, and reacted to the intricate shades of green in the same way I had.

"My, this is lovely."

She held the fabric against her cheek, one of the swirls of color an exact match to her eyes.

"I found it in one of those artist cooperatives. Allegedly the woman who does these makes her own dyes from plants that she grows."

She replaced the scarf in the box and reached for a paté-topped cracker. "What great adventure comes next?"

My attempt at humility quickly dissolved in my excitement to tell her of the work I had lined up. "I have an assignment for one of the Philadelphia publications to photograph some historical buildings, and you'll like this, next week I run up to New York to have an interview with one of the major gardening magazines. They're looking at a series featuring the gardens of New England starting with Maine."

Amelia nodded with what I took as approval. "With all this success, you'll be getting a swelled head. Let's finish up here, and then, I've got a new hybrid rose to show you."

This one-day visit followed our usual pattern. An afternoon preferably spent on the terrace, indoors if required. Wine, cheese, and paté, perhaps tea and pastries depending on Amelia's mood. If a single book or dish had been moved, I could not tell it; her life was unchanged, except I noticed when we walked that her pace had slowed. When I commented that she seemed thinner, she said I was imagining things.

I stayed at the Dolphin Inn and had early dinner with Jed and Susie, their three children stairstepped in age. He passed on news of the others, politely asked about my work, and paid little attention to my response. Within an hour or two, we had both reached the awkward stage where it was easier for me to depart than try to find anything else to talk about. As usual, I stopped by the cemetery, leaving fresh flowers and lingering to describe a trip to Mamma if no one was close enough to hear me talking to the simple headstone.

I idly thought about the distance between my family and me and compared us to Christina's family as I drove across Currituck Sound the next morning. Theresa, Christina's mother, had swept me into a startling embrace the first time we met, vowing that I was to become one of them when I entered their three-story brick home near Rittenhouse Square. Although Christina had warned me that the Donnettis' big Sunday lunches tended toward chaos, I was not prepared for the crescendo of laughter and simultaneous talk of fifteen relatives seated around the massive dining table. Mounded bowls of food passed between hands, wine flowed, and everyone blithely dispensed advice about each other's lives. I managed to escape too much attention by smiling a great deal, and in truth, there was an element of amusement in observing the gathering. I didn't catalogue all the names in the beginning—that was to come later.

"Don't be ridiculous—you cannot possibly spend Christmas alone," Christina announced. Holidays or simply the traditional Sunday lunch, Theresa insisted that their door was open to me, and she would be brokenhearted if I did not join them. I did enjoy the invariably cheerful tumult as long as I parceled out my attendance—something akin to indulging in rich desserts. I couldn't have managed a weekly dose.

I learned the names, the sprawling history of four generations, beginning with the two brothers who had left their impoverished village in the hills of Umbria. The America where their fortunes could be made did not reveal her treasures immediately. A tiny food store in Philadelphia's Italian Market and an apprenticeship on Tailor's Row laid the foundation. Unceasing work and an eye for opportunity as they expanded, clinging tightly to each other through the Great Depression, and firming their footing through the World War II years had built the Donnetti family success. The community, fervent in its patriotism, had sent sons to fight for freedom, and those too old to serve had moved the family business into restaurants and clothing stores. It was Christina's father's generation that made the leap into the higher end boutiques and fine dining restaurants—the family gaining the American dream of prosperity after all. It was not a matter of idle wealth, but a well-established hold with adequate positions for Christina and her multiple brothers, sisters, and cousins to follow in the businesses if they chose to do so.

And unlike my family, their arguments were quickly dealt with on an emotional spectrum that ran from screeches of indignation to lavish makeup hugs and kisses. Open emotional display might be healthier than repression, but the intensity of their affections jangled at times. I found a comfortable balance in limiting the number of times I joined them; my schedule provided a ready excuse that would not hurt Theresa's generous feelings.

Christina understood my intermittent attendance, and while she made certain that I knew of any special gathering, she was not usually pushy when I declined. "Having your space is one thing; too much being alone and you're likely to become a hermit," she remarked two days after my return to Philadelphia when we met for drinks. She'd spent the day making the rounds of her father's four stores, talking with the managers. Even though she no longer worked full time, nothing escaped her about fashion news, and she served as the major consultant about the clothing lines they carried. "Listen, we're having a party Saturday and don't you dare tell me no. We're having about twenty people. It's not a sit-down dinner, so you can escape when you're ready. Uncle G is catering, and it's some of the neighbors as well as people from Richard's office and a few others that should be interesting to talk to. It's not black tie, but wear something nice."

I rolled my eyes. "That's your code for having a man there you want me to meet."

"He's different from the last few—nothing pretty boy about him; he's got that kind of rugged look, and he's new to Richard's poker group." She stirred the ice in her vodka tonic. "Besides, it's your own fault. If you would find a guy for yourself, I wouldn't have to bother."

I motioned for another round, draft Yuengling for me. "How many times have we had this conversation? I am quite content to be single, and my career is not conducive to relationships. It doesn't bother me in the least to go out for dinner alone, and I am capable of opening jars and changing light bulbs. I do not have anything against men, per se—I simply don't feel the need for constant male companionship."

She nudged the bowl of snack mix toward me. "Indulge me. The food will be great, it's a decent mix of guests, and if you think the guy is a toad, you can leave after thirty minutes."

I sighed. "Are you going to nag me until Saturday unless I agree?"

She gave me that smartass grin that meant I was right. "You bet. Multiple telephone calls every day."

"Fine, I'll be there and I'll wear a dress."

"You know it's no problem if you want a new outfit," she said slyly. "In fact, we could make an afternoon of it Friday, run by the flagship shop, pick something out, lunch, salon."

I narrowed my eyes in a mock threat. "Don't push your luck. It will be the Givenchy, the Chanel, or the Versace, and no, I will not buy some silly tottering heels to wear."

"Thank God the city is not filled with women who think

like you," she said in surrender. "Pops would have to go into
appliance sales." She glanced at her watch. "Listen, I have to
run. See you Saturday and no last-minute excuses like you've
got an assignment and have to fly to the Arctic Circle."

I held my hand up in promise and offered my cheek for
a kiss. What the hell—half an hour wouldn't kill me, and I
didn't have any plans. I finished my beer and set off for the
walk to my place. One of several reasons for buying my converted store was that, except when ice made for slippery footing, I could walk to virtually everything I needed. I had my
choice of numerous restaurants from fine dining to a cramped
Chinese takeout that knew my standing order. I was close to
the Kimmel Center, which also meant I was within an easy
stroll of the Walnut Theater and others. It was a short cab ride
to the train station or to the airport if I didn't want to drive and
park. The Italian Market was convenient since I rarely bought
more than a couple of bags of food at a time, and the liquor
store I frequented either carried what I liked or ordered it for
me. If I was in the mood for the architecture of the historical
section, it was accessible by foot. When Richard urged me to
buy, I had been briefly tempted by the thought of develop-
ments on the Delaware River to be on the water again and then
realized that having my own studio outweighed the desire for
waterfront, not to mention the price difference.

Either the aroma from Mama Sophie's or the idea of Uncle
G—Giovanni's—catering on Saturday lured me into the restaurant for a to-go serving of eggplant parmesan with freshly
baked garlic rolls and a salad. It wasn't that I couldn't cook or
didn't like to; it was more that cooking anything substantial
required planning ahead and that wasn't enough of a priority
for me to bother with most nights. I let myself in through the
studio and looked around contentedly, as I often did.

It was a working studio. I had no placard or lettering on the two large front windows that indicated my craft. I opted instead for heavy-duty deep green shutters downstairs, which I didn't mind opening and closing each day. I had replaced the recessed glass front doors with a pair of solid oak ones that had been salvaged from another home and refinished in a slightly darker red than the brick of the building. I'd found a bronze lion's head doorknocker during a trip to the Brandywine Valley and affixed it as an added touch. We had rightly suspected that the durable linoleum downstairs and the stained carpet upstairs covered wooden floors, so when the old layers were stripped away, the maple planks required only minor repairs and refinishing. I did install industrial strength rubberized matting in the darkroom that had once been the refrigeration section. I kept the wide open front area and mounted soapstone topped cabinets that ran the length of one wall. A long, three-shelf bookcase separated a wooden work table and a drafting table against the other wall with pendant task lighting augmenting the central overhead fixture. The bronze and frosted glass fixtures had been the result of another successful salvage hunt.

Upstairs was similarly, sparsely furnished with reclaimed items. I enjoyed poking around used furniture places and spotting the potential in battered pieces that simply required someone with patience. A sander, a scraper, a multi-bit hand tool, a variety of paint brushes, a heavy-duty stapler for upholstery— and every piece that I owned was restored to a warmth that you couldn't find outside of pricey antique stores. The area rugs in muted colors were likewise extracted from rolled bundles in thrift shops and made presentable with a few hours of serious cleaning. Saving money wasn't the real objective. Transforming pieces that others had set aside or given up on gave me a sense of satisfaction.

I deposited dinner in the galley kitchen, a tiered breakfast bar with an overhang dividing it from the den. The almond-colored appliances were new, but I'd lucked into limestone counters that someone had ordered and returned because they were the wrong size. The sections fit beautifully into my smaller kitchen, and I'd created a backsplash of travertine tile that I got for a bargain price at a going-out-of-business sale. Unlike downstairs, where I needed plain white walls to properly display my photos, I used the rugs as my palette for painting my living space; sage and butter yellow for the kitchen flowed into a muted gold with a marbling effect for the den. I had chosen different shades of blue with splashes of green for accent for the bedroom and decent-size bath.

I put on a BB King album and succumbed to the idea of an early dinner. I transferred the parmesan-laden eggplant casserole, rolls, and salad to stoneware dishes; poured a glass of Chianti; and took everything to the square wooden pub table that seated two. I understood that Christina and, no doubt, Theresa were well-intentioned albeit misguided in their concern that I had no man in my life.

Aside from my very real point that most men did not want a girlfriend or wife who spent nearly two hundred days a year on the road, traveling that much had given me plenty of experience with how men behaved on the road. I never knew if it was more pathetic for a guy to take off his wedding ring, oblivious to other clear signals of his marital status, or for a guy to trot out tired lines to rationalize his infidelity. *Oh, I never mess around in the town where we live; the marriage has been over a long time; we only stay together for the kids; my wife and I have an understanding about these things.* Single guys had their own issues, telegraphing their aversion to commitment before you were halfway through the first date—*I just want to make sure you know this is just for fun,* or conversely, dropping immediate hints that they were ready to settle down and were actively seeking the right one. With divorced men, it was the tricky balance of them trying the dating scene too soon or having been out of circulation so long that they were incredibly awkward. It was easy for romantic comedies to assure women that love was waiting around the corner and easier for me to view men as occasional treats when the time and place coincided. I wasn't cynical to the point of saying *no, never,* but I saw no reason to spend any degree of emotion on the subject, nor was my biological clock ticking at a noticeable rate.

I savored the final bite of eggplant and decided that the film I planned to develop could wait until tomorrow. Brewing a cup of tea and watching *The Thomas Crowne Affair* again was a better option. I chuckled at the thought of calling Christina and asking her if the guy she wanted me to meet was like Steve McQueen.

A steady rain kept me inside for a couple of days, and I caught up on all my darkroom work as well as dealt with a stack of sorting and filing that I'd been putting off. By Saturday evening, I was ready for a night out. As I stood in front of the full-length mirror in the bedroom, I was momentarily startled at the effect of the Givenchy. Felice had convinced me that a few classic pieces of high-quality designer clothes were truly necessary in my line of work. Slouching around in jeans when I attended receptions wasn't really appropriate, and the incredible discounts that Felice managed to get for me made it silly to refuse her suggestion. This dress was a long-sleeved, knee-length sheath in a purple so dark that it looked black except when the light caught it. The rounded neckline showed off a strand of polished amethyst beads, and I added matching earrings. Sensibly low black Italian leather pumps fit well, and I located the black cashmere wrap that Christina had given me one Christmas.

The party was still at a manageable noise level when I arrived, Richard answering the door with a highball glass in hand. A towering mixed flower bouquet on a marble-topped wrought iron table lightly scented the arched foyer.

"Whoa, don't you look terrific," he said, planting a kiss on my forehead and finding a hanger for my wrap in the long, narrow closet. The accordion doors had a paint effect that made them blend with the cream-colored plaster walls. "Let's get you a drink. Christina's in the dining room. I'll introduce you around if you'd like, or the Bentons are here if you want to make straight for them."

"White wine is fine," I said and followed him to the amply stocked wet bar staffed with a young bartender whom I recognized from one of Uncle G's restaurants. Someone called Richard's name, and I gave him a little shove. "Go, I'll be fine."

A woman with an empty tray moved in the direction of the kitchen. I turned and surveyed the guests, who were arrayed in small groups, a cousin of Christina the only one that I knew. Chairs from the dining room and extra small round tables draped in white cloths were placed throughout the room to relieve people of the need to juggle small plates, napkins, and glasses. I mentally framed the photo that could appear in the city magazine with a caption of *Thirty-something successful urbanites found in their natural setting.* I spotted the Bentons, an older neighbor couple who often attended Christina's parties. They were seated on one of the two sofas that formed a rectangular arrangement with a pair of chairs on each end and tables that were reminiscent of a hotel lobby. Actually the entire house, done in understated Italianate, could have passed for a small inn. Thankfully, Christina had not adopted the overly ornate style with overwhelming amounts of gold leaf and curlicues on every piece of furniture. The softened tones of gold, red, cream, blue, and green were repeated throughout the house that was definitely not furnished from restored bargain items.

"Why hello, Maggie, how have you been?" Tom Benton stood to clasp my free hand.

Joyce Benton smiled warmly and asked, "What great adventure have you been on lately?"

I took one of the chairs by the sofa, struck by her question, so similar to what Amelia had asked me. Of course, they were of the same age, and when I met them, we'd found a common topic in discussing Paris. Mr. Benton had been a part of the liberation in World War II, and they had returned there for their thirtieth anniversary.

"I was in St Croix in the U.S. Virgin Islands not long ago. It was my first time in the Caribbean."

"We haven't been there," Joyce said, "although we enjoy the Grand Bahamas, and we did try Bermuda. What were you working on?"

We chatted for a few minutes, and when I saw Mr. Benton's smile widen, I knew Christina was behind me.

"Maggie, you made it." A thin gentleman with a close-cropped graying beard and mustache was at her side. He had the look of an academic about him.

I stood to exchange hugs. It was no surprise that she looked gorgeous in a silken peacock green pair of wide legged slacks and a V-neck hip-length tunic. Opals were her choice of jewelry for the evening, and she wore a pair of strappy green shoes that I couldn't have stood on much less glided regally on as she did. Christina may have given up modeling as a career, but the bearing of a model was an ingrained part of her.

She motioned to the chair where I had been sitting. "This is Dr. Nathan Wilford, who will be moving into the house on the corner," she said by way of introduction. "Maggie Stewart, an old friend of mine, and the Bentons, who live four houses down. Nathan has joined the staff at the Museum of Art. Tom, Joyce, I'll send over fresh drinks for you if you want to fill Nathan in on all the good stuff. I'll steal Maggie away for a bit if you don't mind."

"I was coming to find you, honest," I said, her hand beneath my elbow. "Richard diverted me with wine."

We were in the momentarily empty dining room, the oval table that seated twelve and the buffet on the far wall providing more photo perfect displays of bite-size delicacies interspersed with votive candles in greenery. Chafing dishes kept lobster-stuffed ravioli, tiny crab cakes, small rolls with thinly sliced roast beef, and bacon-wrapped scallops warm; a silver bowl of crushed ice held chilled spiced shrimp, while fresh fruit provided a balance to a large platter of who knew how many cheeses. The dessert layout was enticing with chocolate-dipped strawberries accenting the various little cakes and tarts.

"Not one morsel of food until you've met John," Christina warned, as she gave me a quick inspection. "I have no idea why you carry on about getting dressed up—you look great."

I gazed at the table with a sudden surge of hunger and dared a sip of wine. "I didn't notice a guy who seemed to be unattached."

"He was hiding out in Richard's study, and I've planted him with Bradley and Monica. Bradley's in the poker group, and Monica's the one who linked you up with that editor who hired you on the historic banks of Philadelphia piece, so it's perfectly natural for you to say hello to her."

"Can't I just go up to John and say, *Hi, Christina won't let me eat until I've met you. Let's hit the buffet?*"

"No, you may not," she said through a smile, nodding to a man heading toward us. "Make sure you try the ravioli," she advised, her eye on the trio by the French doors that led outside. If the temperature had been warmer, the party would have expanded onto the covered terrace and into the landscaped yard within manicured hedges that concealed the black iron fence.

"Bradley, Monica, you remember Maggie, and John, I don't believe the two of you have met."

"Of course, Maggie, the brilliant photographer," Monica cooed so quickly that I wondered if she was in on the conspiracy. "It's been ages. How are you?"

She turned to John before I could answer. "Maggie did the photographs for the historic banks layout last year, and she's done just tons of other things. Flies about all over the country, well, out of the country, too, I guess. Oh goodness, Bradley, we both need a drink, don't we? John, are you okay?"

He tilted his almost full beer and grinned. "I'm fine, thanks."

"Well, come on," Christina said, still smiling. "Let's go get you two taken care of."

"John McConnell," he said to fill in what could have been an awkward silence. "I have to admit that was a smooth hand-off. You must be Christina's friend whom she met in France."

He had a broad shoulder build, but nicked in at under six feet; a nose that had once been broken; a small scar on his chin; and a tiny chip on his bottom front tooth. His hand was calloused, although not rough. "Richard alerted me that I was to be on extra good behavior," he said in a low voice, laughter in his brown eyes.

Not a pretty boy indeed. He was the only man in our age

group who wasn't wearing a designer suit. Gray slacks, a herring-bone jacket, and a navy blue turtleneck. "Christina wouldn't let me eat until she introduced us. She probably thought I'd get something stuck in my teeth."

"She tracked me down in Richard's study, even though he really did take me in there to see his signed first edition of *The Sea-Wolf.* He mentioned that you gave it to him."

"You never know what you'll find rummaging around in used bookstores," I said. "Are you a Jack London fan?"

"Isn't every boy at some point or other?" He held up his hand at the woman with the tray and motioned her to me.

"Pesto chicken rounds and brie in pastry," she explained, as I popped one in my mouth and took another.

The tanned skin around his eyes was slightly creased. "Unless you were planning an immediate escape, why don't we make a round of the buffet and refresh drinks?"

"I can handle that," I agreed. "I was told you are in the poker group, but I assume that's a pastime rather than a profession."

"Sportswriter," he said, one step behind me. "I wound up in a foursome with Richard at a charity tournament a couple of months ago. After a while, Richard said they were losing one of the poker regulars and invited me in for a game."

"You're a golfer?" We piled our plates with a similar selection and threaded through the growing crowd to the bar.

"Not really," he replied, leaning closer in because of shrieks of laughter coming from a knot of people. "Our golf guys were out, and we were expected to provide someone. I can manage to not completely embarrass myself, but I'm a football guy and everything else is in descending order. I confess to the snobbery of football, basketball, and baseball as the only true sports, and all else is merely entertainment."

We captured one of the small tables and traded occupational

stories between bites and sips. Full glasses appeared at one point, and when I looked around, Christina waved happily from across the room.

"They always mean well, you know," John said as he caught the gesture. "The friends and relatives who are convinced that you need their help in finding that right person they are equally convinced you need in the first place."

"I can accept that," I said after a moment's reflection, "as long as they don't pout when I'm not enthralled with their suggestion." I paused and continued guiltily, "I'm certain that came out badly."

He laughed. "I have a thicker skin than that. I have the feeling that if you had wanted to, you'd have been out of here after the first drink."

I was well past my thirty minutes and realized that, despite it being a setup, I was having a good time.

A cautious look crossed his face, and before I could reply to his assessment, he asked, "Do you like jazz by any chance?"

I nodded, wondering at the change in subject. "Classic and New Age and rhythm and blues as long as you don't define that too broadly."

He gave me a half-smile that hinted of shyness. "The brother of one of the guys at work has a nice jazz ensemble, mostly classic stuff, and they're playing downtown. At the risk of misinterpreting the fact that you haven't bolted from the party yet, would you be interested in dinner tomorrow night?"

"Uh, yeah, that would be nice," I said. I didn't even mind that I knew I was letting myself in for a big *I told you so* from Christina and lunch on Monday to give her all the details.

# Chapter Twenty-one

"If you had told me the news beforehand, we would be having champagne," Amelia said with a small wag of her finger. "Not that your career has been lacking, but work in both *Society of National Geography* and *Island Hopping* in the same year is quite the accomplishment."

I brushed cracker crumbs off my jeans. "It took awhile to sink in, even after I got the checks. I mean, it's not like they want to put me on staff or anything, but it does put me on pretty solid footing as a freelancer. In fact, I'm actually turning down assignments now that I can't get to. I never thought I'd see that day. Do you know that I might need part-time help?"

"Are you still working out of your downstairs studio?"

"Yes, and that's one of the reasons I'm hesitant to hire an assistant. The place isn't really set up for two people, and then there are the employer-to-employee hassles to deal with. There's a company downtown that offers the kind of support that I think I want—someone to handle initial scheduling, invoicing, packaging, and mailing plus a couple of conference rooms if you need a place for meetings. They have everything computerized. I'm going to check them out when I get back."

Amelia turned her mouth down. "Computers. Beastly things, I think."

"Considering that you've never owned a television, I'm not

surprised," I laughed. "John has one, and he swears it won't be long before everyone will have one, but I'm not sold on the idea for me."

"Ah, yes, your young man, John. It's been what, well over a year?"

"Close to two," I said and scratched my chin. "It's hard to believe. I mean, we both stay so busy that I guess time just slips by and you don't realize it's been so long. He's on the road a fair amount, too, and he's certainly up to his eyeballs in football from training camp time through the Super Bowl. So I guess he knows it would be hypocritical to object to me being gone a lot."

She raised an eyebrow. "He would hardly be the first man to promote a double standard."

"True," I agreed. "He's, I don't know, he's not like any other guy I've known. Christina doesn't understand why we aren't 'moving to the next level' as she calls it."

Amelia shifted slightly in her chair and looked at me over the top of her wineglass. "Is that supposed to be marriage since you're already living together?"

"We aren't living together," I said quickly. "I mean, we aren't seeing other people either, but I think that's as much because, well, I'm not sure why exactly. We've never talked about it."

"From what you have told me of Christina, I assume she *is* referring to marriage. Do you fundamentally have something against the concept?"

It was my turn to shift now so I could fully face her, plus it gave me a moment to think through my response. "I don't think so, I mean, not in the sense of I don't believe in it. I'm thirty-one, and while, okay, that's older than when some women get married, it's not as if I'm out of time. John is a super guy, and we have a really good thing going, but how do I know it will last?"

She finished her wine before she answered. "You want some sort of guarantee from life?"

"Well, no, I wouldn't put it that way. After all, though, you never married, did you? And it isn't as if my parents acted like the happiest people in the world, and God knows I have no desire to get stuck in something I'd have to figure a way out of."

"You mean extricate yourself from the clutches of a man you're currently living with?"

"We aren't living together," I corrected again. "That's my point exactly. I have my own space, my own place. I can pack up and leave any time I want."

Amelia's voice softened, the look in her eyes hard to read. "Do you love him?"

That was a tough one, and I was slow with my reply. "I'm very comfortable with John. I enjoy him, we do great things together, the sex is terrific, and we laugh a lot. I haven't lost my breath while thinking of him or had butterflies in my stomach, so I don't know, do I love him or not?"

She shook her head. "Maggie, you must surely understand that love comes in different packages. Rockets exploding and bells pealing are not the only ways to recognize it. You're an adult, capable of making up your own mind. But it sounds to me like this young man is worthwhile. You may be well served by examining what you seem to be defining as freedom. If there is something wrong with him, that is one thing. If you are holding back, consciously or otherwise, because you feel a commitment would ensnare you, that is altogether a different matter."

I gave her an exasperated look. "Quite an observation from the most independent woman I've ever run across."

She started to say something and changed her mind. "Yes,

well, that may be. I lived my life as I chose, and you should do the same, but enough of that. Let's carry these things inside, and then I want to show you my plans for returning much of the garden back to meadow. It's time for me to cut back on high-maintenance plants."

Apparently, discussion of my love life was over. Not that Amelia had ever been one to probe into or linger over feelings.

Our conversation, brief though it had been, returned to mind as I drove north the next morning, the sun pale yellow in its early rise. John. How did I really feel about him? For that matter, how did he feel about me? If we hadn't exchanged *I love you*, was it because we didn't love each other? I was serious about him not being like other men I'd known.

At first, I thought that maybe some hidden repugnant characteristic would pop out when I let my guard down, but John had maddeningly persisted in being a great guy. Even though he displayed no inclination toward undue sentimental trappings, he would surprise me with spontaneous bouquets of flowers and little presents. He was almost as well-versed in music and reading as he was in sports, was arguably a better cook than I, and understood that Marc Chagall was not a French racecar driver. He complimented me on my successes, admired my work, and never indicated he needed more attention than I could give. He didn't press for details about my past but listened on those occasions when I talked about my family or Amelia.

I suppose it was the lack of fireworks that confused me. Not that I was convinced that there was such a thing as love at first sight or some indefinable mystical aura surrounding *the one*, but when you considered the thousands of poets, lyricists, and novelists who described great love, it seemed you should have some kind of sign that pointed to, "Yes, yes, this is it, no question." If my parents had ever exchanged words of love, it wasn't within hearing of us. I couldn't even remember ever seeing them hold hands or touch each other tenderly.

I didn't know if love could move in quietly, settling around two people like a football stadium blanket. Were those routine moments of cooking together, sitting at the breakfast table absorbed in separate parts of the newspaper, and greeting each other with a kiss at the airport as much love as were the grand passions of famous romances?

What about John's divorce? He rarely discussed his first wife, except to say they had been a bad match. He said it had been one of those opposites attract situations that began to fracture during the first year of their marriage when she wanted him to cancel his trip to the Super Bowl and attend a benefit for the symphony instead. They hung on for another year and then both admitted it had been a mistake. He sounded philosophical rather than bitter, and I had no reason to want to know more about her. At least they'd gotten divorced.

I hadn't told John or Amelia about the last time I'd had lunch with Christina. She was going on vacation to Cancun, and when I made a comment about too bad Richard couldn't get away, I noticed a twist to her mouth that was almost a smirk.

"That would be a waste of a good vacation."

"Oh, you mean you're planning a lot of girl stuff," I said automatically.

She looked at me quizzically. "You don't know, do you? You haven't picked up on it? Well, we do work to keep up appearances."

Her matter-of-fact tone startled me. "You mean that you and Richard are..."

She nodded. "We got tired of pretending with each other,"

she said calmly. "He has his interests, and I have mine. Our schedules are busy, and the house is big enough that quite frankly, we see each other surprisingly little. That makes it easier to handle the social things. The kids don't know, and Richard is a good father, even though he's seldom around. Lots of client entertaining in the real estate development business."

"Uh, I . . ." What was I supposed to say?

Her laugh was flat. "You look a little shocked, Maggie. It's just one of those things. After the new wore off, we discovered that we really didn't have much in common beyond the superficial elements. We look good together; we enjoy the circles we move in; our families don't believe in divorce. It's not as if we fight or anything. We have a very civilized approach to this, and separate vacations are a part of the unspoken agreement." She leaned in for a moment. "You'd be surprised how small a town Philadelphia can be, and we don't need complications. I like Cancun; Richard likes Las Vegas. They're far enough away so that stories don't get back."

"Oh, I see," I said, searching Christina's face for hidden pain. Isn't that what I should be seeing?

She shrugged and lifted her martini. "This isn't a big deal, Maggie. We're not the only couple in the same situation by any stretch of the imagination. Actually, once you adjust your idea of what *happily ever after* means, it's pretty easy. Anyway, tell me about this assignment to photograph the lighthouses of North Carolina. How cool is that?"

I shook my head to clear my thoughts and pulled into a convenience store for gas and coffee. Christina's and Richard's arrangement was apparently working for them, but her revelation had genuinely surprised me. Oh, well, it was their business, not mine.

The day after my return from visiting Amelia, I plunged

into an assignment for a local interior design group, and that was followed by a chance to go into Maryland's horse country to photograph championship trotters. I had more or less lost track of our two-year mark together until a Tuesday morning when neither of us had to be anywhere before noon.

John took mugs into the kitchen and refilled them from the new French press that I had found in a coffee shop that had just opened a block over. He set mine in front of me and scooted his chair until his knee touched mine. "Maggs, I've been wondering about something with us."

I paused, the mug partway to my mouth. "Wondering what?"

Keeping eye contact, he stretched his free hand toward me, his fingertips light against my skin. "We're coming up on two years together, and well, you know, we haven't talked about anything like, you know, getting married."

I was stunned into silence and lowered the mug to the table. "What? What do you mean getting married? Why would you bring that up? I thought we were fine together just the way we are."

He didn't flinch. "I do like the way we are, Maggs, but it's not like we're children. We're grownups, and grownups do things like get married. We've had enough time together to know we're good for each other, and that's a pretty important component to marriage. I thought you might be ready to take the next step."

I felt a surprising sense of not being able to take a full breath. I repositioned my hand to grip the edge of the table as I took two shallow breaths and kept my voice steady. "Look, we do get along great. Why do we want to risk changing that? I mean, it's not like your first try at marriage worked out. And what's next—that I stop work and become a housewife, pop out a couple of kids maybe?"

He didn't completely stop a grin and held both hands up. "Slow down, Maggs. I get your point, and no, I am not trying to clip your wings if that's what you think. I just want you to understand that I've got nothing against commitment. Marriage with the right person is a partnership, not a control issue, but if you don't want to, I'm not going anywhere anytime soon. We haven't really talked about it, but I guess now I've got my answer. We'll scratch the wedding question. Do you want to move in together and give that a try?"

I did push back this time, my toes digging into the floor. "Christ, what is this?" I could hear my voice rising.

John stood up, walked behind me, and started to massage my shoulders. "Hey, Maggs, take it easy," he said quietly. "All I'm trying to do is tell you that I think we're awfully good with each other and we've been together for two years. I don't have any burning need to change our status, but I don't have anything against it either. I'm not a flowery speech kind of guy. I figured this was a good way to let you know how I feel. Maybe I should just say that I love you and stop there. We can go on like we are until we do want a change and maybe that won't be for a long time."

His hands felt good, as they always did, and the tension lessened. I leaned into him and allowed my stomach to unclench. "Sorry I went off like that; I don't know why, really. You just took me by surprise. My career is important to me, and I can't deal with the idea of disrupting that."

"Not a problem for me. You're one of the best around at what you do, and I don't intend to interfere with that. But as far as distracting you goes, how about an hour to make amends?"

His hands slipped down my back, kneading the muscles, then moved back up to my neck. I breathed slowly, losing myself to the sensation.

"Well, that would probably be good for me, reduce my stress level and all."

He pulled my chair out the rest of the way so I could stand and took me into his arms. I felt a flash of guilt when I realized that I hadn't responded to his profession of love: *Maybe I should just say that I love you and stop there.*

"It's okay," he whispered, as if reading my mind. "I don't need to hear anything else. Come on, let's go work out that stress."

# Chapter Twenty-two

The next morning I made two telephone calls.

The editor who was a steady client warned, "This is no-kidding remote. The dig is in northern Belize, the archeologist in charge has a reputation for being a pain in the ass, and I think they sleep in tents or huts. It's rustic for sure."

"That's fine, I don't mind."

The second call was to a travel agent. "Yeah, I think the ecotourism thing has real potential," she said, "and we're thinking about specializing in it, but we don't have a lot of details yet. There are people in Costa Rica who have ideas up in the rain forest and other areas scattered around the country. I've got the contact information for a woman that I think you met once, although from what I understand, the road network is limited. I'm not sure how easy it is to get around."

"Not a problem. I've got work in Belize, and then I'll make my way down. I'll do up a nice pictorial, take good notes of contacts, and give you my on-the-ground impressions."

I spent the rest of the day making preparations and called John's office. He was out, and I left a cowardly message that I would be out of the country for a while, maybe as long as three or four weeks. No, he didn't need to call me back. I would send him a card once I had a better idea of my schedule.

Many of my assignments were to accompany writers, but

for stories that weren't time sensitive, it was useful for editors to have a ready source of good quality photographs. Since I specialized in inanimate objects rather than people, my stock pieces provided background for a variety of topics, particularly for short-notice travel sections. Even though this would be my first trip to Central America, I knew other photographers who had spent time there and I'd done some research, knowing that I would probably make my way beyond Mexico at some point. I had a couple of decent guide books on hand, and I'd picked up travel-related conversational Spanish, along with Italian and German, while I lived in France. Belize's former status as British Honduras meant I wouldn't need Spanish until I got to Costa Rica. Catching up on the phrase book would be a good way to occupy my evenings. It had been a long time since I had trudged through the North Carolina wetlands in sweltering summer heat, but I still recalled the intense humidity, swarming bugs, slithering snakes, and sweat that drenched every inch of fabric. I didn't think it would be much different in either Belize or Costa Rica. I needed rugged surroundings, not luxurious resorts, to occupy my mind and absorb my focus. Belize and Costa Rica would be perfect.

The flight to Dallas, another into Belize, and making arrangements to rent a sturdy Jeep took up most of the first day so I stayed overnight in Belize City and set out early the following day for the pre-Columbian Mayan center. My arrival was met with thinly veiled disdain until I assured the professor in charge of the archeological crew that I could work quietly without personally disturbing him or blundering aimlessly about. I nodded sympathetically about the importance of controlling access to the site and mentioned that I had experience taking photographs of a dig in Birnie, Scotland. As further proof that I wasn't there to be disruptive, I told him that I had booked into a small hotel in Orange Walk Town, the sizeable town seven miles to the south. I came logistics-free, merely an observer admiring their work. He accepted my credentials in clipped sentences and collared the most junior member of the team to explain what they were doing. I was able to spend nearly three full days on-site among the two groups of buildings and ten plazas. The view of the nearby river from the limestone ridge was superb, and I shot it at different times of the day. My temporary assistant was excited about the fact that this center contained construction from multiple periods in history, and I dutifully catalogued terms of pre-classic and classic Mesoamerican chronology. I had brought two fresh journals for the trip, one for each country. Detailing topography, plants, animals, history, cultural notes, and practical travel matters would help prolong the trip and occupy my time.

My two official assignments would not stretch for much more than a week, so the remaining time was mine to spend with native flora and fauna, geographic features, or essentially anything that caught my eye. The British ex-patriot couple who owned the hotel where I was staying consulted with the housekeeper, Maria, and she brought in her middle son, Juan, to serve as my guide for as long as I wished. Juan, fourteen or so, was a skinny kid who was thrilled to be bouncing around in the Jeep. His knowledge of the area was impressive, and I spent ten days roaming the river banks, other Mayan ruins, and forested acres with toucans flying about and abundant tropical flowers. Despite more than passable English, Juan cheerfully reminded me that Spanish was common for locals, and he helped me work on useful sentences. I scrawled a quick postcard to John the day before I left for my next destination, vague about exactly when I was returning.

Maria took care of booking my flight from Belize City to

San Jose, and the approach into Costa Rica was a beautiful view of foliage-covered peaks sweeping toward azure seas, wide expanses of forest, valleys, cities, and towns. As much as I love the sea, I didn't want beaches for this trip. I wanted the interior, although as I had been told and saw from the air, there did not appear to be much of a highway system.

I was feeling the sense of adventure that comes from being away from urban areas, and I decided that another ten days should be about right. I wasn't certain of what communications support I would have once I left San Jose, so I booked my return flight and then took a taxi to the hotel. I was scheduled to have dinner with Miranda Ramirez, a woman from a major travel agency, who would link me up with transportation to the *Bosque Corazon*—a place called Heart of the Forest, which sounded like what I was looking for. When we met in the lobby of the hotel, I thanked her for recommending the lovely side street inn that had been converted from an old mansion.

"I thought perhaps you would like this better than one of your major chains," she said in lightly accented English. Her thick, straight black hair was cut into a pageboy, and with only faint wrinkles around the eyes and chin, it was difficult to determine her age. Although as the head of the travel agency, I assumed she was in her early forties. She was dressed in a mocha-colored, belted dress with wooden buttons down the front; leather strappy sandals; and simple gold and amber jewelry for accessories.

I had the foresight to pack one wrinkle-resistant, sleeveless, all-purpose ankle length black jersey dress and a pair of flat black woven sandals that had been with me since my time in Spain. I hadn't bothered with jewelry for a trip like this.

Her rapid Spanish to the hostess resulted in a table in the courtyard that featured large pottery containers of orchids, bromeliads, and other plants I didn't immediately recognize.

We enjoyed a cocktail and the first course as we exchanged small talk. Miranda and I originally had met at a travel symposium where the panelists were discussing the fledging ecotourism industry.

"You are interested in the idea for yourself?"

"Not in the way you mean," I said truthfully. "I've been in much of Europe, in other places of the Caribbean, and all over the United States. I thought it was time to see Central America."

"We are not a wealthy country, yet stable and without the political problems of others. We have a great beauty here with the Caribbean to one side, the Pacific to the other, rain forests, mountains, waterfalls, volcanoes, wildlife, and many, many birds. It is ideal if we can bring in tourists to see our beauty, but protect it, too. I have a cousin on the tourist board, and this is our dream."

"It was a beautiful view flying in," I agreed.

Miranda handed me a heavy-duty mailing envelop. "I have made a list with a map of four projects people are working on. If these are successful, there will be many more, we hope. Two are by the ocean, which you said you did not want; one is not yet ready for guests; and the fourth is Bosque Corazon, where you are going. The owners, husband and wife Javier and Angela Rodriguez, have plans to build a central lodge with a restaurant, but for now it is small with only six cabins and a dining hall. Their son, Ricardo, will pick you up here at eight o'clock in the morning. You could drive, although the directions are a little difficult to explain. They have many acres of their own for you to explore, and they are close to a national forest. They will take you to the volcano as well and other places if you wish." She nodded at the waiter who appeared with our meals. "They have small baths in the cabins, but it is not luxurious. No telephone, fax, or television."

Aromatic steam wisped from the bowl of seafood stew that Miranda had suggested I try. "I appreciate all your help," I said, lifting a spoon. "Getting away from crowds is what I am looking for right now."

"Then I think this will be a correct choice," she said. "And to end the meal, I will introduce you to Costa Rican coffee. That is something else we take pride in."

If the Bosque Corazon and the Rodriguez family were examples of Costa Rica's ecotourism industry, it should have a bright future. Ricardo was a sturdier version of my teenaged Belize companion, and like him, he was cheerfully determined to take care of my needs. He apologized for his heavy mixture of Spanish among misplaced English words. I laughingly told him that his English was much better than my Spanish and was rewarded with a crooked-tooth grin. The slow pace of our drive on marginal roads, which we shared with cumbersome vehicles as well as donkey-drawn carts, gave him time to explain that his oldest brother was at university learning to speak excellent English and to be excellent in business. His father, also a good mechanic, knew more plants and animals than anyone else; his mother was an excellent cook; his two older sisters were married and no longer lived with them; and his younger sister helped his mother. He, Ricardo, was an excellent guide and driver and would take me to see everything, and oh yes, his mother made a lotion to keep away bugs that was most excellent and I should use it. And, if I was not in fear of the dark, he would take me to see ocelots "for my camera." I bought us both Coca-colas, which I agreed were excellent, to use what was apparently Ricardo's favorite adjective, when we stopped at the single store in a tiny village to pick up a few supplies.

We had been steadily climbing up a twisting road, when we finally turned onto a gravel road that I would have likely missed and Ricardo began gleefully honking the horn. A green wooden sign with Bosque Corazon painted in yellow letters was affixed to an iron gate. A man in loose-fitting clothes and a broad-brimmed hat sauntered through the trees and swung the gate open with a wave and wide smile in his creased brown face.

"Luis who is help to my father," Ricardo said, as we bounced up the short drive and broke into a clearing. He leapt out and pointed to a building basically in the center of the compound. "My mother is there to say welcome. I take your bag to the cabin. It is number three, an excellent cabin that I helped to build with my father." He handed me my backpack. I looked toward the rambling wooden house, which was partially visible through the foliage up a broad incline. Two paths led in the opposite direction from the house, gently winding into more foliage, and I thought I saw part of a roof line. As soon as Ricardo cut the engine, I became aware of the clatter of stiff palm fronds and the flash of birds. Yellow butterflies flitted past me, and a woman held open a screen door of the building that Ricardo had indicated.

"*Hola!* You are Senorita Stewart?" She was a head shorter than I, and there was a distinct Indian mix in her cheekbones and dark eyes. Her largish nose was not quite in proportion to her round, smooth face. Her black hair was pulled back into a braid. She wore a brightly colored floral ankle-length skirt and a simple, bright blue cotton top with three-quarter-length sleeves. "I am Angela, and we welcome you. It was a good ride?"

"Yes, thank you." I stepped inside the building that was the dining hall, the interior dim compared to the bright sunshine outside. Heavy wooden beams supported the ceiling; the windows had screening instead of glass and wooden shutters that could be closed from inside. Different types of wood had been used, all of which I suspected were native taken from the grounds. Mahogany for sure and I didn't know the others. Two wooden-bladed ceiling fans turned overhead, and lights suspended from them were not on. Square pottery candleholders with thick round reddish candles sat on the single long wooden table in the center of the room, six armless chairs on each side, a chair with arms at the head and foot. A bar with no stools was to the right of the table, an old, scratched refrigerator behind it. A thick shelf held bottles of rum, gin, and a brown unlabeled one. A buffet with doors was against the other wall, pottery pieces atop it. All the furniture had the hewn look of handmade work. I assumed the kitchen was at the far end of the building behind a set of swinging doors.

"The meals are together here. There is the Coca-cola, juice of fruits, water, beers, and ice," Angela said, gesturing to the refrigerator. A wooden box with a slot cut into the top sat next to a writing pad. A handwritten sign that probably had the prices was taped to the side of the box. "For each day, you put the name and the drink and the paper in the box, please."

An honor bar. "Yes, certainly," I replied. "Ricardo was very helpful to me."

"That boy, he talks much," she said with a soft smile. "I tell him not to talk too much to make you not work. He is good to show you the forest."

"Oh, yes, thank you," I said quickly.

"Come, we go to your cabin. It is easy for the pictures."

I nodded, thinking I understood what she meant. The six cabins appeared to be the same size, three along each path, spaced about twenty feet apart. A mass of ferns, flowering plants, and trees waited a mere forty feet beyond the third cabin. A profusion of different colored butterflies graced a bush between my cabin and the forest, and I was certain I heard monkeys in a canopy tree on the other side of the path.

Two square columns supported the corrugated tin roof of the porch that was large enough for two chairs. The cabin was the same type of construction as the dining hall with screened, shuttered windows and chunky furniture. The double bed on a low wooden platform looked comfortable, and the wardrobe had plenty of space for what I'd brought. I was glad to see a table with two chairs and a lamp with a pottery base of the same color as the candlestick holders that I'd seen. A single bedside table had a lamp with a greenish blue base. There was no overhead light or fan, but I could feel the breeze through the screens. Trees and shrubs kept direct sunlight from the cabins. Angela showed me the bathroom with the pedestal sink, toilet, and shower, no tub. It reminded me of the one in my apartment in Paris.

"I will leave you now. Dinner is seven o'clock, and if you come before, there is little bites," Angela said. "If there is something not good for you, you come to see me." She swept her hand toward the table. "There is book about here. I think tomorrow is time for Ricardo to help, but today is for you to learn the grounds."

The ten days I allotted at the Bosque Corazon flowed smoothly, a pattern quickly emerging. The other people in residence were a German couple in their early sixties, who were there for bird watching, and a honeymoon couple from London. None were inquisitive of my solo status or wanted to engage me in lengthy discussions. We simply enjoyed the varied, delicious food that Angela and her daughter Juanita prepared and served; meals with fresh, local ingredients, flavored with herbs and fruits grown on the grounds. Angela was happy to provide portable lunches of fruits, bread, cheese, and sausage. I was usually gone immediately after breakfast, sometimes alone on the marked trails, other times with Ricardo, who was indeed an excellent guide. He was also correct in that Angela's homemade lotion was not only effective against bugs, but soothing to the skin.

Hummingbirds were a constant presence as were parrots and three or four varieties of monkey. Dozens of other birds, frogs, iguanas, and bats were plentiful, and Ricardo was good to his word to expertly lead me one night to a stream where I captured ocelots on film. Exotic flowers were in such abundance that it was difficult to choose what to feature, and the day trip to a nearby volcano was a completely new experience for me.

My body had forgotten the exertion of extended outdoor shoots, and I spent several evenings falling into bed, soundly asleep not long after dinner. Three nights before I was scheduled to leave, Angela urged me to take an opened bottle of wine to the cabin. I moved one of the chairs onto the porch, the night black outside the separate pools of light from the dining hall, the other cabins, and the lit torches along the paths. The air was still, although not oppressive. Floral scents mingled with earthier ones, frogs sounded, trees rustled with unseen movement, and the howler monkeys' noise was muffled rather than shockingly loud.

I was lulled by nature's offering and gingerly gave in to the thought that John would enjoy being here. He owned a tuxedo because he was occasionally required to attend that type of social function, but he preferred relaxed jeans, worn sweatshirts, and sneakers. He would sit through a ballet if I asked him to and would have easily made today's four-mile hike to a waterfall and series of stone pools. All right, I had forced myself to focus on anything except John, and now that I cracked the door open, it swung wider than I intended. What the hell, I needed to face this, didn't I?

I sipped the red Chilean wine and slowly unreeled highlights of our two years. Is it possible that we hadn't had a fight? I couldn't think of one unless I counted walking out on him because he asked if I wanted to get married. Sure, why wouldn't that upset me? How many women in the world at that moment were complaining about men being afraid of commitment? On the other hand, how many women, if they were being honest, were afraid of commitment? I wasn't thinking of strident women who viewed all men with derision, but of women who held no special grudges. In other words, women like me. As I told Amelia, it wasn't that I objected to marriage in general. I mean, I suppose that at some point, I guessed I would get married. Except, maybe I did distrust the whole idea. I thought of the other guests. The older couple certainly seemed happy together. As for the newlyweds, would they return here for some future anniversary, or discover they did better with separate vacations, locked into a marriage they couldn't bring themselves to end? Would they join the ranks of the divorced, admitting failure of a love they had once declared to the world?

*You want some kind of guarantee?* Isn't that what Amelia had asked?

And while Amelia's withdrawal from people was an extreme, it wasn't as if she led a miserable life alone. My mother, with her marriage and we kids, was that really her choice or simply the outcome expected by her upbringing? Had she and my father really loved each other? Why hadn't Amelia ever married? Or had she and simply wiped out all traces of it?

I took another sip of wine. Stop, one issue at a time. John.

John was the issue. Or rather how I felt about him. He hadn't delivered an ultimatum—he had offered me a choice, well, two choices. Actually, three choices if you counted keeping things as they were between us. Why in the hell had that upset me? Because he surprised me with it? My wineglass was empty, and I upended the bottle, glad to see another half glass flow. I wasn't ready for a change. There, it was simple. Change was risk. Risk of making a wrong decision, risk of upsetting a balance. If I had let him, John would have said, "I love you," in a more definitive way. Did I love him? Quite possibly, but how was I supposed to know if I really did or if it was just an automatic response? If I did love him, why did the thought disturb me? Was it because I thought the statement came with too many strings attached? Saying "I love you" didn't necessarily lead to marriage. After all, people lived together for years without taking that step. Wasn't that part of the whole argument about living together? You were supposed to find out if you were genuinely compatible? Except, was living together that much different from being married?

I shifted in the chair as the lights at the dining hall were turned off. If John were here, perhaps we would wander back to the clearing to see the sparkle of stars made brilliant with no city lights to obscure them. I felt it then, a stirring rather than a crescendo, the desire to have him next to me, his lips, his hands. It wasn't some silly notion that I couldn't live without him, or the kind of urgency that made me want to rouse Ricardo and get to the airport to take the first airplane out. It was a pleasant sensation, not an overwhelming need, and the image of a winter evening came to mind. We were at John's place, tongues of flame flaring, or dying depending on what part of the logs was burning.

"You can't get really good wood here," John said, shifting the position of the logs with a poker, sending sparks and burning chunks tumbling to the glowing base. "Seasoned hardwood, that makes the kind of fire that will go for hours. My dad has this dedicated woodshed where he rotates the logs to make sure he puts the fresh ones deeper in to let them dry longer."

I hadn't given it much thought at the time, but he was right. The driftwood fires from when I grew up burned quickly, not dense enough to last and softwoods like pine crackled with resin. Maybe love was like that. Kindling and paper blazed hotly and burned out quickly, greener wood lasted a little longer. You had fire and enjoyed it in either case. If what you wanted was the continual, cleaner burn, though, you brought in the seasoned hardwoods and tended your fire properly. Maybe that's where I was with John. Our fire wasn't the blazing, roaring type, and I didn't know if it would last. It could turn out that we didn't have the right sort of wood or that we walked away and let it die from lack of attention, or hell, maybe we would douse it for some reason. It wasn't the most romantic of analogies, but I was okay with that. John had made me offers, not demands, but I hadn't seen it that way. I had lashed out at him, feeling put on the spot, immediately looking for a hidden motive when that wasn't what he intended. I knew that now, now that I had time to step back and think through the scene.

I set the wineglass on the porch, stood, and stepped down to listen to croaks, rustlings, a faint snuffling within the tree line. I breathed in deeply, watching the far torch splutter into darkness. I was ready to return. I sheltered my new awareness during my last two days and was sincere in my praise when Angela hugged me good-bye. Ricardo weakly protested the size of the tip I gave him and extracted a promise that I would come for another visit. I enlisted him to help me manage a telephone call from the airport and left a message for John with my arrival information.

The flights were uneventful, and I deplaned, peering around people in front of me to see John waiting, holding a single red rose.

His smile was wide without any hesitation. He reached for my backpack, drew us away from the crowd, dropped the bag next to his feet, and held out the rose. "It's all good, Maggs, but you really didn't have to be gone this long to get the point across."

I took the flower, sniffed it gently, and swallowed hard. "I did sort of overreact."

He opened his arms, still smiling. "You're here, and you called me. That's what counts."

I pressed against him then pulled back enough to look up into his eyes, not caring if anyone was staring. "Is it enough if I tell you that I think I love you?"

He pressed his lips to my forehead. "Works for me. You want to go somewhere fancy for dinner tonight to celebrate?"

I could feel the grin cross my face and lowered my voice. "How about a hot shower and we order pizza instead?"

"That works even better. Come on, let's get your bag, and you can fill me in on Mayan pottery or monkeys or macaws or whatever it was that you were doing."

"All of the above," I said and took his hand as we headed to baggage claim. "By the way, I brought you some fantastic coffee, and I've got so many great shots that it will take me a week to develop the film."

John squeezed my hand lightly. "Speaking of fantastic and great, you look terrific."

I wasn't ready to talk about my new perspective. "It's amazing what trekking around in jungles will do for you," I said, "but it's good to be home, too."

# Part Three

*Amelia's Secrets*

**April 1992**

# Chapter Twenty-three

I gripped the receiver too tightly, my fingers showing white, my mind involuntarily remembering that long ago call from Jed. Except this time, it was Doc Rundle.

"Suicide? Are you sure? I mean, couldn't it have been accidental?" Of course, it hadn't been accidental—Amelia wouldn't have made a mistake like that—not when she could make a choice instead.

"You know Amelia; everything was in order, including detailed instructions for the ceremony or lack of one would be more like it. She went to see Harvey Trotter and Stan Grayling last week, although, of course, neither one of them knew what she was planning, no more than I did."

The doctor, lawyer, and banker. How like her.

"What did she want done about a ceremony?"

He hesitated briefly. "Not much. Her note said she didn't want a bunch of hypocrites crying crocodile tears. Just a cremation and then you're to place her ashes somewhere on the property. The note also said if you're too angry with her, I'm to take care of it."

I struggled to speak without snarling. Of course, I was angry with her.

"No, it's not a problem. Look, I'm going to try and book a flight this afternoon. I'll pick up a car and be in around eight.

Can you call the Dolphin Inn for me?"

"Sure, but there's a nice new Hilton in Nags Head if you'd rather."

"No, no, I always stay at the Dolphin. I know it will be a little late, but will you, or Harvey, or Stan be able to meet with me?"

"None of us mind, Maggie, but it will be Harvey. Amelia left some papers or something specifically for him to give you as soon as you arrive. Do you need anything else?"

It was my turn to hesitate—the question could wait. But then, knowing the answer might make the trip a little easier.

"Just one more thing, actually."

"Yes?"

I forced the tears back until I had time for them. "Had it gotten that much worse? Seems like only a few months ago she was doing okay."

"The pain was more frequent and of greater intensity. I couldn't promise her she was going to be able to stay on her own. Awfully risky, a woman her age living alone like that." Another pause as we both thought.

Walt's voice was reflective. "Maybe I should have said it differently."

"It wouldn't have mattered, Walt, you know that. You did everything you could. You tried to get her to see the specialists, to go for therapy. You explained the odds if she didn't."

"Yes, well, I like to think so anyway. How many nights do you want the room?"

"Tonight and then I'll work it out. Give me Harvey's home phone number so I can call him when I get in, since I really don't know how long it will take."

I slowly released my grip, my hand trembling, moments from the past year careening through my mind. Had it been a year? Where had the months gone? Why had Amelia lied to me? She'd told me the medications were working, that as long as she slowed down and didn't do too much each day, it was manageable. For all she knew, Doc Rundle might have misdiagnosed, or maybe she was one of those lucky ones who would go into remission. She dismissed my suggestions to move—come be with me or let me find her an appropriate facility. She had told me she intended to die right where she was. I hadn't realized she meant it in this way.

I rose slowly, pressing the tips of my fingers to my temples, not wanting to waste time with crying. Amelia had lied to me for the same reason that I trusted what she said. It was what we both wanted to hear. I picked up the telephone again, not bothering to sit. With the flight and rental car arranged, I called John and managed the conversation calmly. No, no, thank you, it was sweet to offer to take off and drive me, but I wasn't sure of anything and it would be better if I went alone. Yes, I would call once I knew more.

Thank God, I was in a gap of assignments—one more quick telephone call to the agency to tell them I would be out of town and keep my schedule clear for the next week; no, make that two.

Dealing with practical matters got me through the next few hours, and when I boarded the airplane, I was grateful the cabin wasn't full. I didn't want the feel of a crowd, the distraction of a seatmate. I needed to think. I had gotten over the initial shock of suicide, but why hadn't she called or done something to say good-bye?

The stewardess stopped at my seat. "Would you like a drink, ma'am?"

"Gin and tonic, please."

I mixed the drink from the little bottle and held the glass

for a moment before taking a sip, a sip that invoked the memory of Amelia teaching me to make a martini.

"Gin and tonic is easy if you remember to squeeze a bit of lime juice in first, but it takes more practice to do this correctly," she said. "The ability to pour bourbon into a Coke bottle is not considered a necessary skill beyond the borders of the South. Mixing a good martini is more useful."

I couldn't get a flight into Norfolk until morning so I settled for Patrick Henry Airport in Newport News with its slightly longer drive. Landing in Newport News also meant that I wouldn't have to fight the tedious afternoon Washington, D.C. area bumper-to-bumper traffic. Traffic from Newport News would be light for another two months when the tourists and summer homeowners would appear by the hundreds. That economic boost predicted in the seventies by a few visionaries, an idea my family and many other residents of the Outer Banks had incorrectly ridiculed, had come. I focused on these changes as the plane carried me southward, less painful than thoughts of Amelia.

The Outer Banks' small cottages designed for the shore fishermen and single-story motels with kitchenettes were indeed being steadily replaced by franchised chains, condominiums, and larger rental beach houses advertised as ideal for two or more families to split for a week. A conscious decision had been made by the developers to maintain a family-oriented atmosphere on the Outer Banks. The ample number of miniature golf courses, water slides, and real golf courses combined with the absence of casinos and the boardwalks of other seaside towns kept the college population to a minimum and held nothing to attract the gambling crowd.

My hometown, though, the village of Duck, had so far refused the expansion of hotels, content to have the tourists long

enough to shop and dine but leave again at night for the sprawl
of Kitty Hawk, Kill Devil Hills, and Nags Head. The lesser
level of revenue was considered a fair trade-off by those who
valued quiet more than money.

I was on the road in less than thirty minutes from the time
we landed, which included a stop to grab a cup of coffee. I
wasn't hungry even though I couldn't remember if I had eaten
lunch. Probably not.

I started on I-64, noting construction of new buildings,
more growth of Newport News, Portsmouth, and Norfolk.
There was a time when the cities had been distinguishable enti-
ties, but I wasn't sure how much longer that would last.

Once I turned onto Highway 168, the few changes were
hidden within the darkness, small towns set between the cities
and the shores offering little to visitors except the occasional
antique shop, gas stations that closed not long after sundown,
and authentic North Carolina barbecue joints. That was one
of the few things I genuinely missed. For all of Philadelphia's
enticing restaurants, and taking nothing away from a Philly
cheese steak, a proper barbecue sandwich was hard to find.

Amelia dead. Cognitively, I knew it was true, and I understood the process of death. Mamma, then Daddy, and now
Amelia. I hadn't bothered to call Jed; I imagine word had spread
rapidly. I would talk to him at some point, and even though
he had never had the hostility of my sister, Ruth Ann, he'd
never understood my relationship with Amelia. Mamma was
the only one who'd come close, and hers had been more an acceptance than an understanding.

I stopped once briefly for a bathroom break and another
coffee, unable to think of food. A few cars dotted the streets of
Duck as I passed into Southern Shores. When I turned into the
Dolphin parking lot, I could see faint lights of the newer hotels

further down the beach; nationally known names, a familiar sameness for visitors who wished to minimize the chance of surprise in their lodgings.

I sat in the car for a few minutes and noticed scaffolding to the side that meant the Wilsons were probably in the process of restaining the shingled exterior. They seemed content to maintain the rambling look of the two-story seaside motel built after World War II, all rooms guaranteed a beach view and individual window air-conditioners, which varied in the amount of noise and cool air they could produce. A man I didn't recognize was alone in the small lobby. He glanced at me and laid a key on the counter.

"You must be Maggie Stewart. Walt said you'd be in about now, and Harvey said to give him a call once you got settled. Put you down in number eighteen—understand that's the room you like."

I signed the register. "Thanks. Are you one of the Wilsons?"

"Garner, actually. One of the sons-in-law. Married to Becky, the middle girl. Want me to ring up Harvey for you?"

"No, that's okay; I'll call from the room. How much?"

"This time of year, twenty-seven dollars plus tax. Don't need anything till you check out. Is it just for tonight?"

"I think so, but it may be another day or so depending on a couple of things. I guess that won't be a problem then."

"Nope, booked well for the summer, but kinda quiet for now. Need help with your luggage?"

I picked up my backpack and lightly packed duffle bag. "I'm fine, this is all I brought."

"Ice and Coke machines are still in the middle stairwell. Call if you need anything."

I nodded and went out. Room eighteen. The same age I'd been when I left Duck. The first time I had stayed at the

Dolphin, it had been a coincidence, and I suppose after that, it became a symbol for me.

The Wilsons might not be able to match the amenities of the larger places, but business seemed adequate. The paint on the walls was new, the mattress firm, no cigarette burns on the carpet. I opened the large window facing the water to let sea smells compete with the odor of pine-scented cleaner.

Harvey picked up the telephone on the second ring.

"Everything okay at the motel?"

"It's fine. Walt said you could fill me in tonight. I know it's a little late."

"Been expecting you. You eat yet, by the way?"

"No, I haven't been very hungry."

"Truth of the matter is, I've got a house full of company that I wouldn't mind leaving for a while and you need to eat whether you think you do or not. We've got a new place open that's not bad. The Pelican's Roost, back up the highway this direction. Meet you there in twenty minutes, unless that's too soon."

"No, that's fine. Is it beachside or across the way?"

"Right on the beach—bought out old Dean Johnson's place. See you shortly."

I replaced the receiver and decided to grab a quick shower. Johnson's place gone, too. Not that it had been much, just a snack shop really. An old-fashioned Coke box, the chest kind filled with ice where you drew out a bottle, chips of ice clinging to it, and used the bottle opener built into the chest. Racks within the shack held salty snacks, cookies, candy bars, and a sno-cone machine. No fancy flavors, strictly lime, cherry, and grape. Oh, yes, moon pies and a big jar of bubble gum. I wondered briefly if Mr. Johnson had died, too.

I leaned my head against the front wall of the shower, let

the warm water massage my back, and tried to release some of the tension. As the steam filled the space around me, I was able to place Amelia's last telephone call. When had it been—two weeks ago, maybe three?

"Any chance you could come down next week? I thought you might need a break, and we could spend some time looking for seashells before the tourists start pouring in," she'd said after assuring me she was fine. That had obviously been a lie.

"I'd love to, but I'm swamped with projects. Are you having trouble? I can make some calls and try to rearrange some things."

"Nothing that I can't manage. Take a look at your calendar and let me know when would be good for you. No hurry."

My God, it had been a month ago! I had wrapped up a piece on the Philadelphia zoo on Monday and intended to call to let Amelia know that I would have a few days free, but something happened and I forgot. Shit, shit! Had she been planning this even then? If I had come then, would it have made a difference? Goddamn it, had she ever asked me specifically to come see her? No, not in all the years I'd known her. Why hadn't that occurred to me at the time? The questions repeated in my mind as I dressed and drove to meet Harvey. Could I have stopped her if I had just come when she called?

# Chapter Twenty-four

We sat in the bar of the Pelican's Roost, the kind of place you expect to find on a beach. A maritime theme with brass railing, hanging plants, and pelicans etched on the big glass doors. It was the new look of the Outer Banks, a less ramshackle one, which I had not yet become accustomed to.

I didn't know Harvey in the way I knew Walt Rundle—my family had little need for lawyers. His silver hair was still full, and he hadn't developed either an old-man paunch or a pronounced slump to his shoulders. His gray eyes were clear in a wrinkled face that was lean without being gaunt. Even in this relaxed atmosphere, he wore a pair of knife-edged navy pants, a blue and white striped shirt, and a navy cotton V-neck sweater. He refused to open his briefcase until I agreed to eat a bowl of shrimp bisque, but my impatience dissolved after the first bite. This was not the stuff of amateurs. Real butter, cream, and plentiful shrimp with a balance of seasonings that I think included a dash of nutmeg.

I sipped a glass of pilsner from Manteo's microbrewery, the Weeping Radish. It couldn't compare in size with the giant drinking halls in Bavaria, but it did capture the spirit with an outdoor beer garden and waitresses in dirndls. The Weeping Radish was very much attuned to the increase in the tourist industry of the Outer Banks, and despite more Bavarian blue and white décor than I cared for, I couldn't fault the quality of its beers.

"Okay, Harvey, I've had a meal. Now can we get down to business?"

He took one more swallow of Jack Daniels and water and extracted a sheet of paper and an envelope from the briefcase. He handed me the envelope and tactfully glanced away while I blinked my eyes as I recognized Amelia's handwriting.

"I'll open this when I get back to the hotel," I said quietly. "What's the rest?"

"She left letters for Walt, Stan, and me with her instructions. I would imagine that's what yours is as well. Maybe we should discuss the will first."

I held up my hand. "Let's don't start there. Start by telling me what the hell happened. Walt didn't say too much, and I would like some answers."

Harvey laid the paper down and picked up his tumbler. He instinctively looked around to see if anyone was paying attention to us and shifted his chair closer before beginning to speak. His voice was steady, the longtime lawyer handling one more death of someone he had known for decades.

"Amelia called me out to the cottage last Tuesday, said she wanted to update her will, and make sure everything was in order. She seemed tired, but nothing led me to believe she was in really bad shape. I did notice the place looked like it had been cleaned top to bottom, and the garden was better than usual for this time of year, but I didn't give it any thought at the time. We spent an hour or so working out a couple of changes she wanted made, nothing major. I took care of it, and she even agreed to come into the office for signature, which was a surprise, but I guess she had planned her trip to the bank to coincide. Stan said she came in, verified her holdings, and wrote a couple of checks. Turns out one of them was for a funeral home in Nags Head. She prepaid everything."

He paused for another drink. "Anyway, she called Walt late Monday and said she needed to see him on Tuesday, which was yesterday, but that she would be busy in the morning, so come around noon." Harvey exhaled what could have been a sigh. "So Walt arrived and saw a note taped to the door. She didn't want him to just walk in like that."

"It was too late?"

"Yes. Way Walt figures it, she must have gotten up early, probably walked along the beach, came back, and took the pills around eight o'clock." He smiled a half-smile, a sign of reluctant admiration. "I don't know if he told you, but she washed the pills down with Moet and Chandon. It should have been pretty quick."

I closed my eyes and clenched my jaw until I could feel the pain. I could see her sitting there, carefully, deliberately swallowing the capsules. What was quick in a case like that? How long did you sit there, waiting for unconsciousness to take over? Maybe it had at least been painless.

"The four letters were on the table with her, our three pretty much alike. Told Walt about the funeral home and not to feel guilty, told Stan to help you settle the last of the accounts, told me to give you your letter and not to screw around with lengthy probate. But there are a few steps we can't ignore, you know."

I nodded. I hadn't noticed Harvey's signal to the waiter, but he appeared with new drinks.

"So she's there now? At the funeral home?"

"Tomorrow. One of those steps we can't ignore is an autopsy. Even though there was no real question, it's the law. Walt called in a favor to make it a priority. They finished this afternoon." He cleared his throat, his eyes calm.

"Amelia was specific. She didn't want you to see the . . ., to see her like this. She wanted the cremation as quickly as possible. That's why she chose the funeral home she did; they have the only crematorium in this area."

I emptied my glass and reached for the new one. Not see her? How could I not see her? It wasn't like I'd never seen a dead body. What would I have to remember if I didn't see her?

"I'm not sure I can agree to that, Harvey. It's hard enough for me to accept she's gone. I think I need to see her just to be sure, to be certain this isn't some kind of absurd joke she's playing. I don't give a damn how irrational that sounds."

The smile was sympathetic. "Can't say I'm surprised. I've had cases when the family couldn't have closure for one reason or the other, and it does seem to help to be able to see for yourself. If you'd like, you can come to the office at ten; we'll take care of reading the will and then go to the funeral home."

I looked around the room to avoid speaking until I could control my voice. A few people who had the look of regular patrons were at the bar, two other couples and a group of four kept the noise level low.

"Is there anyone else to notify? I know she doesn't have any family left, but was there someone from her time in Europe that I don't know about?"

Harvey shook his head and pulled his glasses to the end of his nose, referring to the paper. "You know how isolated she was. There was a banker in Paris, a Bernard Sancerre, and believe it or not, a nun, Sister Agnes Elizabeth, at a convent in Switzerland. I sent a telegram to both of them this morning in accordance with Amelia's instructions."

"A nun? In a convent in Switzerland? I know Amelia spent some time there around the end of World War II, but I don't know how long and she never mentioned anything about a convent. Was there any explanation?"

"She was no more forthcoming about this than she ever has been about anything else, Maggie. In all the years I knew her, I helped settle the Thornhill estate once we were notified of her inheritance; I maintained her will and handled the paperwork for your trip when she sent you off to Paris. We talked very little when I first met her and not much more since that day. I respected her privacy and ignored all the rumors. The French banker, Sancerre, was the contact I used in the Thornhill business, but it was all by wire and telephone, and I don't have the slightest idea about the nun."

I nodded silently. It must have been someone important, although I was certain Amelia had never returned to Europe after she moved to Duck.

"So how are you doing?"

I paused before answering Harvey's question. "Mostly numb, a little tired, and I think I'm angry. Why couldn't she have waited? Maybe if she had told me it was this bad, I could have talked her into getting help or moving in with me."

He reached out his hand and patted my knee. "You can talk to Walt about the medical particulars, but I don't recommend feeling guilty. Amelia had made her decision, and I don't think you could have stopped her." He pointed to the unopened envelope. "I'm sure she explained in the letter."

I bit my lower lip, partly to keep it from quivering. "I hope so," I said and drained my glass. The waiter started toward the table, but I shook my head. I wanted to go back to my room and see what was in the letter.

"Maggie, you go on. I want one more bourbon before I face my sister-in-law again. I'll take care of the bill and see you in the morning." He stood up with me and stretched out his hand.

I took it and pulled close for a quick hug. "I almost forgot, is your office in the same place?"

He laughed. "None of us have moved, Maggie. We let the new folks have all the fancy places, although Stan's bank has opened a branch. You try and get some rest."

"Sure," I said and walked him to the bar where he transferred to one of the empty stools. I stepped out into the parking lot, the evening breeze cooler than when I entered. There were no other cars on the road.

I could see the top of Becky's husband's head as I passed the motel office. He was watching something on television, all but one of the lights turned off. He probably wasn't expecting any other guests at this hour.

The scent of the sea had filled the room while I was gone, night smells different from those during the day, a difference you didn't notice with the occasional visit to the shore. It was a difference you understood if you'd been raised along the water; if you'd spent years wandering around the piers, watching fishing boats launch and dock, inhaling the odor of fresh catch mingled with diesel, sweat, rotting fish heads, and yards of wet netting.

I breathed in those memories of my childhood and sat at the small desk, the envelope in my hand. *For Maggie* it said in Amelia's familiar script. I tore the end open and slid a single sheet of stationery out. The ivory parchment paper I had given her last Christmas, probably written with the Waterman pen I'd brought her from London.

*My Dear Maggie,*

*I don't know when you will read this, but I'm certain you will be angry with me when you do. I hope Walt, or Harvey, or Stan will have talked to you a bit and that you try to understand I made this choice without regret. I am sorry for how you will feel, and perhaps, in the future, you will come to recognize it was the right decision for me.*

*I am also sorry we didn't get to have one last visit together, but on the other hand, this might be best. I am not going to explain much in this note, but I have left a packet for you on the dresser in my bedroom. I think it will answer all of your questions. I told the others it was not to be disturbed as they did whatever chores they needed to do. If I have calculated your schedule correctly, you should have a few days to spend at the house, although you may not wish to. If not, just take those items you want to keep and have Harvey or Stan give the rest to some charity. The house is yours, of course, in case you haven't seen the will yet.*

*Again, I am sorry for the grief this will cause you, and I hope the contents of the packet will help you through this time.*

*All my love,*
*Amelia*

I blinked rapidly, trying to remember my conversations with Walt and Harvey. A packet? Neither one of them had mentioned a packet. What could possibly be in it to help? Explanations? Mementos? I read the note again.

*. . . you should have a few days to spend . . .*

I struggled against the urge to wad the page. Why couldn't she have waited?

*. . . this was the right decision for me.* And for me? Hadn't that mattered to her?

I stood up abruptly, my eyes beginning to sting. Weeping was not my style anymore than it had been Amelia's. *All my love.* Had she ever said those words to me before? Or I to her, for that matter? I couldn't recall a single time that we had actually spoken that way to each other.

The sound of the waves outside called to me. A walk along the sand was what I needed, the stretch of sand, water, sky, stars, moon, and clouds. I pulled a sweater from my suitcase, a hooded woolen piece I bought in a little shop on the Isle of Skye. I slipped into it and let the hood hang behind me so the wind could catch my hair. I walked for more than an hour, remembering the ocean's rhythm. The beach was less than five miles from Amelia's, the topography identical to the section she walked every day, except in the midst of a hurricane. The section she *had* walked, I corrected myself.

I thought of the years between age sixteen and eighteen when Amelia became the center of my life and the years since. What was it going to be like with her gone? The woman who had been a substitute grandmother, a second mother, a mentor, a demanding teacher. A woman who altered my life inexorably, a woman who had chosen her own path, who had cared nothing for the eyebrows she raised around the village. A woman I never understood.

I returned to the room, and to my surprise, sleep came quickly, a welcome blackness, a natural anesthetic to dull the pain.

# Chapter Twenty-five

I stood in front of the cottage, keys in hand, not ready to unlock the door. I walked around for a few minutes instead, trying to accustom myself to the fact that I would not see Amelia once I stepped inside. I could see what Harvey meant about the way it looked. The remaining beds and containers had been weeded, but the meadow was untouched, wildflowers and tall grasses moving with the breeze. Returning the entire meadow to a more natural state was part of the plan Amelia had shown me when she decided to slow down with her gardening.

I crossed onto the flagstone terrace and stopped at the edge of the low stone wall. I loved this spot, where the dune sloped into the beach. If you turned toward the cottage, the French doors led into Amelia's den. My den now. I wasn't really surprised to be the primary heir, but I wasn't prepared to accept either the finality, or what it meant to me financially.

Her will was indeed straightforward—I was to receive the bulk of her estate with no strings attached. The amount of the estate had been another matter altogether. I was stunned when I met with Stan at the bank, and he laid it all out for me without hesitation, the sums no surprise to him. I more or less knew the increase in local land prices brought the value of the house and two acres to more than half a million dollars, but I had not realized her investment portfolio exceeded another seven hundred thousand dollars, nor had I opened the safe deposit box. Thank God, Christina had recommended a good accountant when my career had started bringing in real income. He would be busy for a few weeks.

Like Harvey, I was puzzled by the twenty-five thousand dollars she had bequeathed to Our Lady of the Mountain convent near Zermatt, Switzerland, although it was logically connected to the time she spent there after World War II. The same amount bequeathed to the March of Dimes Foundation was no doubt in honor of Ronny Blackwell, or rather for future Ronny Blackwells, since he died in his early twenties. He had succumbed to the congenital heart problem Doc Rundle had diagnosed at about the same time he explained that Ronny would never be quite "right," never be able to grasp the things his brother and sister could. I listened to the surf and thought of how Ronny had unintentionally served as the catalyst to bring Amelia and me together. Poor Ronny and the bunny rabbits, his joy in something as simple as having lemonade and cookies with "Miss Melly."

A mass of clouds drifted across the sun and brought my mind back to the present, to the feel of the keys in my hand. I retraced my steps, unlocked the front door, and immediately sensed the temperature difference between the sun against my back and the coolness held in by stone walls.

I opened the French doors both to allow fresh air in and because Amelia closed them only during the coldest part of the winter months. From the moment she took her coffee in the morning until the sun set, the doors remained open to the scent of seawater and flowers. The silence brought me no comfort; I had rarely been inside without the sound of classical music, jazz, or blues. A Vivaldi album was on the turntable, and I wondered if Amelia had played it at the end. Or had she wanted only the natural noises from the garden and ocean?

It was so hard to believe she wasn't here, so easy to think she would emerge from the bedroom, laughing at me for having believed something so nonsensical as her death. I closed my eyes and inhaled a deep breath, hoping to at least catch the lingering fragrance of her perfume. The odor of cigarettes, no doubt from the sheriff, and cleaning fluids filled my nostrils. There was something out of place, though, something that didn't fit.

I walked into the kitchen and realized what it was. The not yet faded smell of chlorine was especially concentrated around the sink. Harvey had mentioned that like the outside, the house had appeared cleaned, not simply clean as Amelia kept it, but thoroughly scrubbed. There were no stains on the counters, no smudges on the appliances, even the baseboards were clear of collected dirt.

I opened a cabinet and saw the same pattern—the seals on everything were intact. There wasn't much: a few cans of soup, a can of tuna, a box of pasta, a box of crackers, three jars of Amelia's homegrown tomatoes, a small jar of French sea salt, another of whole peppercorns, and a package of wild and brown rice mix.

The refrigerator was similar with a pint of milk, a container of whipped butter, a half-carton of eggs, packages of hard salami and Black Forest ham, a block of white cheddar cheese, a container of brie, a jar of gourmet mustard, a jar of cornichons, six packs of Diet Coke and Weeping Radish beer, two bottles of an Alsatian Pinot Gris, and a loaf of bread. I checked the expiration dates but knew what I would find. The groceries had probably been delivered a day or two before she called Walt.

*If I've calculated correctly, you should have a few days to spend* . . . That had been in her note to me.

I pushed the door shut, leaned against it, and felt the shudder from my shoulders to my knees. God, she had even thought to order groceries for me.

I caught the tears before they rolled down my cheeks; I had other tasks to accomplish. I checked the second bedroom and smaller bath, although I waited to enter Amelia's room. I wasn't ready to face her most private of spaces. Nothing was out of place, nothing had been left undone; a real estate agent could have easily shown the house to any prospective buyer.

"Amelia was hoping you would keep the place, but she said she would understand if you wanted to sell," Harvey said, after he explained the will.

I was almost speechless. "Sell it? Sell the cottage? Why in God's name would she think I would do that?"

Harvey smiled. "Didn't think you would, but as you can tell, she covered all the bases pretty well. She didn't want you to have to deal with too many details, Maggie."

I wandered as I had during those first visits and looked at the furniture, the paintings, the Persian rugs, the collections of porcelain and crystal. I ran my finger across the leather-bound books in the bookshelf, recently dusted. Amelia alternated between shame and bribes to lure me to the point until I needed no urging to read the classics that she wanted me to be able to discuss. In this cottage, this created, or recreated, piece of French countryside, I had slipped into the dimensions of art, history, music, and extraordinary cuisine.

I pulled her copy of *Journey to the Center of the Earth* from the shelf and thumbed through the pages. An old leather bookmark was in it, the handmade quality of Italian work, Roman or Florentine, from the style. I replaced the book and looked toward the window as a gust of wind rattled the shutters. It was supposed to rain in the late afternoon, and I thought about bringing my bag in. I had already checked out of the motel in an effort to force myself to stay at the cottage.

I sighed and looked at the photograph on the wall. It was the first photograph I had taken of Amelia, a black and white shot of her sitting on the stone wall, her straw hat in her lap, skirt billowed to one side, fine wisps of hair blown across her forehead, longer strands broken loose from the bun she always wore, a bouquet of iris in her right hand. The light had been soft enough to capture her features with little focus on her wrinkles, making it difficult to guess her age. But then, I'd never known how old she was anyway, not until today.

Amelia's face in the photograph chided me for avoiding her bedroom. I flexed my shoulders and walked quickly, purposefully through the door and halted at the foot of the bed. Here, the scent was more familiar with faint traces of the perfume I sought earlier. Little had been disturbed since the officials would have been primarily interested in the notes that had been left on the dining table. The smell of disinfectant was minimal, for I was certain Amelia would have done this cleaning herself.

The package, a large envelope actually, on the dresser drew my attention. This was the one she mentioned in her note. The package that she said contained answers to my questions. I approached it as though it might spring open in some macabre fashion.

The envelope's inanimate state did not alter, and I saw the note attached to the outside, my name in script and a printed warning, "*Walt, you and Harvey don't need to touch this, so leave it for Maggie.*"

I smiled in reaction and wondered if Walt had, too. I lifted it from the dresser and noticed it was not sealed. My willingness to stay in the bedroom waned so I carried it into the dining nook and laid it on the table.

I hesitated again and steadied my hands as I emptied the contents onto the table. Two single sheets of paper scattered across the surface, and another letter, this one sealed, fell in front of me.

Why had Amelia gone to all the trouble to arrange things in this way? Had she begun to suffer some sort of dementia in the last few days or even weeks? Why couldn't she have explained everything in the note Harvey gave me?

I gathered the loose pages and began to read, hoping I could find some comfort in them, some comprehension of what had been going through her mind during the final days before she chose to kill herself.

*My Dear Maggie,*

*By now, you may well be wondering about my mental state, but I assure you, it was sound as I wrote this. Hopefully, the first note Harvey or Walt gave you helped a bit, and I would like to think you are at the house now.*

*The packet you should have in front of you contains the letter you are reading and one more sealed letter, which holds my final words to you. If he has not done so already, a French gentleman, Monsieur Bernard Sancerre, will be contacting you. Harvey knows of him, even though they have never met.*

*I want you to allow Monsieur Sancerre to speak with you at great length and then read the last letter when he has told you all that he can. You may, of course, choose to follow another sequence, but it is genuinely important to me that you do as I ask. Why?*

*Because, a very long time ago, Sarah Thornhill told me that if at no other time in your life you are willing to face truth, you should do so as Death approaches. I didn't understand what she* meant for many years, but as I walked these beaches since then, I came to agree with her, and although I didn't wait as long as she did to face truth, I have invited Death to come sit at my table and there is a story you need to hear.

I have recently realized that for all I tried to do for you, I unintentionally set certain things into motion, which may not have been in your best interest, and you will not be able to fully understand that unless you also understand what Monsieur Sancerre tells you. It is somewhat like a two-edged sword, however, since you may become dismayed by what you hear and wonder if I lied to you from the very beginning.

I have never agreed that lies of omission are the same as commission, nor do I now. I did not reveal the secrets of my past to you, or to others for that matter, because it would have served no purpose. Walt, Harvey, and Stan are the only ones in town who know that certain events occurred during my time in Europe and led to my life of virtual solitude and that my wealth also stemmed from that source. Even they do not know the details, nor have they any need. The only two people who know what you will be told are Sister Agnes of Our Lady of the Mountains convent and Bernard.

Once you have spoken with Bernard, you may open the last letter. No matter how you may feel, no matter how disappointed you may be, please remember, I cared for you as if you were my own daughter. If I had understood the one mistake I made with you, I would have explained these things to you in person, but I am out of time, Maggie. One cannot invite Death and then ask to keep him waiting.

With all my love,
Amelia

I read the letter again, slowly, and held the second envelope, the last words she'd written, in my hand. It felt like two or three pages, but Amelia had scrawled a note on the outside— *I hope you've spoken with Bernard.* I laid the envelope on the table, wondering what to do. I understood what she wanted me to do, but what I didn't understand was why it needed to be this way.

I walked into the kitchen and opened a bottle of beer. The answers to why Amelia lived the life she had, the answers to her life in Europe, revelation of the mysteries she'd wrapped herself in for decades. Answers to questions I had learned not to ask. Answers she had refused to me, to everyone. No, not everyone. The unexplained Sister Agnes and the Frenchman I was to meet knew, or at least knew a great deal more than anyone else. More than anyone except me, if I followed Amelia's instructions.

I stepped out onto the terrace again. I had fantasized of what Amelia's life had been like when she wouldn't tell me. I had resented her refusal then decided it didn't matter. A two-edged sword she said in her note—the chance I would be upset with what I heard.

God knows I was upset with what she'd done, did I want to risk more at this moment? *Unintentionally set things into motion not in my best interest?* How could that be?

Amelia had done things for me beyond my teenage imaginings. It was Amelia who led me, forced me, tempted me to dream, and then put those dreams within my reach. She gave me Paris; she gave me the beginning of my career; she gave me a reason to leave. I was successful, financially secure, even before today, and I was content. If I was not as close to family as I could have been, that was not of Amelia's doing, not really. While she may have given me the means to leave, that long ago comment she made that I would have eventually found my own way was true. What is it that she could have done that was not in my best interest?

But a chance to understand Amelia, a chance to exclusive knowledge, how could I not want that? She obviously wanted me to know; she had certainly gone to a great deal of trouble to arrange this setting. It was important to her and that should be enough for me. But why had she waited until now? Whatever it was, why couldn't she have told me before? If it was important, why did it take her so long to recognize it?

*If I had understood the one mistake I made with you, I would have explained these things to you in person, but I am out of time, Maggie.*

Perhaps that sentence, that need had been the real reason she had called me to ask if I could come for a visit. A visit I was too busy to make. If she had meant to offer me an explanation, did I have any right to now ignore her wishes? But what if the information Monsieur Sancerre possessed was too painful? I had just lost her. Did I want to risk losing what I had known of her? Or at least, what I had accepted as what I knew?

I shaded my eyes as a sailboat came into view several hundred yards distant. It was a nice-size boat, a forty-footer, if not larger. The sails were billowed almost full, running south. Bound for where? Further down the coast, or all the way to Florida? Maybe even the Caribbean. Places I had visited and would again. And if it had not been for Amelia, I would have perhaps made it to Florida, but the Caribbean? It was hard to say.

I turned from the wall of the terrace and strolled back to the rose section of the garden. At this point in April, only a few early blossoms showed; most of the buds were tightly wrapped.

Roses were not Amelia's favorite, but she always said no respectable gardener would refuse to plant them, and although she particularly enjoyed new hybrids, she also kept the classic American Beauty and some pink English tea roses.

I made a mental note to make arrangements for the continued upkeep of what had been an extension of her, even though I would have to meet face-to-face with the intended caretaker before any final agreement was reached. I could hardly allow just anyone access to Amelia's prized grounds. No, it had to be someone who embraced the artistry as well as the science of horticulture.

A pair of yellow butterflies passed over the roses toward the more abundant iris in mixed colors of deep purple, white, and lavender. Iris, the symbol of France. France. Paris. Europe. Amelia's mysterious time there as a young woman. Amelia's letter. The man who could tell me about Amelia.

I drank the last swallow of beer, my decision made. I would follow her instructions as she wished and hope I didn't discover something unbearable. For whatever happened on another continent in the years she had obscured, whatever led to her eccentric seclusion in this spot, none of that could alter what she had done for me. The part of her I knew, the woman I thought of as a second mother, those feelings could surely stand up to whatever I learned of past, or imagined, wrongs, committed in a time before I was born. At least that was what I told myself as I stood in the garden.

# Chapter Twenty-six

Neither Harvey nor Stan had mentioned that I was to meet with Bernard Sancerre, but wouldn't Amelia have told one of them he was to contact me? How? And when? Or did she perhaps tell him to call me directly?

I dialed Harvey first, but he was out of the office. I left a message and tried Stan. His secretary said he was in a meeting and would call me as soon as he finished.

I read Amelia's letter once more and stared at the sealed envelope, fighting the urge to tear it open. How important was it really that I wait? Suppose this Monsieur Sancerre didn't contact me? After all, not everyone Amelia knew was willing to carry out her instructions. Well actually, I guess everyone did.

Sudden hunger pangs sent me to the refrigerator for a sandwich. It was the first time in three days anything tasted good, so I thought I would try some cheese as well. I was reaching for the box of crackers when the telephone rang. It was Stan.

I explained what I needed as well as I could considering my confusion and told him Harvey was possibly the one who would know, but I wasn't sure. He was silent for several seconds.

"That's certainly interesting," he said. "I was, in fact, meeting with Mr. Bernard Sancerre when you called."

I paused. "Here's here?"

"He is indeed. He's with the Banque Francaise and received

a letter from Amelia last week to contact either Harvey or me in order to find out where you would be. His signal was the telegraph I sent. Even though he dealt with Harvey years ago, he wanted to talk with me about some of Amelia's foreign holdings."

"What did he tell you?"

"Not a great deal about you, but we did have a nice discussion about Amelia's finances. He was quite discreet."

"So what did you tell him?"

"I told him I would call you and let you decide what to do. He's staying at the Sanderling. He's probably there now if he went straight back."

"Let me have the number," I said. "Stan, didn't you pry anything out of him?"

"I'm a banker, Maggie, been one all of my life. We don't pry; it's not good business. How are you doing by the way?"

"All right, I guess. Did you know Amelia left other letters for me?"

"Walt told me about the package on the dresser, and it makes sense she would have much more to say to you than to us. Anything you have problems with or can't handle?"

"I guess not," I said reluctantly. "I just wish she had talked to me instead of concocting this craziness." The words were out before I could stop. "Speaking of which, was she really in full possession of her senses during the . . . well, you know, toward the . . . I mean last week."

Stan sighed. "Maggie, I know it's hard, and I don't understand why Amelia set it up this way, maybe some last streak of orneriness. But yes, she was fully alert and nitpicky as hell when she came to see me. You've just got to trust that she had a good reason. It hardly seems likely that Mr. Sancerre would have flown from Paris just for the hell of it."

That did make sense—I mean why would a man whom I had never met travel across the Atlantic to see me unless it served a real purpose? "Yeah, I guess you're right. Thanks, Stan, I'll call him and let you know what happens."

I dialed the number without hanging up the telephone. Monsieur Sancerre was in, sounded like a polished gentleman, and thankfully agreed to take a taxi immediately. I paced slowly in front of the gate and tried to remain calm when I saw the cab stop. The gentleman in question paid the driver, executed an elegant pivot, and extended his hand.

"I am Bernard Sancerre of the Banque Francaise at your service," he said formally, with the barest of accents. "And you are Maggie, of course."

I smiled. "Yes, I am. It is a pleasure, although I must admit that I am somewhat confused at this point, Monsieur Sancerre."

His smile was practiced, the banker you could entrust with your fortune. "Please call me Bernard. Some perplexity is to be expected, dear young lady. Our Amelia could be irritatingly opaque, despite her other charms. I am honored she requested that I be the one to come and visit you. But first, if you do not object, may I take a moment to walk around Amelia's house?"

"Certainly, we'll go around back and in through the terrace. It's quite lovely and unique for this area. I do know Amelia had it built like someplace she used to visit in France."

He nodded without speaking, and I led the way by the garden, past the garage. He was a little over a head taller than I, slender in the way older men are who have taken care of themselves, had pure white hair combed back with only a slightly receding hairline, and wore an expensive dark suit, very much the picture of a successful banker. I knew he must be in his late seventies or early eighties, but his stride and carriage were that of a man several years younger.

He stopped at the wall and stared out to sea. "A stone cottage overlooking the Atlantic Ocean. How appropriate," he said quietly.

"Excuse me?"

He shook his head. "It is nothing, my dear, merely the memories of an old man."

We went inside where I motioned him toward the sofa. I handed him Amelia's letter, while I quickly prepared a tray with two glasses of wine.

He was finished reading when I took the chair across from him. There was an undisguised look of sadness on his face.

"Is all you know of my visit what is written here?"

"Yes, although there was another note, which briefly explained why she made the decision she did, that requested I come here to the cottage, and told me where I would find the package with the other two letters. As you can see, she wants me to wait to open the last letter. What did she ask you to do?"

He took a sip of wine, giving it his unspoken approval. "It is complicated, as you might expect. But before I begin to pass along to you what Amelia wanted me to say, I must acknowledge you are not unknown to me. You see, I am Jean-Claude's uncle."

I stared at him, my mouth dropping open despite myself. He nodded slowly, as if to verify his statement while pieces to the puzzle locked into place.

"The job! The bank account! It was you?"

"At Amelia's request, naturally. I often wished to meet you, but Amelia insisted that I not, for she was certain your curiosity would have been overwhelming at your age, and she did not wish you to know of her past with me."

"Excuse me, I need a moment," I said almost abruptly, feeling a sensation in my stomach like when you peer down too quickly from a great height. I walked out onto the terrace to the wall and gazed to the sea where sky and water became indistinguishable. There were no boats in sight, not even birds. An ageless vista, except I knew what lay beyond my view. I had flown above the wide expanse at Amelia's urging, unaware that another person had been a part of her plan for me, or her vision of what I could be. An unknown, unseen guardian right there in Paris with me? Evidently, and he was sitting in the cottage waiting for me to regain my composure.

Bernard rose as I joined him.

"I'm sorry," I said. "It was such a surprise. I feel as though I should thank you for what you did."

He waved his hand in the French gesture of dismissal and settled onto the sofa again. "It could have been nothing less than a shock, and you owe me nothing. It has been enjoyable observing your professional growth over the years. I am quite a fan, you know. And since the secret has been revealed, perhaps I can persuade you to autograph one of your marvelous photographs for me."

"Of course, that's the least I can do."

"And now, I believe that we must speak of Amelia."

"Where do you start?"

He handed me the other glass of wine.

"This is not a quick or simple story. And as Amelia wrote in her letter, it is expected that you will become distressed, although with what I know of you, I think you will understand in the end. But if you could tell me what you do know of her life in Europe, it would give me a proper point from which to begin."

I frowned with concentration, trying to piece together my

infrequent glimpses into Amelia's past. "I was told by someone other than Amelia that she had a difficult childhood and came to work for Mrs. Thornhill after her parents died. She went to Paris with Mrs. Thornhill and remained there when Mrs. Thornhill died unexpectedly. It is my impression that there was a man she fell in love with, and I think he was probably wealthy, but something happened and she left Paris and went to Germany, not realizing the political situation. What Amelia told me over the years was that she lived in Paris for a time, stayed in Germany until almost the end of the war, then was in Switzerland, somehow came back here, had this place built, and became our local eccentric recluse."

I paused for a sip of wine. "Doesn't seem like much to know considering our relationship, does it?"

He smiled. "On the contrary, Amelia must have thought a great deal of you to tell you what she did. Did she ever mention she was a somewhat celebrated singer in the Parisian cabaret circles?"

I raised my eyebrows. "Amelia, a singer? An entertainer in front of audiences? That's difficult to imagine."

"Well then, we have our starting point, for it was Amelia's time as a singer which was the beginning of what followed. So I will talk and you can tell me when to stop."

I nodded, leaned forward, and in listening to Bernard, stepped back with him to Paris in 1935.

# Chapter Twenty-seven

B ernard's voice segued from conversational to that of telling a story. "I think it is best to begin with an explanation of myself, Emil de Montrat, and Henri Greville. You see, we were close companions, all the same age, twenty-three; the age when young men know they will soon have to fulfill family expectations and, therefore, are inclined to seek many pleasures before domestic obligations rein them in. The difference in us, however, was that Emil and Henri belonged to a more privileged class than I, their family names a part of France's aristocracy, while my family was well-to-do and accepted, but not considered of the same social value, shall we say. Despite a lack of titles, however, clever financiers have always been needed, and thus we were often invited into the more refined circles."

"You mean Amelia was involved with a duke or something?" I interrupted.

"Not precisely, but the de Montrats had been a presence at court from the time of Henri IV and the Grevilles almost as long. Naturally, there had been some reversal of fortune during the Revolution, but both families recovered remarkably well. At any rate, the history is merely to put their status into perspective. I became friends with Emil and Henri during our days at the university, and as I said, proper marriages and following in our fathers' footsteps were soon to be our fate, so we decided to enjoy a libertine life as long as possible. Despite the economic woes in the world, our families were protected. We left the internal power struggles to the wisdom of our elders and were too self-indulgent to understand the political winds brewing across the Saar River. Besides, like all patriotic Frenchmen, we believed in the strength of the Maginot Line. It was an impenetrable defense against any future advances of Germany."

He paused for a sip of wine and I tried to curb my impatience. I could sense it was important to understand the chronology of what he had to say.

"Despite my constant companionship with Emil and Henri, I happened to be with other friends the night we went to La Femme d'Or. They had engaged a new singer, an American girl, who was said to be both lovely and quite talented. The way she sang 'Billie's Blues' was surpassed only by her beauty. Her hair was golden then, her eyes, of course, that green not quite like the emeralds. I was enchanted and, in looking back, realized I should have waited before I insisted Henri and Emil come with me to hear her."

"Billie Holiday," I said. "She has, I mean had, all her records."

"Yes, I took care of them for her when she left Paris, one of the few things she knew she would want to keep."

"So, you met her that night?"

He smiled, the loss not faded by passing decades. "Unfortunately no, for like many men, I did not have the confidence in approaching a beautiful woman immediately, but instead spoke of her the next day and, in my admiration, sparked Emil's interest. Possessing an arrogance which seems to be common among his class, he thought to purchase a diamond bracelet before we attended the show. He sent it to Amelia backstage and requested she join us after the performance. Her attraction to him was therefore understandable, although ultimately regrettable," he said, flickering his eyes down to his hands, then back up to me.

"A diamond bracelet to a woman he hadn't met? Wasn't that a bit extravagant?"

"Oh, very much so, and Henri chastised him later about not giving us a chance. Emil's response was that victory belongs to the daring."

"But Amelia was a nightclub singer, hardly a suitable match for someone like the way you describe de Montrat."

Bernard lifted one eyebrow. "My dear, surely you are familiar with the concept of the type of women men marry and those they do not intend to."

I frowned in spite of my impractical resolve to try and listen objectively.

"Amelia was simply a conquest then? Another opportunity for one-up-manship?"

"A perceptive comment, yet as we both know, our Amelia was not without surprises, even at her youthful age. She appeared at our table afterwards, inquired as to which one was Emil, handed him the box, and said, 'It is a wonderful bracelet, monsieur, but if you wish to bed me, I don't come that inexpensively.'"

I failed to hide my shock. "She said it like that? Just straight out like that? And his response?"

"He laughed and told her to keep it while he thought of a suitable gift. She did accept our invitation to dinner, was witty and charming, her French good with a delightful accent. If you paid attention, you could tell she was not entirely comfortable with luxurious surroundings, although she conducted herself well. She displayed a fascinating blend of false sophisticate, waif, seductress, and innocent, an altogether irresistible

Charlie Hudson

combination. It seemed reasonable she came from a humble background, but she would say only that she was an American who had fallen in love with Paris. She refused to allow us to take her to her apartment, and when we returned her to the club, she politely kissed each of us good-night and said we must decide for ourselves who would continue the pursuit. She had no shortage of admirers but thought we demonstrated more possibility than the others."

"Just like that?"

"Ah, yes, an unforgettable comment."

"And?"

"We assured her we would decide by the time she took to the stage the next evening. We left and went to one of the other clubs we frequented. It was heartbreaking for me to acknowledge, but I concluded my lesser financial status was probably a limitation. Therefore, it was between Emil and Henri. Emil reminded us he had taken the first step, but that's when Henri pointed out that Amelia had not accepted his offer. So in the fashion of those days, they called for the dice cup and agreed the winner would be given one opportunity only to suitably impress her, and if he failed, the other could step in."

Bernard paused, shrugged, and continued. "Emil won, and he had a matching diamond necklace and earrings delivered to the club along with a new dress from one of the most exclusive designer houses in Paris. Once again, it was a gesture that was outrageous, and I never knew if he was genuinely captivated by Amelia or he was determined to best Henri. We arrived at the club the next night, but Amelia refused to see us until after her performance. When she joined us, she was wearing the ensemble Emil had given her."

"She sold herself?" I struggled to hold back a feeling of dismay.

Bernard set his glass down and reached to pat my hand. "Please, Maggie, do not think in that way."

I exhaled a deep breath. "It's pretty obvious."

"Not really," he countered. "You know from your time in Europe that we view such arrangements more liberally than you Americans. I did not think of Amelia in those terms, for I understood it was the way of the world. I was not so foolish as to hope I could have her heart, and yet, I sensed that perhaps I could fill a special role, that of a sort of teacher and confidant. After all, I knew that Emil was not a man of patience, and if she wished to not make the social mistakes, she would require someone to help her with these things. She was reluctant at the beginning, not wishing to risk the relationship with Emil, but I promised I would behave honorably. I upheld that promise, and within time, she told me stories of her upbringing. You know I believe, that it was quite tragic, for her to have a father so cruel, to lose her brothers and sister and then even her mother. I think if you know more of that sadness, it will be easier to understand."

I nodded, trying to sort through my conflicting emotions.

Bernard shifted his position. "Like many who grow up in poverty, Amelia valued security highly. Her employment with Mrs. Thornhill was entered into under less than ideal circumstances, and while she did provide Amelia the chance to learn how to behave properly within upper class society, she was still, for all practical purposes, a servant. From what Amelia told me, the woman was not unkind to her but was quite demanding until near the end when she softened. That will play an important part, but comes much later in the story. At the time it occurred, Mrs. Thornhill's unanticipated death was a blow to Amelia. Another example of how easily the foundation could disappear beneath her."

"You've lost me," I admitted. "What does Mrs. Thornhill's death have to do with Amelia singing in a Parisian cabaret and looking for security?"

"Yes, of course, I did leave out that part when I began with the night I met Amelia. You remember I mentioned Mrs. Thornhill was a formidable woman? Apparently, she alienated her two children after her husband died. I understand that it was her beach house which was once a part of these grounds."

"That's correct. It was a huge house but burned down in 1950 maybe. I was told both the Thornhill son and daughter died in an airplane crash around that time, so the estate was in quite a mess, but then somehow Amelia was a part of it. Does all of this eventually make sense?"

Bernard smiled gently at my frustration. "Yes, it does but not in a straightforward manner. Shall I continue?"

"Yes, please, I'll try not to interrupt."

"All right, where was I? Ah, yes, Mrs. Thornhill. I was never sure of the reason she came to Paris, but Amelia, as she told us, embraced the city from the moment they arrived. Mrs. Thornhill was active during the first several months, and Amelia accompanied her to galleries, salons, the parks, and so forth. Fortunately, the housekeeper Mrs. Thornhill hired took a liking to Amelia and helped her learn to speak an acceptable level of French rather quickly. The pleasant sojourn came to an end when Mrs. Thornhill contracted influenza and, too weak to return to America, reluctantly sent for her son."

I suddenly remembered the passage from Amelia's letter: *Because, a very long time ago, Sarah Thornhill told me that if, at no other time in your life, you are willing to face truth, you should do so as Death approaches.* A reaction must have reflected on my face for Bernard stopped speaking. I motioned for him to resume.

"Apparently Mrs. Thornhill called Amelia in, told her she was dying, and that in gratitude for the service she had rendered, she wanted Amelia to take the sum of three hundred dollars and remain in Paris for a while if she wished. Amelia didn't believe the situation was quite so serious, but it soon became obvious. Amelia accepted the money, and Mrs. Thornhill died three days later. The son arrived only the day before her death, terminated the lease on the house, and informed everyone, including Amelia, that they had lived off his mother long enough and they would receive not a dime more from him."

"What was Amelia to do?"

"The son didn't care, nor did he know of Mrs. Thornhill's bequest to Amelia. Had he known, he would have perhaps found a way to deprive her of it. She kept silent and let the younger Mr. Thornhill leave the country as quickly as possible.

"The housekeeper did not know of the money, and even if she had, that sum would not last for too long a time. She had often heard Amelia sing to her employer, knew the owner of La Femme d'Or, and arranged a meeting. He was in a bit of difficulty because one of his singers had eloped, so he agreed to hire Amelia temporarily. As I mentioned earlier, she was genuinely talented and rapidly became popular. Business at the club increased, the owner was happy, and then I wandered in and we are back to my beginning."

"With no better an explanation of why Amelia was willing to be essentially purchased. If she was a success, why did she need Emil?"

The Frenchman sighed. "Ah, Maggie, the times were different then. It was not easy for a woman to be alone. There were no career women then, no independent structure outside a family life, and Amelia knew her popularity could disappear with no notice. She might be given an offer by one of the larger clubs, but there was no guarantee by any means. It was commonplace for singers, dancers, and actresses to catch the eye of a wealthy man, a man who would be willing to keep them in a comfortable style. You can surely understand what it was like for a young woman with no family and little money to want the sort of security a man such as Emil could provide."

"She must have known it couldn't last."

Bernard spread his hands philosophically. "That is why she was looking for someone of Emil's financial status. She thought his demonstrations of affection, shall we say, would allow her to build what I believe you call a 'nest egg'."

He hesitated with the term, and I indicated he was using the correct idiom.

"You see, Maggie, Amelia was young, beautiful, desired by men, and for the first time in her life, able to, what is your expression, 'call the shots'? It would have been a great temptation for anyone, and I can assure you, Emil enjoyed displaying his riches. His indulgences were well known. The diamonds he gave her were to him the same as giving a bouquet of roses would be for me. Why should not Amelia take advantage of it?"

I exhaled again. His point was difficult to argue with. Was this what Amelia thought I might find disturbing? Well, didn't I? On the other hand, it was really only the idea she'd chosen Emil for his money that bothered me, and wasn't that absurdly judgmental considering her circumstances?

I tried a smile. "I suppose when you look at it realistically, Amelia probably selected a sensible course," I said. "I mean, you're right, becoming a wealthy man's mistress is hardly a new concept." I realized I was missing something when I saw the depth of sadness in Bernard's eyes. "But that's not all, is it?"

He stood before answering, walked to the bookcase, and

picked up Amelia's photograph. He stared at it without speaking then turned to me.

"No, Maggie, Amelia's selection of Emil as her benefactor was in fact, only the tip of the iceberg, I believe is the term. I was anxious to talk to you, but now seeing you here, seeing how much you felt for Amelia, perhaps she and I were wrong about what you should know. The human frailties one can accept tend to increase when you are my age. Perhaps it is best to stop now and leave you to your personal memories, undisturbed by stories of her past."

I practically leapt from the chair. "You can't be serious! You tell me this much, and then you want to stop? I admit I had misgivings when I read her letter, but no matter what you tell me, it shouldn't change how I feel about her, and it can't change what she did for me. No, Bernard, we've opened this box, and I want to see what's inside."

"Very well," he said, "if it is not bothersome, I think another glass of wine and moving to the terrace would be in order. The next part of the story is quite complex, and I wish to tell it accurately, in the most fitting way."

"That's not a bad idea. Please go out to the table, and I'll join you in a few minutes."

I refilled the glasses and added cheese, slices of the ham, and crackers to a tray. I carefully carried it outside, as I reassured myself I was ready to hear the rest of Amelia's secrets.

# Chapter Twenty-eight

Bernard was seated at the table, and he looked around with an odd air of familiarity. "Amelia told you this was like a place she had been to in France?"

"Yes, but I don't remember where."

His voice was reflective, reaching into another part of the story. "Bretagne; Brittany, as it is said in English. There is an impressive lodge only a few kilometers from Nantes. This is the guest cottage, or rather, a remarkable duplication of it. The stone wall, the design of the garden, all of it."

"It was a property of the de Montrats?"

"Oh, yes, it was one of Emil's favorite places. His mother, a grand dame in the finest French tradition, ruled the Parisian house without question; his sister preferred their chalet in the Alps; and his father spent most of his time traveling on business. Emil used the lodge as his escape when his exploits raised the ire of his mother or when he wished to hold particularly hedonistic parties, shall we say."

I didn't think I needed too many details of the parties. "Why did Emil's mother tolerate his affair with a singer with, what I'm sure she must have considered, an unworthy background?"

Bernard tilted his head. "Emil was the oldest son, and Madame de Montrat always indulged him within rather broad limits. He understood that when it came time for a marriage,

his parents, his mother in particular, would present him with a
list of candidates from which he was permitted to select. Until
that time, he was allowed to take certain liberties with his behavior. Like the rest of us, she presumed Amelia would soon be
cast aside for a new interest."

"And that didn't happen?"

Bernard was surprisingly quiet as he appeared to think
of how to answer my question. "As I said before, Amelia was
charmed by Emil, yet held no illusions about her role in his
life. At least, not at first. I have asked myself many times since
then about their feelings, and I have come to believe that, for
Amelia, Emil was simply more than she ever expected. And for
Emil, Amelia's unique character was beguiling, stronger than
he anticipated."

He paused for a sip of wine. "You see, despite an attempt
at detachment, at pretending she could, what is your phrase,
'take things in stride', she was impressionable. Emil took pleasure in surprising her, and unlike some of the other women of
unworthy background to use your term, Amelia possessed a
taste for culture. She was willing—no, eager—to learn and an
avid reader." A smile came and faded. "When I first offered to
help teach the social graces she was lacking, I did so as a way
to be close to her, and then, it was difficult for me not to take
pride in seeing how quickly she took to the lessons. Within a
few months, it was impossible to tell during a normal encounter that Amelia had not been born into the life of the wealthy.
She had an excellent eye for artistic objects, and she advised
Emil well on some purchases when he took her to three or four
auctions."

"It's funny, but I can remember how I thought the cottage
looked like a museum the first time I stepped inside. I'd never
seen anything like it except maybe in the movies."

Bernard nodded. "Amelia could probably have been a marvelous decorator or art dealer if she'd had the opportunity. She occasionally discussed the possibility of Emil buying her a gallery or bookstore when their affair would inevitably end, and at the time, I had no reason to believe she did not understand that it *would* end. You see, the early part of the relationship went according to how these affairs go. Emil literally showered her with expensive presents, moved her into a lovely apartment, and took her to lavish late night dinners while Henri, never one to sit idle, took up with an Italian actress. I contented myself with admiring Amelia, secure in my role of friend and confidant, something she had never had before. In retrospect, the change began when Emil decided Amelia should stop singing so she could travel with him."

"She agreed?"

"They had a bit of a row. Amelia asked what was to happen to her if Emil decided he too preferred Italian actresses, or more likely, when Madame de Montrat decided he should marry properly to enhance the family's standing. Emil told her she meant more to him than that, no Italian actress could compare, and no matter what happened, he would see to her future. He said he would buy her a cabaret if she wished, just as we predicted. And, of course, Amelia knew, as did we all, that she could retain her status as Emil's mistress once he was married if he exercised a degree of discretion."

"No marriage to Amelia, of course?"

Bernard sighed. "At that point, they both still understood what was expected. It was, if I recall correctly, during a trip to Rome that Amelia confided to me that she thought Emil might consider risking his family's anger for her sake."

"What was your reaction?"

"I was stunned, naturally. I asked her why she would think

that, and she told me Emil was growing tired of his mother's old-fashioned ways. He had told her that it was 1936, not 1836, and he should be free to marry who he wished. I tried to gently dissuade her, as was only sensible, but she assured me she would keep her wits about her. She did not intend to press the subject, but to continue to enhance her knowledge of things and social bearing, in what I too late realized was her belief that she could ultimately be accepted by the de Montrats."

"You talked to Emil afterwards?"

"But naturally, my dear, and he confirmed he had said such nonsense to her. He laughed at my concerns and told me to enter the modern age. Oh certainly, he would take his time, get his father on his side, and so forth. I took his willingness to wait as a good sign, but perhaps, even then, I knew the outcome could not possibly be fortunate. Had I understood the tragedy that awaited, I would have done more. I truly thought Emil would delay Amelia, recognize the unlikelihood of defying his parents' wishes, and then, ah Maggie, in the deepest part of my heart, I think I expected Amelia to eventually turn to me for solace. I could never provide for her in the same style as Emil, but I could have given her a moderately wealthy, secure home. She would have been safe with me."

I watched him as he spoke and was certain that this must have been the first time in years he had articulated his thoughts. The reminiscences of youth, his obvious love for Amelia, the pain of whatever was to come, and loss were woven together as surely as if he had penned the words to a poem.

The hint of a sigh escaped his lips as he resumed his narrative. "And so, for months we continued to enjoy ourselves, insulated from reality with the protection of money. We traveled in the manner of the rich: skiing in the Alps, trips on the Orient Express, parties while in Paris, weekends at the lodge in Bretagne. I had begun to work with my father in the financial world and, therefore, was more aware of the political rumblings, but discounted the events in Germany, as did many people. Oh, yes, there were those who warned of waiting dangers, but others, knowledgeable in global affairs, who seemed assured Europe was under control. Even today with all I know, I sometimes wonder how we could have chosen to see so little."

His voice trailed to nearly a whisper, the last sentence spoken almost to himself. He shook his head and half-smiled an apology. "Neither Emil nor Amelia said anything further of their intentions, and I wrongly concluded they had both realized the improbability of a marriage. Again in looking back, the signs were there, the way Amelia would sometimes speak of a larger apartment in Paris, or of how she might wish to redecorate the lodge. Emil said nothing to me, but I could hear them arguing late at night and held my hope the day of their separation would come. It did not, and somehow we celebrated the passage into 1937, the spring. April. April the twenty-second to be precise."

"April the twenty-second? How odd, that's the same day that Amelia . . . that was her last day," I said, startled. "What a coincidence."

Bernard lifted one eyebrow in a look I couldn't read. "It had been a cold winter in spite of our ability to escape for periods to warmer climates, and we were grateful for the pleasantness of spring. A call for more celebration, the traditional time for thoughts of romance."

He faltered, and I was momentarily alarmed, whether for his sake or mine, I couldn't say. He took a couple of steadying breaths.

"Are you all right?"

"Yes, but now I arrive at one of the difficult parts."

*One of the difficult parts?*

"We were in the de Montrats' Paris house. Madame de Montrat was visiting her sister for the evening and was not expected to return. It was after midnight, and Emil had, as usual during his mother's absence, hosted a party. It was a somewhat sedate gathering by Emil's standards, although Amelia had been cross with him for much of the evening, almost ignoring him. Finally, the four of us—Emil, Henri, Amelia, and I—were alone as often happened when these parties ended. Henri was out of sorts because his latest conquest had been disappointing, and he was in between women. Again in retrospect, I think he had never truly forgiven Emil for his easy win of Amelia. Granted, she flirted with Henri constantly, and it was upon occasion the source of harsh words with Emil, but it always passed as a minor thing. On this night, though, she had been more attentive of Henri than usual during the party."

I wanted him to get to the point, sensing the importance of what he was about to say.

"So, here we were, and Henri began to complain that he should have to go home alone and that if Emil were a true friend, he would either allow Amelia to go with him or they would engage in a *ménage à trois* or *quatre*, if I wished to join, that surely after all our escapades together, we were ready to engage in such pleasures. Emil gave him a churlish response, and Amelia rather coolly pronounced she might be agreeable. I was nearly speechless and quickly tried to deflect the course of the conversation by reminding Henri that the pretty Mademoiselle Bonant had made her availability known to him.

"I clearly remember his words, 'She is nothing compared to Amelia,' because they were spoken with an unusual degree of vehemence."

I swallowed, seeing the scene as he described it. "Sounds as if the friendship was becoming strained."

Bernard nodded slowly. "How little we understand human passions. Emil turned to Amelia and said she must stop teasing Henri, that she belonged to him, and he would have no more of this talk. Amelia was strangely silent as Henri said it was Amelia's decision as it had always been. Amelia said, and for the love of God I cannot tell you why, that if they were men, they would fight for her."

"What?"

Bernard's face twisted. "Those were the very words she used. It was then that it happened, a moment that even now, it is difficult for me to believe that Emil's rage came so swiftly. He turned, any thought of friendship consumed into a sudden fury, and snatched a pair of dueling swords from the wall. Tossing one to Henri, he lunged for him. I thought so many times after that how few seconds passed from our life together and that terrible moment. I found myself frozen at their anger and dared not step between them. I begged Amelia to stop them, but she looked at me and said they would tire before they harmed one another and we should allow them their amusement. Again, I do not know why she refused to acknowledge what was happening in front of her. It was no harmless play."

I felt frozen myself, unsure of what to say.

"It was a terrible sight, for they each drew blood from several cuts. I think they must have lost touch with their surroundings, for their faces were locked into battle, the faces of enemies, not friends. I do not remember how many minutes passed; I tried to think of some way to intervene. Emil had always been the more accomplished fencer, and with a powerful slash, Henri collapsed, his neck nearly separated from his head."

"Oh my God!"

Bernard breathed deeply, raggedly. "The blow caused Emil

to stop at last. He realized what he'd done, dropped the sword, and began to tend to Henri, who had lost consciousness. Blood soaked into the carpet as Emil tried to staunch the flow. *Mon Dieu*, the blood! I telephoned my doctor, a man of great discretion, who lived nearby. He arrived as quickly as possible, but I think we all knew it was too late."

My voice had dropped to a loud whisper. "What did Amelia do?"

"She too was in a state of shock, unable to speak or move. We stood there, praying the doctor could help, when Madame de Montrat entered the room. I presumed the secretary had called her."

"Well, what did she do? Panic, fly into a fit?"

Bernard's eyes were stricken, the memory undimmed. "Ah, Maggie, either of those might have been better. No, in all the years I had known Madame de Montrat, never had I seen her so completely glacial. She looked around the room, called the doctor away from Henri into the hallway, spoke with him for a moment, and then directed the removal of Henri by the servants. The doctor left with him, and she returned to us. Emil started to speak, but she told him to keep silent."

Bernard visibly braced himself. "She stared at Emil and said she had permitted his adolescent, irresponsible behavior too long. Now she would make matters right, and he would keep quiet while she took care of this mess. She turned to Amelia and said she would have her taken to the train station, that once she was safely out of the country, neither the police nor the press would have anyone to contradict Emil. Naturally, Amelia said she would never do anything to hurt Emil, but Madame de Montrat said Amelia was a fool if she thought she would allow her to stay with her son for so much as another minute."

"And you, did she forget about you?"

"I was from their circle, Maggie; yes, the fringes, but still within the circle. Madame de Montrat knew I would play by their rules. Amelia was the only outsider involved, as well as the cause of all that had happened, as far as Madame was concerned."

"And Emil had no blame?" I tried to control my rising anger, but the privileges granted to the privileged who could afford them were always difficult to stomach.

Bernard shrugged. "Not within the world of the de Montrats. His payment would be extracted in other ways. For now, the avoidance of a scandal was all important, and the Grevilles would feel the same. Whether it was right or wrong, fair or unfair, Madame de Montrat knew the actions to take. She pulled an envelope from her handbag and said it contained fifty thousand francs for Amelia to take with her. She would send more if it was needed. I watched as Amelia composed herself until she was almost as icy as Madame. She said that she didn't believe Emil would let her go, and if he was willing to do so, she certainly didn't need Madame's money."

I searched his face, beginning to understand. "I can't imagine that had much impact."

"You are correct. Madame turned to Emil and told him he could choose right then if he wished to be disowned as a de Montrat or permit Amelia to leave. She made it clear, that there was to be no quarter given, no chance for him to think about his response."

I wondered what it must have been like for Amelia, one man killed in front of her, the man she loved ready to betray her, and another man who had declared himself to be her friend apparently powerless to help her.

If I had photographed Bernard's face at that moment, anyone looking at it would have seen the sadness. "Emil could not even speak, would not reach out to Amelia. He stared at the blood on the floor and looked away in shame, leaving the struggle between the two women. Then suddenly, perhaps because Emil's weakness was embarrassing, Madame de Montrat said to Amelia in an almost gentle tone, 'My dear, I have no doubt you actually love my son, and in a way, he may love you, but that is simply not important. Whether you accept the money or not is of no consequence to me, nor shall it alter my opinion of you one way or the other. I should think, however, it would be in your best interest to take it. As you must surely see, Emil has made his choice.'"

I wanted to weep for Amelia.

Bernard almost stumbled in his telling. "I can clearly remember the words between the women, the strength in Amelia's voice, the reflection in her eyes, when she reached for the envelope. 'I suppose there are certain cold realities in life we cannot be shielded from.' Then she turned and asked if I would accompany her to the railroad station."

"You went with her?"

"How could I not? Madame de Montrat signaled for the chauffeur, and Amelia strode from the room without a glance to Emil. I followed her, and once we were in the car, the glass partition closed, she leaned against my shoulder and wept for only a few minutes until she pulled herself away, her face determined. She dried her tears long enough to stop at the apartment for only two suitcases and her jewelry box. She asked me to keep her records until she sent for them, burn the rest, or give it to charity; she didn't want anything else as a reminder."

"Where did you go after that?"

"When we arrived at the station, there were early morning trains to Rome, Frankfurt, Amsterdam, Madrid, Munich, Copenhagen, Innsbruck, to connect to London, and other cities

I suppose. I asked her if she wanted to return to America, but she said there was nothing for her there. I suggested London for the language, but she said it was too gray. She said she had a gentleman friend she had met from Munich who had insisted she come for a visit someday. The status of politics was not on my mind at that moment, or I would have insisted on anywhere except Germany. She also gave me half the money from the envelope and told me to use my marvelous banking skills and do something worthy with it. She would let me know where she was in a few days."

Bernard took another breath. "I do not believe I can properly explain what it was like to stand on the platform and watch her board the train. I wanted desperately to do what was right, but I did not know what it was. I wanted to tell her that I loved her, that I could come for her later, but, Maggie, I could not speak those words. All I could think of was to do as she instructed. I have never felt such a moment of pain, not even when I saw Henri die in Emil's arms."

We were both silent, he lost in his memories, me with tumultuous emotions fighting to emerge.

Did I feel sorry for Amelia or did I blame her for taking the path she did? I'd been warned the truth was distressing, yet I had told myself I could handle it. I had not imagined something like this. I tried to keep my voice from quavering when I spoke.

"My God, what a story! No wonder you were unsure of how much to tell me. Of all places, she picked Munich in 1937! Well, that helps explain how she eventually went to Switzerland, and I suppose her money must have come from whatever investments you made for her. Her refusal to discuss her past makes a lot more sense now. But even so, and I'm not saying what she did was right, I can't see how all of that led to her decision to withdraw from the rest of the world. And that still doesn't answer how she came back here, to this piece of property."

Bernard set his glass on the table, rose, and walked to the stone wall. He stared out at the ocean a moment then turned toward me, his voice bleak. "Unfortunately, Maggie, there is more tragedy to be told, more pieces of the puzzle to fit together."

# Chapter Twenty-nine

I knew Bernard was observing my reaction, no doubt attempting to determine my emotional state. I had long ago learned to hide feelings I could not avoid in a family that had no use for open displays of emotion. I funneled my passion into my photographs instead, a fact that Jean-Claude had noted almost immediately when I began work as his apprentice.

At this moment I had no camera to shield me, nor would it help if I did. I could not step back and rearrange this scene to suit me, or wait for the light to be perfect. As with a wild subject of nature, I could only capture it, not change it, not control it.

"I know of no way to be more gentler, Maggie," Bernard said quietly, walking back to the table. He sat again, facing me.

It was my turn to sigh, to search for words. "I don't know what I expected you to tell me. Oh sure, a torrid love affair, I guessed that not long after I met Amelia. I suppose I fantasized that she might have been involved in some government scandal, hidden an illegitimate child or an abortion, maybe even been a spy during the war, something more . . . something less . . . well, not this."

I drained my glass and refilled both of them. "It's not as if Amelia was a woman overflowing with warmth; she was a recluse, for God's sake. And we didn't sit around discussing our affection for each other, but she cared about me, Bernard, and I for her. I can believe parts of this, while other things just don't match. I'm neither naïve nor overly sheltered; it's just that the Amelia you're telling me about is so different from the one I knew. It was pretty obvious all along that something haunted her, something kept her from marrying, and she was stubborn as she could be, but she never seemed to be viciously manipulative. This woman you're describing, this girl who kidded herself into thinking she could join high society, who goaded her rich lover into killing another man, is someone else. She has to be."

Bernard nodded once. "I understand what you're saying, and that is why you should probably hear the rest since we have gone this far. I think it is only then that you can grasp how she came to be the woman you knew. Are you ready?"

I inhaled shallowly and exhaled a long breath. "I might as well be. All right, she left Paris for Munich. What then?"

"I received a telegram to tell me she arrived safely, and then there was nothing for weeks. She finally sent a short letter and told me she was singing again, she was well, and she knew about Emil."

"Knew what?"

"Madame de Montrat had moved quickly. Emil's engagement to Mademoiselle Bernadette de Chandon was announced within barely a month. She was the daughter of a notable family."

"So Madame de Montrat succeeded in preventing a scandal in spite of Henri's death?"

"You mean 'the unfortunate, tragic accident which brought grief to two prominent Parisian families', as the newspapers reported? The investigation was personally handled at the highest levels within the police department, influential people who felt the de Montrats and Grevilles had already suffered enough."

"I see. And you, did you also take an appropriate wife?"

Bernard's smile combined sadness and irony. "Not as quickly as Emil, but it seemed to be best under the circumstances. It was difficult for me to admit that I had abandoned Amelia almost as cowardly as had Emil, and I suppose in a way, I thought a proper marriage would bring me to a state of less emotion. Mathilde was a plain, good woman, the daughter of one of my father's friends, a woman who could in no way compete with thoughts of Amelia. She was an excellent home-maker, a wonderful mother, completely devoid of imagination. She was my calm harbor after the storm of the sea and a good wife. She died last March, and three months ago, I summoned enough courage to call Amelia to tell her I wished to meet with her again, thinking that perhaps it would be possible to take a chance together despite the so many years gone by. That is when she told me of the cancer. I offered to bring her to the European clinics if she preferred instead of receiving treatment in the United States. You can imagine her answer."

What was that like, to love someone for so long, to lose that person, to think you might, just might have a second chance, and discover death beat you to it?

"I'm sure you had no more influence than I did. How sad it must have been for you."

The lines in his face seemed to deepen for a moment, then he, too, exhaled audibly. "Yes, well, at least I am able to fulfill this one final request for her. So, shall we go on with the story? As the war began, it was difficult to communicate, but word got through occasionally. She stayed in Munich until the bombing reached such deadly proportions that one of her German lovers arranged for passage to a convent near Zermatt, Switzerland."

"Our Lady of the Mountains," I said.

"You know it?"

"I didn't, not until Amelia's will was read. I'm sure you know she left some money to them, and that would be the Sister Agnes she mentioned?"

Bernard nodded. "I did not know where she was until late in 1947 when, at last, she wrote to say she was safe, but something had happened in Munich and she intended to remain at the convent with no further contact for an unspecified period of time. She said if I attempted to find her, she would leave. I explained to her that I had, as she instructed, made sound investments with the money she'd left in my care and her fortune was now sizable, but she told me to keep it in whatever I deemed most prudent. She said to send ten thousand francs only; that was all she needed for the time being."

"Surely she wasn't planning to become a nun?"

Bernard touched his glass with his forefinger but didn't pick it up. "I did not know, although I admit I wondered the same thing. It seemed improbable, but the war had a devastating effect on millions. Rejecting worldly goods and turning to God would not seem so unusual compared to the madness that was the war and what we learned in its aftermath. No, I discovered the reason later, in 1951, when a young American lawyer, your Mr. Harvey Trotter, made inquiries as to whether or not I could assist him in locating Miss Amelia Louise Hatcher."

"That's right, Harvey had something to do with the Thornhill estate."

"Yes, the story now returns to Mrs. Thornhill, the part I told you was important and would come later. You may recall she gave Amelia a small bequest for her service? That was not all, however. For reasons we can only speculate about, she also bequeathed her the beach house and this land, the spot where we sit at this moment. It would seem likely she felt a special bond with Amelia if you know the story of Amelia's parents. Perhaps Mrs. Thornhill thought the land would provide Amelia with some sort of dowry. You also recall, however, the attitude of the Thornhill son toward Amelia? It seems as though he successfully hid the fact that his mother had made a new will, but when he and his sister were killed with no other direct beneficiaries to the estate, it was left entirely in the hands of the Thornhill attorneys. They, in turn, discovered his deceit and involved Mr. Trotter since the property was located here."

What a convoluted series of events. "That's amazing."

"Quite, and I do not know exactly how he came to know of me, but you can imagine my delight when he approached me for assistance. It was a great trouble for him to find me, and it was as if the perfect excuse to see Amelia had fallen to me like a gift. When I wired her, she sent a telegram to say that I and Paris had been on her mind, and yes, she was ready to speak with me. I left the very next day with the papers Mr. Trotter had sent. Amelia booked me into a hotel in Zermatt and promised to come and meet me the following morning. I hardly slept; I was so excited at the prospect. I was to see my beautiful Amelia again!"

"After fourteen years, you thought she would not have changed?"

Bernard took a sip before he answered. "Foolishness of the heart, Maggie, but to me she was still the girl who stood in the spotlight and enchanted me that night in Paris with her golden hair and green satin dress. When I saw her, I tried to hide my shock, but I could not. She was much too thin, and her blonde hair was almost as white as mine is now. Fortunately, her eyes were the same, her smile enough to give me hope. She let me tell her about the property, asked me of my welfare, and then took me for coffee and pastry at a nearby café. She said she wanted to tell me about the years since we'd parted, wanted me to understand what she was going to do."

"Were you apprehensive?"

"A little, for I knew the war could not have been easy for her, the inhumanity of it could not have by-passed her entirely. She escaped before the worst of the bombing, but even so, she had elected to stay at the convent rather than return to a more social life, shall we say. I knew women were permitted to be in residence, even if they were not planning to take vows, and all I could think was that Amelia wanted refuge from whatever had happened."

"You said there was one more tragedy? This is why she stayed?"

Bernard's face became still, his lack of expression oddly disturbing. What emotion was he trying to control? "Yes. Amelia told me she had rented a small apartment when she arrived in Munich, her gentleman friend willing to help, but unlike Emil, he was reluctant to keep a mistress in the same town as his wife. He did, however, assist her with an audition, which, of course, led to her being engaged once again as a singer. It was a club that many of the Wermacht officers frequented, and as a blonde-haired, green-eyed beautiful woman, her popularity grew quickly. She became fluent in German as easily as she had French."

"Nazis? She was involved with Nazis?"

"Maggie, please try to remember. Amelia was not a creature of politics, and at any rate, the clientele was predominantly Wermacht, many of whom despised the Nazis. No, for the most part, the officers were from elite German families, patriotic, committed to restoring Germany to her rightful place as a power in Europe. They were soldiers, not the thugs of the

Nazi Party. And for Germany, the beginning years of the war were times of celebration, euphoric; they were unstoppable. Austria was reunited, Germany's strength regained. The nightclubs and cabarets would have reflected the enjoyment of the victorious."

I felt my jaw tighten. "And the treatment of the Jews?"

"Joseph Goebbels's merit as a master of propaganda was well deserved. It took little effort to believe the official version of events—that no mistreatment was occurring, that the Jews themselves were to blame for any violence directed against them. And Amelia at that point was not concerned with the welfare of others. Her life had hardly been one of privilege, and the circumstances under which she left Paris did nothing to make her feel secure. No, as she explained to me, she re-entered her role as an admired singer, one whose favors were sought after by handsome German officers, more easily than she expected—it was like the life she had before Emil."

"Did she ask about him, talk about him?"

He gave one sharp shake of his head. "Not a single word. She told me that she was hesitant to become involved with any one man, but instead divided her interest among three or four gentlemen, careful to keep them all guessing as to which one she might eventually choose."

"And accepting appropriate gifts in the meantime?" I managed the question with more neutrality than I felt.

Bernard shrugged. "I did not ask the question of her, but I suspect such was the case. Remember, at that time, Amelia was unaware of what I was doing with the money she had entrusted to me. For all she knew, I was not brilliant with her funds, and her future welfare depended solely upon her own efforts. She told me that in the club where she worked, there were two other singers, although Amelia had become the most requested. Apparently, however, one of the women was a rival to Amelia, and they did not like each other. One evening in a fit of pique, Amelia let it be known to a man who was an officer with political connections that the rival singer had changed her name and was actually half-Jewish."

"You said Amelia had no political understanding."

Bernard wrapped his fingers around the stem of the glass, his eyes gazing past me. "She did not. I genuinely think she was not fully aware of what she'd done until it was too late, very much like the night with Henri and Emil. I think she merely expected the woman to be fired, unable to find other work once her origins were known. Our Amelia, my Amelia, still could not look beyond her own needs."

My voice was lower than I intended. "What happened?"

"The woman disappeared the next night after her performance. In the beginning of the deportation of the Jews, it was more common for someone to be carried away during the early morning hours, unlike later when the mass arrests occurred. Amelia said she was surprised but told herself for a long time that it was all right. Then, as rumors of the camps circulated, she told herself it couldn't be true. She could not believe the Germans capable of such planned, monstrous killing of the Jews. Her denial was no different than the majority of citizens and a part of why the Nazis could develop and implement a plan to eradicate the Jews and other undesirables."

I fought back a shudder. "As an American, didn't she have problems when the United States entered the war?"

"Remember, she came from Paris, spoke fluent French, and she did not think of the Germans as a direct threat to her homeland. Few people knew she was American, and Amelia's view of the war was really quite naive. She considered it to be male bravura gone awry, a European struggle for power which would somehow work itself out. A friend took care of papers for her, and although she was questioned one time by the local Gestapo, her connections through the nightclub and her obvious lack of political thought convinced them that she was harmless. She did not fully comprehend the impact of the war until the bombing began. She said the stench of burning buildings mixed with charred bodies became almost unbearable, and the day she helped remove what was left of a child so the mother could give him a Christian burial, she agreed to leave the city. It was one of the Wermacht officers who arranged for her to be taken to the convent in Switzerland. His family had often skied in Zermatt before the war, and he thought Amelia would be safe there. Like many such places, the nuns gave shelter for wounded, sick, and transient refugees, mostly women and children. Amelia had no real home to go to after the war ended, and she volunteered to stay and help."

"But for almost five years?"

Bernard's face twisted slightly. "Ah, Maggie, people now think it was land at Normandy, conquer the Germans, and poof!, the war is over, everything is normal again. There was still much chaos with food, medical, and fuel shortages—even clothes were difficult to find. The occupation, the destruction from the bombing, the danger of the Russians, the Nuremburg Trials. Too many forget why the great Marshall Plan was needed. Hundreds of thousands of people were destitute or displaced; literally every institution of any social nature was overwhelmed for several years. The stories of atrocities were discussed openly as former internees and prisoners searched for what might be left of their families and came to terms with what they had seen and been subjected to. It was during this time that Amelia learned the fate of Gretchen, the rival singer."

"Was she certain it was Gretchen? From what I've read,

it would have been difficult to pinpoint what happened to individuals."

"Not as much so as you think. A need emerged among the survivors to remember as many details as possible, to be able to tell the truth afterwards, to ensure those responsible could be held accountable. If you had a name, or knew when someone had been taken, you could often find someone who was with them for at least a part of the time. I do not know if Amelia tried to find out what happened to Gretchen or if she became aware by accident."

I braced myself. "This is the other thing you have to tell me?"

"The part which kept Amelia at the convent. Gretchen and her son had been taken but separated immediately. He was mentally defective in some way and was sent to a center where he died, either as a result of medical experiments, neglect, or as a part of the early executions to purify the German race."

"Ronny," I said without thinking. No wonder Amelia had been so protective of him.

Bernard looked puzzled. "Amelia did not tell me his name; I do not believe she knew it."

I didn't want to explain about Ronny. "No, I mean, it was nothing, please go on."

"Gretchen was young and pretty so she was assigned to one of the officers' brothels rather than a work camp. The women were allowed to stay until they were no longer useful, then they were sent on or killed. Gretchen apparently contracted an unusual strain of venereal disease, which the doctors could not treat. She was shot once they determined she was not curable."

I blinked my eyes rapidly. "Maybe it was a mistake, maybe it wasn't Gretchen. You said yourself hundreds of women were sent to those places."

"No, the woman who told Amelia of Gretchen had been transported to the brothel with her, had been with her when one of the guards told her of the death of her son. Gretchen was shot in front of the other women as a reminder of what happened when you could no longer fulfill your purpose. There was no doubt the woman told the truth."

I found myself feeling nauseous and momentarily covered my face with my hands. My God, what had Amelia done! I don't know how long I sat that way, but I looked up to see Bernard waiting patiently. I nodded without speaking.

"Amelia finally understood what she had caused to happen, and she was repulsed, convinced she was damned. Henri, Gretchen, and a child she never met, all dead because of a part she played. She worked harder than anyone in the convent, went for long walks in the mountains, and at last confided in Sister Agnes, but she still found no peace, no absolution. As it happens, only a few days before I contacted her, Sister Agnes had told Amelia she could not hide from the world forever. Amelia said she took this occurrence as a sign that she should return to America."

"What did you say to her?"

"As before, I had no answers for her. Naturally, I tried to tell her that perhaps everything would have happened in due course without her hand in it, but she gave me a look of such misery, I recoiled from the pain. She said she would take her demons and live with them by the sea, away from people, alone where she could do no more harm. I knew it would be futile to argue with her."

"My God," I repeated aloud.

"I was able to put her in touch with Mr. Trotter, who took care of the legal matters. I think you probably know the rest

from the talk of the townspeople. She built this house and isolated herself. While she resumed her taste for luxuries such as
books, food, and wine, she remained a virtual prisoner to her
guilt. The proverbial bird in the gilded cage, shall we say, except
it was a cage of her own making."

I found myself gripping my wineglass, as Bernard was, and
forced my fingers to relax. "When did you see her last?"

His sigh was longer this time, his voice sad to the point of
breaking. "I ignored her protests and came to the dock when
she sailed from Calais. Not that it would have mattered, but
I wish I had known I would never see her again, perhaps I
would have said something differently, done something for
once. I suppose that I always somehow believed that I could
have Amelia without the risk of losing my family, my position.
And so once more, I failed to speak, to tell her that I loved her.
I kissed her good-bye and let her go again. Oh, I received word
from her every year or two, and when she wrote me of you, I
thought surely she would relent and come visit you in Paris. I
was certain she would want to see you, especially as recognition
of your talent grew, yet she proved resolute to the end."

I rose from the table, took a long breath, and rubbed the
back of my neck, unable to release the knotted muscles.

"My God, Bernard, it suddenly seems I knew so little of
Amelia. Maybe I didn't know her at all; maybe I was wrong and
nothing I knew was true."

Bernard's voice became firm. "No, Maggie, I cannot permit
you to have those thoughts. You understood Amelia as well as
she would allow. I do not know exactly how it was between
you, but I do know in her letter to me asking for my assistance
she said you were very special, as close to a daughter as she
would ever have, and she wanted me to watch over you accord-
ingly. That was part of why I was disappointed to be kept from

you. I wanted to meet the one person Amelia allowed to come close to her, and I see she made a good choice."

I tried to smile and failed. "I could have done more for her. Not when I was a teenager, God, I was ignorant then. But later, when I was older, if she had told me, I could have consulted therapists, could have found someone to help her."

"I think you did far more than you will ever know. She was an intelligent, literate woman. She could have sought treatment, just as she could have for the cancer. No, Maggie, Amelia condemned herself and would seek no pardon."

The length of the shadows reminded me that the afternoon was nearly over. "It's much later than I realized, and I must admit, I don't know what to say now."

"I hope I have not been wrong in what I have told you, but Amelia said it was important to bring you the truth, although I do not know precisely why. I would suppose she wished to finally release her burden of sad memories, and I think you have the strength to accept it in spite of its unpleasant nature. As you said earlier this afternoon, nothing I have said changes what Amelia did for you. And now, I think my task is completed. If it is not inconvenient, could you telephone a taxi cab for me?"

I was disconcerted with Bernard's impending departure, and I didn't want him to leave, even if there was nothing more he could tell me.

"Good Lord, Bernard, there's no need for a cab; I'll drive you back."

"I do not wish to impose," he said quickly.

"Really, it's no imposition," I assured him. "Would you like to take a few minutes before we go?"

"That is very kind of you. Yes, I would like to walk around a bit."

"I just thought of something I need to do," I said. "Take your time."

I hurried inside and went to Amelia's desk. I found what I was looking for in the middle drawer—another photograph I'd taken of her not quite two years ago on her birthday. It was a candid shot, a frontal frame of her laughing at a Monarch butterfly that had landed on the large bouquet of iris she was holding. I scrawled my name across the bottom, careful not to detract from the view of Amelia.

When I silently handed it to Bernard, he gazed at it, not trying to hide the slow tears that leaked down his face, and gallantly gave me his handkerchief to dry my own trickle. We tried to laugh awkwardly then, two people brought together by our love for a woman who we would both miss. Neither of us spoke as I drove him to the resort.

"I will leave tomorrow," he said in parting. "You will let me know when you come to Paris again?"

"Of course," I said, "and do give me love to Jean-Claude."

He smiled and kissed me good-bye, a kiss to each cheek. I stayed until he walked through the lobby and felt a sensation of loss when he disappeared, a man I had met only hours ago.

I drove away, my face wet, my vision blurred. It seemed only right to grieve, to grieve for my Amelia, for Bernard's Amelia, for the Amelia who could have been.

# Chapter Thirty

The silence in the cottage seemed strange after spending the afternoon with Bernard. I understood now why she selected the twenty-second of April and Moet and Chandon champagne as an ironic gesture in taking her life. I meandered through the rooms once more, but with different eyes. Each item brought to mind the question of its history. Was it a symbol of a place Amelia shared with Emil? She'd left everything in Paris, but over the decades had she acquired her *objets d'art* in an attempt to recapture their voyages, just as she had recreated the cottage itself? If she had exiled herself to this plot of land, was she reaching out to the world in the only way she allowed herself?

I realized I was avoiding the envelope on the table. Amelia said I would understand once Bernard talked to me, but what else was there for her to say? Some mistake she'd made with me, was what she'd written. I assumed it was her explanation for why she'd never told me the truth. Or could there possibly be a secret she'd kept from Bernard? And if that was it, I didn't know if I could handle any further revelations. The ringing of the telephone shattered the quiet and jarred my thoughts.

"Maggs? Maggie, is that you?"

My mind went momentarily blank.

"Maggs, it's John."

"Oh God, I'm sorry, the connection was a little unclear," I lied. "I can hear you fine now. How are you?"

"I'm okay. You were going to call two days ago and I waited, then I wanted to make sure you were all right. I got the number from Doctor Rundle. He said you probably had a lot to do at the house."

Oh God, John! I had told him I would call as soon as I knew what was going on! Christ, almost three years with the man and I'd forgotten to call! "Yeah, John, I'm really sorry. I meant to call last night, but it has been kind of crazy with trying to get everything settled. I mean, Amelia tied up all kinds of loose ends, but there are still a number of things to take care of."

"Well, these situations are always tough no matter what. You sound exhausted. Have you gotten any sleep since you left?"

"Enough," I said with what I hoped was a reassuring tone. Lack of sleep wasn't my problem.

"Look, I know you don't like me to coddle you, but do you need me to come down and help with anything? I can take four or five days off with no problem. Do any heavy lifting for you or whatever."

His voice held a strength I could use right now. "No, I'm okay. I mean there's really no reason for you to make the trip. I'm not sure how much longer I'll be, although I expect I can wrap everything up by the end of the week."

I sensed he wanted to say more in the short pause that followed. "Okay, whatever you think is best. My schedule is pretty light, and I'll be either at the apartment or the office. I'm just a phone call away if you change your mind and think of something you need. Take care of yourself, and maybe we'll go out to Brandeywine Valley for the weekend when you get back."

"That sounds like a good idea. I'll give you a call for sure to let you know when I'm flying in." Maybe he would offer one more time to join me.

"See you then, Maggs. Don't stay away too long."

"I won't," I said and held the receiver to my shoulder long after we had been disconnected.

The idea of asking John to come to the cottage was tempting, but I resisted the urge to call back. He knew some of how I felt about Amelia, knew about our background, knew why he'd not been allowed to meet her, or at least knew what I had told him, which was the truth until a few hours ago. Well, wasn't it still essentially the truth? Amelia as a recluse, my benefactress, a woman who never asked to meet my significant other? None of that had changed. Yet, the reasons for her withdrawal were not the convenient ones that I had unconsciously created. That was the part I was struggling with. Would John's presence help me sort through my tangled emotions or add to my confusion?

The sky faded into gray, clouds losing faint tinges of color and the approaching darkness reminding me of the times I'd sat at the table watching Amelia prepare dinner. The smell of unfamiliar spices, the enticing aroma of a dish I couldn't pronounce, the lessons in how to select a wine.

Lessons she had learned in order to lift herself from a life of poverty. Lessons that had not protected her from tragedy. Tragedy she could not be considered blameless in.

I sighed, mental fatigue threatening to erupt into a headache. I needed a hot shower, a respite from the burdens of Amelia's past before I opened the remaining envelope. I turned the stall into a virtual steam bath until I was obscured within the vaporous heat. The temperature was as close to scalding as I could stand, as though I could warm the internal chill that touched me.

I toweled off, roughly rubbing my short hair until it was nearly dry, and slipped on a pair of light blue sweats that were now a pale memory of the original color. My favorite sweats that I could roll tightly to fit into a backpack or a tiny space in my duffle. Durable, comfortable, shapeless, reliable. I'd worn these in more places than I could count, whether I was sitting by a campfire in Arizona or on the balcony of the Ritz-Carlton in Rome.

I delayed a little longer as I decided against another glass of wine and brewed a cup of tea instead. I filled the cup to the brim, barely allowed it to steep, and nearly spilled it when I sat at the table. I tore off the end of the last envelope, crumpled the strip of paper into a ball, and pulled the letter out gently. The salutation was the same as the others, *My Dear Maggie*. The last time Amelia would write those words, the last time she would use that phrase.

*My Dear Maggie,*

*I am going to trust you have spoken with Bernard and he has told you of Paris, of Emil, of Henri, of Munich, and of my return to Duck. I know what he told you will have been difficult for you to hear, but I am also going to trust you will believe me when I say I wanted to keep the truth from you, to not burden you with my personal demons. It was the thought that I had unintentionally influenced you in matters of the heart that caused me to ask Bernard to come and tell you the truth of what happened.*

*I know you probably think it was a selfish decision to end my life as I have, although I hope you understand I simply could not face the idea of dying in an institution or here with strangers attending to me. Walt's assurances of advances in treatments were tainted by what we both recognized as the inevitable outcome.*

*No, Maggie, as I walked along the beach thinking of all that had happened to me, and all that I had caused to happen, I knew that you were the one truly good thing I could claim.*

*The afternoon we met, the days that followed when I saw within you the kind of spirit that needed to be released, I knew at last that I had an opportunity to enhance another human being. While I suspect I could have handled the lessons I gave you in a different fashion, you nonetheless grew into a young woman I could not have been more proud of.*

*As the years passed, I became concerned when you did not find someone to share your success and your dreams with. I understood initially you were occupied with perfecting your skills. You were cautious of the deceptive nature of sexual magnetism disguised as love, but your caution was too deep, a shield you wrapped yourself in, and now, I worry that I unconsciously taught you that, also.*

*That is why it was important for you to understand that my isolation was deliberate, but not what I would have chosen if I had lived my life differently. When I was willing to accept Madame de Montrat's opinion of me, when it was no longer possible for me to deny the truth of the consequences of my behavior and I sought refuge here, I shut myself away where people could neither harm me nor be harmed by me. The world I created for myself was one of the only happy times I'd known, a time I wanted to lose myself in until I could perhaps start over. I thought if I walked enough, if I watched the sun rise and set enough, I would find a way to undo what I had done.*

*But instead, I sank further into the image that I created. Between the beach, the garden, my music, and my books, I lost the desire, and later the ability, to step beyond the boundaries I had established.*

*What you saw as eccentricity, independence, self-reliance was as much fear and imprisonment as anything else. All the times you* asked me to come visit and I turned you down were not because I didn't want to, but because I no longer could.

At any rate, I am digressing. Maggie, I cannot leave this earth and allow you to think the way I chose was the right one. Oh, I know you have friends, acquaintances, and a lover you care for, but I also know you don't allow them to come close, especially John, who sounds to me like the kind of man you need.

Needing someone is not giving in, Maggie; it is not a sign of weakness; it is not something to be afraid of. If I had been willing to need the right things, perhaps I would have made other choices when I was young. That isn't particularly important now, for I cannot alter what has been. You have the capacity to care, to express your passion—I've seen it in you from the time you were sixteen. I wrongly assumed if I sent you to Paris under better circumstances, if I urged you on to adventure with a safety net beneath you, you would experience life free of entanglements. I didn't mean for you to experience those things alone.

It's like the cottage, Maggie. I hope you keep it, but as a haven, as a romantic get-away, as an interlude, not as a retreat into solitude.

I don't know what other words to use, and if you haven't understood by now, then repeating myself won't serve any purpose. More than anything in the world, I want you to be happy, Maggie, not just secure. You must look inward, my dear. You must see for yourself where the empty spots are, and you must not follow my pattern thinking to fill them.

As I finish this letter, knowing I will not be here to answer any questions you have, knowing I will have brought you pain in the end, I hope I have made the right decision about telling you the truth.

And if, after all, you should choose a life without a partner, do so because you can find no one deserving, not because you think it is not worth the risk, and not because you misunderstood the reasons I did so.

All my love,
Amelia

# Chapter Thirty-one

I felt as if I couldn't breathe, my heart accelerating. I had to get outside, away from these words. I dropped the letter, thrusting away from the table, sloshing tea from the cup, nearly toppling the chair. I almost tripped on the door sill and caught my footing, not stopping until I felt the beach beneath my feet. My God, this was her truth? Her notion that I was some sort of atonement—a goddamn social experiment? She screwed her life up, and now, now, in this way, she was telling me what I was supposed to do with mine?

The beach was deserted, a thin crescent moon moving in and out of the clouds. I gulped air until I forced myself to slow down, to inhale slowly, exhale deeply, moving along the sand. I veered from packed sand into looser stuff, sloughing through it instead of lifting my feet. Waves periodically washed over my shoes, sometimes up to my calves, pants absorbing the water.

Images, scenes, conversations tore through my mind in no particular order, crashing upon one another. *All my love*—the same in each letter—words that she hadn't said to me and perhaps couldn't, no more than I did to her. Words my own mother hadn't been able to utter to me as I sat by her side before she died—words I hadn't spoken either. Love me—had Amelia loved me after all? Or had I simply been a convenient outlet that had stumbled into her life? An amusement, a diversion—*can I use my money and connections to make this person into something that I failed to be?*

All the while that I was in awe of her, striving to meet her demands, thinking that she was the only person who understood me, she was setting me on a path that she controlled—watching to see how I would react. Okay, maybe when I was young I couldn't have understood, but why couldn't she have shared some of her past with me later? Not all at once, but at least in pieces? Why didn't she talk with me, trust me?

I barely registered the breeze lifting my hair, plastering my damp pants to my legs. My thoughts swirled in the onslaught of what I'd learned, logic trying to break through the emotional haze. Amelia had gone to extraordinary lengths to reveal things to me, and until I opened the last letter, I was disturbed, yet willing to accept what Bernard had told me, willing to try and view her actions from his devoted perspective. Why did I feel such a surge of betrayal in this last letter?

"Because you aren't sure if I have told you the truth even now." I could hear Amelia's voice as if she hovered around me. "Because you unconsciously created a history for me and you see that history wasn't real. You never imagined me to be as flawed as I was. If I could be as carelessly cruel as I was then, can you believe that I actually sought redemption? Can you believe that I cared about you as a person? Was everything I did for my own sake?"

The sob might as well have been wrenched from my chest, and I stopped, unable to see through the tears. I stood, weeping, sand shifting beneath my shoes, arms wrapped round myself, until I felt my knees weaken and I rocked back to keep from collapsing. I heard my choking, wet sounds, and may have howled my distress. I lost sense of time until I drew a shuddering breath and another one. I shakily lifted my shirt, twisted it to grab the side, and wiped my nose, then used my sleeve to blot my eyes.

That was it. In the absence of knowing about Amelia, I had woven a past for her—a woman who had given her heart to a foreigner and for some reason been left bereft, unable to ever love again, mired in eccentricity and solitude. Yet despite being outwardly snappish, there beat the good-heartedness of a fairy godmother. It was a scripted part that fit neatly into my imagination. The role did not call for a woman clawing her way from poverty regardless of who she hurt. Could I accept that she had been both?

I pivoted awkwardly and stood facing the water, the waves not visible until they broke near my feet, their sound carrying in the stillness—no night birds in the forest, no croaking frogs. This ocean with waves that deposited sand or ripped out expanses of it in winter storms. We had seen that as kids, the width of the beach changing, sometimes by season. That was how it had been for thousands of years, tens of thousands, the ocean in its vastness. Waves that gently lapped, rhythmically rolled, or thundered onto shore—the same ocean in her changeable moods. Humans, once mystified by waters seemingly without end, had ventured onto those waters, learned to navigate, built airplanes to fly over it. Yet, had we conquered the ocean? Not really—not when Mother Nature could snarl back with raging winds and towering waves as a reminder of her power. And yet, it returned to beauty when the storm passed, this vista of water that reflected back the blue of a cloudless sky or the steel of an overcast one.

Was this so different than what was churning inside me? Wasn't what Amelia had written much the same—a pounding, tearing storm that could destroy a beach shack and leave a well-constructed lighthouse intact? What was our relationship built on, or of, for that matter? Wood that splintered or concrete and rock?

My feet moved slowly, my thoughts yielding to a drained calm that was taking hold. I focused on Bernard's voice, the way he spoke of what had happened, his unmistakable sadness, his suggestion that I stop, that I not hear of Munich. His undeniable pleasure when he explained about helping me at Amelia's request. If she had lied to me about why I should go to Paris, she had lied to Bernard, also. Her explanation made sense, and like the time when John had offered commitment, my heated suspicion of her motives was probably an overreaction. My real truth was that I didn't like to be surprised by the expression of emotion. The past two days had been filled with shocks, and Amelia's last letter was the tipping point. When presented with raw, touching emotion, I had lashed out just as I had at John, except that I didn't need a month in Central America to regain my balance. And since I was being honest about my actions, I had to acknowledge that I had never discussed the emotional distances within my own family. Why would Amelia have assumed that others around me had been lacking in sentimentality, unwilling to exhibit or deal with tenderness? Why wouldn't she have thought that her own behavior was the primary influence on me? I thought of that telephone call to me, of my failure to come see her. I don't know if we could have actually spoken of the things in her letters, if I could have heard the words from her that I did through Bernard. The fact was that I did not come, and what I learned from Bernard was hardly the stuff of a telephone conversation. Her decision to leave me the letters and involve Bernard took a level of courage that I had no right to dismiss.

My truth with Amelia, despite whatever came before it, was that she gave me opportunities that no one else had offered, opportunities that I might not have managed on my own. If she sought redemption in my success, that was little to give in exchange for what she had done for me. The matter of my future with John or any other man was a subject I didn't want to dwell on. I could understand Amelia's concern, but it was simply too much to deal with on top of everything else.

I hadn't realized how far I'd walked, and when I saw the lights of the cottage, the last trickle of anger dissipated, and I shivered at the damp cloth clinging to my legs, my sodden shoes. I straightened in the dark, and if I did not clamor up the steps, at least I didn't drag myself the remaining distance into the cottage. I stripped naked, brought some warmth back with another brisk towel rub, threw my clothes over the shower curtain rod, and set my shoes and soaked socks on the edge of the tub. I climbed into bed and relinquished my body to the darkened room.

Mercifully, I slept dreamlessly and emerged groggily, sunshine slanting through the crack where the curtains met. My calf muscles protested as I swung my legs over, and I blinked twice looking at my travel clock. Jesus, it was almost noon. The first cup of coffee brought me around, and I was savoring a second, wondering what I should do next, when the telephone rang.

"Hi, Maggs, I know I'm calling a little early."

I rubbed the back of my neck. "Uh, that's okay. I mean I've got some things to do, and I haven't decided what to start on first."

John hesitated then cleared his throat. "Well, how about giving me directions? I'm at the last gas station before I cross Currituck Sound."

Had I heard him correctly? "You're here? I mean, almost here?"

"Yep. You sounded terrible last night, and I caught a plane this morning. I know you told me not to come, and if you really don't want me to, I'll turn around and catch a flight back, but I'd like to stay."

"You flew down because I sounded terrible?"

Hs voice was steady. "Yes. I know you're tough and independent and all that, but, Maggs, I want to be with you for this. I don't think you should have to do this alone."

"I—I—I'm glad you're here," I said softly.

I gave him directions, refilled my mug, and opened the French doors to sun and fresh air, the high clouds thin and scattered today. I wandered to the table and sat, clasping the mug in both hands. I could think clearly, either from a decent night's sleep or from the release of tears.

John was coming. I felt a smile, a lightness that I didn't bother to deny. I wanted him here with me, here in the cottage. I wanted to show it to him, tell him what it meant to me. We would have wine on the terrace and talk about, well, about a lot of things. I would call Jed and see if they wanted to have dinner with us tomorrow.

And while John was here with me, we would take Amelia's ashes and bury them in with the iris. That was the right place for them.

The End

# Questions and Points of Discussion

1.  What are your thoughts about why Maggie is not content with the idea of settling down even though she loves the Outer Banks of North Carolina?

2.  What comes to mind about Amelia's past when Mrs. Pinkham tells Maggie about the Hatcher family?

3.  Have you ever had the experience of striking out on your own to a completely new place with no friends or family nearby? If so, did you respond in the same way that Maggie did?

4.  Do you think that Maggie's reluctance to become emotionally involved with people has been influenced by Amelia, by her family, or it is just a part of her personality?

5.  As Amelia's secrets were revealed, were you surprised? What had been your thoughts as to why she had withdrawn from people?

6.  Do you think that Maggie's reaction to Amelia's last request was understandable?

CPSIA information can be obtained at www.ICGtesting.com
Printed in the USA
LVOW032031201011

251431LV00004B/3/P